THE
CHRISTMAS
READER

COMPILED AND INTRODUCED BY

GODFREY SMITH

VIKING

for
Bertie and Joyce
with love

VIKING

Penguin Books Ltd, Harmondsworth, Middlesex, England
Viking Penguin Inc., 40 West 23rd Street, New York, New York 10010, U.S.A.
Penguin Books Australia Ltd, Ringwood, Victoria, Australia
Penguin Books Canada Ltd, 2801 John Street, Markham, Ontario, Canada L3R 1B4
Penguin Books (N.Z.) Ltd, 182–190 Wairau Road, Auckland 10, New Zealand

First published 1985

Compilation, Introduction and commentary Copyright © Godfrey Smith, 1985

Copyright information for individual
extracts and illustrations is given
on pages 324–326.

Filmset in Monophoto Palatino by
Northumberland Press Ltd, Gateshead, Tyne and Wear

Printed in Great Britain by
Hazell, Watson & Viney, Ltd,
Member of the BPCC Group, Aylesbury, Bucks

Designed by Judith Gordon

British Library Cataloguing in Publication Data

The Christmas reader.
1. Short stories, English
I. Smith, Godfrey
823'.01'08[FS]   PR1309.S5

ISBN 0–670–80814–8

Adeste, fideles,
Laeti triumphantes;
Venite, venite in Bethlehem . . .

O come, all ye faithful,
Joyful and triumphant,
O come ye, O come ye to Bethlehem . . .

CONTENTS

Contents 9

INTRODUCTION

John Simmons had a problem. He belongs to a supper club, and had read them an extract from *A Christmas Carol* the previous December. What could he read them this year anything like as good? He put the problem to me, and I put it to readers of my *Sunday Times* column. The answers cascaded in. Soon we had enough to keep John Simmons in readings till AD 2050. It seemed a pity not to gather this cornucopia together between covers: here it is – and a good deal more besides.

On the face of it, the notion of reading aloud to an audience sounds outmoded. Surely the audio-visual revolution has overtaken such gentle and unsophisticated delights? Who wants to listen to Dickens when he can watch James Bond on the box? Many people, I suspect. First, the literate audience is vastly larger than it was when in mid-Victorian England Dickens himself was a reader of titanic clout. More enticements clamour for our time – radio, film, records, tape, video – but there are infinitely more people able to share those delights. Besides, the arrival of the video camera, enabling any family to shoot its own home movies and play them back on the television screen, has rekindled interest in exploiting family talents and making one's own pleasures. Yet over and above these massive forces, I detect a resurgence of interest in reading out loud for its own sake. The visual image locks imagination: the spoken work unlocks it. That, at any rate, has been the experience in my own family. So I hope that readers will not only read this book to themselves for their own pleasure, but also to others for the shared enjoyment it uniquely brings. Here are a few tentative tips for those trying the experiment of family reading.

First, it is far better to be invited to read than to inflict your text on an uncaring audience. Obviously there has to be a first time, but once the idea has caught on always wait until your family are ready, waiting and indeed eager for a reading. This usually will not happen until after they have eaten; but that is a good moment, as the digestive process does its mysterious work, and the drink has its mellifluous effect.

Next, cut, cut and cut again. When someone sits in an armchair reading a book he can stop, scratch, get up, yawn, walk about – and skip to his heart's content. A captive audience cannot do that. So take a pencil and score it ruthlessly through diversions and circumlocutions. It will have to be a fine passage indeed that will hold a family audience for more than six or seven minutes. That is six or seven hundred words or two pages of an average book. Not many passages in *The Christmas Reader* fall naturally into that ambit; but they can be made to do so.

Next, don't be afraid to practise. You will have to be a very remarkable reader not to hesitate or stumble over some unexpectedly difficult word or phrase; besides, even when the text is crystal clear, you have to think out how to vary your pitch, speed and emphasis to squeeze the most effect from it.

Don't be afraid to introduce what you are going to read with a word or two of explanation. If you are going to include the carol-singing scene from *Under the Greenwood Tree*, dip first into Hardy's introduction to the book and explain that even when he wrote, he was reaching back into a past he could hardly remember himself; a time before the arrival of the church organ, when villagers made their own music and when their music books often contained comical mixtures of the sacred and profane. Just to launch cold into the text puts an extra strain on your listeners; play them in gently.

Be conservative in your choice of text. Christmas is one time when no one is interested in the avant-garde. The three pieces most often named by readers trying to solve the problem for John Simmons are the three we give first: by Laurie Lee, Dylan Thomas and Thomas Hardy. Note that all three are carol-singing scenes; all three involve snow; though no doubt we could prove very simply and boringly that snow in hard fact is a minority weather at Christmas.

I have tried in *The Christmas Reader* to spread my net widely. Thus, we have three examples of Christmas in France; two of Celtic Christmases, in Ireland and Wales respectively; and four marvellously wrought accounts of the American Christmas. It will not take anyone examining them long to realize that certain threads run right through the entire gamut. First, the religious basis of Christmas is still manifest. This is at first surprising, for a good case could be made out to show that our modern Christmas is the apotheosis of materialism.

It focuses the minds of our children not on what they can give but on what they can get (though we have two charming stories from books by Winifred Foley and Keith Waterhouse, to show that even the most wretched gifts can sometimes become precious for considerations over and above their surface worth). It is the time for laying up precisely those material treasures on earth that the proponent of treasures in heaven so eloquently despised. What would the man who gave us the parable of the rich man and the eye of the needle say to Harrods in Christmas week?

I think it is because of a revulsion against the corrupt modern Christmas that so many people like to equate their observance of it with a balancing and cleansing recourse to Christmas past. Go back as far as you will in this book, and someone will regret the passing of an earlier kind of Christmas. Belloc in the 1920s calls out eloquently for the certainties and safeties of Christmas past; so, if we read between the lines, does Harold Macmillan. Yet when we cast our minds back to the romantic, idealized country Christmas of the 1820s captured for us by Washington Irving, what do we find? An old English squire profoundly regretting Christmas two centuries before that. And so on, I suspect, in an infinite regress.

I have tried not to omit the voices of dissent (Bernard Shaw) and doubt (Noël Coward); and to let Christmas act as the vehicle for the black comedy of Kingsley Amis. I have also included several examples of what we might call vernacular Christmas; the kind every Englishman has running in his subconscious along with more noble intimations of the holy time: 'Christmas Day in the Workhouse' and Stanley Holloway's great monologue 'Old Sam's Christmas Pudding'. And then, to lighten the mixture still further, I have thrown in a good measure of poetry. The Nativity itself does tend to over-awe many poets; I have tried to include only those who have something fresh or remarkable to say about it like Herrick or Chesterton, Serraillier or Swinburne. Yet another change of pace is supplied by the cross-section of Christmas letters, ranging from the palace gossip of the young Victoria to the unbearable poignancy of the letter from No-Man's-Land in 1914.

Yet the final mood of *The Christmas Reader* is, I trust, quite otherwise, and nobody should surely rise from it without a renewed sense of the common thread that runs through all our Christmases: that shivery intimation that, whether infidels or believers, we are dwellers all in time and space.

Godfrey Smith
Malmesbury, summer 1985

GOLDEN GIFTS
FOR ALL

We begin with the book most often named by readers: Laurie Lee's magical slice of autobiography, Cider with Rosie. *A million copies have been sold in paperback alone and it is not hard to see why. H. E. Bates called it a prose poem that flashes and winks like a prism. This carol-singing sequence is wry, comic, rich and strange: could it really be that in the Cotswolds between the wars not a single person came out to see the boys and wish them a Happy Christmas? Did the old squire turn away without saying a single word? The passage has the ring of truth; there is no pretence that the singing was much good, yet the sense of Christmas made manifest is very real: 'the stars were bright to guide the Kings through the snow; and across the farmyard we could hear the beasts in their stalls.'*

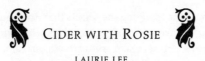

CIDER WITH ROSIE

LAURIE LEE

The week before Christmas, when snow seemed to lie thickest, was the moment for carol-singing; and when I think back to those nights it is to the crunch of snow and to the lights of the lanterns on it. Carol-singing in my village was a special tithe for the boys, the girls had little to do with it. Like hay-making, blackberrying, stone-clearing, and wishing-people-a-happy-Easter, it was one of our seasonal perks.

By instinct we knew just when to begin; a day too soon and we should have been unwelcome, a day too late and we should have received lean looks from people whose bounty was already exhausted. When the true moment came, exactly balanced, we recognized it and were ready.

So as soon as the wood had been stacked in the oven to dry for the morning fire, we put on our scarves and went out through the streets, calling loudly between our hands, till the various boys who knew the signal ran out from their houses to join us.

One by one they came stumbling over the snow, swinging their lanterns around their heads, shouting and coughing horribly.

'Come carol-barking then?'

We were the Church Choir, so no answer was necessary. For a year we had praised the Lord out of key, and as a reward for this service – on top of the Outing – we now had the right to visit all the big houses, to sing our carols and collect our tribute.

To work them all in meant a five-mile foot journey over wild and generally snowed-up country. So the first thing we did was to plan our route; a formality, as the route never changed. All the same, we blew on our fingers and argued; and then we chose our Leader. This was not binding, for we all fancied ourselves as Leaders, and he who started the night in that position usually trailed home with a bloody nose.

Eight of us set out that night. There was Sixpence the Tanner, who had never sung in his life (he just worked his mouth in church); the brothers Horace and Boney, who were always fighting everybody and always getting the worst of it; Clergy Green, the preaching maniac; Walt the bully, and my two brothers. As we went down the lane other boys, from other villages, were already about the hills, bawling 'Kingwenslush', and shouting through keyholes 'Knock on the knocker! Ring at the Bell! Give us a penny for singing so well!' They weren't an approved charity as we were, the Choir; but competition was in the air.

Our first call as usual was the house of the Squire, and we trouped nervously down his drive. For light we had candles in marmalade-jars suspended on loops of string, and they threw pale gleams on the towering snowdrifts that stood on each side of the drive. A blizzard was blowing, but we were well wrapped up, with Army puttees on our legs, woollen hats on our heads, and several scarves around our ears.

As we approached the Big House across its white silent lawns, we too grew respectfully silent. The lake near by was stiff and black, the waterfall frozen and still. We arranged ourselves shuffling around the big front door, then knocked and announced the Choir.

A maid bore the tidings of our arrival away into the echoing distances of the house, and while we waited we cleared our throats noisily. Then she came back, and the door was left ajar for us, and we were bidden to begin. We brought no music, the carols were in our heads. 'Let's give 'em "Wild Shepherds",' said Jack. We began in confusion, plunging into a wreckage of keys, of different words and tempo; but we gathered our strength; he who sang loudest took the rest of us with him, and the carol took shape if not sweetness.

This huge stone house, with its ivied walls, was always a mystery to us. What were those gables, those rooms and attics, those narrow windows veiled by the cedar trees. As we sang 'Wild Shepherds' we craned our necks, gaping into that lamplit hall which we had never entered; staring at the muskets and untenanted chairs, the great tapestries furred by dust – until suddenly, on the stairs, we saw the old Squire himself standing and listening with his head on one side.

He didn't move until we'd finished; then slowly he tottered towards us, dropped two coins in our box with a trembling hand, scratched his name in the book we carried, gave us each a long look with his moist blind eyes, then turned away in silence.

As though released from a spell, we took a few sedate steps, then broke into a run for the gate. We didn't stop till we were out of the grounds. Impatient, at last, to discover the extent of his bounty, we squatted by the cowsheds, held our lanterns over the book, and saw that he had written 'Two Shillings'. This was quite a good start. No one of any worth in the district would dare to give us less than the Squire.

Steadily we worked through the length of the valley, going from house to house, visiting the lesser and the greater gentry – the farmers, the doctors, the merchants, the majors, and other exalted persons. It was freezing hard and blowing too; yet not for a moment did we feel the cold. The snow blew into our faces, into our eyes and mouths, soaked through our puttees, got into our boots, and dripped from our woollen caps. But we did not care. The collecting-box grew heavier, and the list of names in the book longer and more extravagant, each trying to outdo the other.

Mile after mile we went, fighting against the wind, falling into snowdrifts, and navigating by the lights of the houses. And yet we never saw our audience. We called at house after house; we sang in courtyards and porches, outside windows, or in the damp gloom of hallways; we heard voices from hidden rooms; we smelt rich clothes and strange hot food; we saw maids bearing in dishes or carrying away coffee-cups; we received nuts, cakes, figs, preserved ginger, dates, cough-drops, and money; but we never once saw our patrons. We sang as it were at the castle walls, and apart from the Squire, who had shown himself to prove that he was still alive, we never expected it otherwise.

We approached our last house high up on the hill, the place of Joseph the farmer. For him we had chosen a special carol, which was about the other Joseph, so that we always felt that singing it added a spicy cheek to the night. The last stretch of country to reach his farm was perhaps the most difficult of all. In these rough bare lanes, open to all winds, sheep were buried and wagons lost. Huddled together, we tramped in one another's footsteps, powdered snow blew into our screwed-up eyes, the candles burnt low, some blew out altogether, and we talked loudly above the gale.

Crossing, at last, the frozen mill-stream — whose wheel in summer still turned a barren mechanism — we climbed up to Joseph's farm. Sheltered by trees, warm on its bed of snow, it seemed always to be like this. As always it was late; as always this was our final call. The snow had a fine crust upon it, and the old trees sparkled like tinsel.

We grouped ourselves round the farmhouse porch. The sky cleared, and broad streams of stars ran down over the valley and away to Wales. On Slad's white slopes, seen through the black sticks of its woods, some red lamps still burned in the windows.

Everything was quiet; everywhere there was the faint crackling silence of the winter night. We started singing, and we were all moved by the words and the sudden trueness of our voices. Pure, very clear, and breathless we sang:

> As Joseph was a walking
> He heard an angel sing;
> 'This night shall be the birth-time
> Of Christ the Heavenly King.
>
> He neither shall be bornèd
> In Housen nor in hall,
> Nor in a place of paradise
> But in an ox's stall . . .'

And two thousand Christmases became real to us then; the houses, the halls, the places of paradise had all been visited; the stars were bright to guide the Kings through the snow; and across the farmyard we could hear the beasts in their stalls. We were given roast apples and hot mince-pies, in our nostrils were spices like myrrh, and in our wooden box, as we headed back for the village, there were golden gifts for all.

While Laurie Lee was growing up in the remote Cotswolds another poet and magician born the same year — 1914 — was growing up eighty miles away in Swansea. Yet while Lee is incontrovertibly English, Thomas quintessentially Welsh, the experience each offers of Christmas remembered is similar. 'It was always snowing,' Thomas tells us in 'A Child's Christmas in Wales', and though we could no doubt produce the record books to question his literal truth, we take his poetic meaning. Again, a vividly remembered sketch of the pleasures and terrors of carol-singing; and though the experience is now urban rather than rural, the sense of mystery and fear is the same. Whose was that 'small, dry, eggshell voice'? Probably simply a householder's, someone on the receiving end of 'Good King Wenceslas', anxious but unable to communicate. The religious undertow recurs: '. . . I got/into bed. I said some words to the close and/holy darkness, and then I slept.'

A Child's Christmas in Wales

DYLAN THOMAS

... Bring out the tall tales now that we told
by the fire as the gaslight bubbled like a diver.
Ghosts whooed like owls in the long nights
when I dared not look over my shoulder; animals
lurked in the cubbyhole under the stairs where the
gas meter ticked. And I remember that we went
singing carols once, when there wasn't the shaving
of a moon to light the flying streets. At the end
of a long road was a drive that led to a large
house, and we stumbled up the darkness of the drive
that night, each one of us afraid, each one holding
a stone in his hand in case, and all of us too brave
to say a word. The wind through the trees
made noises as of old and unpleasant and maybe
webfooted men wheezing in caves. We reached
the black bulk of the house.

'What shall we give them? Hark the Herald?'

'No,' Jack said, 'Good King Wenceslas.
I'll count three.'

One, two, three, and we began to sing,
our voices high and seemingly distant in the
snow-felted darkness round the house that
was occupied by nobody we knew. We stood
close together, near the dark door.

Good King Wenceslas looked out
On the Feast of Stephen . . .

And then a small, dry voice, like the voice
of someone who has not spoken for a long time,
joined our singing: a small, dry, eggshell voice
from the other side of the door: a small dry voice
through the keyhole. And when we stopped running
we were ouside *our* house; the front room was lovely;
balloons floated under the hot-water-bottle-gulping gas;
everything was good again and shone over the town.

'Perhaps it was a ghost,' Jim said.

'Perhaps it was trolls,' Dan said,
who was always reading.

'Let's go in and see if there's any jelly left,'
Jack said. And we did that.

Always on Christmas night there was music.
An uncle played the fiddle, a cousin sang
'Cherry Ripe', and another uncle sang 'Drake's Drum'.
It was very warm in the little house.
Auntie Hannah, who had got on to the parsnip
wine, sang a song about Bleeding Hearts and Death,
and then another in which she said her heart
was like a Bird's Nest; and then everybody
laughed again; and then I went to bed.
Looking through my bedroom window, out into
the moonlight and the unending smoke-coloured snow,
I could see the lights in the windows
of all the other houses on our hill and hear

the music rising from them up the long, steadily
falling night. I turned the gas down, I got
into bed. I said some words to the close and
holy darkness, and then I slept.

Swansea, where Dylan Thomas first sang his songs, Slad, where Laurie Lee first fell in love, and Stinsford, where Thomas Hardy set the scene for his best-read book, Under the Greenwood Tree, *form three sides of an equilateral triangle each some eighty miles long. Here Celtic and Saxon mythologies mingle; here Wessex and Cymru and Cotswolds hinge together; here, at each corner, lived in one mortal frame a poet and magician. Hardy's fine carol-singing sequence is set much earlier than the other two — the 1840s rather than the 1920s — and the village musicians, soon to be replaced by the organ, much to Hardy's regret, still make their own music. Yet here too it snows; here too the carol-singers wait expectantly for some — any — reaction to their song; and here at last they are rewarded. With that cinematic quality that marks all his work, and makes him so easily adaptable to television and film, Hardy brings his heroine Fanny Day to the window to thank the carol-singers. Dick Dewy has met his future wife: 'As near a thing to a spiritual vision as ever I wish to see!' The hymn that brought her to the window is ancient and time worn, transmitted orally from one generation to the next; and encapsulating what Hardy calls 'a quaint Christianity'.*

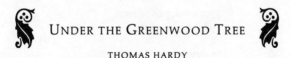

UNDER THE GREENWOOD TREE

THOMAS HARDY

Just before the clock struck twelve they lighted the lanterns and started. The moon, in her third quarter, had risen since the snowstorm; but the dense accumulation of snow-cloud weakened her power to a faint twilight which was rather pervasive of the landscape than traceable to the sky. The breeze had gone down, and the rustle of their feet and tones of their speech echoed with an alert rebound from every post, boundary-stone, and ancient wall they passed, even where the distance of the echo's origin was less than a few yards. Beyond their own slight noises nothing was to be heard save the occasional bark of foxes in the direction of Yalbury Wood, or the brush of a rabbit among the grass now and then as it scampered out of their way.

By this time they were crossing to a gate in the direction of the school which, standing on a slight eminence at the junction of three ways, now rose in unvarying and dark flatness against the sky. The instruments were retuned, and all the band entered the school enclosure, enjoined by old William to keep upon the grass.

'Number seventy-eight,' he softly gave out as they formed round in a semicircle, the boys opening the lanterns to get a clearer light, and directing their rays on the books.

Then passed forth into the quiet night an ancient and time-worn hymn, embodying a quaint Christianity in words orally transmitted from father to son through several generations down to the present characters, who sang them out right earnestly:

> Remember Adam's fall,
>   O thou Man:
> Remember Adam's fall
>   From Heaven to Hell.
> Remember Adam's fall;
> How he hath condemn'd all
> In Hell perpetual
>   There for to dwell.
>
> Remember God's goodnesse,
>   O thou Man:
> Remember God's goodnesse,
>   His promise made.
> Remember God's goodnesse;
> He sent His Son sinlesse
> Our ails for to redress;
>   Be not afraid!
>
> In Bethlehem He was born,
>   O thou Man:
> In Bethlehem He was born,
>   For mankind's sake.
> In Bethlehem He was born,
> Christmas-day i' the morn:
> Our Saviour thought no scorn
>   Our faults to take.
>
> Give thanks to God alway,
>   O thou Man:
> Give thanks to God alway
>   With heart-most joy.
> Give thanks to God alway

On this our joyful day:
Let all men sing and say,
Holy, Holy!

Having concluded the last note they listened for a minute or two, but found that no sound issued from the schoolhouse.

'Four breaths, and then, "O, what unbounded goodness!" number fifty-nine,' said William.

This was duly gone through, and no notice whatever seemed to be taken of the performance.

'Good guide us, surely 'tisn't a' empty house, as befell us in the year thirty-nine and forty-three!' said old Dewy.

'Perhaps she's just come from some musical city, and sneers at our doings?' the tranter whispered.

' 'Od rabbit her!' said Mr Penny, with an annihilating look at a corner of the school chimney, 'I don't quite stomach her, if this is it. Your plain music well done is as worthy as your other sort done bad, a' b'lieve, souls; so say I.'

'Four breaths, and then the last,' said the leader authoritatively. ' "Rejoice, ye Tenants of the Earth," number sixty-four.'

At the close, waiting yet another minute, he said in a clear loud voice, as he had said in the village at that hour and season for the previous forty years:

'A merry Christmas to ye!'

*

When the expectant stillness consequent upon the exclamation had nearly died out of them all, an increasing light made itself visible in one of the windows of the upper floor. It came so close to the blind that the exact position of the flame could be perceived from the outside. Remaining steady for an instant, the blind went upward from before it, revealing to thirty concentrated eyes a young girl framed as a picture by the window architrave, and unconsciously illuminating her countenance to a vivid brightness by a candle she held in her left hand, close to her face, her right hand being extended to the side of the window. She was wrapped in a white robe of some kind, whilst down her shoulders fell a twining profusion of marvellously rich hair, in a wild disorder which proclaimed it to be only during the invisible hours of the night that such a condition was discoverable. Her bright eyes were looking into the grey world outside with an uncertain expression, oscillating between courage and shyness, which, as she recognized the semicircular group of dark forms gathered before her, transformed itself into pleasant resolution.

Opening the window, she said lightly and warmly:

'Thank you, singers, thank you!'

Together went the window quickly and quietly, and the blind started downward on its return to its place. Her fair forehead and eyes vanished; her little mouth; her neck and shoulders; all of her. Then the spot of candlelight shone nebulously as before; then it moved away.

'How pretty!' exclaimed Dick Dewy.

'If she'd been rale wexwork she couldn't ha' been comelier,' said Michael Mail.

'As near a thing to a spiritual vision as ever I wish to see!' said tranter Dewy.

'O, sich I never, never see!' said Leaf fervently.

All the rest, after clearing their throats and adjusting their hats, agreed that such a sight was worth singing for.

WE DON'T WANT YOUR CHRISTMAS PUDDING...

A Merry Christmas

The Christmas pudding has a powerful role in the English subconscious, not simply as a necessary sequel to the turkey on Christmas Day, but as an enormously strong symbol of distaste and rejection. 'Then up spoke one old pauper', as the vernacular tradition has it, 'With a face as bold as brass/We don't want your Christmas pudding . . .' but there is surely no need to labour the quatrain's specific and colourful prescription for the pud. The fons et origo of this robust mode of renunciation is a Victorian monologue recited with immense success and absolutely au pied de la lettre on the Victorian music hall stage by George R. Sims: playwright, social reformer, criminologist and bon viveur. Though the original must now strike us as ludicrously melodramatic, there is no denying its emotional force either. It is hard to remember now the fear and loathing in which the workhouse was held by working people. 'Cold as charity' as another snatch of vernacular has it, 'and that's pretty chilly/But not as cold as our poor Willy/He's dead poor bugger . . .' and so on. Exactly when the workhouse saga turned from straight-faced melodrama to burlesque comedy is not certain; probably during the First World War. Certainly by the 1920s Billy Bennett was having vast success with his parody 'Christmas Day in the Cookhouse'. Yet the Christmas pud also had a starring role in the repertoire of that other great master of the monologue, Stanley Holloway, whose rendition of Marriott Edgar's 'Old Sam's Christmas Pudding' celebrated another enduring quality of the archetypal English artefact — its durability. Finally in this section, the Christmas pud as cause célèbre between Edmund Gosse and his rigidly God-fearing father, to whom any permutation of the accepted regimen of everyday life for Christ's Mass was idolatry. Here alas, the pud bites the dust: but the questions that led to the elder Gosse's precipitate action have not gone away.

CHRISTMAS DAY IN THE WORKHOUSE

GEORGE R. SIMS

It is Christmas Day in the Workhouse,
    And the cold bare walls are bright
With garlands of green and holly,
    And the place is a pleasant sight:
For with clean-washed hands and faces,
    In a long and hungry line
The paupers sit at the tables,
    For this is the hour they dine.

And the guardians and their ladies,
    Although the wind is east,
Have come in their furs and wrappers,
    To watch their charges feast;
To smile and be condescending,
    Put pudding on pauper plates,
To be hosts at the workhouse banquet
    They've paid for – with the rates.

Oh, the paupers are meek and lowly
    With their 'Thank'ee kindly, mum's;
So long as they fill their stomachs,
    What matter it whence it comes?
But one of the old men mutters,
    And pushes his plate aside:
'Great God!' he cries; 'but it chokes me!
    For this is the day *she* died.'

The guardians gazed in horror,
    The master's face went white;
'Did a pauper refuse their pudding?'
    'Could their ears believe aright?'
Then the ladies clutched their husbands,
    Thinking the man would die,
Struck by a bolt, or something,
    By the outraged One on high.

But the pauper sat for a moment,
   Then rose 'mid a silence grim,
For the others had ceased to chatter,
   And trembled in every limb.
He looked at the guardians' ladies,
   Then, eyeing their lords, he said,
'I eat not the food of villains
   Whose hands are foul and red:

'Whose victims cry for vengeance
   From their dank, unhallowed graves.'
'He's drunk!' said the workhouse master.
   'Or else he's mad, and raves.'
'Not drunk or mad,' cried the pauper,
   'But only a hunted beast,
Who, torn by the hounds and mangled,
   Declines the vulture's feast.

'I care not a curse for the guardians,
   And I won't be dragged away.
Just let me have the fit out,
   It's only on Christmas Day

That the black past comes to goad me,
   And prey on my burning brain;
   I'll tell you the rest in a whisper —
I swear I won't shout again.

'Keep your hands off me, curse you!
   Hear me right out to the end.
You come here to see how paupers
   The season of Christmas spend.
You come here to watch us feeding,
   As they watch the captured beast.
Hear why a penniless pauper
   Spits on your paltry feast.

'Do you think I will take your bounty,
   And let you smile and think
You're doing a noble action
   With the parish's meat and drink?
Where is my wife, you traitors —
   The poor old wife you slew?
Yes, by the God above us,
   My Nance was killed by you!

'Last winter my wife lay dying,
   Starved in a filthy den;
I had never been to the parish —
   I came to the parish then.
I swallowed my pride in coming,
   For, ere the ruin came,
I held up my head as a trader,
   And I bore a spotless name.

'I came to the parish, craving
   Bread for a starving wife,
Bread for the woman who'd loved me
   Through fifty years of life;
And what do you think they told me,
   Mocking my awful grief?
That "the House" was open to us,
   But they wouldn't give "out relief".

'I slunk to the filthy alley —
　　'Twas a cold, raw Christmas eve —
And the bakers' shops were open,
　　Tempting a man to thieve;
But I clenched my fists together,
　　Holding my head awry,
So I came to her empty-handed,
　　And mournfully told her why.

'Then I told her "the House" was open;
　　She had heard of the ways of *that*,
For her bloodless cheeks went crimson,
　　And up in her rags she sat,
Crying, "Bide the Christmas here, John,
　　We've never had one apart;
I think I can bear the hunger —
　　The other would break my heart."

'All through that eve I watched her,
　　Holding her hand in mine,
Praying the Lord, and weeping
　　Till my lips were salt as brine.
I asked her once if she hungered,
　　And as she answered "No,"
The moon shone in at the window
　　Set in a wreath of snow.

'Then the room was bathed in glory,
　　And I saw in my darling's eyes
The far-away look of wonder
　　That comes when the spirit flies;
And her lips were parched and parted,
　　And her reason came and went,
For she raved of our home in Devon,
　　When our happiest years were spent.

'And the accents, long forgotten,
　　Came back to the tongue once more,
For she talked like the country lassie
　　I woo'd by the Devon shore.

Then she rose to her feet and trembled,
And fell on the rags and moaned,
And, "Give me a crust — I'm famished —
For the love of God!" she groaned.

'I rushed from the room like a madman,
And flew to the workhouse gate,
Crying, "Food for a dying woman!"
And the answer came, "Too late".
They drove me away with curses;
Then I fought with a dog in the street,
And tore from the mongrel's clutches
A crust he was trying to eat.

'Back, through the filthy by-lanes!
Back, through the trampled slush!
Up to the crazy garret,
Wrapped in an awful hush.
My heart sank down at the threshold,
And I paused with a sudden thrill,
For there in the silv'ry moonlight
My Nance lay, cold and still.

'Up to the blackened ceiling
The sunken eyes were cast —
I knew on those lips all bloodless
My name had been the last;
She'd called for her absent husband —
O God! had I but known! —
Had called in vain, and in anguish
Had died in that den — *alone*.

'Yes, there, in a land of plenty,
Lay a loving woman dead,
Cruelly starved and murdered
For a loaf of the parish bread.
At yonder gate, last Christmas,
I craved for a human life.
You, who would feast us paupers,
What of my murdered wife!

'There, get ye gone to your dinners;
   Don't mind me in the least;
Think of the happy paupers
   Eating your Christmas feast;
And when you recount their blessings
   In your smug parochial way,
Say what you did for *me*, too,
   Only last Christmas Day.'

 ## CHRISTMAS DAY IN THE COOKHOUSE

BILLY BENNETT

'Twas Christmas Day in the cookhouse, and the place
      was clean and tidy,
   The soldiers were eating their pancakes – I'm a liar,
      that was Good Friday.
In the oven a turkey was sizzling and to make it look
      posh, I suppose,
   They fetched the Battalion Barber, to shingle its
      parson's nose!

Potatoes were cooked in their jackets, and carrots in
      pants – how unique!
   A sheep's head was baked with the eyes in, as it had
      to see them through the week.
At one o'clock 'Dinner Up' sounded, the sight made an
      old soldier blush,
   They were dishing out Guinness for nothing, and
      fifteen got killed in the crush!

A jazz band played in the mess-room, a fine lot of
      messers it's true,
   We told them to go and play Ludo, and they all
      answered 'Fishcakes' to you!

In came the old Sergeant Major, he'd walked all the
way from his billet,
His toes were turned in, his chest was turned out,
with his head back in case he'd spill it.

He wished all the troops 'Merry Xmas', including the
poor Orderly Man;
Some said 'Good Old Sergeant Major', but others
said 'San Fairy Ann'.
Then up spoke one ancient warrior, his whiskers a nest
for the sparrows,
The old man had first joined the army when the
troops used to use bows and arrows.

His grey eyes were flashing with anger, he threw down
his pudden' and cursed,
'You dare to wish me a Happy New Year, well, just
hear my story first.
Ten years ago, as the crow flies, I came here with my
darling bride,
It was Christmas Day in the Waxworks, so it must be
the same outside.

We asked for some food, we were starving – you gave
    us pease pudden' and pork.
My poor wife went to the Infirmary, with a pain in
    her Belle of New York.
You're the man that stopped bacon from shrinking, by
    making the cook fry with Lux,
And you wound up the cuckoo clock backwards, and
    now it goes "oo" fore it "cucks".

So thank you, and bless you, and b–low you, you just
    take these curses from me,
May your wife give you nothing for dinner, and
    then warm it up for your tea.
Whatever you eat, may it always repeat – be it soup,
    fish, entrée, or horse doovers,
May blue bottles and flies descend from the skies
And use your bald head for manoeuvres.

May the patent expire on your evening dress shoes,
    may your Marcel waves all come uncurled,
May your flannel shirt shrink up the back of your
    neck and expose your deceit to the world.
And now that I've told you my story, I'll walk to the
    clink by the gate,
And as for your old Xmas Pudden', stick that – on
    the next fellow's plate.'

OLD SAM'S CHRISTMAS PUDDING

STANLEY HOLLOWAY

It was Christmas Day in the trenches
In Spain in Penninsula War,
And Sam Small were cleaning his musket
A thing as he ne'er done before.

They'd had 'em inspected that morning,
And Sam had got into disgrace
For when Sergeant had looked down the barrel
A sparrow flew out in his face.

The Sergeant reported the matter
To Lieutenant Bird then and there.
Said Lieutenant 'How very disgusting
The Duke must be told of this 'ere.'

The Duke were upset when he heard,
He said 'I'm astonished, I am.
I must make a most drastic example
There'll be no Christmas pudding for Sam.'

When Sam were informed of his sentence
Surprise rooted him to the spot —
'Twere much worse than he had expected,
He thought as he'd only be shot.

And so he sat cleaning his musket,
And polishing barrel and butt,
Whilst the pudding his mother had sent him
Lay there in the mud at his foot.

Now the centre that Sam's lot were holding
Ran around a place called Badajoz
Where the Spaniards had put up a bastion
And ooh what a bastion it was!

They pounded away all the morning
With canister, grape shot and ball,
But the face of the bastion defied them
They made no impression at all.

They started again after dinner
Bombarding as hard as they could;
And the Duke brought his own private cannon
But that weren't a ha'pence o' good.

The Duke said 'Sam, put down thy musket
And help me to lay this gun true.'
Sam answered 'You'd best ask your favours
From them as you give pudding to.'

The Duke looked at Sam so reproachful
'And don't take it that way,' said he,
'Us Generals have got to be ruthless
It hurts me more than it did thee.'

Sam sniffed at these words kind of sceptic,
Then looked down the Duke's private gun
And said 'We'd best put in two charges
We'll never bust bastion with one.'

He tipped cannon ball out of muzzle,
He took out the wadding and all,
He filled barrel chock full of powder,
Then picked up and replaced the ball.

He took a good aim at the bastion
Then said 'Right-o, Duke, let her fly.'
The cannon nigh jumped off her trunnions
And up went the bastion, sky high.

The Duke he weren't 'alf elated,
He danced round the trench full of glee
And said 'Sam, for this gallant action
You can hot up your pudding for tea.'

Sam looked round to pick up his pudding,
But it wasn't there, nowhere about.
In the place where he thought he had left it
Lay the cannon ball he'd just tipped out.

Sam saw in a flash what 'ad happened:
By an unprecedented mishap
The pudding his mother had sent him
Had blown Badajoz off the map.

That's why Fuisilliers wear to this moment
A badge which they think's a grenade,
But they're wrong – it's a brass reproduction
Of the pudding Sam's mother once made.

FATHER AND SON

EDMUND GOSSE

My Father's austerity of behaviour was, I think, perpetually accentuated by his fear of doing anything to offend the consciences of these persons, whom he supposed, no doubt, to be more sensitive than they really were. He was fond of saying that 'a very little stain upon the conscience makes a wide breach in our communion with God', and he counted possible errors of conduct by hundreds and by thousands. It was in this winter that his attention was particularly drawn to the festival of Christmas, which, apparently, he had scarcely noticed in London.

On the subject of all feasts of the Church he held views of an almost grotesque peculiarity. He looked upon each of them as nugatory and worthless, but the keeping of Christmas appeared to him by far the most hateful, and nothing less than an act of idolatry. 'The very word is Popish', he used to exclaim, 'Christ's Mass!' pursing up his lips with the gesture of one who tastes assafoetida by accident. Then he would adduce the antiquity of the so-called feast, adapted from horrible heathen rites, and itself a soiled relic of the abominable Yule-Tide. He would denounce the horrors of Christmas until it almost made me blush to look at a holly-berry.

On Christmas Day of this year 1857 our villa saw a very unusual sight. My Father had given strictest charge that no difference whatever was to be made in our meals on that day; the dinner was to be neither more copious than usual nor less so. He was obeyed, but the servants, secretly rebellious, made a small plum-pudding for themselves. (I discovered afterwards, with pain, that Miss Marks received a slice of it in her boudoir.) Early in the afternoon, the maids – of whom we were now advanced to keeping two – kindly remarked that 'the poor dear child ought to have a bit, anyhow', and wheedled me into the kitchen, where I ate a slice of plum-pudding. Shortly I began to feel that pain inside which in my frail state was inevitable, and my conscience smote me violently. At length I could bear my spiritual anguish no longer, and bursting into the study I called out: 'Oh! Papa, Papa, I have eaten of flesh offered to idols!' It took some time, between my sobs, to explain what had happened. Then my Father sternly said: 'Where is the accursed thing?' I explained that as much as was left of it was still on the kitchen table. He took me by the hand, and ran with me into the midst of the startled servants, seized what remained of the pudding, and with the plate in one hand and me still tight in the other, ran till we reached the dust-heap, when he flung the idolatrous confectionery on to the middle of the ashes, and then raked it deep down into the mass. The suddenness, the violence, the velocity of this extraordinary act made an impression on my memory which nothing will ever efface.

The key is lost by which I might unlock the perverse malady from which my Father's conscience seemed to suffer during the whole of this melancholy winter. But I think that a dislocation of his intellectual system had a great deal to do with it. Up to this point in his career, he had, as we have seen, nourished the delusion that science and revelation could be mutually justified, that some sort of compromise was possible. With great and ever greater distinctness, his investigations had shown him that in all departments of organic nature there are visible the evidences of slow modification of forms, of the type developed by the pressure and practice of aeons. This conviction had been borne in upon him until it was positively irresistible. Where was his place, then, as a sincere and accurate observer? Manifestly, it was with the pioneers of the new truth, it was with Darwin, Wallace and Hooker. But did not the second chapter of 'Genesis' say that in six days the heavens and earth were finished, and the host of them, and that on the seventh day God ended his work which he had made?

Here was a dilemma! Geology certainly *seemed* to be true, but the Bible, which was God's word, *was* true. If the Bible said that all things in Heaven and Earth were created in six days, created in six days they were, in six literal days of twenty-four-hours each.

My Father, although half suffocated by the emotion of being lifted, as it were, on the great biological wave, never dreamed of letting go his clutch of the ancient tradition, but hung there, strained and buffeted. It is extraordinary that he – an 'honest hodman of science', as Huxley once called him – should not have been content to allow others, whose horizons were wider than his could be, to pursue those purely intellectual surveys for which he had no species of aptitude. As a collector of facts and marshaller of observations, he had not a rival in that age; his very absence of imagination aided him in this work. But he was more an attorney than philosopher, and he lacked that sublime humility which is the crown of genius. For, this obstinate persuasion that he alone knew the mind of God, that he alone could interpret the designs of the Creator, what did it result from if not from a congenital lack of that highest modesty which replies 'I do not know' even to the questions which Faith, with menacing finger, insists on having most positively answered?

THIS
MOST TREMENDOUS TALE
OF ALL

*Now four poets, each making his obeisance to Christmas, each making his reservations. The
line of thought in Betjeman and Hardy is wellnigh identical. 'And is it true,' asks Betjeman
'This most tremendous tale of all?' Hardy meantime, dramatizing the old country belief that
the animals kneel at midnight on Christmas Eve, confesses that he too would go to see it happen
if invited: 'Hoping it might be so'. Cecil Day Lewis celebrates the Christmas tree as fable, as
phoenix in evergreen; while Louis MacNeice sees the finger of the future beckoning beyond the
tinsel and gewgaws. Note how he introduces the image of the blue flame dancing round the
brandied plum-pudding: it will occur over and again in this book.*

CHRISTMAS

JOHN BETJEMAN

The bells of waiting Advent ring,
    The Tortoise stove is lit again
And lamp-oil light across the night
    Has caught the streaks of winter rain
In many a stained-glass window sheen
From Crimson Lake to Hooker's Green.

The holly in the windy hedge
    And round the Manor House the yew
Will soon be stripped to deck the ledge,
    The altar, font and arch and pew,
So that the villagers can say
'The church looks nice' on Christmas Day.

Provincial public houses blaze
    And Corporation tramcars clang,
On lighted tenements I gaze
    Where paper decorations hang,
And bunting in the red Town Hall
Says 'Merry Christmas to you all'.

And London shops on Christmas Eve
    Are strung with silver bells and flowers
As hurrying clerks the City leave
    To pigeon-haunted classic towers,
And marbled clouds go scudding by
The many-steepled London sky.

And girls in slacks remember Dad,
    And oafish louts remember Mum,
And sleepless children's hearts are glad,
    And Christmas-morning bells say 'Come!'
Even to shining ones who dwell
Safe in the Dorchester Hotel.

And is it true? And is it true,
　　This most tremendous tale of all,
Seen in a stained-glass window's hue,
　　A Baby in an ox's stall?
The Maker of the stars and sea
Become a Child on earth for me?

And is it true? For if it is,
　　No loving fingers tying strings
Around those tissued fripperies,
　　The sweet and silly Christmas things,
Bath salts and inexpensive scent
And hideous tie so kindly meant,

No love that in a family dwells,
　　No carolling in frosty air,
Nor all the steeple-shaking bells
　　Can with this single Truth compare –
That God was Man in Palestine
And lives to-day in Bread and Wine.

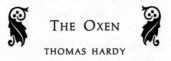

THE OXEN

THOMAS HARDY

Christmas Eve, and twelve of the clock.
　　'Now they are all on their knees,'
An elder said as we sat in a flock
　　By the embers in hearthside ease.

We pictured the meek mild creatures where
　　They dwelt in their strawy pen,
Nor did it occur to one of us there
　　To doubt they were kneeling then.

So fair a fancy few would weave
   In these years! Yet, I feel,
If someone said on Christmas Eve,
   'Come; see the oxen kneel

'In the lonely barton by yonder coomb
   Our childhood used to know,'
I should go with him in the gloom,
   Hoping it might be so.

 THE CHRISTMAS TREE

C. DAY LEWIS

Put out the lights now!
Look at the Tree, the rough tree dazzled
In oriole plumes of flame,
Tinselled with twinkling frost fire, tasselled
With stars and moons – the same
That yesterday hid in the spinney and had no fame
Till we put out the lights now.

Hard are the nights now:
The fields at moonrise turn to agate,
Shadows are cold as jet;
In dyke and furrow, in copse and faggot
The frost's tooth is set;
And stars are the sparks whirled out by the north wind's fret
On the flinty nights now.

So feast your eyes now
On mimic star and moon-cold bauble:
Worlds may wither unseen
But the Christmas Tree is a tree of fable,
A phoenix in evergreen,

And the world cannot change or chill what its mysteries mean
To your hearts and eyes now.

The vision dies now
Candle by candle; the tree that embraced it
Returns to its own kind,
To be earthed again and weather as best it
May the frost and the wind.
Children, it too had its hour – you will not mind
If it lives or dies now.

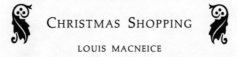 CHRISTMAS SHOPPING

LOUIS MACNEICE

Spending beyond their income on gifts for Christmas –
Swing doors and crowded lifts and draperied jungles –
What shall we buy for our husbands and sons
    Different from last year?

Foxes hang by their noses behind the plate glass –
Scream of macaws across festoons of paper –
Only the faces on the boxes of chocolates are free
    From boredom and crowsfeet.

Sometimes a chocolate-box girl escapes in the flesh,
Lightly manoeuvres the crowd, trilling with laughter;
After a couple of years her feet and her brain will
    Tire like the others.

The great windows marshal their troops for assault on the purse
Something-and-eleven the yard, hoodwinking logic,
The eleventh hour draining the gurgling pennies
    Down to the conduits

Down to the sewers of money – rats and marshgas –
Bubbling in maundering music under the pavement;

Here go the hours of routine, the weight on our eyelids –
    Pennies on corpses'.

While over the street in the centrally heated public
Library dwindling figures with sloping shoulders
And hands in pockets, weighted in the boots like chessmen,
    Stare at the printed

Columns of ads, the quickset road to riches,
Starting at a little and temporary but once we're
Started who knows whether we shan't continue,
    Salaries rising,

Rising like a salmon against the bullnecked river,
Bound for the spawning-ground of care-free days –
Good for a fling before the golden wheels run
    Down to a standstill.

And Christ is born – The nursery glad with baubles,
Alive with light and washable paint and children's
Eyes, expects as its due the accidental
    Loot of a system.

Smell of the South – oranges in silver paper,
Dates and ginger, the benison of firelight,
The blue flames dancing round the brandied raisins,
    Smiles from above them,

Hands from above them as of gods but really
These their parents, always seen from below, them-
Selves are always anxious looking across the
    Fence to the future –

Out there lies the future gathering quickly
Its blank momentum; through the tubes of London
The dead winds blow the crowds like beasts in flight from
    Fire in the forest.

The little firtrees palpitate with candles
In hundreds of chattering households where the suburb
Straggles like nervous handwriting, the margin
    Blotted with smokestacks.

Further out on the coast the lighthouse moves its
Arms of light through the fog that wads our welfare,
Moves its arms like a giant at Swedish drill whose
   Mind is a vacuum.

NOW ONE TIME
IT COMES
ON CHRISTMAS...

Now four American stories, all beautifully written, all varieties of frontier experience. Willa Cather was born in Virginia in 1873 where her ancestors had farmed the land for generations. When she was eight her father bought a ranch in Nebraska, then still immigrant territory. One of the people who interested her most in her childhood was the Bohemian hired girl of a neighbouring family. She is the Ántonia of this story. Mr Shimerda exemplifies Catholic piety, Grandfather the home-grown Protestant variety; but it is Mr Shimerda's kneeling body, shaped like an S as he prays, which lingers in the mind. Truman Capote was born in New Orleans and raised in various parts of the South — winters in New Orleans, summers in Alabama and New Georgia. His short stories were first published when he was fourteen, and it is not hard to see why when one feels the assurance of 'A Christmas Memory'. Prohibition, a nightmare that was to haunt America for thirteen long years, casts its shadow here and is of course central to the action in Damon Runyon's 'Dancing Dan's Christmas': 'For a while some people try making hot Tom and Jerry without putting rum in it, but somehow it never has the same old holiday spirit...' Fortunately, however, Doc Moggs has a capital remedy: '...there is nothing better for rheumatism than rye whisky, especially if it is made up in a hot Tom and Jerry'. The grand old Christmas spirit is made manifest even on West Forty-seventh Street. Finally in this quartet, O. Henry's 'The Gift of the Magi', exploring one American experience with which we are decreasingly familiar: poverty. It is said to be his best story.

Alistair Cooke's account of Christmas in Vermont with his daughter is not fiction, but is appended here as yet another lapidary mutation of frontier experience. His son-in-law proposes a toast to the bounty of nature with some justice; for nothing they ate during the three days had been, as they say in New England, 'store boughten'; they had lived off the good earth.

My Ántonia

WILLA CATHER

During the week before Christmas, Jake was the most important person of our household, for he was to go to town and do all our Christmas shopping. But on the twenty-first of December, the snow began to fall. The flakes came down so thickly that from the sitting-room windows I could not see beyond the windmill – its frame looked dim and grey, unsubstantial like a shadow. The snow did not stop falling all day, or during the night that followed. The cold was not severe, but the storm was quiet and resistless. The men could not go farther than the barns and corral. They sat about the house most of the day as if it were Sunday; greasing their boots, mending their suspenders, plaiting whip-lashes.

On the morning of the twenty-second, grandfather announced at breakfast that it would be impossible to go to Black Hawk for Christmas purchases. Jake was sure he could get through on horseback, and bring home our things in saddle-bags; but grandfather told him the roads would be obliterated, and a newcomer in the country would be lost ten times over. Anyway, he would never allow one of his horses to be put to such a strain.

We decided to have a country Christmas, without any help from town. I had wanted to get some picture books for Yulka and Ántonia; even Yulka was able to read a little now. Grandmother took me into the ice-cold storeroom, where she had some bolts of gingham and sheeting. She cut squares of cotton cloth and we sewed them together into a book. We bound it between pasteboards, which I covered with brilliant calico, representing scenes from a circus. For two days I sat at the dining-room table, pasting this book full of pictures for Yulka. We had files of those good old family magazines which used to publish coloured lithographs of popular paintings, and I was allowed to use some of these. I took 'Napoleon Announcing the Divorce to Josephine' for my frontispiece. On the white pages I grouped Sunday-School cards and advertising cards which I had brought from my 'old country'. Fuchs got out the old candle-moulds and made tallow candles. Grandmother hunted up her fancy cake-cutters and baked gingerbread men and roosters, which we decorated with burnt sugar and red cinnamon drops.

On the day before Christmas, Jake packed the things we were sending to the Shimerdas in his saddle-bags and set off on grandfather's grey gelding. When he mounted his horse at the door, I saw that he had a hatchet slung to his belt, and he gave grandmother a meaning look which told me he was planning a surprise for me.

That afternoon I watched long and eagerly from the sitting-room window. At last I saw a dark spot moving on the west hill, beside the half-buried cornfield, where the sky was taking on a coppery flush from the sun that did not quite break through. I put on my cap and ran out to meet Jake. When I got to the pond, I could see that he was bringing in a little cedar tree across his pommel. He used to help my father cut Christmas trees for me in Virginia, and he had not forgotten how much I liked them.

By the time we had placed the cold, fresh-smelling little tree in a corner of the sitting-room, it was already Christmas Eve. After supper we all gathered there, and even grandfather, reading his paper by the table, looked up with friendly interest now and then. The cedar was about five feet high and very shapely. We hung it with the gingerbread animals, strings of popcorn, and bits of candle which Fuchs had fitted into

pasteboard sockets. Its real splendours, however, came from the most unlikely place in the world – from Otto's cowboy trunk. I had never seen anything in that trunk but old boots and spurs and pistols, and a fascinating mixture of yellow leather thongs, cartridges, and shoemaker's wax. From under the lining he now produced a collection of brilliantly coloured paper figures, several inches high and stiff enough to stand alone. They had been sent to him year after year, by his old mother in Austria. There was a bleeding heart, in tufts of paper lace; there were the three kings, gorgeously apparelled, and the ox and the ass and the shepherds; there was the Baby in the manger, and a group of angels, singing; there were camels and leopards, held by the black slaves of the three kings. Our tree became the talking tree of the fairy tale; legends and stories nestled like birds in its branches. Grandmother said it reminded her of the Tree of Knowledge. We put sheets of cotton wool under it for a snow-field, and Jake's pocket-mirror for a frozen lake.

I can see them now, exactly as they looked, working about the table in the lamplight: Jake with his heavy features, so rudely moulded that his face seemed, somehow, unfinished; Otto with his half-ear and the savage scar that made his upper lip curl so ferociously under his twisted moustache. As I remember them, what unprotected faces they were; their very roughness and violence made them defenceless. These boys had no practised manner behind which they could retreat and hold people at a distance. They had only their hard fists to batter at the world with. Otto was already one of those drifting, case-hardened labourers who never marry or have children of their own. Yet he was so fond of children!

On Christmas morning, when I got down to the kitchen, the men were just coming in from their morning chores – the horses and pigs always had their breakfast before we did. Jake and Otto shouted 'Merry Christmas!' to me, and winked at each other when they saw the waffle-irons on the stove. Grandfather came down, wearing a white shirt and his Sunday coat. Morning prayers were longer than usual. He read the chapters from Saint Matthew about the birth of Christ, and as we listened, it all seemed like something that had happened lately, and near at hand. In his prayer he thanked the Lord for the first Christmas, and for all that it had meant to the world ever since. He gave thanks for our food and comfort, and prayed for the poor and destitute in great cities, where the struggle for life was harder than it was here with us. Grandfather's prayers were often very interesting. He had the gift of simple and moving expression. Because he talked so little, his words had a peculiar force; they were not worn dull from constant use. His prayers reflected what he was thinking about at the time, and it was chiefly through them that we got to know his feelings and his views about things.

After we sat down to our waffles and sausage, Jake told us how pleased the Shimerdas had been with their presents; even Ambrosch was friendly and went to the creek with him to cut the Christmas tree. It was a soft grey day outside, with heavy clouds working across the sky, and occasional squalls of snow. There were always odd jobs to be done about the barn on holidays, and the men were busy until afternoon. Then Jake and I played dominoes, while Otto wrote a long letter home to his mother. He always wrote to her on Christmas Day, he said, no matter where he was, and no matter how long it had been since his last letter. All afternoon he sat in the dining-room. He would write for a while, then sit idle, his clenched fist lying on the table, his eyes following the pattern of the oilcloth. He spoke and wrote his own language so seldom that it came to him awkwardly. His effort to remember entirely absorbed him.

At about four o'clock a visitor appeared: Mr Shimerda, wearing his rabbit-skin cap and collar, and new mittens his wife had knitted. He had come to thank us for the presents, and for all grandmother's kindness to his family. Jake and Otto joined us from the basement and we sat about the stove, enjoying the deepening grey of the winter afternoon and the atmosphere of comfort and security in my grandfather's house. This feeling seemed completely to take possession of Mr Shimerda. I suppose, in the crowded clutter of their cave, the old man had come to believe that peace and order had vanished from the earth, or existed only in the old world he had left so far behind. He sat still and passive, his head resting against the back of the wooden rocking-chair, his hands relaxed upon the arms. His face had a look of weariness and pleasure, like that of sick people when they feel relief from pain. Grandmother insisted on his drinking a glass of Virginia apple-brandy after his long walk in the cold, and when a faint flush came up in his cheeks, his features might have been cut out of a shell, they were so transparent. He said almost nothing, and smiled rarely; but as he rested there we all had a sense of his utter content.

As it grew dark, I asked whether I might light the Christmas tree before the lamp was brought. When the candle-ends sent up their conical yellow flames, all the coloured figures from Austria stood out clear and full of meaning against the green boughs. Mr Shimerda rose, crossed himself, and quietly knelt down before the tree, his head sunk forward. His long body formed a letter 'S'. I saw grandmother look apprehensively at grandfather. He was rather narrow in religious matters, and sometimes spoke out and hurt people's feelings. There had been nothing strange about the tree before, but now, with some one kneeling before it – images, candles ... Grandfather merely put his finger-tips to his brow and bowed his venerable head, thus Protestantizing the atmosphere.

We persuaded our guest to stay for supper with us. He needed little urging. As we sat down to the table, it occurred to me that he liked to look at us, and that our faces were open books to him. When his deep-seeing eyes rested on me, I felt as if he were looking far ahead into the future for me, down the road I would have to travel.

At nine o'clock Mr Shimerda lighted one of our lanterns and put on his overcoat and fur collar. He stood in the little entry hall, the lantern and his fur cap under his arm, shaking hands with us. When he took grandmother's hand, he bent over it as he always did, and said slowly, 'Good wo-man!' He made the sign of the cross over me, put on his cap and went off in the dark. As we turned back to the sitting-room, grandfather looked at me searchingly. 'The prayers of all good people are good,' he said quietly.

A Christmas Memory

TRUMAN CAPOTE

Imagine a morning in late November. A coming of winter morning more than twenty years ago. Consider the kitchen of a spreading old house in a country town. A great black stove is its main feature; but there is also a big round table and a fireplace with two rocking chairs placed in front of it. Just today the fireplace commenced its seasonal roar.

A woman with shorn white hair is standing at the kitchen window. She is wearing tennis shoes and a shapeless grey sweater over a summery calico dress. She is small and sprightly, like a bantam hen; but, due to a long youthful illness, her shoulders are pitifully hunched. Her face is remarkable – not unlike Lincoln's, craggy like that, and tinted by sun and wind; but it is delicate too, finely boned, and her eyes are sherry-coloured and timid. 'Oh my,' she exclaims, her breath smoking the windowpane, 'it's fruitcake weather!'

The person to whom she is speaking is myself. I am seven; she is sixty-something. We are cousins, very distant ones, and we have lived together – well, as long as I can remember. Other people inhabit the house, relatives; and though they have power over us, and frequently make us cry, we are not, on the whole, too much aware of them. We are each other's best friend. She calls me Buddy, in memory of a boy who was formerly her best friend. The other Buddy died in the 1880s, when she was still a child. She is still a child.

'I knew it before I got out of bed,' she says, turning away from the window with a purposeful excitement in her eyes. 'The courthouse bell sounded so cold and clear. And there were no birds singing; they've gone to warmer country, yes indeed. Oh, Buddy, stop stuffing biscuit and fetch our buggy. Help me find my hat. We've thirty cakes to bake.'

It's always the same: a morning arrives in November, and my friend, as though officially inaugurating the Christmas time of year that exhilarates her imagination and fuels the blaze of her heart, announces: 'It's fruitcake weather! Fetch our buggy. Help me find my hat.'

The hat is found, a straw cartwheel corsaged with velvet roses out-of-doors has faded: it once belonged to a more fashionable relative. Together, we guide our buggy, a dilapidated baby carriage, out to the garden and into a grove of pecan trees. The buggy is mine; that is, it was bought for me when I was born. It is made of wicker, rather unravelled, and the wheels wobble like a drunkard's legs. But it is a faithful object;

springtimes, we take it to the woods and fill it with flowers, herbs, wild fern for our porch pots; in the summer, we pile it with picnic paraphernalia and sugar-cane fishing poles and roll it down to the edge of a creek; it has its winter uses, too: as a truck for hauling firewood from the yard to the kitchen, as a warm bed for Queenie, our tough little orange and white rat terrier who has survived distemper and two rattlesnake bites. Queenie is trotting beside it now.

Three hours later we are back in the kitchen hulling a heaping buggyload of windfall pecans. Our backs hurt from gathering them: how hard they were to find (the main crop having been shaken off the trees and sold by the orchard's owners, who are not us) among the concealing leaves, the frosted, deceiving grass. Caarackle! A cheery crunch, scraps of miniature thunder sound as the shells collapse and the golden mound of sweet oily ivory meat mounts in the milk-glass bowl. Queenie begs to taste, and now and again my friend sneaks her a mite, though insisting we deprive ourselves. 'We mustn't, Buddy. If we start, we won't stop. And there's scarcely enough as there is. For thirty cakes.' The kitchen is growing dark. Dusk turns the window into a mirror: our reflections mingle with the rising moon as we work by the fireside in the firelight. At last, when the moon is quite high, we toss the final hull into the fire and, with joined sighs, watch it catch flame. The buggy is empty, the bowl is brim-full.

We eat our supper (cold biscuits, bacon, blackberry jam) and discuss tomorrow. Tomorrow the kind of work I like best begins: buying. Cherries and citron, ginger and vanilla and canned Hawaiian pineapple, rinds and raisins and walnuts and whisky and oh, so much flour, butter, so many eggs, spices, flavourings: why, we'll need a pony to pull the buggy home.

But before these purchases can be made, there is the question of money. Neither of us has any. Except for skinflint sums persons in the house occasionally provide (a dime is considered very big money); or what we earn ourselves from various activities: holding rummage sales, selling buckets of hand-picked blackberries, jars of home-made jam and apple jelly and peach preserves, rounding up flowers for funerals and weddings. Once we won seventy-ninth prize, five dollars, in a national football contest. Not that we know a fool thing about football. It's just that we enter any contest we hear about: at the moment our hopes are centred on the fifty-thousand-dollar Grand Prize being offered to name a new brand of coffee (we suggested 'A.M.'; and, after some hesitation, for my friend thought it perhaps sacrilegious, the slogan 'A.M.! Amen!'). To tell the truth, our only *really* profitable enterprise was the Fun and Freak Museum we conducted in a backyard wood-shed two summers ago. The Fun was a stereopticon with slide views of Washington and New York lent us by a relative who had been to those places (she was furious when she discovered why we'd borrowed it); the Freak was a three-legged biddy chicken hatched by one of our own hens. Everybody hereabouts wanted to see that biddy: we charged grown-ups a nickel, kids two cents. And took in a good twenty dollars before the museum shut down due to the decease of the main attraction.

But one way and another we do each year accumulate Christmas savings, a Fruitcake Fund. These moneys we keep hidden in an ancient bead purse under a loose board under the floor under a chamber pot under my friend's bed. The purse is seldom removed from this safe location except to make a deposit, or, as happens every Saturday, a withdrawal; for on Saturdays I am allowed ten cents to go to the picture show. My friend has never been to a picture show, nor does she intend to: 'I'd rather hear you tell the story, Buddy. That way I can imagine it more. Besides, a person my age shouldn't squander their eyes. When the Lord comes, let me see him clear.' In addition to never having seen a movie, she has never: eaten in a restaurant, travelled more than five miles from home, received or sent a telegram, read anything except funny papers and the Bible, worn cosmetics, cursed, wished someone harm, told a lie on purpose, let a hungry dog go hungry. Here are a few things she has done, does do: killed with a hoe the biggest rattlesnake ever seen in this county (sixteen rattles), dip snuff (secretly), tame hummingbirds (just try it) till they balance on her finger, tell ghost stories (we both believe in ghosts) so tingling they chill you in July, talk to herself, take walks in the rain, grow the prettiest japonicas in town, know the recipe for every sort of old-time Indian cure, including a magical wart-remover.

Now, with supper finished, we retire to the room in a faraway part of the house where my friend sleeps in a scrap-quilt-covered iron bed painted rose pink, her favourite colour. Silently, wallowing in the pleasures of conspiracy, we take the bead purse from its secret place and spill its contents on the scrap quilt. Dollar bills, tightly rolled and green as May buds. Sombre fifty-cent pieces, heavy enough to weight a dead man's eyes. Lovely dimes, the liveliest coin, the one that really jingles. Nickels and quarters, worn smooth as creek pebbles. But mostly a hateful heap of bitter-odoured pennies. Last summer others in the house contracted to pay us a penny for every twenty-five flies we killed. Oh, the carnage of August: the flies that flew to heaven! Yet it was not work in which we took pride. And, as we sit counting pennies, it is as though we were back tabulating dead flies. Neither of us has a head for figures; we count slowly, lose track, start again. According to her calculations, we have $12.73. According to mine, exactly $13. 'I do hope you're wrong, Buddy. We can't mess around with thirteen. The cakes will fall. Or put somebody in the cemetery. Why, I wouldn't dream of getting out of bed on the thirteenth.' This is true: she always spends thirteenths in bed. So, to be on the safe side, we subtract a penny and toss it out the window.

Of the ingredients that go into our fruitcakes, whisky is the most expensive, as well as the hardest to obtain: State laws forbid its sale. But everybody knows you can buy a bottle from Mr Haha Jones. And the next day, having completed our more prosaic shopping, we set out for Mr Haha's business address, a 'sinful' (to quote public opinion) fish-fry and dancing café down by the river. We've been there before, and on the same errand; but in previous years our dealings have been with Haha's wife, an iodine-dark Indian woman with brassy peroxided hair and a dead-tired disposition. Actually, we've never laid eyes on her husband, though we've heard that he's an Indian too. A giant with razor scars across his cheeks. They call him Haha because he's so gloomy, a man who never laughs. As we approach his café (a large log cabin festooned inside and out with chains of garish-gay naked light bulbs and standing by the river's muddy edge under the shade of river trees where moss drifts through the branches like grey mist) our steps slow down. Even Queenie stops prancing and sticks close by. People have been murdered in Haha's café. Cut to pieces. Hit on the head. There's a case coming up in court next month. Naturally these goings-on happen at night when the coloured lights cast crazy patterns and the victrola wails. In the daytime Haha's is shabby and deserted. I knock at the door, Queenie barks, my friend calls: 'Mrs Haha, ma'am? Anyone to home?'

Footsteps. The door opens. Our hearts overturn. It's Mr Haha Jones himself! And he *is* a giant; he *does* have scars; he *doesn't* smile. No, he glowers at us through Satan-tilted eyes and demands to know: 'What you want with Haha?'

For a moment we are too paralysed to tell. Presently my friend half-finds her voice, a whispery voice at best: 'If you please, Mr Haha, we'd like a quart of your finest whisky.'

His eyes tilt more. Would you believe it? Haha is smiling! Laughing, too. 'Which one of you is a drinkin' man?'

'It's for making fruitcakes, Mr Haha. Cooking.'

This sobers him. He frowns. 'That's no way to waste good whisky.' Nevertheless, he retreats into the shadowed café and seconds later appears carrying a bottle of daisy yellow unlabelled liquor. He demonstrates its sparkle in the sunlight and says: 'Two dollars.'

We pay him with nickels and dimes and pennies. Suddenly, jangling the coins in his hand like a fistful of dice, his face softens. 'Tell you what,' he proposes, pouring the money back into our bead purse, 'just send me one of them fruitcakes instead.'

'Well,' my friend remarks on our way home, 'there's a lovely man. We'll put an extra cup of raisins in *his* cake.'

The black stove, stoked with coal and firewood, glows like a lighted pumpkin. Eggbeaters whirl, spoons spin round in bowls of butter and sugar, vanilla sweetens the air, ginger spices it; melting, nose-tingling odours saturate the kitchen, suffuse the house, drift out to the world on puffs of chimney smoke. In four days our work is done. Thirty-one cakes, dampened with whisky, bask on window sills and shelves.

Who are they for?

Friends. Not necessarily neighbour friends: indeed the larger share are intended for persons we've met maybe once, perhaps not at all. People who've struck our fancy. Like President Roosevelt. Like the Reverend and Mrs J. C. Lucey, Baptist missionaries to Borneo who lectured here last winter. Or the little knife grinder who comes through town twice a year. Or Abner Packer, the driver of the six o'clock bus from Mobile, who

exchanges waves with us every day as he passes in a dust-cloud whoosh. Or the young Wistons, a California couple whose car one afternoon broke down outside the house and who spent a pleasant hour chatting with us on the porch (young Mr Wiston snapped our picture, the only one we've ever had taken). Is it because my friend is shy with everyone *except* strangers, that these strangers, and merest acquaintances, seem to us our truest friends? I think yes. Also, the scrapbooks we keep of thank-you's on White House stationery, time-to-time communications from California and Borneo, the knife-grinder's penny postcards, make us feel connected to eventful worlds beyond the kitchen with its view of a sky that stops.

Now a nude December fig branch grates against the window. The kitchen is empty, the cakes are gone; yesterday we carted the last of them to the post office, where the cost of stamps turned our purse inside out. We're broke. That rather depresses me, but my friend insists on celebrating – with two inches of whisky left in Haha's bottle. Queenie has a spoonful in a bowl of coffee (she likes her coffee chicory-flavoured and strong). The rest we divide between a pair of jelly glasses. We're both quite awed at the prospect of drinking straight whisky; the taste of it brings screwed-up expressions and sour shudders. But by and by we begin to sing, the two of us singing different songs simultaneously. I don't know the words to mine, just: *Come on along, come on along, to the dark-town strutters' ball.* But I can dance: that's what I mean to be, a tap dancer in the movies. My dancing shadow rollicks on the walls; our voices rock the chinaware; we giggle: as if unseen hands were tickling us. Queenie rolls on her back, her paws plough the air, something like a grin stretches her black lips. Inside myself, I feel warm and sparky as those crumbling logs, carefree as the wind in the chimney. My friend waltzes round the stove, the hem of her poor calico skirt pinched between her fingers as though it were a party dress: *Show me the way to go home*, she sings, her tennis shoes squeaking on the floor. *Show me the way to go home.*

Enter: two relatives. Very angry. Potent with eyes that scold, tongues that scald. Listen to what they have to say, the words tumbling together into a wrathful tune: 'A child of seven! whisky on his breath! are you out of your mind? feeding a child of seven! must be loony! road to ruination! remember Cousin Kate? Uncle Charlie? Uncle Charlie's brother-in-law? shame! scandal! humiliation! kneel, pray, beg the Lord!'

Queenie sneaks under the stove. My friend gazes at her shoes, her chin quivers, she lifts her skirt and blows her nose and runs to her room. Long after the town has gone to sleep and the house is silent except for the chimings of clocks and the sputter of fading fires, she is weeping into a pillow already as wet as a widow's handkerchief.

'Don't cry,' I say, sitting at the bottom of her bed and shivering despite my flannel nightgown that smells of last winter's cough syrup, 'don't cry,' I beg, teasing her toes, tickling her feet, 'you're too old for that.'

'It's because', she hiccups, 'I *am* too old. Old and funny.'

'Not funny. Fun. More fun than anybody. Listen. If you don't stop crying you'll be so tired tomorrow we can't go cut a tree.'

She straightens up. Queenie jumps on the bed (where Queenie is not allowed) to lick her cheeks. 'I know where we'll find real pretty trees, Buddy. And holly, too. With berries big as your eyes. It's way off in the woods. Farther than we've ever been. Papa used to bring us Christmas trees from there: carry them on his shoulder. That's fifty years ago. Well, now: I can't wait for morning.'

Morning. Frozen rime lustres the grass; the sun, round as an orange and orange as hot-weather moons, balances on the horizon, burnishes the silvered winter woods. A wild turkey calls. A renegade hog grunts in the undergrowth. Soon, by the edge of knee-deep, rapid-running water, we have to abandon the buggy. Queenie wades the stream first, paddles across barking complaints at the swiftness of the current, the pneumonia-making coldness of it. We follow, holding our shoes and equipment (a hatchet, a burlap sack) above our heads. A mile more: of chastizing thorns, burrs, and briers that catch at our clothes; of rusty pine needles brilliant with gaudy fungus and moulted feathers. Here, there, a flash, a flutter, an ecstasy of shrillings remind us that not all the birds have flown south. Always, the path unwinds through lemony sun pools and pitch vine tunnels. Another creek to cross: a disturbed armada of speckled trout froths the water round us, and frogs the size of plates practise belly flops; beaver workmen are building a dam. On the farther shore, Queenie shakes herself and trembles. My friend shivers, too: not with cold but enthusiasm. One of her hat's ragged roses sheds a petal as she lifts her head and inhales the pine-heavy air. 'We're almost there; can you smell it, Buddy?' she says, as though we were approaching an ocean.

And, indeed, it is a kind of ocean. Scented acres of holiday trees, prickly-leafed holly. Red berries shiny as Chinese bells: black crows swoop upon them screaming. Having stuffed our burlap sacks with enough greenery and crimson to garland a dozen windows, we set about choosing a tree. 'It should be', muses my friend, 'twice as tall as a boy. So a boy can't steal the star.' The one we pick is twice as tall as me. A brave handsome brute that survives thirty hatchet strokes before it keels with a crackling rending cry.

Lugging it like a kill, we commence the long trek out. Every few yards we abandon the struggle, sit down, and pant. But we have the strength of triumphant huntsmen; that and the tree's virile, icy perfume revive us, goad us on. Many compliments accompany our sunset return along the red clay road to town; but my friend is sly and non-committal when passers-by praise the treasure perched in our buggy: what a fine tree and where did it come from? 'Yonderways,' she murmurs vaguely. Once a car stops and the rich mill owner's lazy wife leans out and whines: 'Giveya two-bits cash for that ol tree.' Ordinarily my friend is afraid of saying no; but on this occasion she promptly shakes her head: 'We wouldn't take a dollar.' The mill owner's wife persists. 'A dollar, my foot! Fifty cents. That's my last offer. Goodness, woman, you can get another one.' In answer, my friend gently reflects: 'I doubt it. There's never two of anything.'

Home: Queenie slumps by the fire and sleeps till tomorrow, snoring loud as a human.

A trunk in the attic contains: a shoebox of ermine tails (off the opera cape of a curious lady who once rented a room in the house), coils of frazzled tinsel gone gold with age, one silver star, a brief rope of dilapidated, undoubtedly dangerous candy-like light bulbs. Excellent decorations, as far as they go, which isn't far enough: my friend wants our tree to blaze 'like a Baptist window', droop with weighty snows of ornament. But we can't afford the made-in-Japan splendours at the five-and-dime. So we do what we've always done: sit for days at the kitchen table with scissors and crayons and stacks of coloured paper. I make sketches and my friend cuts them out: lots of cats, fish too (because they're easy to draw), some apples, some watermelons, a few winged angels devised from saved-up sheets of Hershey-bar tin foil. We use safety pins to attach these creations to the tree; as a final touch, we sprinkle the branches with shredded cotton (picked in August for this purpose). My friend, surveying the effect, clasps her hands together. 'Now honest, Buddy. Doesn't it look good enough to eat?' Queenie tries to eat an angel.

After weaving and ribboning holly wreaths for all the front windows, our next project is the fashioning of family gifts. Tie-dye scarves for the ladies, for the men a home-brewed lemon and liquorice and aspirin syrup to be taken 'at the first Symptoms of a Cold and after Hunting'. But when it comes time for making each other's gift, my friend and I separate to work secretly. I would like to buy her a pearl-handled knife, a radio, a whole pound of chocolate-covered cherries (we tasted some once, and she always swears: 'I could live on them, Buddy, Lord yes I could – and that's not taking His name in vain'). Instead, I am building her a kite. She would like to give me a bicycle (she's said so on several million occasions: 'If only I could, Buddy. It's bad enough in life to do without something *you* want; but confound it, what gets my goat is not being able to give somebody something you want *them* to have. Only one of these days I will, Buddy. Locate you a bike. Don't ask how. Steal it, maybe.'). Instead, I'm fairly certain that she is building me a kite – the same as last year, and the year before: the year before that we exchanged slingshots. All of which is fine by me. For we are champion kite-fliers who study the wind like sailors; my friend, more accomplished than I, can get a kite aloft when there isn't enough breeze to carry clouds.

Christmas Eve afternoon we scrape together a nickel and go to the butcher's to buy Queenie's traditional gift, a good gnawable beef bone. The bone, wrapped in funny paper, is placed high in the tree near the silver star. Queenie knows it's there. She squats at the foot of the tree staring up in a trance of greed: when bedtime arrives she refuses to budge. Her excitement is equalled by my own. I kick the covers and turn my pillow as though it were a scorching summer's night. Somewhere a rooster crows: falsely, for the sun is still on the other side of the world.

'Buddy, are you awake?' It is my friend, calling from her room, which is next to mine; and an instant later she is sitting on my bed holding a candle. 'Well, I can't sleep a hoot,' she declares. 'My mind's jumping like a jack rabbit. Buddy, do you think Mrs Roosevelt will serve our cake at dinner?' We huddle in the bed, and she squeezes my hand I-love-you. 'Seems like your hand used to be so much smaller. I guess I hate to see you grow up. When you're grown up, will we still be friends?' I say always. 'But I feel so bad, Buddy. I wanted so bad to give you a bike. I tried to sell my cameo Papa gave me. Buddy' – she hesitates, as though embarrassed – 'I made you another kite.' Then I confess that I made her one, too; and we laugh. The candle burns too short to hold. Out it goes, exposing the starlight, the stars spinning at the window like a visible carolling that slowly, slowly daybreak silences. Possibly we doze; but the beginnings of dawn splash us like cold water: we're up, wide-eyed and wandering while we wait for others to waken. Quite deliberately my friend drops a kettle on the kitchen floor. I tap-dance in front of closed doors. One by one the household emerges, looking as though they'd like to kill us both; but it's Christmas, so they can't. First, a gorgeous breakfast: just everything you can imagine – from flapjacks and fried squirrel to hominy grits and honey-in-the-comb. Which puts everyone in a good humour except my friend and me. Frankly, we're so impatient to get at the presents we can't eat a mouthful.

Well, I'm disappointed. Who wouldn't be? With socks, a Sunday-school shirt, some handkerchiefs, a hand-me-down sweater, and a year's subscription to a religious magazine for children. *The Little Shepherd.* It makes me boil. It really does.

My friend has a better haul. A sack of Satsumas, that's her best present. She is proudest, however, of a white wool shawl knitted by her married sister. But she *says* her favourite gift is the kite I built her. And it *is* very beautiful; though not as beautiful as the one she made me, which is blue and scattered with gold and green Good Conduct stars; moreover, my name is painted on it, 'Buddy'.

'Buddy, the wind is blowing.'

The wind is blowing, and nothing will do till we've run to a pasture below the house where Queenie has scooted to bury her bone (and where, a winter hence, Queenie will be buried, too). There, plunging through the healthy waist-high grass, we unreel our kites, feel them twitching at the string like sky fish as they swim into the wind. Satisfied, sun-warmed, we sprawl in the grass and peel Satsumas and watch our kites cavort. Soon I forget the socks and hand-me-down sweater. I'm as happy as if we'd already won the fifty-thousand-dollar Grand Prize in that coffee-naming contest.

'My, how foolish I am!' my friend cries, suddenly alert, like a woman remembering too late she has biscuits in the oven. 'You know what I've always thought?' she asks in a tone of discovery, and not smiling at me but a point beyond. 'I've always thought a body would have to be sick and dying before they saw the Lord. And I imagined that when He came it would be like looking at the Baptist window: pretty as coloured glass with the sun pouring through, such a shine you don't know it's getting dark. And it's been a coloured glass with the sun pouring through, such a spooky feeling. But I'll wager it never happens. I'll wager at the very end a body realizes the Lord has already shown Himself. That things as they are' – her hand circles in a gesture that gathers clouds and kites and grass and Queenie pawing earth over her bone – 'just what they've always seen, was seeing Him. As for me, I could leave the world with today in my eyes.'

This is our last Christmas together.

Life separates us. Those who Know Best decide that I belong in a military school. And so follows a miserable succession of bugle-blowing prisons, grim reveille-ridden summer camps. I have a new home too. But it doesn't count. Home is where my friend is, and there I never go.

And there she remains, puttering around the kitchen. Alone with Queenie. Then alone. ('Buddy dear,' she writes in her wild hard-to-read script, 'yesterday Jim Macy's horse kicked Queenie bad. Be thankful she didn't feel much. I wrapped her in a Fine Linen sheet and rode her in the buggy down to Simpson's pasture where she can be with all her Bones . . .') For a few Novembers she continues to bake her fruitcakes single-handed; not as many, but some: and, of course, she always sends me 'the best of the batch'. Also, in every letter she encloses a dime wadded in toilet paper: 'See a picture show and write me the story.' But gradually in her letters she tends to confuse me with her other friend, the Buddy who died in the 1880s; more and more thirteenths are not the only days she stays in bed: a morning arrives in November, a leafless birdless coming of winter morning, when she cannot rouse herself to exclaim: 'Oh my, it's fruitcake weather!'

And when that happens, I know it. A message saying so merely confirms a piece of news some secret vein had already received, severing from me an irreplaceable part of myself, letting it loose like a kite on a broken string. That is why, walking across a school campus on this particular December morning, I keep searching the sky. As if I expected to see, rather like hearts, a lost pair of kites hurrying towards heaven.

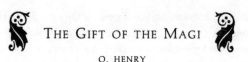

THE GIFT OF THE MAGI

O. HENRY

One dollar and eighty-seven cents. That was all. And sixty cents of it was in pennies. Pennies saved one and two at a time by bulldozing the grocer and the vegetable man and the butcher until one's cheeks burned with the silent imputation of parsimony that such close dealing implied. Three times Della counted it. One dollar and eighty-seven cents. And the next day would be Christmas.

There was clearly nothing to do but flop down on the shabby little couch and howl. So Della did it. Which instigates the moral reflection that life is made up of sobs, sniffles, and smiles, with sniffles predominating.

While the mistress of the home is gradually subsiding from the first stage to the second, take a look at the home. A furnished flat at $8 per week. It did not exactly beggar description, but it certainly had that word on the lookout for the mendicancy squad.

In the vestibule below was a letter-box into which no letter would go, and an electric button from which no mortal finger could coax a ring. Also appertaining thereunto was a card bearing the name 'Mr James Dillingham Young'.

The 'Dillingham' had been flung to the breeze during a former period of prosperity when its possessor was being paid $30 per week. Now, when the income was shrunk to $20, the letters of 'Dillingham' looked blurred, as though they were thinking seriously of contracting to a modest and unassuming D. But whenever Mr James Dillingham Young came home and reached his flat above he was called 'Jim' and greatly hugged by Mrs James Dillingham Young, already introduced to you as Della. Which is all very good.

Della finished her cry and attended to her cheeks with the powder rag. She stood by the window and looked out dully at a grey cat walking a grey fence in a grey backyard. Tomorrow would be Christmas Day, and she had only $1.87 with which to buy Jim a present. She had been saving every penny she could for months, with this result. Twenty dollars a week doesn't go far. Expenses had been greater than she had calculated. They always are. Only $1.87 to buy a present for Jim. Her Jim. Many a happy hour she had spent planning for something nice for him. Something fine and rare and sterling – something just a little bit near to being worthy of the honour of being owned by Jim.

There was a pier-glass between the windows of the room. Perhaps you have seen a pier-glass in an $8 flat. A very thin and very agile person may, by observing his reflection in a rapid sequence of longitudinal strips, obtain a fairly accurate conception of his looks. Della, being slender, had mastered the art.

Suddenly she whirled from the window and stood before the glass. Her eyes were shining brilliantly, but her face had lost its colour within twenty seconds. Rapidly she pulled down her hair and let it fall to its full length.

Now, there were two possessions of the James Dillingham Youngs in which they both took a mighty pride. One was Jim's gold watch that had been his father's and his grandfather's. The other was Della's hair. Had the Queen of Sheba lived in the flat across the airshaft, Della would have let her hair hang out the window some day to dry just to depreciate Her Majesty's jewels and gifts. Had King Solomon been the janitor, with all his treasures piled up in the basement, Jim would have pulled out his watch every time he passed, just to see him pluck at his beard from envy.

So now Della's beautiful hair fell about her rippling and shining like a cascade of brown waters. It reached below her knee and made itself almost a garment for her. And then she did it up again nervously and quickly. Once she faltered for a minute and stood still while a tear or two splashed on the worn red carpet.

On went her old brown jacket; on went her old brown hat. With a whirl of skirts and with the brilliant sparkle still in her eyes, she fluttered out the door and down the stairs to the street.

Where she stopped the sign read: 'Mme Sofronie. Hair Goods of All Kinds.' One flight up Della ran, and collected herself, panting. Madame, large, too white, chilly, hardly looked the 'Sofronie'.

'Will you buy my hair?' asked Della.

'I buy hair,' said Madame. 'Take yer hat off and let's have a sight at the looks of it.'

Down rippled the brown cascade.

'Twenty dollars,' said Madame, lifting the mass with a practised hand.

'Give it to me quick,' said Della.

Oh, and the next two hours tripped by on rosy wings. Forget the hashed metaphor. She was ransacking the stores for Jim's present.

She found it at last. It surely had been made for Jim and no one else. There was no other like it in any of the stores, and she had turned all of them inside out. It was a platinum fob chain simple and chaste in design, properly proclaiming its value by substance alone and not by meretricious ornamentation – as all good things should do. It was even worthy of The Watch. As soon as she saw it she knew that it must be Jim's. It was like him. Quietness and value – the description applied to both. Twenty-one dollars they took from her for it, and she hurried home with the 87 cents. With that chain on his watch Jim might be properly anxious about the time in any company. Grand as the watch was, he sometimes looked at it on the sly on account of the old leather strap that he used in place of a chain.

When Della reached home her intoxication gave way a little to prudence and reason. She got out her curling irons and lighted the gas and went to work repairing the ravages made by generosity added to love. Which is always a tremendous task, dear friends – a mammoth task.

Within forty minutes her head was covered with tiny, close-lying curls that made her look wonderfully like a truant schoolboy. She looked at her reflection in the mirror long, carefully, and critically.

'If Jim doesn't kill me,' she said to herself, 'before he takes a second look at me, he'll say I look like a Coney Island chorus girl. But what could I do – oh! what could I do with a dollar and eighty-seven cents?'

At 7 o'clock the coffee was made and the frying-pan was on the back of the stove hot and ready to cook the chops.

Jim was never late. Della doubled the fob chain in her hand and sat on the corner of the table near the door that he always entered. Then she heard his step on the stair away down on the first flight, and she turned white for just a moment. She had a habit of saying little silent prayers about the simplest everyday things, and now she whispered: 'Please God, make him think I am still pretty.'

The door opened and Jim stepped in and closed it. He looked thin and very serious. Poor fellow, he was only twenty-two – and to be burdened with a family! He needed a new overcoat and he was without gloves.

Jim stopped inside the door, as immovable as a setter at the scent of quail. His eyes were fixed upon Della, and there was an expression in them that she could not read, and it terrified her. It was not anger, nor surprise, nor disapproval, nor horror, nor any of the sentiments that she had been prepared for. He simply stared at her fixedly with that peculiar expression on his face.

Della wriggled off the table and went for him.

'Jim, darling,' she cried, 'don't look at me that way. I had my hair cut off and sold it because I couldn't have lived through Christmas without giving you a present. It'll grow out again – you won't mind, will you? I just had to do it. My hair grows awfully fast. Say "Merry Christmas!" Jim, and let's be happy. You don't know what a nice – what a beautiful, nice gift I've got for you.'

'You've cut off your hair?' asked Jim, laboriously, as if he had not arrived at that patent fact yet even after the hardest mental labour.

'Cut it off and sold it,' said Della. 'Don't you like me just as well, anyhow? I'm me without my hair, ain't I?'

Jim looked about the room curiously.

'You say your hair is gone?' he said, with an air almost of idiocy.

'You needn't look for it,' said Della. 'It's sold, I tell you – sold and gone, too. It's Christmas Eve, boy. Be good to me, for it went for you. Maybe the hairs of my head were numbered,' she went on with a sudden serious sweetness, 'but nobody could ever count my love for you. Shall I put the chops on, Jim?'

Out of his trance Jim seemed quickly to wake. He enfolded his Della. For ten seconds let us regard with discreet scrutiny some inconsequential object in the other direction. Eight dollars a week or a million a year – what is the difference? A mathematician or a wit would give you the wrong answer. The magi brought valuable gifts, but that was not among them. This dark assertion will be illuminated later on.

Jim drew a package from his overcoat pocket and threw it upon the table.

'Don't make any mistake, Dell,' he said, 'about me. I don't think there's anything in the way of a haircut or a shave or a shampoo that could make me like my girl any less. But if you'll unwrap that package you may see why you had me going a while at first.'

White fingers and nimble tore at the string and paper. And then an ecstatic scream of joy; and then, alas! a quick feminine change to hysterical tears and wails, necessitating the immediate employment of all the comforting powers of the lord of the flat.

For there lay The Combs – the set of combs, side and back, that Della had worshipped for long in a Broadway window. Beautiful combs, pure tortoise shell, with jewelled rims – just the shade to wear in the beautiful vanished hair. They were expensive combs, she knew, and her heart had simply craved and yearned over them without the least hope of possession. And now, they were hers, but the tresses that should have adorned the coveted adornments were gone.

But she hugged them to her bosom, and at length she was able to look up with dim eyes and a smile and say: 'My hair grows so fast, Jim!'

And then Della leaped up like a little singed cat and cried, 'Oh, oh!'

Jim had not yet seen his beautiful present. She held it out to him eagerly upon her open palm. The dull precious metal seemed to flash with a reflection of her bright and ardent spirit.

'Isn't it a dandy, Jim? I hunted all over town to find it. You'll have to look at the time a hundred times a day now. Give me your watch. I want to see how it looks on it.'

Instead of obeying, Jim tumbled down on the couch and put his hands under the back of his head and smiled.

'Dell,' said he, 'let's put our Christmas presents away and keep 'em a while. They're too nice to use just at present. I sold the watch to get the money to buy your combs. And now suppose you put the chops on.'

The magi, as you know, were wise men – wonderfully wise men – who brought gifts to the Babe in the manger. They invented the art of giving Christmas presents. Being wise, their gifts were no doubt wise ones, possibly bearing the privilege of exchange in case of duplication. And here I have lamely related to you the uneventful chronicle of two foolish children in a flat who most unwisely sacrificed for each other the greatest treasures of their house. But in a last word to the wise of these days let it be said that of all who give gifts these two were the wisest. Of all who give and receive gifts, such as they are wisest. Everywhere they are wisest. They are the magi.

DANCING DAN'S CHRISTMAS

DAMON RUNYON

Now one time it comes on Christmas, and in fact it is the evening before Christmas, and I am in Good Time Charley Bernstein's little speakeasy in West Forty-seventh Street, wishing Charley a Merry Christmas and having a few hot Tom and Jerrys with him.

This hot Tom and Jerry is an old-time drink that is once used by one and all in this country to celebrate Christmas with, and in fact it is once so popular that many people think Christmas is invented only to furnish an excuse for hot Tom and Jerry, although of course this is by no means true.

But anybody will tell you that there is nothing that brings out the true holiday spirit like hot Tom and Jerry, and I hear that since Tom and Jerry goes out of style in the United States, the holiday spirit is never quite the same.

The reason hot Tom and Jerry goes out of style is because it is necessary to use rum and one thing and another in making Tom and Jerry, and naturally when rum becomes illegal in this country Tom and Jerry is also against the law, because rum is something that is very hard to get around town these days.

For a while some people try making hot Tom and Jerry without putting rum in it, but somehow it never has the same old holiday spirit, so nearly everybody finally gives up in disgust, and this is not surprising, as making Tom and Jerry is by no means child's play. In fact, it takes quite an expert to make good Tom and Jerry, and in the days when it is not illegal a good hot Tom and Jerry maker commands good wages and many friends.

Now of course Good Time Charley and I are not using rum in the Tom and Jerry we are making, as we do not wish to do anything illegal. What we are using is rye whisky that Good Time Charley gets on a doctor's prescription from a drug store, as we are personally drinking this hot Tom and Jerry and naturally we are not foolish enough to use any of Good Time Charley's own rye in it.

The prescription for the rye whisky comes from old Doc Moggs, who prescribes it for Good Time Charley's rheumatism in case Charley happens to get any rheumatism, as Doc Moggs says there is nothing better for rheumatism than rye whisky, especially if it is made up in a hot Tom and Jerry. In fact, old Doc Moggs comes around and has a few seidels of hot Tom and Jerry with us for his own rheumatism.

He comes around during the afternoon, for Good Time Charley and I start making this Tom and Jerry early in the day, so as to be sure to have enough to last us over

Christmas, and it is now along towards six o'clock, and our holiday spirit is practically one hundred per cent.

Well, as Good Time Charley and I are expressing our holiday sentiments to each other over our hot Tom and Jerry, and I am trying to think up the poem about the night before Christmas and all through the house, which I know will interest Charley no little, all of a sudden there is a big knock at the front door, and when Charley opens the door who comes in carrying a large package under one arm but a guy by the name of Dancing Dan.

This Dancing Dan is a good-looking young guy, who always seems well-dressed, and he is called by the name of Dancing Dan because he is a great hand for dancing around and about with dolls in night clubs, and other spots where there is any dancing. In fact, Dan never seems to be doing anything else, although I hear rumours that when he is not dancing he is carrying on in a most illegal manner at one thing and another. But of course you can always hear rumours in this town about anybody, and personally I am rather fond of Dancing Dan as he always seems to be getting a great belt out of life.

Anybody in town will tell you that Dancing Dan is a guy with no Barnaby whatever in him, and in fact he has about as much gizzard as anybody around, although I wish to say I always question his judgment in dancing so much with Miss Muriel O'Neill, who works in the Half Moon night club. And the reason I question his judgment in this respect is because everybody knows that Miss Muriel O'Neill is a doll who is very well thought of by Heine Schmitz, and Heine Schmitz is not such a guy as will take kindly to anybody dancing more than once and a half with a doll that he thinks well of.

This Heine Schmitz is a very influential citizen of Harlem, where he has large interests in beer, and other business enterprises, and it is by no means violating any confidence to tell you that Heine Schmitz will just as soon blow your brains out as look at you. In fact, I hear sooner. Anyway, he is not a guy to monkey with and many citizens take the trouble to advise Dancing Dan that he is not only away out of line in dancing with Miss Muriel O'Neill, but that he is knocking his own price down to where he is no price at all.

But Dancing Dan only laughs ha-ha, and goes on dancing with Miss Muriel O'Neill any time he gets a chance, and Good Time Charley says he does not blame him, at that, as Miss Muriel O'Neill is so beautiful that he will be dancing with her himself no matter what, if he is five years younger and can get a Roscoe out as fast as in the days when he runs with Paddy the Link and other fast guys.

Well, anyway, as Dancing Dan comes in he weighs up the joint in one quick peek, and then he tosses the package he is carrying into a corner where it goes plunk, as if there is something very heavy in it, and then he steps up to the bar alongside of Charley and me and wishes to know what we are drinking.

Naturally we start boosting hot Tom and Jerry to Dancing Dan, and he says he will take a crack at it with us, and after one crack, Dancing Dan says he will have another crack, and Merry Christmas to us with it, and the first thing anybody knows it is a couple of hours later and we are still having cracks at the hot Tom and Jerry with Dancing Dan, and Dan says he never drinks anything so soothing in his life. In fact, Dancing Dan says he will recommend Tom and Jerry to everybody he knows, only he does not know anybody good enough for Tom and Jerry, except maybe Miss Muriel O'Neill, and she does not drink anything with drugstore rye in it.

Well, several times while we are drinking this Tom and Jerry, customers come to the door of Good Time Charley's little speakeasy and knock, but by now Charley is commencing to be afraid they will wish Tom and Jerry, too, and he does not feel we will have enough for ourselves, so he hangs out a sign which says 'Closed on Account of Christmas', and the only one he will let in is a guy by the name of Ooky, who is nothing but an old rum-dum, and who is going around all week dressed like Santa Claus and carrying a sign advertising Moe Lewinsky's clothing joint around in Sixth Avenue.

This Ooky is still wearing his Santa Claus outfit when Charley lets him in, and the reason Charley permits such a character as Ooky in his joint is because Ooky does the porter work for Charley when he is not Santa Claus for Moe Lewinsky, such as sweeping out, and washing the glasses, and one thing and another.

Well, it is about nine-thirty when Ooky comes in, and his puppies are aching, and he is all petered out generally from walking up and down and here and there with his sign, for any time a guy is Santa Claus for Moe Lewinsky he must earn his dough. In fact, Ooky is so fatigued, and his puppies hurt him so much, that Dancing Dan and Good Time Charley and I all feel very sorry for him, and invite him to have a few mugs of hot Tom and Jerry with us, and wish him plenty of Merry Christmas.

But old Ooky is not accustomed to Tom and Jerry, and after about the fifth mug he folds up in a chair, and goes right to sleep on us. He is wearing a pretty good Santa Claus make-up, what with a nice red suit trimmed with white cotton, and a wig, and false nose, and long white whiskers, and a big sack stuffed with excelsior on his back, and if I do not know Santa Claus is not apt to be such a guy as will snore loud enough to rattle the windows, I will think Ooky is Santa Claus sure enough.

Well, we forget Ooky and let him sleep, and go on with our hot Tom and Jerry, and in the meantime we try to think up a few songs appropriate to Christmas, and Dancing Dan finally renders My Dad's Dinner Pail in a nice baritone and very loud, while I do first-rate with Will You Love Me in December — As You Do in May? But personally I always think Good Time Charley Bernstein is a little out of line trying to sing a hymn in Jewish on such an occasion, and it causes words between us.

While we are singing many customers come to the door and knock, and then they read Charley's sign, and this seems to cause some unrest among them, and some of them stand outside saying it is a great outrage, until Charley sticks his noggin out the door and threatens to bust somebody's beezer if they do not go on about their business and stop disturbing peaceful citizens.

Naturally the customers go away, as they do not wish their beezers busted, and Dancing Dan and Charley and I continue drinking our hot Tom and Jerry, and with each Tom and Jerry we are wishing one another a very Merry Christmas, and sometimes a very Happy New Year, although of course this does not go for Good Time Charley as yet, because Charley has his New Year separate from Dancing Dan and me.

By and by we take to waking Ooky up in his Santa Claus outfit and offering him more hot Tom and Jerry, and wishing him Merry Christmas, but Ooky only gets sore and calls us names, so we can see he does not have the right holiday spirit in him, and let him alone until along about midnight when Dancing Dan wishes to see how he looks as Santa Claus.

So Good Time Charley and I help Dancing Dan pull off Ooky's outfit and put it on Dan, and this is easy as Ooky only has this Santa Claus outfit on over his ordinary clothes, and he does not even wake up when we are undressing him of the Santa Claus uniform.

Well, I wish to say I see many a Santa Claus in my time, but I never see a better-looking Santa Claus than Dancing Dan, especially after he gets the wig and white whiskers fixed just right, and we put a sofa pillow that Good Time Charley happens to have around the joint for the cat to sleep on down his pants to give Dancing Dan a nice fat stomach such as Santa Claus is bound to have.

In fact, after Dancing Dan looks at himself in a mirror awhile he is greatly pleased with his appearance, while Good Time Charley is practically hysterical, although personally I am commencing to resent Charley's interest in Santa Claus, and Christmas generally, as he by no means has any claim on these matters. But then I remember Charley furnishes the hot Tom and Jerry, so I am more tolerant towards him.

'Well,' Charley finally says, 'it is a great pity we do not know where there are some stockings hung up somewhere, because then,' he says, 'you can go around and stuff things in these stockings, as I always hear this is the main idea of a Santa Claus. But,' Charley says, 'I do not suppose anybody in this section has any stockings hung up, or if they have,' he says, 'the chances are they are so full of holes they will not hold anything. Anyway,' Charley says, 'even if there are any stockings hung up we do not have anything to stuff in them, although personally,' he says, 'I will gladly donate a few pints of Scotch.'

Well, I am pointing out that we have no reindeer and that a Santa Claus is bound to look like a terrible sap if he goes around without any reindeer, but Charley's remarks seem to give Dancing Dan an idea, for all of a sudden he speaks as follows:

'Why,' Dancing Dan says, 'I know where a stocking is hung up. It is hung up at Miss Muriel O'Neill's flat over here in West Forty-ninth Street. This stocking is hung up by nobody but a party by the name of Gammer O'Neill, who is Miss Muriel O'Neill's grandmamma,' Dancing Dan says. 'Gammer O'Neill is going on ninety-odd,' he says, 'and Miss Muriel O'Neill tells me she cannot hold out much longer, what with one thing and another, including being a little childish in spots.

'Now,' Dancing Dan says, 'I remember Miss Muriel O'Neill is telling me just the other night how Gammer O'Neill hangs up her stocking on Christmas Eve all her life, and,' he says, 'I judge from what Miss Muriel O'Neill says that the old doll always believes Santa Claus will come along some Christmas and fill the stocking full of beautiful gifts. But,' Dancing Dan says, 'Miss Muriel O'Neill tells me Santa Claus never does this, although Miss Muriel O'Neill personally always takes a few gifts home and pops them into the stocking to make Gammer O'Neill feel better.

'But, of course,' Dancing Dan says, 'these gifts are nothing much because Miss Muriel O'Neill is very poor, and proud, and also good, and will not take a dime off of anybody, and I can lick the guy who says she will, although,' Dancing Dan says, 'between me, and Heine Schmitz, and a raft of other guys I can mention, Miss Muriel O'Neill can take plenty.'

Well, I know that what Dancing Dan states about Miss Muriel O'Neill is quite true, and in fact it is a matter that is often discussed on Broadway, because Miss Muriel O'Neill cannot get more than twenty bobs per week working in the Half Moon, and it is well known to one and all that this is no kind of dough for a doll as beautiful as Miss Muriel O'Neill.

'Now,' Dancing Dan goes on, 'it seems that while Gammer O'Neill is very happy to get whatever she finds in her stocking on Christmas morning, she does not understand why Santa Claus is not more liberal, and,' he says, 'Miss Muriel O'Neill is saying to me that she only wishes she can give Gammer O'Neill one real big Christmas before the old doll puts her checks back in the rack.

'So,' Dancing Dan states, 'here is a job for us. Miss Muriel O'Neill and her grandmamma live all alone in this flat over in West Forty-ninth Street, and,' he says, 'at such an hour as this Miss Muriel O'Neill is bound to be working, and the chances are Gammer O'Neill is sound asleep, and we will just hop over there and Santa Claus will fill up her stocking with beautiful gifts.'

Well, I say, I do not see where we are going to get any beautiful gifts at this time of night, what with all the stores being closed, unless we dash into an all-night drug store and buy a few bottles of perfume and a bum toilet set as guys always do when they forget about their ever-loving wives until after store hours on Christmas Eve, but Dancing Dan says never mind about this, but let us have a few more Tom and Jerrys first.

So we have a few more Tom and Jerrys, and then Dancing Dan picks up the package he heaves into the corner, and dumps most of the excelsior out of Ooky's Santa Claus sack, and puts the bundle in, and Good Time Charley turns out all the lights but one, and leaves a bottle of Scotch on the table in front of Ooky for a Christmas gift, and away we go.

Personally, I regret very much leaving the hot Tom and Jerry, but then I am also very enthusiastic about going along to help Dancing Dan play Santa Claus, while Good Time Charley is practically overjoyed, as it is the first time in his life Charley is ever mixed up in so much holiday spirit. In fact, nothing will do Charley but that we stop in a couple of spots and have a few drinks to Santa Claus's health, and these visits are a big success, although everybody is much surprised to see Charley and me with Santa Claus, especially Charley, although nobody recognizes Dancing Dan.

But of course there are no hot Tom and Jerrys in these spots we visit, and we have to drink whatever is on hand, and personally I will always believe that the noggin I have on me afterwards comes of mixing the drinks we get in these spots with my Tom and Jerry.

As we go up Broadway, headed for Forty-ninth Street, Charley and I see many citizens we know and give them a large hello, and wish them Merry Christmas, and some of these citizens shake hands with Santa Claus, not knowing he is nobody but Dancing Dan, although later I understand there is some gossip among these citizens because they claim a Santa Claus with such a breath on him as our Santa Claus has is a little out of line.

And once we are somewhat embarrassed when a lot of little kids going home with their parents from a late Christmas party somewhere gather about Santa Claus with shouts of childish glee, and some of them wish to climb up Santa Claus's legs. Naturally, Santa Claus gets a little peevish, and calls them a few names, and one of the parents comes up and wishes to know what is the idea of Santa Claus using such language, and Santa Claus takes a punch at the parent, all of which is no doubt most astonishing to the little kids who have an idea of Santa Claus as a very kindly old guy. But of course they do not know about Dancing Dan mixing the liquor we get in the spots we visit with his Tom and Jerry, or they will understand how even Santa Claus can lose his temper.

Well, finally we arrive in front of the place where Dancing Dan says Miss Muriel O'Neill and her grandmamma live, and it is nothing but a tenement house not far back of Madison Square Garden, and furthermore it is a walk-up, and at this time there are no lights burning in the joint except a gas jet in the main hall, and by the light of this jet we look at the names on the letter-boxes, such as you always find in the hall of these joints, and we see that Miss Muriel O'Neill and her grandmamma live on the fifth floor.

This is the top floor, and personally I do not like the idea of walking up five flights of stairs, and I am willing to let Dancing Dan and Good Time Charley go, but Dancing Dan insists we must all go, and finally I agree because Charley is commencing to argue that the right way for us to do is to get on the roof and let Santa Claus go down a chimney, and is making so much noise I am afraid he will wake somebody up.

So up the stairs we climb and finally we come to a door on the top floor that has a little card in a slot that says O'Neill, so we know we reach our destination. Dancing

Dan first tries the knob, and right away the door opens, and we are in a little two- or three-room flat, with not much furniture in it, and what furniture there is is very poor. One single gas jet is burning near a bed in a room just off the one the door opens into, and by this light we see a very old doll is sleeping on the bed, so we judge this is nobody but Gammer O'Neill.

On her face is a large smile, as if she is dreaming of something very pleasant. On a chair at the head of the bed is hung a long black stocking, and it seems to be such a stocking as is often patched and mended, so I can see what Miss Muriel O'Neill tells Dancing Dan about her grandmamma hanging up her stocking is really true, although up to this time I have my doubts.

Well, I am willing to pack in after one gander at the old doll, especially as Good Time Charley is commencing to prowl around the flat to see if there is a chimney where

Santa Claus can come down, and is knocking things over, but Dancing Dan stands looking down at Gammer O'Neill for a long time.

Finally he unslings the sack on his back, and takes out his package, and unties this package, and all of a sudden out pops a raft of big diamond bracelets, and diamond rings, and diamond brooches, and diamond necklaces, and I do not know what all else in the way of diamonds, and Dancing Dan and I begin stuffing these diamonds into the stocking and Good Time Charley pitches in and helps us.

There are enough diamonds to fill the stocking to the muzzle, and it is no small stocking, at that, and I judge that Gammer O'Neill has a pretty fair set of bunting sticks when she is young. In fact, there are so many diamonds that we have enough left over to make a nice little pile on the chair after we fill the stocking plumb up, leaving a nice diamond-studded vanity case sticking out the top where we figure it will hit Gammer O'Neill's eye when she wakes up.

And it is not until I get out in the fresh air again that all of a sudden I remember seeing large headlines in the afternoon papers about a five-hundred-G's stick-up in the afternoon of one of the biggest diamond merchants in Maiden Lane while he is sitting in his office, and I also recall once hearing rumours that Dancing Dan is one of the best lone-hand git-'em-up guys in the world.

Naturally I commence to wonder if I am in the proper company when I am with Dancing Dan, even if he is Santa Claus. So I leave him on the next corner arguing with Good Time Charley about whether they ought to go and find some more presents somewhere, and look for other stockings to stuff, and I hasten on home, and go to bed.

The next day I find I have such a noggin that I do not care to stir around, and in fact I do not stir around much for a couple of weeks.

Then one night I drop around to Good Time Charley's little speakeasy, and ask Charley what is doing.

'Well,' Charley says, 'many things are doing, and personally,' he says, 'I am greatly surprised I do not see you at Gammer O'Neill's wake. You know Gammer O'Neill leaves this wicked old world a couple of days after Christmas,' Good Time Charley says, 'and,' he says, 'Miss Muriel O'Neill states that Doc Moggs claims it is at least a day after she is entitled to go, but she is sustained,' Charley says, 'by great happiness on finding her stocking filled with beautiful gifts on Christmas morning.

'According to Miss Muriel O'Neill,' Charley says, 'Gammer O'Neill dies practically convinced that there is a Santa Claus, although of course,' he says, 'Miss Muriel O'Neill does not tell her the real owner of the gifts, an all-right guy by the name of Shapiro, leaves the gifts with her after Miss Muriel O'Neill notifies him of the finding of same.

'It seems,' Charley says, 'this Shapiro is a tender-hearted guy, who is willing to help keep Gammer O'Neill with us a little longer when Doc Moggs says leaving the gifts with her will do it.

'So,' Charley says, 'everything is quite all right, as the coppers cannot figure anything except that maybe the rascal who takes the gifts from Shapiro gets conscience stricken, and leaves them the first place he can, and Miss Muriel O'Neill receives a ten-G's reward for finding the gifts and returning them. And,' Charley says, 'I hear Dancing Dan is in San Francisco and is figuring on reforming and becoming a dancing teacher, so he can marry Miss Muriel O'Neill, and of course,' he says, 'we all hope and trust she never learns any details of Dancing Dan's career.'

Well, it is Christmas Eve a year later that I run into a guy by the name of Shotgun Sam, who is mobbed up with Heine Schmitz in Harlem, and who is a very, very obnoxious character indeed.

'Well, well, well,' Shotgun says, 'the last time I see you is another Christmas Eve like this, and you are coming out of Good Time Charley's joint, and,' he says, 'you certainly have your pots on.'

'Well, Shotgun,' I say, 'I am sorry you get such a wrong impression of me, but the truth is,' I say, 'on the occasion you speak of, I am suffering from a dizzy feeling in my head.'

'It is all right with me,' Shotgun says. 'I have a tip this guy Dancing Dan is in Good Time Charley's the night I see you, and Mockie Morgan and Gunner Jack and me are casing the joint, because,' he says, 'Heine Schmitz is all sored up at Dan over some doll, although of course,' Shotgun says, 'it is all right now, and Heine has another doll.'

'Anyway,' he says, 'we never get to see Dancing Dan. We watch the joint from six-thirty in the evening until daylight Christmas morning, and nobody goes in all night but old Ooky the Santa Claus guy in his Santa Claus make-up, and,' Shotgun says, 'nobody comes out except you and Good Time Charley and Ooky.

'Well,' Shotgun says, 'it is a great break for Dancing Dan he never goes in or comes out of Good Time Charley's, at that, because,' he says, 'we are waiting for him on the second-floor front of the building across the way with some nice little sawed-offs, and are under orders from Heine not to miss.'

'Well, Shotgun,' I say, 'Merry Christmas.'

'Well, all right,' Shotgun says, 'Merry Christmas.'

CHRISTMAS IN VERMONT

ALISTAIR COOKE

31 December 1976

I spent a four-day Christmas with my daughter in northern Vermont after flying out of New York City on one of those brilliant blue winter days that ring like a bell. There was not a smidgeon of snow anywhere. But very soon after we flew over Long Island Sound and into Connecticut, the smears were lining the roads, and by the time we were over Boston every lake and pond was a white rectangle and the forests were as leafless as a storehouse of telegraph poles, the towns collections of little wooden boxes strewn around bare ground. Then the real snow came in, first fringing the mountains then blanketing them, and as we veered and banked over the white-peppered evergreens the only bare land you could see was the long curving ribbons of cement, of the federal highways snaking through a planet of snow.

When you're not used to it, it's always a shock to get out of a plane and feel that somebody's slapped you in the eyes with a towel. This is simply the first adjustment to the blinding northern light. I went padding towards the tiny airport taking deep breaths of oxygen as sharp as ammonia. I was met by my daughter and son-in-law and grandson, a grinning Brueghel trio if ever I saw one. It had been fourteen below zero when they woke up, and though it had gone up to a suffocating twenty above, their outlines were thickened by the snow boots and the billowing pants and those parkas that look like balloons but weigh about an ounce and are warmer than all the wool and sweaters in the world. My family, in short, looked like the first family of spacemen out there to greet a wan man-creature from remote New York.

With suspicious casualness, my daughter told me to put my bag in the back of the station wagon. I found it was impossible, because rearing up there and making a frightful honking sound were two of the fattest geese outside the *Christmas Carol*. About twenty minutes later, when we'd arrived at the graceful little white wooden eighteenth-century box they call home, I should say not more than ten minutes after we'd arrived, the two fat geese honked no more. They had departed this life, having had their necks wrung by my son-in-law and my son – a flown-in refugee from another distant planet, California. I didn't see these two for the next hour or two, which is just as well for a squeamish city type, since they'd been busy cleaning and plucking the birds against the Christmas feast.

The kitchen, which on any working farm is the centre of things, was dense with odours and tottering with platters and bowls, and my wife and daughter up to their elbows in parsley and onions and forcemeat and chanterelles, and pans bubbling with morelles (plucked, according to a sacred tradition of my children, from dark corners in the woods by the light of a waning moon). The only time I ever saw anything like it was in rural France when I was invited to see what was brewing in the recesses of one of those country restaurants that manage to snag three stars from the Parisian dictators of such things.

My daughter and son-in-law lead a hard – but on these occasions and strictly to an outsider what looks like an idyllic – life. The food is not everything in some families but it happens to be my daughter's passion. And why not? After all, she has a lot of time hanging on her hands. She gets up before six, feeds, dresses and civilizes two small children, then goes out to see to the chickens and – in summer and fall – the raising of the fruits and vegetables. All that's left is to clean the house, stack the wood for the stoves, clean the barns, shovel the knee-high, fresh snow into parapets so as to be able to get to the big sleeping polar bear which tomorrow, the next day maybe, will turn into an automobile. Ferry the four-year-old over the ice and snow to school, and put in an hour or so campaigning for the public (non-commercial) television station. So this leaves her ample time to prepare three meals a day, which are never snacks, at any time of the year. The first night, we started – started, mind – with a platter of smoked bluefish, one of a dozen thirteen-pounders her husband had caught in the summer off the end of Long Island. We smoked them within hours of the catch and they froze beautifully. After that came the irresistible piece of resistance: venison. Ten days before, my son-in-law had shot a doe and I'm happy to say I was not on hand to watch him and my daughter spend the next six hours skinning, de-gutting and butchering it before leaving it for the statutory week or so to hang.

I ought to say that I've had venison in farmhouses in Scotland and in lush restaurants in London and Paris. And, with an immense to-do and gaudy promises of food for the gods, in Texas. Texas does not, like any other region, simply have indigenous dishes. It proclaims them. It congratulates you, on your arrival, at having escaped from the slop-pails of the other forty-nine States. Welcome to Texas, and the incomparable three dishes of the Lone Star State: venison, *chili con carne*, and rattlesnake. (To the goggling unbeliever, they say – as people always say about their mangier dishes – 'But it's just like chicken, only tenderer.' Rattlesnake is, in fact, just like chicken, only tougher.)

Well, about venison and its hunters and preparers, I can only say that they all wag their fingers against their noses and confide to you, as a privileged guest, their dark and secret recipes for hanging and cooking and having it 'come out just right'. And it's always smelly and gamey and a little tough. In a restaurant, you can let the whole thing go with a sickly nod at the waiter. But the Texans are nothing if not considerate and eager hosts. They always beg you to tell them truthfully if you've ever eaten venison like that. The true answer is yes, unfortunately, always. But they are kindly people and you have to think up some variation on old Sam Goldwyn's line when he was pressed

for an opinion by a brother film producer who'd just shown him his latest masterpiece in a sneak preview. 'Louis,' Goldwyn used to say, looking the man square in the eye, 'only you could 'eff made a movie like thet.'

Well, I want to tell you that that first evening I had naturally assigned the venison to Christmas day and the big feast. I started to slice into a very fine tenderloin steak. It was so tender you could have eaten it with a spoon. But a round of uh-ums alerted me, rather late, to the fact that this was the venison. With delicate chanterelle sauce. A salad with raw mushrooms. Then Susie's fat and creamy cheesecake, with some of the fruit of the 270 strawberry plants I'd seen her putting in earlier in the year, up to her knees in mud on some idle day. Just to keep things in the family, the wine was a remarkable claret from the vineyard my stepson farms in the beautiful Alexander Valley eighty miles north of San Francisco.

Well, it went on like that. And on Christmas day, we had the geese, succulent and very serene in death. And a billowing cheese soufflé. And from time to time, there wafted in from the kitchen the scent of the four sorts of bread my daughter had baked. I once said to her, 'Any day now, Susie, you'll be making your own soap.' It was too late. She'd done it.

At the Christmas feast, with old Thomas Beecham whipping his orchestra and principals into proving once again that he is the Handel master of all time, I was asked to turn it down a shade while my son-in-law – a New England version of Gary Cooper – proposed a toast. He is not a gabby type, and this extraordinary initiative must have been inspired by the Alexander Valley grapes. Anyway, he said he didn't know what a proper toast should be but all he could think of with – 'well, pride I guess you can call it' – was the fact that everything we'd eaten in three days had lived or roamed or been grown right there, or in the woods that rise from the long meadow that goes up to the hills. Nothing, as they say in New England, had been 'store boughten'. And, he ended, 'If it doesn't sound pretentious' – wriggling at the fear that it might be – 'I think we should drink to the bounty of nature.' A very weird thing to toast in the last quarter of the twentieth century, when you can hardly buy a tomato that hasn't been squirted a chemical red, and chickens are raised in little gravel cages, and since they are immobile from birth and failing fast, must for our protection be injected with antibiotics and God knows what. (I know a very knowledgeable food writer in France who says he now recalls that the last time he tasted a chicken – a real free-range chicken – in a restaurant was in 1952.)

That evening we sang carols, in close if creaky harmony, with the four-year-old Adam piping 'God Rest Ye Merry, Gentlemen' right on pitch. Next morning, I woke up and he was out on his skis. They are small skis and he got them a year ago. He was plumping up the hills and skimming down them with the poles helping him on the turns. And I thought, what an extraordinary childhood. He was born in twenty below zero (outside; of course he was born inside). Winter brings about 100–120 inches of snow. May is the squishy month, when the thaw sets in. Summer bangs in with ninety degrees. Fall is a fountain of scarlet and gold, and inky forests of evergreens on the mountains. And here, at four, he's skiing over the deep and crisp and even like a Disney doll. And this is all the life Adam knows.

One day he will grow up and, I'm afraid, taste of the forbidden fruit. One day, he will read the *New York Times*. And Adam will be out of the Garden of Eden, out of Vermont, for ever.

Indeed, our Fathers were Very Wise ...

Now three memories of traditional English Christmas. The last decade of Belloc's life was clouded by illness and the last half of it darkened by bereavement; he lost his adored wife when she was forty and a son in each world war. His enormous œuvre is little read now; but the new biography by A. N. Wilson has done much to help us understand him. In this essay from his 1928 Conversations with an Angel, we find many of the things Belloc held closest to his heart: a profound belief in antiquity; a love of the countryside and country life; a pervasive faith in Roman Catholicism. Yet the Protestant reader, coming to this impassioned defence of a traditional Catholic Christmas, will find almost nothing strange to him except the midnight Mass; and even that may be familiar to him too if he is a practising Anglican. Belloc's style is not everyone's; but there is no denying the simple power with which he paints his scene and puts his case. Then we move north from this Catholic fastness to a Protestant stronghold as we celebrate Christmas at Chatsworth with Harold Macmillan. The period is the same — the 1920s — but the scale has opened up and a hundred and fifty people celebrate under the palatial aegis of his father-in-law, the Duke of Devonshire. Yet the actual ingredients are no different: the tree, the stockings, the presents. And Belloc's ancient house in the Sussex Weald, the Devonshire's venerable pile in the Derbyshire dales, had one other attribute in common: a chapel in which each family could celebrate the great festival in its own Christian mode. Finally we reach back another century for Washington Irving's romantic account of an English country Christmas soon after Waterloo. Here again, family prayers have been already said in the chapel; here again, though the revelries strike us as traditional enough, the old Squire regrets the passing of traditional England, and does all he can to preserve it. Reverence for the past, it seems, has no retrospective frontier; and Christmas is the moment when that reverence unfailingly reaches its apogee.

A Remaining Christmas

HILAIRE BELLOC

The world is changing very fast, and neither exactly for the better or the worse, but for division. Our civilization is splitting more and more into two camps, and what was common to the whole of it is becoming restricted to the Christian, and soon will be restricted to the Catholic half.

That is why I have called this article 'A Remaining Christmas'. People ask themselves how much remains of this observance and of the feast and its customs. Now a concrete instance is more vivid and, in its own way, of more value than a general appreciation. So I will set down here exactly what Christmas still is in a certain house in England, how it is observed, and all the domestic rites accompanying it in their detail and warmth.

This house stands low down upon clay near a little river. It is quite cut off from the towns; no one has built near it. Every cottage for a mile and more is old, with here and there a modern addition. The church of the parish (which was lost of course three and a half centuries ago, under Elizabeth) is as old as the Crusades. It is of the twelfth century. The house of which I speak is in its oldest parts of the fourteenth century at least, and perhaps earlier, but there are modern additions. One wing of it was built seventy years ago at the south end of the house, another at the north end, twenty years ago. Yet the tradition is so strong that you would not tell from the outside, and hardly from the inside, which part is old and which part is new. For, indeed, the old part itself grew up gradually, and the eleven gables of the house show up against the sky as though they were of one age, though in truth they are of every age down along all these five hundred years and more.

The central upper room of the house is the chapel where Mass is said, and there one sees, uncovered by any wall of plaster or brick, the original structure of the house which is of vast oaken beams, the main supports and transverse pieces half a yard across, mortised strongly into each other centuries ago, and smoothed roughly with the adze. They are black with the years. The roof soars up like a high-pitched tent, and is supported by a whole fan of lesser curved oaken beams. There is but one window behind the altar. Indeed, the whole house is thus in its structure of the local and native oak, and the brick walls of it are only curtains built in between the wooden framework of that most ancient habitation.

Beneath the chapel is the dining-room, where there is a very large open hearth which can take huge logs and which is as old as anything in the place. Here wood only is burnt, and that wood oak.

Down this room there runs a very long oaken table as dark with age almost as the beams above it, and this table has a history. It came out of one of the Oxford Colleges when the Puritans looted them three hundred years ago. It never got back to its original home. It passed from one family to another until at last it was purchased (in his youth and upon his marriage) by the man who now owns this house. Those who know about such things give its date as the beginning of the seventeenth century. It was made, then, while Shakespeare was still living, and while the faith of England still hung in the balance; for one cannot say that England was certain to lose her Catholicism finally till the first quarter of that century was passed. This table, roughly carved at the side, has been polished with wax since first it began to bear food for men, and now the surface shines like a slightly, very slightly, undulating sea in a calm. At night the brass candlesticks (for this house is lit with candles, as the proper light for men's eyes) are reflected in it as in still brown water; so are the vessels of glass and of silver and of pewter, and the flagons of wine. No cloth is ever spread to hide this venerable splendour, nor, let us hope, ever will be.

At one end of the house, where the largest of its many outer doors (there are several such) swings massively upon huge forged iron hinges, there is a hall, not very wide; its length is as great as the width of the house and its height very great for its width. Like the chapel, its roof soars up, steep and dark, so that from its floor (which is made of very great and heavy slabs of the local stone) one looks up to the roof-tree itself. This hall has another great wide hearth in it for the burning of oak, and there is an oaken staircase, very wide and of an easy slope, with an oaken balustrade and leading up to an open gallery above, whence you look down upon the piece. Above this gallery is a statue of Our Lady, carved in wood, uncoloured, and holding the Holy Child, and beneath her many shelves of books. This room is panelled, as are so many of the rooms of the house, but it has older panels than any of the others, and the great door of it opens on to the high road.

Now the way Christmas is kept in this house is this:

On Christmas Eve a great quantity of holly and of laurel is brought in from the garden and from the farm (for this house has a farm of a hundred acres attached to it and an oak wood of ten acres). This greenery is put up all over the house in every room just before it becomes dark on that day. Then there is brought into the hall a young pine tree, about twice the height of a man, to serve for a Christmas tree, and on this innumerable little candles are fixed, and presents for all the household and the guests and the children of the village.

It is at about five o'clock that these last come into the house, and at that hour in England, at that date, it has long been quite dark; so they come into a house all illuminated with the Christmas tree shining like a cluster of many stars seen through a glass.

The first thing done after the entry of these people from the village and their children (the children are in number about fifty – for this remote place keeps a good level through the generations and does not shrink or grow, but remains itself) is a common meal, where all eat and drink their fill in the offices. Then the children come in to the Christmas tree. They are each given a silver piece one by one, and one by one, their presents. After that they dance in the hall and sing songs, which have been handed down to them for I do not know how long. These songs are game-songs, and are sung to keep time with the various parts in each game, and the men and things and animals which you hear mentioned in these songs are all of that countryside. Indeed, the tradition of Christmas here is what it should be everywhere, knit into the very stuff of the place; so that I fancy the little children, when they think of Bethlehem, see it in their minds as though it were in the winter depth of England, which is as it should be.

These games and songs continue for as long as they will, and then they file out past the great fire in the hearth to a small piece adjoining where a crib has been set up with images of Our Lady and St Joseph and the Holy Child, the Shepherds, and what I will call, by your leave, the Holy Animals. And here, again, tradition is so strong in this house that these figures are never new-bought, but are as old as the oldest of the children of the family, now with children of their own. On this account, the donkey has lost one of its plaster ears, and the old ox which used to be all brown is now piebald, and of the shepherds, one actually has no head. But all that is lacking is imagined. There hangs from the roof of the crib over the Holy Child a tinsel star grown rather obscure after all these years, and much too large for the place. Before this crib the children (some of them Catholic and some Protestant, for the village is mixed) sing their carols; the one they know best is the one which begins: 'The First Good Joy that Mary had, it was the joy of One.' There are a half a dozen or so of these carols which the children here sing; and mixed with their voices is the voice of the miller (for this house has a great windmill attached to it). The miller is famous in these parts for his singing, having a very deep and loud voice which is his pride. When these carols are over, all disperse, except those who are living in the house, but the older ones are not allowed to go without more good drink for their viaticum, a sustenance for Christian men.

Then the people of the house, when they have dined, and their guests, with the priest who is to say Mass for them, sit up till near midnight. There is brought in a very large log of oak (you must be getting tired of oak by this time! But everything here is oaken, for the house is of the Weald). This log of oak is the Christmas or Yule log and the rule is that it must be too heavy for one man to lift; so two men come, bringing it in from outside, the master of the house and his servant. They cast it down upon the fire in the great hearth of the dining-room, and the superstition is that, if it burns all night and is found still smouldering in the morning, the home will be prosperous for the coming year.

With that they all go up to the chapel and there the three night Masses are said, one after the other, and those of the household take their Communion.

Next morning they sleep late, and the great Christmas dinner is at midday. It is a turkey; and a plum pudding, with holly in it and everything conventional, and therefore satisfactory, is done. Crackers are pulled, the brandy is lit and poured over the pudding till the holly crackles in the flame and the curtains are drawn a moment that the flames may be seen. This Christmas feast, so great that it may be said almost to fill the day, they may reprove who will; but for my part I applaud.

Now, you must not think that Christmas being over, the season and its glories are at an end, for in this house there is kept up the full custom of the Twelve Days, so that 'Twelfth Day', the Epiphany, still has, to its inhabitants, its full and ancient meaning as it had when Shakespeare wrote. The green is kept in its place in every room, and not a leaf of it must be moved until Epiphany morning, but on the other hand not a leaf of it must remain in the house, nor the Christmas tree either, by Epiphany evening. It is all taken out and burnt in a special little coppice reserved for these good trees which have done their Christmas duty; and now, after so many years, you might almost call it a little forest, for each tree has lived, bearing witness to the holy vitality of unbroken ritual and inherited things.

In the midst of this season between Christmas and Twelfth Day comes the ceremony of the New Year, and this is how it is observed:

On New Year's Eve, at about a quarter to twelve o'clock at night, the master of the house and all that are with him go about from room to room opening every door and window, however cold the weather be, for thus, they say, the old year and its burdens can go out and leave everything new for hope and for the youth of the coming time.

This also is a superstition, and of the best. Those who observe it trust that it is as old as Europe, and with roots stretching back into forgotten times.

While this is going on the bells in the church hard by are ringing out the old year, and when all the windows and doors have thus been opened and left wide, all those in the house go outside, listening for the cessation of the chimes, which comes just before the turn of the year. There is an odd silence of a few minutes, and watches are consulted to make certain of the time (for this house detests wireless and has not even a telephone), and the way they know the moment of midnight is by the boom of a gun, which is fired at a town far off, but can always be heard.

At that sound the bells of the church clash out suddenly in new chords, the master of the house goes back into it with a piece of stone or earth from outside, all doors are shut, and the household, all of them, rich and poor, drink a glass of wine together to salute the New Year.

This, which I have just described, is not in a novel or in a play. It is real, and goes on as the ordinary habit of living men and women. I fear that set down thus in our terribly changing time it must sound very strange and, perhaps in places, grotesque, but to those who practise it, it is not only sacred, but normal, having in the whole of the complicated affair a sacramental quality and an effect of benediction; not to be despised.

Indeed, modern men, who lack such things, lack sustenance, and our fathers who founded all those ritual observances were very wise.

CHRISTMAS AT CHATSWORTH

HAROLD MACMILLAN

Christmas at Chatsworth was conducted on traditional lines. Every year was the same, except for the increasing number of children. By the end of the decade these had become a formidable array. The Devonshires' own family consisted, in addition to the Duke and Duchess, of two sons and five daughters, all married. A day or two before the festival, these began to arrive from different parts of the country. The average number of children in each family was about four. These, with their attendant nurses and nurserymaids, amounted therefore to something like fifty souls. Then there were the lady's-maids and valets, bringing the total to at least sixty. In addition there were other guests; sometimes my father and mother or other grandparents; sometimes 'Great-Granny Maud' – the Dowager Lady Lansdowne. There were others, too, who came year after year, by long-established custom. There were generally two or three cousins of the Duke's or Duchess's. In addition, there was Mr Erskine, Deputy Serjeant at Arms, the son of the great Serjeant at Arms who had been a lifelong friend of the Cavendishes; and Mr Mansfield. These two last had been Christmas guests from the times before the Duke succeeded, when he lived at Holker Hall, in Lancashire. They always called the Duchess 'Lady Evie', as a kind of hallmark of long-established friendship. They were reputed intimate cronies of the Duke; he certainly treated them with more than his usual taciturnity. 'Hello Jim', 'Hello Walter', he would say when they arrived and 'Goodbye Jim' and 'Goodbye Walter' when they left. So far as I know, no other conversation passed between them. My much-loved sister-in-law, now Mary, Dowager Duchess, came from a very different home and background. At first, I think, she found the long silences of the Cavendishes somewhat trying; for she was a Cecil and Cecils talk all the time about everything under the sun, with animated and fiercely contested verbal combats. The Duke did not like argument.

With all these Christmas visitors and their attendants, together with the permanent and temporary servants in the household, the number gathered under that vast roof must have been something like one hundred and fifty people. The children, of course, delighted in this strange and exciting world. They were spoilt and pampered by the servants and made many long friendships with them. It was always a new pleasure to be conducted through the great kitchens, the huge pantries, the larders with their stone floors and vaulted roofs; above all, the great building, larger than many butchers' shops, where hung rows of carcasses of oxen and sheep, and game of every kind. Many of the families, including my own, arrived with their ponies. So the stables were a continual source of interest to be visited, each string of animals being accompanied by their attendant grooms. One special treat was to be taken through the plate-rooms. Here was kept, in the care of an old retired under-butler, a great collection, much of it dating from the seventeenth and eighteenth centuries. The beautiful William and Mary dressing-sets were there; and in addition, the gold plate. On certain occasions, at Christmas or at other great parties, the best of the plate was shown in the dining-room. But for the most part, except for the pieces in daily use, these treasures were kept in the vigilant care of their devoted guardian.

The ritual did not differ from year to year. All assembled the day before. As each family arrived, 'Granny Evie' received them at the top of the stairs where the Outer Hall led into the passage leading to the great Painted Hall. My children still remember her greeting each family in turn – always in her place, as the cars passed the lodge – a gracious and dignified figure, dressed in dark colours and long flowing dresses, never changing. Shy and reserved as she was, with the children, like the Duke, she had no inhibitions. The sons-in-law, of course, soon learnt the desirability of sending their families by the early train, and ensuring sufficient important business in London to make it necessary for them to follow later and more comfortably.

Christmas Eve in this, as in every other home throughout the land, was a flurry of mothers filling and hanging stockings, decorating nurseries, and getting to bed very late themselves. All this is still carried on in a modified form in my own home as, happily, in many other houses. Children and grandchildren gather yearly for the great festival.

Christmas Day. Early to church at eight o'clock across the park in the darkness; then breakfast and the morning with the enjoyment of minor presents. Balloons to be inflated, trumpets to be blown, and roller-skates to be tried out. No house is better fitted for roller-skating. The whole course is good, with particularly fast going on the stone floor of the Statue Gallery and the Orangery. Then Matins at the parish church in the park, with a full and overflowing congregation; all the familiar hymns; and a mercifully short sermon. The clergyman likes to be asked to shoot, and the Duke, though he says little, has a good memory. Christmas lunch, to which children over a certain age were allowed – the rules strictly enforced – and then the photograph. In those days the ingenious methods by which these can be taken indoors had not been invented. We all trooped out to a particularly cold and draughty part of the garden – by Flora's Temple, outside the Orangery. When at last all the generations could be brought into some kind of order, the yearly photograph was taken. Each year showed a steady increase

and, happily, no casualties – not yet. A walk in the garden followed, which was supposed to be healthy and after the Christmas cheer was no doubt salutary.

One of the old traditions of Chatsworth scrupulously maintained was Evensong every Sunday in the house chapel. Those who know Chatsworth will remember the great beauty of this masterpiece of late seventeenth-century work, with its lovely altar and the fine ceiling. The village organist and choir came up for the service. Two rows of straight Jacobean chairs stood facing each other. On one side were the men; on the other the women. When the house was full, with all the guests, servants, and visiting servants, there was a goodly company. The service always ended with the same hymn, called the Benediction hymn, sung kneeling:

> Father give us now Thy Blessing,
> Take us now beneath Thy Care;
> May we all enjoy Thy presence,
> And Thy tender mercies share.
>
> Guard us through this night from danger,
> Keep us in Thy heavenly love;
> Through our life do Thou be near us,
> Then receive us all above.

Its origin is unknown.

The weather at Chatsworth was of two kinds and both in an extreme form. Sometimes the glass was low and the temperature mild. Then it was dark, rainy, foggy, and uninviting. Or there could be a high glass, with snow and ice and toboganning and skating. These were the Christmases I remember with the keenest pleasure – the beauty of the great trees in the garden and park, and the house shining with a strangely golden glow in the rays of the low winter sun. The weather played an important part in the daily routine. Following a custom of many generations, every day at breakfast there was placed on one of the splendid Kent side-tables a book recording the temperature, the hours of sunshine, and the rainfall, compiled by one of the gardeners. The Duke studied this every morning, carefully, but without emotion.

After tea on Christmas Day came the ceremony of presents given and received. This took place in the Statue Gallery, where stood the huge tree. First, all the presents to the servants, taken round by the children; then presents from children to grown-ups; then, at last, the children's own presents from all their different relations. They were perhaps not so expensive or so elaborate as they are today, but with the enormous family interchange, they were very numerous.

Boxing Day. Children who survived (there were always some casualties to colds or over-excitement) went off to the meet of the High Peak Harriers at Bakewell. At this time my sister-in-law Maud Baillie and her husband Evan were the Joint Masters. It was a great gathering of local sportsmen, including many children, coming from far and wide. There was no shooting on Boxing Day so that all the men on the place could enjoy their holiday. For those who did not hunt it was, therefore, a day of sleep, or bridge, or reading. During the next few days there was shooting – and good shooting – and then some of the older members of the party began to disperse. But the mothers and children generally stayed on for two or three weeks, the fathers returning each weekend for more shooting. At last, reluctantly, but with a sense of great achievement, this large family party came to an end until the next year.

THE CHRISTMAS DINNER

WASHINGTON IRVING

I had finished my toilet, and was loitering with Frank Bracebridge in the library, when we heard a distant thwacking sound, which he informed me was a signal for the serving up of the dinner. The Squire kept up old customs in kitchen as well as hall; and the rolling-pin, struck upon the dresser by the cook, summoned the servants to carry in the meats.

Just in this nick the cook knock'd thrice,
And all the waiters in a trice
    His summons did obey;
Each serving man, with dish in hand,
March'd boldly up, like our train-band,
    Presented and away.

The dinner was served up in the great hall, where the Squire always held his Christmas banquet. A blazing crackling fire of logs had been heaped on to warm the spacious apartment, and the flame went sparkling and wreathing up the wide-mouthed chimney. The great picture of the crusader and his white horse had been profusely decorated with greens for the occasion; and holly and ivy had likewise been wreathed round the helmet and weapons on the opposite wall, which I understood were the arms of the same warrior. I must own, by the bye, I had strong doubts about the authenticity of the painting and armour as having belonged to the crusader, they certainly having the stamp of more recent days; but I was told that the painting had been so considered time out of mind; and that as to the armour, it had been found in a lumber room, and elevated to its present situation by the Squire, who at once determined it to be the armour of the family hero; and as he was absolute authority on all such subjects in his own household, the matter had passed into current acceptation. A sideboard was set out just under this chivalric trophy, on which was a display of plate that might have vied (at least in variety) with Belshazzar's parade of the vessels of the temple: 'flagons, cans, cups, beakers, goblets, basins, and ewers;' the gorgeous utensils of good companionship, that had gradually accumulated through many generations of jovial housekeepers. Before these stood the two Yule candles beaming like two stars of the first magnitude; other lights were distributed in branches, and the whole array glittered like a firmament of silver.

We were ushered into this banqueting scene with the sound of minstrelsy, the old harper being seated on a stool beside the fireplace, and twanging his instrument with a vast deal more power then melody. Never did Christmas board display a more goodly and gracious assemblage of countenances: those who were not handsome were, at least, happy; and happiness is a rare improver of your hard-favoured visage. I always consider an old English family as well worth studying as a collection of Holbein's portraits or Albert Dürer's prints. There is much antiquarian lore to be acquired; much knowledge of the physiognomies of former times. Perhaps it may be from having continually before their eyes those rows of old family portraits, with which the mansions of this country are stocked; certain it is, that the quaint features of antiquity are often most faithfully perpetuated in these ancient lines; and I have traced an old family nose through a whole picture gallery, legitimately handed down from generation to generation, almost from the time of the Conquest. Something of the kind was to be observed in the worthy company around me. Many of their faces had evidently originated in a Gothic age, and been merely copied by succeeding generations; and there was one little girl, in particular, of staid demeanour, with a high Roman nose, and an antique vinegar aspect, who was a great favourite of the Squire's, being, as he said, a Bracebridge all over, and the very counterpart of one of his ancestors who figured in the court of Henry VIII.

The parson said grace, which was not a short familiar one, such as is commonly addressed to the Deity, in these unceremonious days; but a long, courtly, well-worded one of the ancient school. There was now a pause, as if something was expected; when suddenly the butler entered the hall with some degree of bustle; he was attended by a servant on each side with a large wax-light, and bore a silver dish, on which was an enormous pig's head decorated with rosemary, with a lemon in its mouth, which was placed with great formality at the head of the table. The moment this pageant made its

appearance, the harper struck up a flourish; at the conclusion of which the young Oxonian, on receiving a hint from the Squire, gave, with an air of the most comic gravity, an old carol, the first verse of which was as follows:

Caput apri defero
Reddens laudes Domino.
The boar's head in hand bring I,
With garlands gay and rosemary.
I pray you all synge merily
Qui estis in convivio.

A distinguished post was allotted to 'ancient sirloin,' as mine host termed it; being, as he added, 'the standard of old English hospitality, and a joint of goodly presence, and full of expectation.' There were several dishes quaintly decorated, and which had evidently something traditionary in their embellishments; but about which, as I did not like to appear over-curious, I asked no questions.

I could not, however, but notice a pie, magnificently decorated with peacocks' feathers, in imitation of the tail of that bird, which overshadowed a considerable tract of the table. This the Squire confessed, with some little hesitation, was a pheasant-pie, though a peacock-pie was certainly the most authentical; but there had been such a mortality among the peacocks this season, that he could not prevail upon himself to have one killed.

It would be tedious, perhaps, to my wiser readers, who may not have that foolish fondness for odd and obsolete things to which I am a little given, were I to mention the other makeshifts of this worthy old humorist, by which he was endeavouring to follow up, though at humble distance, the quaint customs of antiquity. I was pleased, however, to see the respect shown to his whims by his children and relatives; who, indeed, entered readily into the full spirit of them, and seemed all well versed in their parts; having doubtless been present at many a rehearsal. I was amused, too, at the air of profound gravity with which the butler and other servants executed the duties assigned them, however eccentric. They had an old-fashioned look; having, for the most part, been brought up in the household, and grown into keeping with the antiquated mansion, and the humours of its lord; and most probably looked upon all his whimsical regulations as the established laws of honourable housekeeping.

When the cloth was removed, the butler brought in a huge silver vessel of rare and curious workmanship, which he placed before the Squire. Its appearance was hailed with acclamation; being the Wassail Bowl, so renowned in Christmas festivity. The contents had been prepared by the Squire himself; for it was a beverage in the skilful mixture of which he particularly prided himself; alleging that it was too abstruse and complex for the comprehension of an ordinary servant. It was a potation, indeed, that might well make the heart of a toper leap within him; being composed of the richest and raciest wines, highly spiced and sweetened, with roasted apples bobbing about the surface.

The old gentleman's whole countenance beamed with a serene look of indwelling delight, as he stirred this mighty bowl. Having raised it to his lips, with a hearty wish of a merry Christmas to all present, he sent it brimming round the board, for everyone to follow his example, according to the primitive style; pronouncing it 'the ancient fountain of good feeling, where all hearts met together.'

There was much laughing and rallying as the honest emblem of Christmas joviality circulated, and was kissed rather coyly by the ladies. When it reached Master Simon he raised it in both hands, and with the air of a boon companion struck up an old Wassail chanson:

> The browne bowle,
> The merry browne bowle,
> As it goes round about-a,
>> Fill
>> Still,
> Let the world say what it will,
> And drink your fill all out-a.
>
> The deep canne,
> The merry deep canne,
> As thou dost freely quaff-a,
>> Sing,
>> Fling,
> Be as merry as a king,
> And sound a lusty laugh-a.

Much of the conversation during dinner turned upon family topics, to which I was a stranger. There was, however, a great deal of rallying of Master Simon about some gay widow, with whom he was accused of having a flirtation. This attack was commenced by the ladies; but it was continued throughout the dinner by the fat-headed old gentleman next the parson, with the persevering assiduity of a slow-hound; being one of those long-winded jokers, who, though rather dull at starting game, are unrivalled for their talents in hunting it down. At every pause in the general conversation, he renewed his bantering in pretty much the same terms; winking hard at me with both eyes whenever he gave Master Simon what he considered a home thrust. The latter, indeed, seemed fond of being teased on the subject, as old bachelors are apt to be; and he took occasion to inform me, in an undertone, that the lady in question was a prodigiously fine woman, and drove her own curricle.

The dinner-time passed away in this flow of innocent hilarity; and, though the old hall may have resounded in its time with many a scene of broader rout and revel, yet I doubt whether it ever witnessed more honest and genuine enjoyment. How easy it is for one benevolent being to diffuse pleasure around him; and how truly is a kind heart a fountain of gladness, making everything in its vicinity to freshen into smiles! The joyous disposition of the worthy Squire was perfectly contagious; he was happy himself, and disposed to make all the world happy; and the little eccentricities of his humour did but season, in a manner, the sweetness of his philanthropy.

When the ladies had retired, the conversation, as usual, became still more animated; many good things were broached which had been thought of during dinner, but which would not exactly do for a lady's ear; and though I cannot positively affirm that there was much wit uttered, yet I have certainly heard many contests of rare wit produce much less laughter. Wit, after all, is a mighty tart, pungent ingredient, and much too acid for some stomachs; but honest good humour is the oil and wine of a merry meeting, and there is no jovial companionship equal to that where the jokes are rather small, and the laughter abundant. The Squire told several long stories of early college pranks and adventures, in some of which the parson had been a sharer; though in looking at the latter, it required some effort of imagination to figure such a little dark anatomy of a man into the perpetrator of a madcap gambol. Indeed, the two college chums presented pictures of what men may be made by their different lots in life. The Squire had left the university to live lustily on his paternal domains, in the vigorous enjoyment of prosperity and sunshine, and had flourished on to a hearty and florid old age; whilst the poor parson, on the contrary, had dried and withered away, among dusty tomes, in the silence and shadows of his study. Still there seemed to be a spark of almost extinguished fire, feebly glimmering in the bottom of his soul; and as the Squire hinted at a sly story of the parson and a pretty milkmaid, whom they once met on the banks of the Isis, the old gentleman made an 'alphabet of faces'.

After the dinner-table was removed, the hall was given up to the younger members of the family, who, prompted to all kind of noisy mirth by the Oxonian and Master Simon, made its old walls ring with their merriment, as they played at romping games. I delight in witnessing the gambols of children, and particularly at this happy holiday-season, and could not help stealing out of the drawing-room on hearing one of their peals of laughter. I found them at the game of blind-man's buff. Master Simon, who was the leader of their revels, and seemed on all occasions to fulfil the office of that ancient potentate, the Lord of Misrule, was blinded in the midst of the hall. The little beings were as busy about him as the mock fairies about Falstaff; pinching him, plucking at the skirts of his coat, and tickling him with straws. One fine blue-eyed girl of about thirteen, with her flaxen hair all in beautiful confusion, her frolic face in a glow, her frock half torn off her shoulders, a complete picture of a romp, was the chief tormentor; and from the slyness with which Master Simon avoided the smaller game, and hemmed this wild little nymph in corners, and obliged her to jump shrieking over chairs, I suspected the rogue of being not a whit more blinded than was convenient.

When I returned to the drawing-room, I found the company seated round the fire, listening to the parson, who was deeply ensconced in a high-backed oaken chair, the work of some cunning artificer of yore, which had been brought from the library for his particular accommodation. From this venerable piece of furniture, with which his shadowy figure and dark weazen face so admirably accorded, he was dealing forth strange accounts of the popular superstitions and legends of the surrounding country, with which he had become acquainted in the course of his antiquarian researches. I am half inclined to think that the old gentleman was himself somewhat tinctured with superstition, as men are very apt to be who live a recluse and studious life in a sequestered part of the country, and pore over black-letter tracts, so often filled with the marvellous and supernatural. He gave us several anecdotes of the fancies of the neighbouring peasantry, concerning the effigy of the crusader which lay on the tomb by the church altar. As it was the only monument of the kind in that part of the country, it had always been regarded with feelings of superstition by the goodwives of the village. It was said to get up from the tomb and walk the rounds of the churchyard in stormy nights, particularly when it thundered; and one old woman, whose cottage bordered on the churchyard, had seen it, through the windows of the church, when the moon shone, slowly pacing up and down the aisles. It was the belief that some wrong had been left unredressed by the deceased, or some treasure hidden, which kept the spirit in a state of trouble and restlessness. Some talked of gold and jewels buried in the tomb, over which the spectre kept watch; and there was a story current of a sexton in old times who endeavoured to break his way to the coffin at night; but just as he reached it, received a violent blow from the marble hand of the effigy, which stretched him senseless on the pavement. These tales were often laughed at by some of the sturdier among the rustics, yet when night came on, there were many of the stoutest unbelievers that were shy of venturing alone in the footpath that led across the churchyard.

From these and other anecdotes that followed, the crusader appeared to be the favourite hero of ghost stories throughout the vicinity. His picture, which hung up in the hall, was thought by the servants to have something supernatural about it; for they remarked that, in whatever part of the hall you went, the eyes of the warrior were still fixed on you. The old porter's wife, too, at the lodge, who had been born and brought up in the family, and was a great gossip among the maid-servants, affirmed, that in her young days she had often heard say, that on Midsummer eve, when it is well known all kinds of ghosts, goblins, and fairies become visible and walk abroad, the crusader used to mount his horse, come down from his picture, ride about the house, down the avenue, and so to the church to visit the tomb; on which occasion the church door most civilly swung open of itself: not that he needed it; for he rode through closed gates and even stone walls, and had been seen by one of the dairymaids to pass between two bars of the great park gate, making himself as thin as a sheet of paper.

All these superstitions I found had been very much countenanced by the Squire, who, though not superstitious himself, was very fond of seeing others so. He listened to every goblin tale of the neighbouring gossips with infinite gravity, and held the porter's wife in high favour on account of her talent for the marvellous. He was himself a great reader of old legends and romances, and often lamented that he could not believe in them; for a superstitious person, he thought, must live in a kind of fairyland.

Whilst we were all attention to the parson's stories, our ears were suddenly assailed by a burst of heterogeneous sounds from the hall, in which was mingled something like the clang of rude minstrelsy, with the uproar of many small voices and girlish laughter. The door suddenly flew open, and a train came trooping into the room, that might almost have been mistaken for the breaking up of the court of Fairy. That indefatigable spirit, Master Simon, in the faithful discharge of his duties as Lord of Misrule, had conceived the idea of a Christmas mummery, or masking; and having called in to his assistance the Oxonian and the young officer, who were equally ripe for anything that should occasion romping and merriment, they had carried it into instant effect. The old housekeeper had been consulted; the antique clothes-presses and wardrobes rummaged and made to yield up the relics of finery that had not seen the light for several generations; the younger part of the company had been privately convened from the parlour and hall, and the whole had been bedizened out, into a burlesque imitation of an antique masque.

Master Simon led the van, as 'Ancient Christmas', quaintly apparelled in a ruff, a short cloak, which had very much the aspect of one of the old housekeeper's petticoats, and a hat that might have served for a village steeple, and must indubitably have figured in the days of the Covenanters. From under this his nose curved boldly forth, flushed with a frost-bitten bloom, that seemed the very trophy of a December blast. He was accompanied by the blue-eyed romp, dished up as 'Dame Mince-Pie', in the venerable magnificence of faded brocade, long stomacher, peaked hat, and high-heeled shoes. The young officer appeared as Robin Hood, in a sporting dress of Kendal green, and a foraging cap with a gold tassel. The costume, to be sure, did not bear testimony to deep research, and there was an evident eye to the picturesque, natural to a young gallant in the presence of his mistress. The fair Julia hung on his arm in a pretty rustic dress, as 'Maid Marian'. The rest of the train had been metamorphosed in various ways; the girls trussed up in the finery of the ancient belles of the Bracebridge line, and the striplings bewhiskered with burnt cork, and gravely clad in broad skirts, hanging sleeves, and full-bottomed wigs, to represent the characters of Roast Beef, Plum Pudding and other worthies celebrated in ancient maskings. The whole was under the control of the Oxonian, in the appropriate character of Misrule; and I observed that he exercised rather a mischievous sway with his wand over the smaller personages of the pageant.

The irruption of this motley crew, with beat of drum, according to ancient custom, was the consummation of uproar and merriment. Master Simon covered himself with glory by the stateliness with which, as Ancient Christmas, he walked a minuet with the peerless, though giggling, Dame Mince-Pie. It was followed by a dance of all the characters, which, from its medley of costumes, seemed as though the old family portraits had skipped down from their frames to join in the sport. Different centuries were figuring at cross hands and right and left; the dark ages were cutting pirouettes and rigadoons; and the days of Queen Bess jigging merrily down the middle, through a line of succeeding generations.

The worthy Squire contemplated these fantastic sports, and this resurrection of his old wardrobe, with the simple relish of childish delight. He stood chuckling and rubbing his hands, and scarcely hearing a word the parson said, notwithstanding that the latter was discoursing most authentically on the ancient and stately dance at the Paon, or Peacock, from which he conceived the minuet to be derived. For my part, I was in a continual excitement, from the varied scenes of whim and innocent gaiety passing before me. It was inspiring to see wild-eyed frolic and warm-hearted hospitality breaking out from among the chills and glooms of winter, and old age throwing off his apathy, and catching once more the freshness of youthful enjoyment. I felt also an interest in the scene, from the consideration that these fleeting customs were posting fast into oblivion, and that this was, perhaps, the only family in England in which the whole of them were still punctiliously observed. There was a quaintness, too, mingled with all this revelry that gave it a peculiar zest; it was suited to the time and place; and as the old Manor House almost reeled with mirth and wassail, it seemed echoing back the joviality of long-departed years.

But enough of Christmas and its gambols; it is time for me to pause in this garrulity. Methinks I hear the questions asked by my graver readers, 'To what purpose is all this? – how is the world to be made wiser by this talk?' Alas! Is there not wisdom enough extant for the instruction of the world? And if not, are there not thousands of abler pens labouring for its improvement? – It is so much pleasanter to please than to instruct – to play the companion rather than the preceptor.

What, after all, is the mite of wisdom that I could throw into the mass of knowledge? or how am I sure that my sagest deductions may be safe guides for the opinions of others? But in writing to amuse, if I fail, the only evil is my own disappointment. If, however, I can by any lucky chance, in these days of evil, rub out one wrinkle from the brow of care, or beguile the heavy heart of one moment of sorrow; if I can now and then penetrate through the gathering film of misanthropy, prompt a benevolent view of human nature, and make my reader more in good humour with his fellow beings and himself, surely, surely, I shall not then have written entirely in vain.

The Frailty

of Father Balaguère

Now three accounts of Christmas in France. In Lawrence Durrell's Monsieur we again are present at a scene potent in its recalled antiquity yet clearly stemming from a common root; note that the father of the house carries in the Yule Log as he does in Belloc's house, though with a child rather than a servant. In du Maurier's Trilby we are invisible guests at a curious mélange of a feast given by English expatriate artists living in the Latin Quarter of Paris in the mid nineteenth century, with traditional English ingredients like turkey and plum-pudding arriving by hamper from London, but no shortage of rillettes, pâtés, and saucissons either. Tennyson, Thackeray and Dickens are all in their prime and each great writer has his health drunk. Then we move south to Provence to cull from Daudet's Lettres de Mon Moulin a delicious Christmas vignette in which Father Balaguère succumbs to the sin of gluttony and gabbles the Mass in order to get at those turkeys stuffed with truffles.

Monsieur

LAWRENCE DURRELL

We sat now, the three of us cross-legged on the floor before the fire, eating chestnuts and drinking whisky and talking about nothing and everything. Never had old Verfeuille seemed so warmly welcoming. If we had an inner pang as we remembered Piers' decisions for the future we did not mention them to each other. It would not have been fair to the time and the place to intrude our premonitions and doubts upon it. But underneath the excitement we were worried, we had a sense of impending departure, of looming critical change in our affairs – in this newly found passion as well. As if sensing this a little Piers said, during a silence 'Cheer up, children. Yesterday we went out and selected the Yule Log – a real beauty this year.' He described to me the little ceremony in which the oldest and the youngest member of the whole household go out hand in hand to choose the tree which will be felled for Christmas, and then return triumphantly to the house bearing it with, of course, the assistance of everyone. It was paraded thrice around the long supper table and then laid down before the great hearth, while old Jan undertook to preside over the ceremony of the libation which he did with great polish, filling first of all a tall jar of *vin cuit*. Describing it Piers acted him to the life, in half-humorous satire – his smiling dignity and serenity as he bowed his head over the wine to utter a prayer while everyone was deeply hushed around him, standing with heads bowed. Then he poured three little libations on the log, to Father, Son and Holy Ghost, before crying out with all the vigour he could muster in his crackly old voice:

> *Cacho-fio!*
> *Bouto-fio!*
> *Alègre! Alègre!*
> *Dieu nous alègre!*

> Yule Log Burn
> Joy Joy
> God give us Joy.

And as he reached the last words of the incantation which were 'Christmas has arrived' a huge bundle of vine-trimmings was set alight under the ceremonial log and the whole fireplace flamed up, irradiating the merry faces of the company, as if they too had caught fire from sympathy with the words; and now everyone embraced anew and clapped hands, while the old man once more filled the ceremonial bowl with wine, but this time passed it about as a loving-cup, beginning with little Tounin the youngest child: and so on in order of seniority until at last it came back to his hand. Then he threw back his head and drained it to the dregs, the firelight flashing on his brown throat. Suddenly Piers, despite himself, was seized with a pang of sadness and tears came into his eyes: 'How the devil am I going to leave them, do you think? And what is going to happen to us, to It?' It was not the time for such questions and I told him so. I finished my drink and consulted my watch. In a little while it would be in order to tackle the second half of the ceremony which consisted in decking out the crèche with the candles and figurines. I was glad of the diversion, for this little aside of his had wakened all kinds of doubts in me – about the future which awaited us, the separations ... Sylvie appeared with her arms full of things, dressed now in the full peasant dress of Avignon and looking ravishing. Everyone clapped her. 'Hurry and dress', she told us, 'before we do the Holy Family.'

It did not take long. My own rooms were on the eastern side of the house. Thoughtful hands had placed a copper warming pan full of coals in my bed, while a small fire, carefully shielded by a guard, crackled in the narrow hearth. I lit my candles and quickly put on the traditional black velvet coat which Piers had given me, with its scarlet silk lining; also the narrow stove-pipe pantaloons, dark sash and pointed black shoes – *tenue de rigueur* for Christmas dinner in Verfeuille. Piers himself would wear the narrow bootlace tie and the ribbon of the *félibre*, the Provençal poet. I hastened, and when I got downstairs Sylvie was already there trying to bring some order into the candle-lighting ceremony which was almost swamped by the antics of high-spirited children flitting about like mice. She managed to control the threatened riot and before long they were all admiring the colour and form of the little figurines as they were unwrapped one by one. Soon a constellation of small flames covered the brown hillsides of Bethlehem and brought up into high prominence the Holy Family in the manger, attended by the utterly improbable kings, gipsies, queens, cowboys, soldiers, poachers and postmen – not to mention sheep, ducks, quail, cattle and brilliant birds. Then came the turn of Piers, who exercised a bit more authority, to unwrap and distribute the wrapped presents, all duly labelled, so that nobody should feel himself forgotten on this memorable eve. Great rejoicing as the paper was ripped and torn away; and so gradually the company drifted slowly away to dinner. This had been laid in the great central hall – the long table ran down the centre with more than enough room for the gathering of that year. We three were seated at a cross-table which formed the cruciform head with Jan and his wife on our right and left respectively. Candles blazed everywhere and the Yule Log by this time had begun to thresh out bouquets of bright sparks into the chimney.

It was not a place or time easy to forget, and I had returned to it so often in my thoughts that it was no surprise to relive all this in my dreams. I must have unconsciously memorized it in great detail without being fully aware of the fact at the time. I know of no other place on earth that I can call up so clearly and accurately by simply closing my eyes: to this very day.

Its floor was laid with large grey stone slabs which were strewn with bouquets of rosemary and thyme: these helped to gather up the dust when one was sweeping, as well as things like the bones which were often thrown to the hunting dogs. The high ceiling was supported by thick smoke-blackened beams from which hung down strings of sausages, chaplets of garlic, and numberless bladders filled with lard. More than a third of the rear wall was taken up by the grand central fireplace which measured some ten feet across and at least seven from the jutting mantelpiece to the floor. In its very centre, with room each side in chimney-corners and angles stood old wicker chairs with high backs, and wooden lockers for flour and salt. The mound of ash from the fires was heaped back against the back of the fireplace which itself was crossed by a pair of high andirons which flared out at the top, like flowers, into little iron baskets, so often used as plate-warmers when filled with live coals. They were furnished with hooks at different levels destined for the heavy roasting spits. From the mantelshelf hung a short red curtain designed to hold the smoke in check when the fire became too exuberant, as it did with certain woods, notably olive. Along the wide shelf above the fire were rows of objects at once utilitarian and intriguing because beautiful, like rows of covered jars

in pure old faience, ranging in capacity from a gill to three pints, and each lettered with the name of its contents — saffron, pepper, cummin, tea, salt, flour, cloves. Tall bottles of luminous olive oil sparked with herbs and spices had their place here. Also a number of burnished copper vessels and a giant coffee-pot. And further along half a dozen tall brass or pewter lamps with wicks that burned olive oil – as in the time of the Greeks and Romans – but rapidly being superseded by the more modern paraffin-burning ones.

To the right of the fireplace was the wide stone sink with rows of shelves above to take a brilliant army of copper pots and pans – a real *batterie de cuisine*. To the left a covered bread-trough above which hung the large salt and flour boxes of immediate use together with the bread-holder – a sort of cage or cradle in dark wood, ornamented with locks and hinges of polished iron.

On the opposite side of the room was the tall curiously carved Provençal buffet, solid and capacious, and shining under its glossy varnish, the colour of salad oil. Then, to the left of it, the grandfather clock – a clock which was so much of a martinet that it assertively struck the hours in duplicate. Some old rush-bottomed chairs stood about awkwardly – for there was no real thought about luxury or even comfort here. The order of things was ancestral, traditional; history was the present, and one did not conceive of altering things, but simply asserting their traditional place in life, and in nature. As well try to alter the course of the planets. Beyond the bread-trough hung a long-shanked steel balance with a brass dish suspended by delicate brass chains, all brilliant with scouring by soap, flour and sand. Then among a straggle of farm implements standing against one wall was an ancient fowling piece resting in wooden crutches driven between two broken flags. The walls were heavily decorated with sentimental lithographs and oleographs, depicting scenes from the local folklore of the region; and, inevitably, with numberless old family pictures, now all faded away into a sepia anonymity – faces of unforgotten people and events, harvests, picnics and bullfights, tree-plantings, bull-brandings, weddings and first communions. A whole life of austere toil and harmless joy of which this room had been the centre, the pivot.

But the wine was going about now and the most important supper of the whole year was in full sail. By old tradition it has always been a 'lean' supper, so that in comparison with other feast days it might have seemed a trifle frugal. Nevertheless the huge dish of *raïto* exhaled a wonderful fragrance: this was a ragout of mixed fish presented in a sauce flavoured with wine and capers. Chicken flamed in Cognac. The long brown loaves cracked and crackled under the fingers of the feasters like the olive branches in the fireplace. The first dish emptied at record speed, and its place was taken by a greater bowl of Rhône pan-fish, and yet another of white cod. These in turn led slowly to the dishes of snails, the whitish large veined ones that feed on the vine-leaves. They had been tucked back into their shells and were extracted with the aid of strong curved thorns, three or four inches long, broken from the wild acacia. As the wine was replenished after the first round, toasts began to fly around.

Then followed the choice supporting dishes like white *cardes* or *cardon*, the delicious stem of a giant thistle which resembles nothing so much as an overgrown branch of celery. These stems are blanched and then cooked in white sauce – I have never tasted them anywhere else. The flavour is one of the most exquisite one can encounter in the southern regions of France; yet it is only a common field-vegetable. So it went on, our last dinner, to terminate at last with a whole anthology of sweetmeats and nuts and winter melons. The fire was restoked and the army of wine-bottles gave place to a smaller phalanx of brandies, Armagnacs and Marcs, to offset the large bowls of coffee from which rose plumes of fragrance.

Now old Jan's wife placed before the three lovers a deep silver sugar bowl full of white sugar. It lay there before them in the plenitude of its sweetness like a silver paunch. The three spoons she had placed in it stood upright, waiting for them to help themselves before the rest of the company. The toasts and the jests now began to subside, sinking towards the ground like expiring fireworks, and the time for more serious business was approaching. By tradition every year Piers made a speech which gave an account of the year's work, bestowing praise or censure as he thought fit. But this time his news was momentous and would affect the fate of everyone in the room. I could see that the idea worried him as much as it did his sister, who glanced at him from time to time with affectionate commiseration. After many hesitations – for he changed places more than once to have a private word with this person and that – he rose – and tapped for silence, to be greeted with loud applause and raised glasses by the very people whom his speech would sadden.

He stood, resigned and a little pale, while he allowed it to subside, before beginning with the Christmas wishes. He then went on by saying that he had been a trifle sad and preoccupied that evening because of the news he had to give them. Not that it was downright tragic, far from that; but all change made one sorry and sad. 'But before I speak of the journey I must make let me speak of the new arrangements which will come into force when I leave. First, I raise my glass to old Jan, closer to me than my father. He will become the *régisseur* of Verfeuille while I am absent *en mission.*' The whole speech was most skilfully executed, and touched everywhere with feeling and thoughtfulness. He reassigned the role of each of the servants, stressing the increase in their responsibilities and according each one a small rise in pay. This caused great joy and satisfaction and much kissing and congratulation followed each announcement. It was a good augury for his diplomatic role to follow – for by the time he came to the sad part of his speech his audience was cheerful, fortified by all this Christmas bounty.

TRILBY

GEORGE DU MAURIER

Christmas was drawing near.

There were days when the whole Quartier Latin would veil its iniquities under fogs almost worthy of the Thames Valley between London Bridge and Westminster, and out of the studio window the prospect was a dreary blank. No Morgue! no towers of Notre Dame! not even the chimney-pots over the way – not even the little medieval toy turret at the corner of the rue Vieille des Trois Mauvais Ladres, Little Billee's delight!

The stove had to be crammed till its sides grew a dull deep red before one's fingers could hold a brush or squeeze a bladder; one had to box or fence at nine in the morning, that one might recover from the cold bath, and get warm for the rest of the day!

Taffy and the Laird grew pensive and dreamy, child-like and bland; and when they talked it was generally about Christmas at home in Merry England and the distant Land of Cakes, and how good it was to be there at such a time – hunting, shooting, curling, and endless carouse!

It was Ho! for the jolly West Riding, and Hey! for the bonnets of Bonnie Dundee, till they grew quite homesick, and wanted to start by the very next train.

They didn't do anything so foolish. They wrote over to friends in London for the biggest turkey, the biggest plum-pudding, that could be got for love or money, with mince-pies, and holly and mistletoe, and sturdy, short, thick English sausages; half a Stilton cheese, and a sirloin of beef – two sirloins, in case one should not be enough.

For they meant to have a Homeric feast in the studio on Christmas Day – Taffy, the Laird, and Little Billee – and invite all the delightful chums I have been trying to describe; and that is just why I tried to describe them – Durien, Vincent, Antony, Lorrimer, Carnegie, Petrolicoconose, l'Zouzou, and Dodor!

The cooking and waiting should be done by Trilby, her friend Angèle Boisse, M et Mme Vinard, and such little Vinards as could be trusted with glass and crockery and mince-pies; and if that was not enough, they would also cook themselves, and wait upon each other.

When dinner should be over, supper was to follow with scarcely any interval to speak of; and to partake of this other guests should be bidden– Svengali and Gecko, and perhaps one or two more. No ladies!

For, as the unsusceptible Laird expressed it, in the language of a gillie he had once met at a servant's dance in a Highland country-house, 'Them wimmen spiles the ball!'

Elaborate cards of invitation were sent out, in the designing and ornamentation of which the Laird and Taffy exhausted all their fancy (Little Billee had no time).

Wines and spirits and English beers were procured at great cost from M.E. Delevingne's, in the rue St Honoré, and liqueurs of every description – chartreuse, curaçoa, *ratafia de cassis*, and anisette; no expense was spared.

Also, truffled galantines of turkey, tongues, hams, *rillettes de Tours*, *pâtés de foie gras*, *fromage d'Italie* (which has nothing to do with cheese), *saucissons d'Arles et de Lyon*, with and without garlic, cold jellies peppery and salt – everything that French *charcutiers* and their wives can make out of French pigs, or any other animal whatever, beast, bird, or fowl (even cats and rats), for the supper; and sweet jellies, and cakes, and sweetmeats, and confections of all kinds, from the famous pastry-cook at the corner of the rue Castiglione.

Mouths went watering all day long in joyful anticipation. They water somewhat sadly now at the mere remembrance of these delicious things – the mere immediate sight or scent of which in these degenerate latter days would no longer avail to promote any such delectable secretion. *Hélas! ahimè! ach weh! ay de mi! eheu! οἴμοι* – in point of fact, *alas!*

That is the very exclamation I wanted.

Christmas Eve came round. The pieces of resistance and plum-pudding and mince-pies had not yet arrived from London – but there was plenty of time.

Les trois Angliches dined at le Père Trin's, as usual, and played billiards and dominoes at the Café du Luxembourg, and possessed their souls in patience till it was time to go and hear the midnight mass at the Madeleine, where Roucouly the great barytone of the Opéra comique, was retained to sing Adam's famous Noël.

The whole Quartier seemed alive with the *réveillon*. It was a clear, frosty night, with a splendid moon just past the full, and most exhilarating was the walk along the quays on the Rive Gauche, over the Pont de la Concorde and across the Place thereof, and up the thronged rue de la Madeleine to the massive Parthenaic place of worship that always has such a pagan, worldly look of smug and prosperous modernity.

They struggled manfully, and found standing and kneeling room among that fervent crowd, and heard the impressive service with mixed feelings, as became true Britons of very advanced liberal and religious opinions; not with the unmixed contempt of the proper British Orthodox (who were there in full force, one may be sure).

But their susceptible hearts soon melted at the beautiful music, and in mere sensuous *attendrissement* they were quickly in unison with all the rest.

For as the clock struck twelve out pealed the organ, and up rose the finest voice in France:

> Minuit, Chrétiens! c'est l'heure solennelle
> Où l'Homme-Dieu descendit parmi nous!

Félicité passée
Qui ne peux revenir,
Tourment de ma pensée,
Que n'ay-je, en te perdant, perdu le souvenir!

Mid-day had struck. The expected hamper had not turned up in the Place St Anatole des Arts.

All Madame Vinard's kitchen battery was in readiness; Trilby and Madame Angèle Boisse were in the studio, their sleeves turned up, and ready to begin.

At twelve the *trois* Angliches and the two fair *blanchisseuses* sat down to lunch in a very anxious frame of mind, and finished a *pâté de foie gras* and two bottles of Burgundy between them, such was their disquietude.

The guests had been invited for six o'clock.

Most elaborately they laid the cloth on the table they had borrowed from the Hôtel de Seine, and settled who was to sit next to whom, and then unsettled it, and quarrelled over it – Trilby, as was her wont in such matters, assuming an authority that did not rightly belong to her, and of course getting her own way in the end.

And that, as the Laird remarked, was her confounded Trilbyness.

Two o'clock – three – four – but no hamper! Darkness had almost set in. It was simply maddening.

They knelt on the divan, with their elbows on the window-sill, and watched the street-lamps popping into life along the quays – and looked out through the gathering dusk for the van from the Chemin de Fer du Nord – and gloomily thought of the Morgue, which they could still make out across the river.

At length the Laird and Trilby went off in a cab to the station – a long drive – and, lo! before they came back the long-expected hamper arrived, at six o'clock.

And with it Durien, Vincent, Antony, Lorrimer, Carnegie, Petrolicoconose, Dodor, and l'Zouzou – the last two in uniform, as usual.

And suddenly the studio, which had been so silent, dark, and dull, with Taffy and Little Billee sitting hopeless and despondent round the stove, became a scene of the noisiest, busiest, and cheerfullest animation. The three big lamps were lit, and all the Chinese lanterns. The pieces of resistance and the pudding were whisked off by Trilby, Angèle, and Madame Vinard to other regions – the porter's lodge and Durien's studio (which had been lent for the purpose); and every one was pressed into the preparations for the banquet. There was plenty for idle hands to do. Sausages to be fried for the turkey, stuffing made, and sauces, salads mixed, and punch – holly hung in festoons all round and about – a thousand things. Everybody was so clever and good-humoured that nobody got in anybody's way – not even Carnegie, who was in evening dress (to the Laird's delight). So they made him do the scullion's work – cleaning, rinsing, peeling, etc.

The cooking of the dinner was almost better fun than the eating of it. And though there were so many cooks, not even the broth was spoiled (cockaleekie, from a receipt of the Laird's).

It was ten o'clock before they sat down to that most memorable repast.

Zouzou and Dodor, who had been the most useful and energetic of all its cooks, apparently quite forgot they were due at their respective barracks at that very moment; they had only been able to obtain *la permission de dix heures*. If they remembered it, the certainty that next day Zouzou would be reduced to the ranks for the fifth time, and Dodor confined to his barracks for a month, did not trouble them in the least.

The waiting was as good as the cooking. The handsome, quick, authoritative Madame Vinard was in a dozen places at once, and openly prompted, rebuked, and bully-ragged her husband into a proper smartness. The pretty little Madame Angèle moved about as deftly and as quietly as a mouse; which of course did not prevent them both from genially joining in the general conversation whenever it wandered into French.

Trilby, tall, graceful, and stately, and also swift of action, though more like Juno or Diana than Hebe, devoted herself more especially to her own particular favourites – Durien, Taffy, the Laird, Little Billee – and Dodor and Zouzou, whom she loved, and *tutoyé'd en bonne camarade* as she served them with all there was of the choicest.

The two little Vinards did their little best – they scrupulously respected the mince-pies, and only broke two bottles of oil and one of Harvey sauce, which made their mother furious. To console them, the Laird took one of them on each knee and gave them of his share of plum-pudding and many other unaccustomed good things, so bad for their little French tumtums.

The genteel Carnegie had never been at such a queer scene in his life. It opened his mind – and Dodor and Zouzou, between whom he sat (the Laird thought it would do him good to sit between a private soldier and a humble corporal), taught him more French than he had learned during the three months he had spent in Paris. It was a specialty of theirs. It was more colloquial than what is generally used in diplomatic circles, and stuck longer in the memory; but it hasn't interfered with his preferment in the Church.

He quite unbent. He was the first to volunteer a song (without being asked) when the pipes and cigars were lit, and after the usual toasts had been drunk – Her Majesty's health, Tennyson, Thackeray, and Dickens; and John Leech.

He sang, with a very cracked and rather hiccupy voice, his only song (it seems) – an English one, of which the burden, he explained, was French:

> Veeverler veeverler veeverler vee
> Veeverler companyee!

And Zouzou and Dodor complimented him so profusely on his French accent that he was with difficulty prevented from singing it all over again.

Then everybody sang in rotation.

The Laird, with a capital barytone, sang:

> Hie diddle dee for the Lowlands low,

which was encored.

Little Billee sang 'Little Billee'.

Vincent sang:

> Old Joe kicking up behind and afore,
> And the yaller gal a-kicking up behind old Joe.

A capital song, with words of quite a masterly scansion.

Antony sang 'Le Sire de Framboisy'. Enthusiastic encore.

Lorrimer, inspired no doubt by the occasion, sang the 'Hallelujah Chorus', and accompanied himself on the piano, but failed to obtain an encore.

Durien sang:

> Plaisir d'amour ne dure qu'un moment;
> Chagrin d'amour dure toute la vie ...

It was his favourite song, and is one of the beautiful songs of the world, and he sang it very well – and it became popular in the Quartier Latin ever after.

The Greek couldn't sing, and very wisely didn't.

Zouzou sang capitally a capital song in praise of *le vin à quat' sous!*

Taffy, in a voice like a high wind (and with a very good imitation of the Yorkshire brogue), sang a Somersetshire hunting ditty, ending:

> Of this 'ere song should I be axed the reason for to show,
> I don't exactly know, I don't exactly know!
> But all my fancy dwells upon Nancy,
> And I sing Tally-ho!

It is a quite superexcellent ditty, and haunts my memory to this day; and one felt sure that Nancy was a dear and a sweet, wherever she lived, and when. So Taffy was encored twice — once for her sake, once for his own.

And finally, to the surprise of all, the bold dragoon sang (in English) 'My Sister Dear', out of *Masaniello*, with such pathos, and in a voice so sweet and high and well in tune, that his audience felt almost weepy in the midst of their jollification; and grew quite sentimental, as Englishmen abroad are apt to do when they are rather tipsy and hear pretty music, and think of their dear sisters across the sea, or their friends' dear sisters.

Madame Vinard interrupted her Christmas dinner on the model-throne to listen, and wept and wiped her eyes quite openly, and remarked to Madame Boisse, who stood modestly close by: 'Il est gentil tout plein, ce dragon! Mon Dieu! comme il chante bien! Il est Angliche aussi, il paraît. Ils sont joliment bien élevés, tous ces Angliches — tous plus gentils les uns que les autres! et quant à Monsieur Litrebili, on lui donnerait le bon Dieu sans confession!'

And Madame Boisse agreed.

Then Svengali and Gecko came, and the table had to be laid and decorated anew, for it was supper-time.

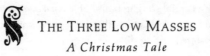

THE THREE LOW MASSES
A Christmas Tale

ALPHONSE DAUDET

I

'Two truffled turkeys, Garrigou?'

'Yes, your Reverence, two magnificent turkeys stuffed with truffles. I know, because I helped stuff them. The skin had been stretched so tightly you would have thought it was going to burst as it was roasting . . .'

'Jesus-Maria! How I do love truffles! Give me my surplice. Quickly, Garrigou . . . And what else did you see in the kitchen, besides the turkeys? . . .'

'Oh, all sorts of good things . . . Since midday they've done nothing but pluck pheasants, larks, pullets, grouse. Feathers flying everywhere . . . Then they brought eels, carp, trout from the pond and . . .'

'How big – the trout, Garrigou?'

'As big as that, your Reverence . . . Enormous!'

'Merciful heavens! You make me see them . . . Have you put the wine in the altar-cruets!'

'Yes, your Reverence, I've put the wine in the altar-cruets . . . But you wait and see! It doesn't compare with what you'll be drinking soon, after Midnight Mass. You should see inside the dining-room at the château: decanters blazing bright with wines of all colours . . . And the silver dishes, the carved dining-table, the flowers, the candelabra! . . . Never will there be a Christmas midnight supper like it. Monsieur le Marquis has invited all the nobility of the neighbourhood. You will be at least forty at table, not counting the bailiff and the scrivener. Ah, you are indeed fortunate to be among them, your Reverence! Just from having sniffed those beautiful turkeys, the smell of the truffles is following me everywhere . . . Myum! . . .'

'Come now, my son. Let us guard ourselves against the sin of gluttony, especially on the eve of the Nativity . . . Off with you, quickly. Light the candles and ring the bell for the first Mass; it is nearly midnight already, and we mustn't be late . . .'

This conversation took place one Christmas Eve in the year of grace sixteen hundred and something, between the Reverend Father Balaguère, formerly Prior of the Barnabites, at present Chaplain to the Lords of Trinquelage, and his little clerk Garrigou, for you must know that the devil, on that very evening, had assumed the round face and nondescript features of the young sacristan, the better to lead the reverend father into temptation and make him commit the terrible sin of gluttony. So, whilst the supposed Garrigou (Hem! hm!) was vigorously jingling the bells of the baronial chapel, the reverend father was hastening to clothe himself in his chasuble in the little sacristy of the château and, already troubled in spirit by all these gastronomic descriptions, he was repeating to himself as he dressed,

'Roast turkeys ... golden carp ... trout as big as that! ...'

Outside, the night wind was blowing, spreading the music of the bells, and gradually lights were appearing in the darkness along the slope of Mont Vertoux, on the top of which rose the age-old towers of Trinquelage. The families of the tenant-farmers were coming to hear Midnight Mass at the château. They sang as they climbed the incline in groups of five or six, the father in front, lantern in hand, the women swathed in their long, brown cloaks under which the children huddled for shelter. In spite of the hour and the cold, all these good folk walked cheerfully, sustained by the thought that when they came out from Mass there would be tables laid for them down in the kitchens, as there were every year. Now and then, on the steep slope, a nobleman's carriage preceded by torch bearers would twinkle its windows in the moonlight, or a mule would trot along tinkling its bells, and by the light of the mist-enveloped lanterns, the tenants would recognize their bailiff and salute him as he passed.

'Good evening, good evening, Master Arnoton!'

'Good evening, good evening, friends!'

The night was clear, the stars gleamed bright in the cold air; the north wind and a fine frozen snow, glancing off the clothes without wetting them, faithfully maintained the tradition of a white Christmas. At the very summit of the slope rose their destination, the château, with its enormous mass of towers and gables, its chapel spire rising into the bluish-black sky, and, at all its windows, little lights that twinkled, bobbing back and forth, and looking, against the dark background of the building, like sparks flashing in the ashes of burnt paper ... Once one was beyond the drawbridge and the postern-gate, to reach the chapel it was necessary to cross the outer courtyard, full of carriages, valets and sedan chairs, all brightly lit by the flames of torches and by the blazing kitchen fires. All around could be heard the chinking click of the turnspits, the clatter of pans, the clink of crystal and silver being set out in preparation for a feast; from up above, a warm vapour which smelt of roast meat and potent herbs used for complicated sauces made not only the tenants, but the chaplain, the bailiff, everybody, say:

'What a fine Christmas supper we are going to have after Mass!'

II

Dingdong-dong! ... Dingdong-dong! ...

So the Midnight Mass begins. In the chapel of the château, a cathedral in miniature, with interlaced arches and oak wainscoting high up the walls, tapestries have been hung, all the candles lit. And the people! The costumes! See first, seated in the carved stalls surrounding the chancel, the Lord of Trinquelage, in salmon-coloured taffeta, and near him all the invited nobility. Opposite, kneeling on prie-Dieus hung with velvet, are the old Dowager Marchioness in her gown of flame-coloured brocade and the young Lady of Trinquelage, wearing on her head the latest fashion of the Court of France: a high tower of fluted lace. Further back, their faces shaved, and wearing black with vast pointed wigs, can be seen the bailiff Thomas Arnoton and the scrivener Master Ambroy, striking two solemn notes among the gaudy silks and brocaded damasks. Then come the fat majordomos, the pages, the grooms, the stewards, the housekeeper with all her keys hung at her side on a fine silver chain. Further back, on benches, are the servants, the maids, and the tenants with their families. And last of all, at the very back, right against the door which they open and shut discreetly, are the scullions who slip in, between sauces, to snatch a little of the atmosphere of the Mass and to bring the smell of the supper into the church, festive and warm with all its lighted candles.

Is it the sight of the scullions' little white caps which distracts the officiating priest? Might it not rather be Garrigou's little bell, that mocking little bell which shakes at the foot of the altar with such infernal haste and seems to keep saying:

'Let's hurry! Let's hurry! The sooner we're finished, the sooner we'll be at supper.'

The fact is that each time this devilish little bell rings, the chaplain forgets his Mass and thinks only of the midnight supper. He imagines the scurrying cooks, the kitchen stoves blazing like blacksmiths' forges, the steam escaping from half-open lids, and, beneath that steam, two magnificent turkeys, stuffed, taut, bursting with truffles . . .

Or still more, he sees pages passing in files carrying dishes surrounded with tempting odours, and he goes with them into the great hall already prepared for the feast. Oh, paradise! He sees the immense table blazing with lights and laden from end to end with peacocks dressed in their feathers, pheasants spreading their wings, flagons the colour of rubies, fruit dazzling bright among green branches, and all the marvellous fish Garrigou was talking about (yes! – Garrigou, of course) displayed on a bed of fennel, their scales pearly as if just from the sea, with bunches of sweet-smelling herbs in their huge nostrils. So real is the vision of these marvels that it seems to Father Balaguère that all these wonderful dishes are served before him on the embroidered altar-cloth, and once – or twice, instead of 'Dominus vobiscum!' he catches himself saying 'Benedicite'. Apart from these slight mistakes, the worthy man recites his office most conscientiously, without missing a line, without omitting one genuflection, and all goes very well until the end of the first Mass; for, as you know, the same priests must celebrate three consecutive Masses on Christmas Day.

'One over!' says the chaplain to himself with a sigh of relief; then, without wasting a moment, he signs to his clerk, or him whom he thinks is his clerk, and –

Dingdong-dong! . . . Dingdong-dong! . . .

So the second Mass begins, and with it begins also the sin of Father Balaguère.

'Quick, quick, let's hurry!' Garrigou's little bell cries to him in its shrill little voice, and this time the unfortunate priest abandons himself on the missal and devours the pages with the avidity of his over-stimulated appetite. Frantically he kneels, rises, makes vague signs of the cross, half-genuflects, cuts short all his gestures in order to finish the sooner. He scarcely extends his arms at the Gospel, or beats his breast at the *Confiteor*. It is between the clerk and himself who will jabber the quicker. Verses and responses patter pell-mell, buffeting each other. Words half-pronounced without opening the mouth which would take too much time, die away in a baffling hum.

'*Oremus ps ... ps ... ps ...*'

'*Mea culpa ... pa ... pa ...*'

Like hurrying wine-harvesters treading the grapes, both splatter about in the latin of the Mass, sending splashes in all directions.

'*Dom ... scum! ...*,' says Balaguère.

'*... Stutuo ...*,' replies Garrigou; and all the time that damned little bell is ringing in their ears, like those bells they put on post-horses to make them gallop quicker. Obviously at this pace a Low Mass is quickly got out of the way.

'Two over!' says the chaplain quite out of breath; then, red and sweating, without pausing to recover, he rushes down the altar steps and ...

Ding-dong! ... Dingdong-dong! ...

So the third Mass begins. It is not far now to the dining hall; but, alas, the nearer the midnight supper approaches, the more the unfortunate Balaguère feels himself seized by a gluttonous madness of impatience. He even sees more distinctly the golden carp, the roast turkeys ... There! ... Yes, and there! ... He touches them ... he ... Oh, merciful

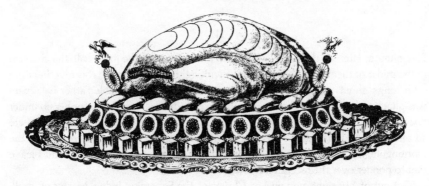

heavens! ... the dishes are steaming, the wines are ambrosial, and, shaking itself madly, the little bell is shrieking at him:

'Quick, quick! Be more quick!'

But how could he go more quickly? His lips are scarcely moving. He is no longer pronouncing the words ... Unless he cheats the good God completely and omits part of the Mass ... And that is exactly what the wretched man does! Falling deeper into temptation, he begins by skipping one verse, then two. Then the Epistle is too long so he doesn't finish it; he skims through the Gospel, passes over the Creed, jumps the Pater, bows distantly to the Preface, and thus by leaps and bounds hurls himself into eternal damnation, closely followed by the infamous Garrigou (*vade, retro, Satanus!*) who cooperates splendidly, holding up his chasuble, turning the pages two at a time, knocking over the desks, upsetting the alter-cruets, and ceaselessly shaking that tiny little bell, louder and louder, quicker and quicker.

The startled faces of the congregation are a sight to behold! Obliged to join in a Mass conducted in dumb-show by a priest whose words they can't hear, some stand up as others are kneeling, or sit when others are rising. And every succeeding part of this extraordinary service results in a confused variety of postures on all the benches. The Star of the Nativity, journeying up there across the sky towards the little stable, paled with apprehension at the sight of such disorder.

'The priest is going too quickly ... you can't keep up with him,' the old Dowager grumbles, shaking her coif angrily.

Master Arnoton, his large steel spectacles on his nose, searches in his prayer-book, wondering where the deuce they are up to. But, on the whole, all these worthy folk are themselves also thinking of the supper, and are not sorry the Mass is going at top speed. And when Father Balaguère, his face shining radiantly, turns towards the congregation and shouts at the top of his voice: '*Ite, missa est*,' the whole chapel replies, as one voice, with a '*Deo Gratias*' so merry and so lively you would have thought they were already at table responding to the first toast.

III

Five minutes later, all the nobles were taking their seats in the great hall, the chaplain in the midst of them. The château, bright with light in every room, was reverberating with songs, shouts, laughter, uproar everywhere; and the venerable Father Balaguère was plunging his fork into the wing of the grouse, drowning remorse for his sin under floods of wine and rich meat gravy. The unfortunate holy man drank so much and ate so much, he died of a stroke that night without even having time to repent. In the morning, he arrived in heaven still all in a stupor after the night's feasting and I leave you to ponder over the reception he was given.

'Get out of My sight, you wicked Christian!' the Sovereign Judge, Master of us all, said to him, 'Your lapse from virtue is so great it outweighs all the goodness of your life. You stole from Me a Midnight Mass. Well, you will pay it back three-hundred-fold. You will not enter Paradise until you have celebrated three hundred Christmas Masses in your own chapel and in the presence of all those who sinned with you and by your fault.'

... Such, in truth, is the legend of Father Balaguère, as you will hear it told in the land of olives. Today the Château de Trinquelage no longer exists, but the chapel still stands on the summit of Mont Ventoux, in a clump of holly oaks. Its disjointed door bangs in the wind, its threshold is overgrown with weeds; there are nests in the corners of the altar and in the recesses of the huge casement windows from which the coloured glass has long since disappeared. Yet it is said that at Christmas every year a supernatural light hovers among these ruins, and that peasants, going to Mass and the midnight supper in the church since built below, see this ghost of a chapel lit with invisible candles which burn in the open air even in wind and snow. You may laugh if you will, but a local vine-grower named Garrigue, a descendant no doubt of Garrigou, has assured me that one Christmas Eve, being slightly drunk, he had lost his way on the mountain near Trinquelage; and this is what he saw ... Until eleven o'clock, nothing. Suddenly, towards midnight, a peal of bells sounded high in the steeple, an old peal not heard for many many years and seeming to come from many leagues away. Soon after, on the path leading upwards, Garrigue saw lights flickering, faint shadows moving. Under the chapel porch there were footsteps, voices whispering:

'Good evening, Master Arnoton!'

'Good evening, good evening, friends!'

When everyone had entered, my vine-grower, who was very brave, approached softly, looked through the broken door, and saw a strange sight. All these people he had seen passing were ranged in rows around the chancel, in the ruined nave, as if the ancient benches were still there. Beautiful ladies in brocade with coifs of lace, handsome noblemen bedecked from head to foot, peasants in flowered jackets such as our grandfathers wore; everything appeared faded, dusty, old and tired. From time to time night birds, the residents now of the chapel, woken by all the lights, came swooping around the candles whose flames burned erect yet nebulous, as if hidden behind a thin veil. And what amused Garrigue greatly was a certain person wearing large steel spectacles who kept shaking his tall black wig on which one of these birds stood, entangled, silently flapping its wings ...

At the far end, a little old man no taller than a child was kneeling in the centre of the chancel, shaking despairingly a little, tongueless, soundless bell; while a priest clothed in old gold moved back and fro before the altar reciting prayers no word of which could be heard ... It was, most surely, Father Balaguère saying his third Low Mass.

A Partridge
in a Pear Tree ...

Next that hardy perennial 'The Twelve Days of Christmas' and two modern variations upon it. New Yorker writer Phyllis McGinley spins a delicate and touching poem from the traditional ingredients — leaping lords, piping pipers and the partridge in a pear tree. John Julius Norwich, on the other hand, had the ingenious notion of rendering the whole sequence as an exchange of letters between lovers which begins all sweetness and light and ends with an exceedingly disagreeable letter from Messrs Sue, Grabbit and Run. Lord Norwich acts as master of ceremonies at the Christmas Carol concert in Liverpool Cathedral where snatches of prose and poetry are intermingled with the music. This enchanting jeu d'esprit *always brings the house down.*

THE TWELVE DAYS OF CHRISTMAS

The first day of Christmas
My true love sent to me
A partridge in a pear tree.

The second day of Christmas.
My true love sent to me
Two turtle doves, and
A partridge in a pear tree.

The third day of Christmas
My true love sent to me
Three French hens,
Two turtle doves, and
A partridge in a pear tree.

The fourth day of Christmas
My true love sent to me
Four colly birds,
Three French hens,
Two turtle doves, and
A partridge in a pear tree.

The fifth day of Christmas
My true love sent to me
Five gold rings,
Four colly birds,
Three French hens,
Two turtle doves, and
A partridge in a pear tree.

The sixth day of Christmas
My true love sent to me
Six geese a-laying,
Five gold rings,
Four colly birds,
Three French hens,
Two turtle doves, and
A partridge in a pear tree.

The seventh day of Christmas
My true love sent to me
Seven swans a-swimming,
Six geese a-laying,
Five gold rings,
Four colly birds,
Three French hens,
Two turtle doves, and
A partridge in a pear tree.

The eighth day of Christmas
My true love sent to me

Eight maids a-milking,
Seven swans a-swimming,
Six geese a-laying,
Five gold rings,
Four colly birds,
Three French hens,
Two turtle doves, and
A partridge in a pear tree.

The ninth day of Christmas
My true love sent to me
Nine drummers drumming,
Eight maids a-milking,
Seven swans a-swimming,
Six geese a-laying,
Five gold rings,
Four colly birds,
Three French hens,
Two turtle doves, and
A partridge in a pear tree.

The tenth day of Christmas
My true love sent to me
Ten pipers piping,
Nine drummers drumming,
Eight maids a-milking,
Seven swans a-swimming,
Six geese a-laying,
Five gold rings,
Four colly birds,
Three French hens,
Two turtle doves, and
A partridge in a pear tree.

The eleventh day of Christmas
My true love sent to me
Eleven ladies dancing,
Ten pipers piping,
Nine drummers drumming,
Eight maids a-milking,
Seven swans a-swimming,

Six geese a-laying,
Five gold rings,
Four colly birds,
Three French hens,
Two turtle doves, and
A partridge in a pear tree.

The twelfth day of Christmas
My true love sent to me
Twelve lords a-leaping,
Eleven ladies dancing,
Ten pipers piping,
Nine drummers drumming,
Eight maids a-milking,
Seven swans a-swimming,
Six geese a-laying,
Five gold rings,
Four colly birds,
Three French hens,
Two turtle doves, and
A partridge in a pear tree.

 ALL THE DAYS OF CHRISTMAS

PHYLLIS MCGINLEY

What shall my true love
Have from me
To pleasure his Christmas
Wealthily?
The partridge has flown
From our pear tree.

Flown with our summers,
Are the swans and the geese.
Milkmaids and drummers

Would leave him little peace.
I've no gold ring
And no turtle dove.
So what can I bring
To my true love?

A coat for the drizzle,
Chosen at the store;
A saw and a chisel
For mending the door;
A pair of red slippers
To slip on his feet;
Three striped neckties;
Something sweet.

He shall have all
I can best afford —
No pipers, piping,
No leaping lord,
But a fine fat hen
For his Christmas board;
Two pretty daughters
(Versed in the role)
To be worn like pinks
In his buttonhole;
And the tree of my heart
With its calling linnet,
My evergreen heart
And the bright bird in it.

The Twelve Days of Christmas
A Correspondence
JOHN   JULIUS   NORWICH

25th December

My dearest darling

That partridge, in that lovely little pear tree! What an enchanting, romantic, poetic present! Bless you and thank you.

Your deeply loving Emily

26th December

My dearest darling Edward

The two turtle doves arrived this morning and are cooing away in the pear tree as I write. I'm so touched and grateful.

With undying love, as always, Emily

27th December

My darling Edward

You do think of the most original presents; whoever thought of sending anybody three French hens? Do they really come all the way from France? It's a pity that we have no chicken coops, but I expect we'll find some. Thank you, anyway, they're lovely.

Your loving Emily

28th December

Dearest Edward

What a surprise — four calling birds arrived this morning. They are very sweet, even if they do call rather loudly — they make telephoning impossible. But I expect they'll calm down when they get used to their new home. Anyway, I've very grateful — of course I am.

Love from Emily

29th December

Dearest Edward

The postman has just delivered five most beautiful gold rings, one for each finger, and all fitting perfectly. A really lovely present — lovelier in a way than birds, which do take rather a lot of looking after. The four that arrived yesterday are still making a terrible row, and I'm afraid none of us got much sleep last night. Mummy says she wants to use the rings to 'wring' their necks – she's only joking, I think; though I know what she means. But I *love* the rings. Bless you.

Love, Emily

30th December

Dear Edward

Whatever I expected to find when I opened the front door this morning, it certainly wasn't six socking great geese laying eggs all over the doorstep. Frankly, I rather hoped you had stopped sending me birds – we have no room for them and they have already ruined the croquet lawn. I know you meant well, but – let's call a halt, shall we?

Love, Emily

31st December

Edward

I thought I said no more birds; but this morning I woke up to find no less than seven swans all trying to get into our tiny goldfish pond. I'd rather not think what happened to the goldfish. The whole house seems to be full of birds – to say nothing of what they leave behind them. Please, please STOP.

Your Emily

1st January

Frankly, I think I prefer the birds. What am I to do with eight milkmaids – AND their cows? Is this some kind of a joke? If so, I'm afraid I don't find it very amusing.

Emily

2nd January

Look here Edward, this has gone far enough. You say you're sending me nine ladies dancing; all I can say is that judging from the way they dance, they're certainly not ladies. The village just isn't accustomed to seeing a regiment of shameless hussies with nothing on but their lipstick cavorting round the green – and it's Mummy and I who get blamed. If you value our friendship – which I do less and less – kindly stop this ridiculous behaviour at once.

Emily

3rd January

As I write this letter, ten disgusting old men are prancing about all over what used to be the garden – before the geese and the swans and the cows got at it; and several of them, I notice, are taking inexcusable liberties with the milkmaids. Meanwhile the neighbours are trying to have us evicted. I shall never speak to you again.

Emily

4th January

This is the last straw. You know I detest bagpipes. The place has now become something between a menagerie and a madhouse and a man from the Council has just declared it unfit for habitation. At least Mummy has been spared this last outrage; they took her away yesterday afternoon in an ambulance. I hope you're satisfied.

5th January

Sir

Our client, Miss Emily Wilbraham, instructs me to inform you that with the arrival on her premises at half-past seven this morning of the entire percussion section of the Liverpool Philharmonic Orchestra and several of their friends she has no course left open to her but to seek an injunction to prevent your importuning her further. I am making arrangements for the return of much assorted livestock.

I am, Sir, Yours faithfully,

G. CREEP

Solicitor-at-Law

I HAVE ACQUIRED

SOME

NICE CHRISTMAS LOOT...

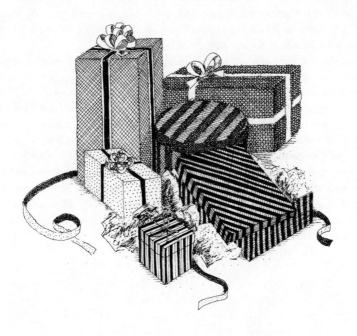

Next, the voice of dissent. Noël Coward lived in a hate–love relationship with Christmas. 'Oh how nice it would be,' he wrote in his diary on Christmas Eve 1954, 'to be a little boy of five again instead of an ageing playwright of fifty-five and look forward to all the high jinks. However, it is no use repining.' And again on Christmas morning 1960: 'This is a day of goodwill to all men and the giving and receiving of presents which nobody particularly wants . . . a commercialized orgy of love without heart. Ah me! I fear I am becoming cynical, but how lovely it would be if it were an ordinary day on which I could get on with my work.' Sometimes, however, Christmas has its old magic; though even at Beverly Hills in 1955 the call of work cuts through his pleasure at the lush Hollywood loot.

Bernard Shaw on the other hand was unequivocal: 'Like all intelligent people, I greatly dislike Christmas.' George Orwell, though, in this 1946 essay, is untypically bonhomous; he sees no harm in a blowout at the winter solstice so long as we do not let it become a habit. The only snag is the nagging voice of conscience: 'In Germany, Austria, Greece and elsewhere, scores of millions of people are existing on a diet which keeps breath in the body but leaves no strength for work.' The war was still that near. How then could we indulge ourselves? So we couldn't have a proper Christmas: that would come in 1947 or 1948. Forty years on no one is starving in Germany, Austria or Greece; but millions, alas, are still starving elsewhere, thus casting a long, uneasy moral shadow over each and every Christmas indulgence. Finally in this section, Kingsley Amis is in top gear as he reaches the dénouement of his black comedy on old age Ending Up: '. . . he took the wrappings off present after useless, insultingly cheap, no doubt intended to be facetious, present.'

DIARY FOR CHRISTMAS DAY
1955

NOËL COWARD

Beverly Hills

In the middle of it all again. This house is really very nice and I have a dusky Jamaican lady to look after me who is lackadaisical and hums constantly. There have been a series of parties as usual, each one indistinguishable from the other, culminating last night in the [Humphrey] Bogarts' Christmas Eve revel which was great fun and highly glamorous to the eye. The Christmas shopping has been frantic as usual. Clifton [Webb] is sweet but inclined to bouts of slightly bibulous self-pity on account of being lonely. Mabelle [Clifton's mother] is indestructible and gets on his nerves, also he has no picture settled, so he is idle. We had a successful reading of the play at the Bogarts' last Sunday and everyone read well. Betty [Lauren] Bacall will be good, I think, and anyhow she is word perfect which is wonderful considering she was shooting a picture until yesterday.

I have acquired some nice Christmas loot. Exquisite gold and ebony monogrammed links from Frank Sinatra, and a lovely black dressing-gown and pyjamas to match from Marlene [Dietrich], and hand-worked bedroom slippers from Merle [Oberon] which are charming. A lot of other nice gifts too, but oh I *do* wish Christmas hadn't coincided with *Blithe Spirit*. There is so much to be done and, it seems, so little time to do it.

'An Atrocious Institution'

GEORGE BERNARD SHAW

The World, 20 December 1893

Like all intelligent people, I greatly dislike Christmas. It revolts me to see a whole nation refrain from music for weeks together in order that every man may rifle his neighbour's pockets under cover of a ghastly general pretence of festivity. It is really an atrocious institution, this Christmas. We must be gluttonous because it is Christmas. We must be drunken because it is Christmas. We must be insincerely generous; we must buy things that nobody wants, and give them to people we don't like; we must go to absurd entertainments that make even our little children satirical; we must writhe under venal officiousness from legions of freebooters, all because it is Christmas – that is, because the mass of the population, including the all-powerful middle-class tradesman, depends on a week of licence and brigandage, waste and intemperance, to clear off its outstanding liabilities at the end of the year. As for me, I shall fly from it all tomorrow or next day to some remote spot miles from a shop, where nothing worse can befall me than a serenade from a few peasants, or some equally harmless survival of medieval mummery, shyly proffered, not advertised, moderate in its expectations, and soon over. In town there is, for the moment, nothing for me or any honest man to do.

'IT IS A DEBAUCH'

GEORGE ORWELL

Tribune, 20 December 1946

An advertisement in my Sunday paper sets forth in the form of a picture the four things that are needed for a successful Christmas. At the top of the picture is a roast turkey; below that, a Christmas pudding; below that, a dish of mince pies; and below that, a tin of ——'s Liver Salt.

It is a simple recipe for happiness. First the meal, then the antidote, then another meal. The ancient Romans were the great masters of this technique. However, having just looked up the word *vomitorium* in the Latin dictionary, I find that after all it does *not* mean a place where you went to be sick after dinner. So perhaps this was not a normal feature of every Roman home, as is commonly believed.

Implied in the above-mentioned advertisement is the notion that a good meal means a meal at which you overeat yourself. In principle I agree. I only add in passing that when we gorge ourselves this Christmas, if we do get the chance to gorge ourselves, it is worth giving a thought to the thousand million human beings, or thereabouts, who will be doing no such thing. For in the long run our Christmas dinners would be safer if we could make sure that everyone else had a Christmas dinner as well. But I will come back to that presently.

The only reasonable motive for not overeating at Christmas would be that somebody else needs the food more than you do. A deliberately austere Christmas would be an absurdity. The whole point of Christmas is that it is a debauch – as it was probably long before the birth of Christ was arbitrarily fixed at that date. Children know this very well. From their point of view Christmas is not a day of temperate enjoyment, but of fierce pleasures which they are quite willing to pay for with a certain amount of pain. The awakening at about 4 am to inspect your stocking; the quarrels over toys all through the morning, and the exciting whiffs of mincemeat and sage-and-onions escaping from the kitchen door; the battle with enormous platefuls of turkey, and the pulling of the wishbone; the darkening of the windows and the entry of the flaming plum pudding; the hurry to make sure that everyone has a piece on his plate while the brandy is still alight; the momentary panic when it is rumoured that Baby has swallowed the threepenny bit; the stupor all through the afternoon; the Christmas cake with almond icing an inch thick; the peevishness next morning and the castor oil on December 27th – it is an up-and-down business, by no means all pleasant, but well worth while for the sake of its more dramatic moments.

Teetotallers and vegetarians are always scandalized by this attitude. As they see it, the only rational objective is to avoid pain and to stay alive as long as possible. If you refrain from drinking alcohol, or eating meat, or whatever it is, you may expect to live an extra five years, while if you overeat or overdrink you will pay for it in acute physical pain on the following day. Surely it follows that all excesses, even a once-a-year outbreak such as Christmas, should be avoided as a matter of course?

Actually it doesn't follow at all. One may decide, with full knowledge of what one is doing, that an occasional good time is worth the damage it inflicts on one's liver. For health is not the only thing that matters: friendship, hospitality, and the heightened spirits and change of outlook that one gets by eating and drinking in good company are also valuable. I doubt whether, on balance, even outright drunkenness does harm, provided it is infrequent — twice a year, say. The whole experience, including the repentance afterwards, makes a sort of break in one's mental routine, comparable to a weekend in a foreign country, which is probably beneficial.

In all ages men have realized this. There is a wide consensus of opinion, stretching back to the days before the alphabet, that whereas habitual soaking is bad, conviviality is good, even if one does sometimes feel sorry for it next morning. How enormous is the literature of eating and drinking, especially drinking, and how little that is worth while has been said on the other side! Offhand I can't remember a single poem in praise

of water, i.e. water regarded as a drink. It is hard to imagine what one could say about it. It quenches thirst: that is the end of the story. As for poems in praise of wine, on the other hand, even the surviving ones would fill a shelf of books. The poets started turning them out on the very day when the fermentation of the grape was first discovered. Whisky, brandy and other distilled liquors have been less eloquently praised, partly because they came later in time. But beer has had quite a good press, starting well back in the Middle Ages, long before anyone had learned to put hops in it. Curiously enough, I can't remember a poem in praise of stout, not even draught stout, which is better than the bottled variety, in my opinion. There is an extremely disgusting description in *Ulysses* of the stout-vats in Dublin. But there is a sort of back-handed tribute to stout in the fact that this description, though widely known, has not done much towards putting the Irish off their favourite drink.

The literature of eating is also large, though mostly in prose. But in all the writers who have enjoyed describing food, from Rabelais to Dickens and from Petronius to Mrs Beeton, I cannot remember a single passage which puts dietetic considerations first. Always food is felt to be an end in itself. No one has written memorable prose about vitamins, or the dangers of an excess of proteins, or the importance of masticating everything thirty-two times. All in all, there seems to be a heavy weight of testimony on the side of overeating and overdrinking, provided always that they take place on recognized occasions and not too frequently.

But ought we to overeat and overdrink this Christmas? We ought not to, nor will most of us get the opportunity. I am writing in praise of Christmas, but in praise of Christmas 1947, or perhaps 1948. The world as a whole is not exactly in a condition for festivities this year. Between the Rhine and the Pacific there cannot be very many people who are in need of ——'s Liver Salt. In India there are, and always have been, about 100 million people who only get one square meal a day. In China, conditions are no doubt much the same. In Germany, Austria, Greece and elsewhere, scores of millions of people are existing on a diet which keeps breath in the body but leaves no strength for work. All over the war-wrecked areas from Brussels to Stalingrad, other uncounted millions are living in the cellars of bombed houses, in hide-outs in the forests, or in squalid huts behind barbed wire. It is not so pleasant to read almost simultaneously that a large proportion of our Christmas turkeys will come from Hungary, and that the Hungarian writers and journalists – presumably not the worst-paid section of the community – are in such desperate straits that they would be glad to receive presents of saccharine and cast-off clothing from English sympathizers. In such circumstances we could hardly have a 'proper' Christmas, even if the materials for it existed.

But we will have one sooner or later, in 1947, or 1948, or maybe even in 1949. And when we do, may there be no gloomy voices of vegetarians or teetotallers to lecture us about the things that we are doing to the linings of our stomachs. One celebrates a feast for its own sake, and not for any supposed benefit to the lining of one's stomach. Meanwhile Christmas is here, or nearly. Santa Claus is rounding up his reindeer, the postman staggers from door to door beneath his bulging sack of Christmas cards, the black markets are humming, and Britain has imported over 7,000 crates of mistletoe from France. So I wish everyone an old-fashioned Christmas in 1947, and meanwhile, half a turkey, three tangerines, and a bottle of whisky at not more than double the legal price.

ENDING UP

KINGSLEY AMIS

Shorty, who had been seeing to drinks, bustled up and, swaying hardly at all, said,

'Couple of carols, Adela? I think the kids might like 'em.'

'Not more than two, Shorty, and not more than, say, four verses. Then we really ought to have the presents, because we don't want to ...'

'I'm right up there with you, Adela.' He was not best pleased at the implication that having carols on Christmas morning was a tiresome and eccentric indulgence of his own. 'If the carols go on too long, that holds up handing out the presents, and holding up handing out the presents means holding up lunch-on, and holding up lunch-on's bad.'

'But surely it's Christmas dinner, isn't it?' asked George. 'I mean, the main meal's usually ...'

'So it is, George, so it is. Once more hath Shorty erred.'

After calling for silence in the manner first of someone imitating a sergeant-major quite well, and then of someone imitating an Oberstürmbannführer almost as well, Shorty introduced the idea of carols in a pan-American accent. He sat down at his piano, played (not too badly) a few bars of *Alexander's Ragtime Band*, apologized, and went into *While Shepherds Watched*. By the end of the first verse, most people were singing, or at least la-la-ing to the tune.

Trevor took in the home-made paper-chains that, falsifying George's prediction that there would be no you stretch them from one corner to the other, met at the partly-intact electrolier at the middle of the room, the holly arranged along the mantelshelf and round the stained oval mirror above it, the Christmas tree (dug up, no doubt, in the woods by Shorty) hung with artificial frost and coloured tin spheres, the pile of variegated parcels and packets at its foot: Adela's planning and her and Shorty's work. A lot of work, done for much less effect. Of eleven people in the room, perhaps two, Adela and George, would positively enjoy the display, two more, Finn and Vanessa, would notice it in full for about half a minute, and another, Marigold, could have been counted on to complain if there had been none. And that was that. Did Adela know of the disparity between her intentions and their results? It made no difference either way: the thought was what counted, and she had simply done what had had to be done. That did not mean that doing as much was negligible or ridiculous or hypocritical.

Tracy saw the same incongruities as Trevor, but they brought to her mind a selection of fairly uncomplicated ironies about good cheer and the festive season, and she felt nothing much more than a mild, inert repulsion.

Keith was not interested in any of that. He threw himself into the singing with as much gusto as he could, short of obvious parody, also with the hope of seeming in retrospect to have enjoyed the day in some part, and was grateful too for another unexpected few minutes' worth of leaning on his spade.

Rachel was fully contented: the children were behaving well, and someone other than herself was doing all the cooking for the whole day.

While Shepherds Watched came to an end with a florid run on the piano not much disfigured by wrong notes. Shorty was having a fine time – bar getting pissed (and he was doing that too) he liked nothing better than a good old sing-song, and here was the chance of one, a rarity in this household. Now he started on *O Come, All Ye Faithful*.

'... Joyful and triumphant,' he sang, and continued at a safe volume, 'The Queen was in the parlour, dopping bread and honey. The maid was in the garden ...' He caught sight of Marigold on her knees between her great-grandchildren, an arm round the restive shoulders of each. The bitch was singing away fit to bust; not only that, but in a way that made out that she had seen to it herself that everybody was having a rare old treat. 'Then along came a bloody great shitehawk,' sang Shorty, slowing down the tempo, 'and chomped ... off ... her nose.'

After that they had the presents. Those from the guests to the hosts were chiefly a disguised dole: tins or pots of more or less luxurious food, bottles of hard liquor, wide-spectrum gift tokens. Hosts showered guests with diversely unwearable articles of clothing: to Keith from Adela, a striped necktie useful for garrotting underbred rivals in his trade; to Tracy from George, a liberation-front lesbian's plastic apron. Under a largely unspoken kind of non-aggression pact, the guests gave one another things like small boxes of chocolates or very large boxes of matches with (say) aerial panoramas of Manhattan on their outsides and containing actual matches each long enough, once struck, to kindle the cigarettes of (say) the entire crew of a fair-sized merchant vessel, given the assembly of that crew in some relatively confined space. Intramural gifts included a bathroom sponge, a set of saucepans, a cushion in a lop-sided cover, a photograph-frame wrought by some vanished hand and with no photograph in it, an embroidered knitting-bag. Keith watched carefully what Bernard gave, half expecting a chestnut-coloured wig destined for Adela, or a lavishly-illustrated book on karate for George, but was disappointed, though he savoured Bernard's impersonation of a man going all out to hide his despondency as he took the wrappings off present after useless, insultingly cheap, no doubt intended to be facetious, present.

I Sing

of a Maiden ...

Now for a miscellany of Christmas poetry. First, one of Shakespeare's very rare references to the season; next, a light-hearted inventory of a Christmas well spent by his gossipy contemporary Nicholas Breton; then 'I Sing of a Maiden', arguably the most beautiful Christmas poem ever written; after that Herrick's 'A Christmas Carol', sung in the King's presence at Whitehall; then Kipling's bitter account of Christmas on the far-flung frontiers of the British raj; and finally, Swinburne's miraculous 'Three Damsels in the Queen's Chamber'.

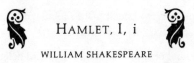

HAMLET, I, i

WILLIAM SHAKESPEARE

Some say that ever 'gainst that season comes
Wherein our Saviour's birth is celebrated,
The bird of dawning singeth all night long,
And then, they say, no spirit dare stir abroad.
The nights are wholesome, then no planets strike,
No fairy takes nor witch hath power to charm,
So hallow'd and so gracious is the time.

A CHRISTMAS SONG

NICHOLAS BRETON

The Christmas now is past, and I have kept my fast,
    With prayer every day;
And, like a country clown, with nodding up and down,
    Have passed the time away.

As for old Christmas games, or dancing with fine dames,
    Or shows or pretty plays;
A solemn oath I swear, I came not where they were,
    Not all these holy-days.

I did not sing one note, except it were by rote,
    Still buzzing like a bee;
To ease my heavy heart of some though little smart,
    For want of other glee.

And as for pleasant wine, there was no drink so fine,
    For to be tasted here;

Full simple was my fare, if that I should compare,
　　The same to Christmas Cheer.

I saw no kind of sight that might my mind delight,
　　Believe me, noble dame.
But everything I saw did fret at woe my maw,
　　To think upon the same.

Upon some bushy balk full fain I was to walk,
　　In woods, from tree to tree,
For want of better room; but since my fatal doom
　　Hath so appointed me;

I stood therewith content, the Christmas full was spent,
　　In hope that God will send
A better yet next year, my heavy heart to cheer;
　　And so I make an end.

I SING OF A MAIDEN

ANON, 15TH CENTURY

I sing of a maiden
　　That is makeles;
King of all kings
　　To her son she ches.

He came al so still
　　There his mother was,
As dew in April
　　That falleth on the grass.

He came al so still
　　To his mother's bour,
As dew in April
　　That falleth on the flour.

He came al so still
 There his mother lay,
As dew in April
 That falleth on the spray.

Mother and maiden
 Was never none but she;
Well may such a lady
 Goddes mother be.

A CHRISTMAS CAROL

ROBERT HERRICK

Sung to the King
in the Presence at White-Hall

Chor. What sweeter musick can we bring,
       Then a Caroll, for to sing
       The Birth of this our heavenly King?

       Awake the Voice! Awake the String!
       Heart, Eare, and Eye, and every thing
       Awake! the while the active Finger
       Runs division with the Singer.

From the Flourish they came to the Song.

  1. Dark and dull night, flie hence away,
      And give the honour to this Day,
      That sees *December* turn'd to *May.*

  2. If we may ask the reason, say;
      The why, and wherefore all things here
      Seem like the Spring-time of the yeere?

  3. Why do's the chilling Winters morne
      Smile, like a field beset with corne?
      Or smell, like to a Meade new-shorne,
      Thus, on the sudden? 4. Come and see
      The cause, why things thus fragrant be:
      'Tis He is borne, whose quickning Birth
      Gives life and luster, publike mirth,
      To Heaven, and the under-Earth.

Chor. We see Him come, and know him ours,
       Who, with His Sun-shine, and His showers,
       Turnes all the patient ground to flowers.

  1. The Darling of the world is come,
      And fit it is, we finde a roome

To welcome Him. 2. The nobler part
Of all the house here, is the heart,

Chor. Which we will give Him; and bequeath
This Hollie, and this Ivie Wreath,
To do Him honour; who's our King,
And Lord of all this Revelling.

The Musicall Part was composed by
M. Henry Lawes.

CHRISTMAS IN INDIA

RUDYARD KIPLING

Dim dawn behind the tamarisks — the sky is saffron-yellow —
As the women in the village grind the corn,
And the parrots seek the river-side, each calling to his fellow
That the Day, the staring Eastern Day, is born.

O the white dust on the highway! O the stenches in the byway!
	O the clammy fog that hovers over earth!
And at Home they're making merry 'neath the white and scarlet berry —
	What part have India's exiles in their mirth?

Full day behind the tamarisks — the sky is blue and staring —
	As the cattle crawl afield beneath the yoke,
And they bear One o'er the field-path, who is past all hope or caring,
	To the ghat below the curling wreaths of smoke.
		Call on Rama, going slowly, as ye bear a brother lowly —
		Call on Rama — he may hear, perhaps, your voice!
	With our hymn-books and our psalters we appeal to other altars,
		And to-day we bid 'good Christian men rejoice!'

High noon behind the tamarisks — the sun is hot above us —
	As at Home the Christmas Day is breaking wan.
They will drink our healths at dinner — those who tell us how they love us,
	And forget us till another year be gone!
		O the toil that knows no breaking! O the *Heimweh*, ceaseless, aching!
		O the black dividing Sea and alien Plain!
	Youth was cheap — wherefore we sold it. Gold was good — we hoped to hold it.
		And to-day we know the fulness of our gain!

Grey dusk behind the tamarisks — the parrots fly together —
	As the Sun is sinking slowly over Home;
And his last ray seems to mock us shackled in a lifelong tether
	That drags us back howe'er so far we roam.
		Hard her service, poor her payment — she in ancient, tattered raiment —
		India, she the grim Stepmother of our kind.
	If a year of life be lent her, if her temple's shrine we enter,
		The door is shut — we may not look behind.

Black night behind the tamarisks — the owls begin their chorus —
	As the conches from the temple scream and bray.
With the fruitless years behind us and the hopeless years before us,
	Let us honour, O my brothers, Christmas Day!
Call a truce, then, to our labours — let us feast with friends and neighbours,
	And be merry as the custom of our caste;
For, if 'faint and forced the laughter,' and if sadness follow after,
	We are richer by one mocking Christmas past.

THREE DAMSELS
IN THE QUEEN'S CHAMBER

ALGERNON SWINBURNE

Three damsels in the queen's chamber,
　The queen's mouth was most fair;
She spake a word of God's mother
　As the combs went in her hair.
　　Mary that is of might,
　　Bring us to thy Son's sight.

They held the gold combs out from her,
　A span's length off her head;
She sang this song of God's mother
　And of her bearing-bed.
　　Mary most full of grace,
　　Bring us to thy Son's face.

When she sat at Joseph's hand,
　She looked against her side;
And either way from the short silk band
　Her girdle was all wried.
　　Mary that all good may,
　　Bring us to thy Son's way.

Mary had three women for her bed,
　The twain were maidens clean;
The first of them had white and red,
　The third had riven green.
　　Mary that is so sweet,
　　Bring us to thy Son's feet.

She had three women for her hair,
　Two were gloved soft and shod;
The third had feet and fingers bare,
　She was the likest God.
　　Mary that wieldeth land,
　　Bring us to thy Son's hand.

She had three women for her ease,
  The twain were good women:
The first two were the two Maries,
  The third was Magdalen.
    Mary that perfect is,
    Bring us to thy Son's kiss.

Joseph had three workmen in his stall,
  To serve him well upon;
The first of them were Peter and Paul,
  The third of them was John.
    Mary, God's handmaiden,
    Bring us to thy Son's ken.

'If your child be none other man's,
  But if it be very mine,
The bedstead shall be gold two spans,
  The bed foot silver fine.'
    Mary that made God mirth,
    Bring us to thy Son's birth.

'If the child be some other man's,
  And if it be none of mine,
The manger shall be straw two spans,

Betwixen kine and kine.'
   Mary that made sin cease,
   Bring us to thy Son's peace.

Christ was born upon this wise,
   It fell on such a night,
Neither with sounds of psalteries,
   Nor with fire for light.
   Mary that is God's spouse,
   Bring us to thy Son's house.

The star came out upon the east
   With a great sound and sweet:
Kings gave gold to make him feast
   And myrrh for him to eat.
   Mary, of thy sweet mood,
   Bring us to thy Son's good.

He had two handmaids at his head,
   One handmaid at his feet;
The twain of them were fair and red,
   The third one was right sweet.
   Mary that is most wise,
   Bring us to thy Son's eyes. Amen.

WHERE WAS THE ECSTASY?

Sometimes Christmas doesn't quite come off; the projected pleasures simply fail to punch their weight. Two great novelists note the phenomenon. In The Mill on the Floss, *George Eliot draws a brilliant, dense and sensuous portrait of Christmas, yet for her hero, Tom Tulliver, something is mysteriously missing from it. In* The Rainbow *D. H. Lawrence puts it with characteristic voltage: 'How passionately the Brangwens craved for it, the ecstasy!'*

Another writer to suffer a diminished Christmas was the contemporary folk hero Adrian Mole. Yet Mole's intrinsic goodness shines through the diary. Rosie is his new baby sister, while Bert, whom he feeds and cleans, is a nonagenarian neighbour. Pandora is his classy girlfriend. Though Mole will be sixteen and three-quarters this Christmas, we fear there may be further slings and arrows in store for him. He is one of life's losers; hence his enormous appeal.

THE MILL ON THE FLOSS

GEORGE ELIOT

Fine old Christmas, with the snowy hair and ruddy face, had done his duty that year in the noblest fashion, and had set off his rich gifts of warmth and colour with all the heightening contrast of frost and snow.

Snow lay on the croft and river-bank in undulations softer than the limbs of infancy; it lay with the neatliest finished border on every sloping roof, making the dark-red gables stand out with a new depth of colour; it weighed heavily on the laurels and fir-trees, till it fell from them with a shuddering sound; it clothed the rough turnip-field with whiteness, and made the sheep look like dark blotches; the gates were all blocked up with the sloping drifts, and here and there a disregarded four-footed beast stood as if petrified 'in unrecumbent sadness;' there was no gleam, no shadow, for the heavens, too, were one still, pale cloud – no sound or motion in anything but the dark river, that flowed and moaned like an unresting sorrow. But old Christmas smiled as he laid this cruel-seeming spell on the out-door world, for he meant to light up home with new brightness, to deepen all the richness of in-door colour, and give a keener edge of delight to the warm fragrance of food: he meant to prepare a sweet imprisonment that would strengthen the primitive fellowship of kindred, and make the sunshine of familiar human faces as welcome as the hidden day-star. His kindness fell but hardly on the homeless – fell but hardly on the homes where the hearth was not very warm, and where the food had little fragrance; where the human faces had no sunshine in them, but rather the leaden, blank-eyed gaze of unexpectant want. But the fine old season meant well; and if he has not learnt the secret how to bless men impartially, it is because his father Time, with ever-unrelenting purpose, still hides that secret in his own mighty, slow-beating heart.

And yet this Christmas day, in spite of Tom's fresh delight in home, was not, he thought, somehow or other, quite so happy as it had always been before. The red berries were just as abundant on the holly, and he and Maggie had dressed all the windows and mantelpieces and picture-frames on Christmas eve with as much taste as ever, wedding the thick-set scarlet clusters with branches of the black-berried ivy. There had been singing under the windows after midnight – supernatural singing, Maggie always felt, in spite of Tom's contemptuous insistence that the singers were old Patch, the parish clerk, and the rest of the church choir: she trembled with awe when their caroling broke in upon her dreams, and the image of men in fustian clothes was always thrust away by the vision of angels resting on the parted cloud. The midnight chant had helped as usual to lift the morning above the level of common days; and then there was the smell of hot toast and ale from the kitchen, at the breakfast hour; the favourite anthem, the green boughs, and the short sermon, gave the appropriate festal character to the church-going; and aunt and uncle Moss, with all their eight children, were looking like so many reflectors of the bright parlour-fire, when the church-goers came back, stamping the snow from their feet. The plum-pudding was of the same handsome roundness as ever, and came in with the symbolic blue flames around it, as if it had been heroically snatched from the nether fires into which it had been thrown by dyspeptic Puritans; the dessert was as splendid as ever, with its golden oranges, brown nuts, and the crystalline light and dark of apple jelly and damson cheese: in all these things Christmas was as it had always been since Tom could remember; it was only distinguished, if by anything, by superior sliding and snowballs.

THE RAINBOW

D. H. LAWRENCE

Gradually there gathered the feeling of expectation. Christmas was coming. In the shed, at nights, a secret candle was burning, a sound of veiled voices was heard. The boys were learning the old mystery play of St George and Beelzebub. Twice a week, by lamplight, there was choir practice in the church, for the learning of old carols Brangwen wanted to hear. The girls went to these practices. Everywhere was a sense of mystery and rousedness. Everybody was preparing for something.

The time came near, the girls were decorating the church, with cold fingers binding holly and fir and yew about the pillars, till a new spirit was in the church, the stone broke out into dark, rich leaf, the arches put forth their buds, and cold flowers rose to blossom in the dim, mystic atmosphere. Ursula must weave mistletoe over the door, and over the screen, and hang a silver dove from a sprig of yew, till dusk came down, and the church was like a grove.

In the cow-shed the boys were blacking their faces for a dress-rehearsal; the turkey hung dead, with opened, speckled wings, in the dairy. The time was come to make pies, in readiness.

The expectation grew more tense. The star was risen into the sky, the songs, the carols were ready to hail it. The star was the sign in the sky. Earth too should give a sign. As evening drew on, hearts beat fast with anticipation, hands were full of ready gifts. There were the tremulously expectant words of the church service, the night was past and the morning was come, the gifts were given and received, joy and peace made a flapping of wings in each heart, there was a great burst of carols, the Peace of the World had dawned, strife had passed away, every hand was linked in hand, every heart was singing.

It was bitter, though, that Christmas Day, as it drew on to evening, and night, became a sort of bank holiday, flat and stale. The morning was so wonderful, but in the afternoon and evening the ecstasy perished like a nipped thing, like a bud in a false spring. Alas, that Christmas was only a domestic feast, a feast of sweetmeats and toys! Why did not the grown-ups also change their everyday hearts, and give way to ecstasy? Where was the ecstasy?

How passionately the Brangwens craved for it, the ecstasy. The father was troubled, dark-faced and disconsolate, on Christmas night, because the passion was not there, because the day was become as every day, and hearts were not aflame. Upon the mother was a kind of absentness, as ever, as if she were exiled for all her life. Where was the fiery heart of joy, now the coming was fulfilled; where was the star, the Magi's transport, the thrill of new being that shook the earth?

 ## THE GROWING PAINS OF ADRIAN MOLE

SUE TOWNSEND

Saturday   December 25th
CHRISTMAS DAY

Got up at 7.30.

Had a wash and a shave, cleaned teeth, squeezed spots then went downstairs and put kettle on. I don't know what's happened to Christmas Day lately, but something has. It's just not the same as it used to be when I was a kid. My mother fed and cleaned Rosie, and I did the same to Bert. Then we went into the lounge and opened our presents. I was dead disappointed when I saw the shape of my present. I could tell at a glance that it didn't contain a single microchip. OK a sheepskin coat is warm but there's nothing you can *do* with it, except wear it.

In fact after only two hours of wearing it, I got bored and took it off. However, my mother was ecstatic about her egg timer; she said, 'Wow, another one for my collection.'

Rosie ignored the chocolate Santa I bought her. That's 79 pence wasted! *This is what I got:*

¾ length sheepskin coat (out of Littlewoods catalogue)
Beano Annual (a sad disappointment, this year's is very childish)
Slippers (like Michael Caine wears, although not many people know that)
Swiss army knife (my father is hoping I'll go out into the fresh air and use it)
Tin of humbugs (supposedly from the dog)
Knitted Balaclava helmet (from Grandma Mole. Yuk! Yuk!)
Boys' Book of Sport (from Grandma Sugden: Stanley Matthews on cover)

I was glad when Auntie Susan and her friend Gloria turned up; at 11 o'clock. Their talk is very metropolitan and daring; and Gloria is dead glamorous and sexy. She wears frilly dresses, and lacy tights, and high heels. And she's got an itsy-bitsy voice that makes my stomach go soft. Why she's friends with Auntie Susan, who is a prison warder, smokes Panama cigars and has got hairy fingers, I'll never know.

The turkey was OK. But would have been better if the giblets and the plastic bag had been removed before cooking. Bert made chauvinist remarks during the carving. He leered at Gloria's cleavage and said, 'Give me a nice piece of breast.' Gloria wasn't a bit shocked, but I went dead red, and pretended that I'd dropped my cracker under the table.

When my mother asked me which part of the turkey I wanted, I said, 'A wing please!' I really wanted breast, leg, or thigh. But wing was the only part of the bird without sexual connotations. Rosie had a few spoons of mashed potato and gravy. Her table manners are disgusting, even worse than Bert's.

I was given a glass of Bull's Blood wine and felt dead sensual. I talked brilliantly and with consummate wit for an hour, but then my mother told me to leave the table, saying, 'One sniff of the barmaid's apron and his mouth runs away with him.'

The Queen didn't look very happy when she was giving her speech. Perhaps she got lousy Christmas presents this year, like me. Bert and Auntie Susan had a disagreement about the Royal Family. Bert said he would 'move the whole lot of 'em into council houses in Liverpool'.

Gloria said, 'Oh Bert that's a bit drastic. Milton Keynes would be more suitable. They're not used to roughing it you know.'

In the evening I went round to see Grandma and my father. Grandma forced me to eat four mincepies, and asked me why I wasn't wearing my new Balaclava helmet. My father didn't say anything; he was dead drunk in an armchair.

Sunday   December 26th
FIRST AFTER CHRISTMAS

Pandora and I exchanged presents in a candlelit ceremony in my bedroom. I put the solid gold chain round her neck, and she put a 70% wool, 10% cashmere, 20% acrylic scarf round my neck.

A cashmere scarf at fifteen!

I'll make sure the label can be seen by the public at all times.

Pandora went barmy about the solid gold chain. She kept looking at herself in the mirror, she said, 'Thank you, darling, but how on earth can you afford solid gold? It must have cost you at least a hundred pounds!'

I didn't tell her that Woolworth's were selling them cheap at two pounds a go.

Monday   December 27th
BOXING DAY, HOLIDAY (UK EXCEPT SCOTLAND). HOLIDAY (CANADA). BANK HOLIDAY (SCOTLAND). HOLIDAY (REPUBLIC OF IRELAND)

Just had a note handed to me from a kid riding a new BMX.

Dear heart,
I'm awfully sorry but I will have to cancel our trip to the cinema to see *ET*.

I woke up this morning with an ugly disfiguring rash around my neck.

Yours sincerely,
Pandora

P.S. I am allergic to non-precious metal.

Everyone Suddenly Burst Out Singing

Now two contrasting accounts of Christmas at war. The unofficial truce in No-Man's-Land still haunts the collective imagination: it formed one of the most effective scenes in Oh! What A Lovely War *and was even used recently as a pop video by Paul McCartney. An excellent new book,* Christmas Truce *by Malcolm Brown and Shirley Seaton, has collated all the evidence and proved beyond question (for it has been sometimes thought an old soldier's story) that it certainly happened and, what is more, all along the line. The famed football match really did take place with the Fritzes beating the Tommies 3–2. The Germans rolled barrels of beer across and swapped them for plum-puddings. A German juggler entertained and a Tommy had his hair cut by his pre-war German barber. Nor were officers immune from the festivities: this letter was written to his wife by a 38-year-old regular officer of the 1/North Staffs called Captain R. J. Armes, who hurried to set down the extraordinary scene while it was fresh in his memory.*

Next we move to the home front in the Second World War and dip into a fascinating slice of social history, How We Lived Then, *compiled by Norman Longmate from thousands of memories sent to him by ordinary men, women and children who had done their best to celebrate Christmas in those dull grey years of bombs, blackouts and rationing.*

CHRISTMAS TRUCE

MALCOLM BROWN AND SHIRLEY SEATON (EDS)

I have just been through one of the most extraordinary scenes imaginable. Tonight is Xmas Eve and I came up into the trenches this evening for my tour of duty in them. Firing was going on all the time and the enemy's machine guns were at it hard, firing at us. Then about seven the firing stopped.

I was in my dugout reading a paper and the mail was being dished out. It was reported that the Germans had lighted their trenches up all along our front. We had been calling to one another for some time Xmas wishes and other things. I went out and they shouted 'no shooting' and then somehow the scene became a peaceful one. All our men got out of the trenches and sat on the parapet, the Germans did the same, and they talked to one another in English and broken English. I got on the top of the trench and talked German and asked them to sing a German *Volkslied* [folk song], which they did, then our men sang quite well and each side clapped and cheered the other.

I asked a German who sang a solo to sing one of Schumann's songs, so he sang 'The Two Grenadiers' splendidly. Our men were a good audience and really enjoyed his singing.

Then Pope and I walked across and held a conversation with the German officer in command. One of his men introduced us properly, he asked my name and then presented me to his officer. I gave the latter permission to bury some German dead who were lying in between us, and we agreed to have no shooting until 12 midnight tomorrow. We talked together, 10 or more Germans gathered round. I was almost in their lines within a yard or so. We saluted each other, he thanked me for permission to bury his dead, and we fixed up how many men were to do it, and that otherwise both sides must remain in their trenches.

Then we wished one another good night and a good night's rest, and a happy Xmas and parted with a salute. I got back to the trench. The Germans sang *'Die Wacht am Rhein'*, it sounded well. Then our men sang quite well 'Christians Awake', it sounded so well, and with a good night we all got back into our trenches. It was a curious scene, a lovely moonlight night, the German trenches with small lights on them, and the men on both sides gathered in groups on the parapets.

At times we heard the guns in the distance and an occasional rifle shot. I can hear them now, but about us is absolute quiet. I allowed one or two men to go out and meet a German or two halfway. They exchanged cigars, a smoke and talked. The officer I spoke to hopes we shall do the same on New Year's Day. I said 'yes, if I am here'. I felt

I must sit down and write the story of this Xmas Eve before I went to lie down. Of course no precautions are relaxed, but I think they mean to play the game. All the same, I think I shall be awake all night so as to be on the safe side. It is weird to think that tomorrow night we shall be at it hard again. If one gets through this show it will be a Xmas time to live in one's memory. The German who sang had a really fine voice.

Am just off for a walk round the trenches to see all is well. Good night.

How We Lived Then

NORMAN LONGMATE (ED.)

Christmas provided the greatest challenge of all. Turkeys were scarce and expensive throughout the war and for an Oldham schoolgirl the privations of wartime were summed up in her family's Christmas dinner in 1944: mutton pie followed by 'wartime

Christmas pudding', made with grated carrots. (The official recipes also suggested grated apples and chopped prunes and dried elderberries to replace the missing dried fruit. The results were rarely very palatable to those old enough to remember the real thing.) One Manchester woman had even more reason than most to remember the great blitz of December 1940, for 'my mother's house in Didsbury had had a direct hit *and* my mother-in-law's house in Chorlton and they all descended on me in my little flat. Our Christmas dinner consisted of corned beef hash and wartime Christmas pudding, but we listened to the wireless, sang, played cards and generally had a good time.' Alcohol of any kind was hard to find. The Radio Doctor, as usual, struck the right note when, broadcasting one wartime Christmas on the possible causes of a hangover, he remarked incredulously: 'It may even be due to too much drink, though if it was I'd like to know where you got it.'

Christmas cards were still sent during the war though most mantelpieces contained more 'official' cards with coats of arms, from the Women's Land Army to the Home Guard, than stage-coaches and snow scenes. A few patriotic people made their own cards by stencilling designs on newspaper, but this was generally felt to be carrying austerity too far.

One might, if fortunate, find a Christmas tree, though one mother still remembers with regret that her child never had the joy of seeing a Christmas tree decorated with electric lights, but decorations of some kind could be improvised and one Essex woman's 'happiest memory' is of 'sitting for hours with my small son making flowers and stars from silver paper to put on an otherwise empty Christmas tree'. Painted egg-shells and fir-cones, and fragments of silver paper from processed cheese packets, were also used as decorations, 'angels' and 'fairy dolls' were made from stiff paper and the blue packets in which cotton wool was sold were opened out and cut into strips for paper chains. Crackers were usually missing, but one East Ham family even succeeded in producing a version of their own, from the cardboard centres of toilet rolls, wrapped in crêpe paper, with, inside each, a home-made paper hat and a fire-cracker left over from Home Guard exercises.

Few Christmas stockings were left unfilled despite the war. A Sheffield girl, two when the war began, eight when it finished, remembers asking in her letter to Santa Claus for '"any little thing you can spare". This touched my mother – but at the time I couldn't see why. It just seemed logical.' A Surrey girl, six in 1939, remembers being put to bed one Christmas Eve in the shelter in the cellar and leaving detailed instructions on the dining room table to Santa Claus, lest he fail to locate this unconventional bedroom. A Liverpool woman remembers how another little girl was made happy that year despite the war:

Christmas 1941. The men were away, except my elder brother who had served in the first world war and was in the Home Guard. My daughter had asked Father

Christmas for a doll's house. We looked at each other in dismay. Then my brother found an old birdcage. During the raids he worked on it: found bits of cardboard for the walls. The office wastepaper basket provided an old file which made the roof. He painted the floors. We hunted for all kinds of bits and pieces and a miracle was achieved.... A piece of hessian, dyed red, fringed, made an elegant carpet. Never will I forget her face that dark Christmas morning and her childish voice piping: 'There'll be blue birds over the white cliffs of Dover' as she saw those tables and chairs, tiny pictures made out of cigarette cards, her cries of joy as she discovered each new thing.

On the whole, very small children probably came off best. Rag dolls, with button eyes, could fairly readily be made from old stockings, old coats could be converted into stuffed animals, seaboot stockings, unravelled, could be reknitted as teddy bears and, in one family in Somerset, an old pair of grey flannel trousers proved the basis for a pull-along elephant. Keen toy-makers hoarded every scrap of material, if not for sewing outside then for stuffing within; one family even saved the small plugs of cotton wool in the tops of aspirin bottles. Cardboard milk bottle tops and large buttons provided the mechanism of 'whizzers', which whirred round when their supporting strings were jerked tight, and in one Yorkshire factory toy-hungry fathers discovered that its basic product, round door-knobs, could serve a new use as yo-yos. A Birmingham builder, posted to London to help in repairs during the flying bomb raids, remembers that his workmates and himself 'made kaleidoscopes in our spare time, using bits of tinfoil, chips of coloured broken glass, etc.', and one mother, evacuated to Exeter with two small girls, brightened their Christmases with cardboard snowmen made from empty Vim canisters, covered with cotton wool and with a black circle of card for a hat, filled 'with little trinkets, sweets, etc., and perhaps an orange'.

Despite all their parents' efforts, many children did miss some of the customary pleasures during the war. One mother still feels sad that her daughter's only dolls were of the cardboard type, with cut-out clothes: the normal china type were simply beyond her means. Inevitably, too, the war deprived children of the pleasure of spending their pocket money as they wished. A Hawick, Roxburghshire, woman witnessed its effects on one small boy in 1944. He had called into the village Post Office to buy a comic, but was told 'They haven't come in this week'. He then asked for sweets, and was told 'No sweeties either' and, after a further question, 'Not even chewing gum'. At this, he asked for a penny stamp, walked out and stuck it on the pillar box outside, remarking 'That Hitler!'

HAD FATHER CHRISTMAS BROUGHT MY DOLL?

Yet it was not only war that brought deprivation and home-made rag dolls. As Winifred Foley explains in her scrumptious memoir, A Child in the Forest, there was no cash in the kitty for for bought presents if you belonged to a miner's family in the Forest of Dean during the 1920s. Few dolls in literature can have been quite so wretched; yet as we see she became just as precious as any glossy hussy bought at Harrods.

Albert, in Keith Waterhouse's charming North Country fable, is a mirror image of the little Forest of Dean girl in Winifred Foley's autobiography. Just as the doll she found on Christmas Day left a great deal to be desired, so the model of the Queen Mary that Albert is given lacks sophistication with its cardboard portholes and cotton reel funnels. Yet, in the end, both presents mean more to their recipients than the most glossy shop-bought equivalents.

Then, of course, not all of us deserve presents – certainly not King John in A. A. Milne's moral tale.

A Child in the Forest

WINIFRED FOLEY

If the chapel treat was the highlight of our life in summer, Christmas was the pinnacle of our winter delight, though most of the joy was in the anticipation. Every year for many years I spent weeks getting excited about a hopeless dream. I wanted – oh how I wanted – a doll. I knew it was quite impossible for Mam and Dad to buy me one. I had no luck praying for one, and it wasn't any good asking Dad to put a word in for me in that quarter, because I'd heard him and his butties argue and come to the conclusion that there couldn't be a God, or at any rate not one who worried about us as individuals.

But Father Christmas was quite a likely benefactor, though he too had his limitations. *My* dad had explained to me that as Father Christmas was such an old man, with his long white beard, he couldn't be expected to carry big things for all the children. I should have to wait my turn for a doll. Meantime I must be satisfied with something small, like a penny box of beads, and an orange if I was lucky. My turn for a doll seemed a long time coming.

My patience ran out one autumn when I was nine years old. Gladys, my best friend, who already had a nice doll, was given the most fantastic doll you ever saw. I didn't begrudge Gladys anything – she let me nurse her doll, and dress and undress it. But that was like being a nanny, not the same as having your own baby. The new doll was the size of a child, had long hair, eyes that opened and shut, and wore socks and shoes. Gladys's dad had won it at Barton fair. The doll was much too grand to play with, and was put on display in their cottage. All the village children, and quite a few grown-ups, called at Gladys's home for the privilege of seeing it.

As far as I was concerned, matters regarding a doll had now come to a head. I couldn't help Father Christmas's decrepitude – he would *have* to bring me a doll this Christmas. I gave him plenty of warning by shouting my request up the chimney weeks in advance of the usual time. Towards Christmas I started to write notes to him as well, with a stub of pencil given me by a neighbour as payment for running errands.

I was puzzling out how best to put my case to him with the limited spelling and vocabulary of a nine-year-old, when Dad came in. I told him I was making a bargain with Father Christmas: providing he brought me a doll this time, he needn't bring me anything else ever. But it had to be a doll big enough to sit on my lap, and have hair, and eyes that opened and shut.

'I be a-feared 'tis no good thee exing Feyther Christmas for that sart o' doll, my wench. 'Im do only take that sart to the rich people's young uns,' Dad warned me kindly.

'You do want to tell the silly old bugger off then. Tell 'im they rich people can afford to buy dolls for their children. It's the likes o' we lot 'im do want to bring the best toys to. Why ever 'aven't 'im got more sense then that?'

Father, who usually had an explanation for everything under the sun, scratched his head and admitted himself 'proper flummoxed'.

Bess said I'd be lucky to get anything if Father Christmas overheard me calling him a silly old bugger. Just because she was gone thirteen years old, and would soon be going into domestic service, she fancied herself too grown-up to ask Father Christmas for anything. Anyway, then she would be rich enough to buy anything she wanted, for my auntie in Bristol was getting her a job with the fantastic wage of five shillings a week.

With hope only slightly diminished, I continued to shout my order up the chimney, and to send up my notes when the draught was strong enough to stop them falling back into the fire.

My little brother fell asleep on Christmas Eve long before I did. I kept poking him awake to keep me company, but it was no good. I must have been awake for hours, when I heard stealthy footsteps coming up the stairs. It must be Father Christmas! Should I look, or shouldn't I? I had the patchwork quilt pulled right up to my eyes – he wouldn't notice, if I just took a peep. I suddenly felt terrified.

It was a bit of an anticlimax when I saw my sister in the doorway! 'Oh gawd! I thought you was Feyther Christmas!' It seemed to me that she was hiding something behind her back.

'If thee doosn't go to sleep Feyther Christmas wunt come at all,' she scolded me.

'I can't,' I wailed, 'thee'lt 'a' to 'it I over the yud wi' the coal 'ammer.'

I banged my obstinate head into the bolster. 'Go to sleep, you silly little bitch,' I told myself crossly.

It was my excited little brother who poked *me* awake in the morning. 'Look – Feyther Christmas a' brought I a tin whistle, a orange, a bag o' marbles an' some sweets.'

I sat bolt upright, like a Jack-in-the-Box. My doll, my doll! Had Father Christmas brought my doll?

At the bottom of my piece of the bed was propped the ugliest apology for a doll one could ever hope not to see.

It looked for all the world like an old, darned, black woollen stocking, lumpily stuffed, with a bit of old ribbon tied tightly round the foot to form its head. The eyes were two odd-sized buttons, and it grimaced from ear to ear with a red woollen gash of a mouth.

After all that cajoling up the chimney, after all the notes I'd written, fancy him bringing me a thing like that! He must think me a horrible little girl to treat me so, but I couldn't be that horrible! Mam came in, looking a bit anxious, but she said, bright

enough, 'Well then, Feyther Christmas didn't forget. 'Im did bring a doll for you.'

'Yes, an' 'im can 'ave the bugger back.'

Mother looked crestfallen. 'It won't break, like one o' they china dolls.'

'It's ugly, an' boss-eyed, an' got no 'air, and 'ow would you like it if the angels sent you a babby as ugly as *that?'*

Then I pulled the quilt over my head, to show I had cut myself off from the season of goodwill, and everyone concerned with it.

But Mam hadn't. After a bit she came back and sat on the bed. She didn't say anything, and my curiosity soon overcame me enough to have a peep at what she was up to.

Her baby boy, born a year after my little brother, had died; I thought he'd gone to heaven to be pampered and fussed over by the angels. Mam had kept a few of his baby clothes, though in general the women in our part of the village pooled their baby clothes to help each other out. Now she was dressing my doll up in a flannel nightdress, a bonnet and a piece of shawl. Held up in Mam's arms and cuddled against her neck, it looked like a real infant from the back. I was tempted to be won round. Mam left it, all snugly wrapped up, on the bed, while she went to get breakfast.

I and the doll were soon downstairs with the rest of the family, sitting at the table. Mam was in a specially good humour with me. We didn't have such things as bacon and eggs even on Christmas Day, but as a great treat old Auntie had given us half a tin of Nestlé's milk to share out on our toast. As if that were not enough, she'd given us each a shiny new penny as well. I felt warmed and loved again. I made a bit of sop in a saucer, with a drop of my tea and a bit of the bread and milk, and pretended to spoon it into my doll's mouth, before taking her out.

I knew that other children might laugh at her ugliness as they did at Lil Wills's poor little looney sister, so I decided to take her for a walk on my own. Miss Phillips, whose cottage garden adjoined ours, was just coming back from the ashmix with an empty bucket.

'My, my, Polly! It looks as though Feyther Christmas 'a' brought you a real big doll this time. Let me 'ave a look at 'er.'

I loved the inside of Miss Phillips' neat, tidy cottage, but none of us were much taken with her – she nagged us for playing noisily, and wouldn't let us play ball where we wanted to. I gave her one of my ferocious scowls to put her off, but she insisted on following me and unwrapping the piece of shawl to see what I'd got.

'Oh my gawd, that'un 'ould do better to frighten the birds off the gyarden. I reckon Feyther Christmas musta took 'im from a crow's nest.'

How dare she! I bridled like an insulted mother! I doubled my scowl, and threw in my monkey face for good measure.

'Never mind,' I said to the doll, when we were out of earshot. ''Er's a nasty old bisom, and your mammy 'ouldn't change you for all the money in the world.'

Miss Phillips' insults cemented my feeling for my new charge. From then, she became the object of my affection.

I had taken squatter's rights of the narrow space between Dad's shed at the bottom of our garden, and the old stone wall of Miss Phillips' garden. Here I played whenever I could. Only my little brother, baby sister and my best friend, Gladys, were allowed to come in without special permission.

One hot, humid summer evening I was minding the two little ones down there, whilst Mam was doing some washing, when an ominous rumble growled across the sky, which had suddenly gone very dark. Almost simultaneously came a vivid flash of lightning that made my little brother jump. Mam had a morbid fear of thunderstorms: she screamed from the doorway for us to come indoors at once. I picked up my toddler sister and shouted at my brother to hurry; we got indoors just as the rain started to come down in a torrent. Mam took us to the coal hole under the stairs. Even here the tiny back window let in the lightning flashes, and the thunder seemed to be concentrating on knocking our cottage down.

Then I remembered! 'Me doll, me doll! I've left her down the bottom of the garden!'

Mother promised me she would be all right, and when the storm was over she would dry her out on the fender. The storm lasted past our bedtime, and though the rumbles got quieter and there weren't so many lightning flashes, Mam wouldn't let me put my nose outside the door.

She promised that Dad would fetch the doll in when he came home from his late shift at the pit. In the morning there was no doll on the fender when I got up. Mam had forgotten, but she ran down to get it before I could put my boots on. She came back with the disintegrating remains.

'Bain't no good you carrying on: it fell to pieces in me 'and.'

Despite a halfpenny and a few currants in a piece of paper, I was still sniffing back the tears when Gladys came to call for me.

'Never mind, Poll,' she said. 'We'll give her a lovely funeral. I'll go back 'ome and ask Mam if we can 'ave some flowers to put on the grave.'

She came back with a bunch of sweet-williams and an old straw hat. "Ere, you be the chief mourner, you can wear this.'

We decided to hold the funeral in private. My little brother would probably only cry, and there was no one else worthy of the honour of attending. Gladys spoke a long sermon, then walked round the grave three times chanting, 'Ashes to ashes, dust to dust, if Gawd won't 'ave her, the devil must.' Then she put a handful of earth on the remains, and we filled up the grave and put the flowers in a jam jar on the top.

'O' course the devil *won't* 'ave 'er,' said Gladys.

It was nice of her to say that, but I never had a doubt where my beloved doll would go.

ALBERT AND THE LINER

KEITH WATERHOUSE

Below the military striking clock in the City Arcade there was, and for all I know still is, a fabulous toyshop.

It was a magic grotto, that shop. A zoo, a circus, a pantomime, a travelling show, a railway exhibition, an enchanted public library, a clockwork museum, an archive of boxed games, a pavilion of sports equipment, a depository of all the joys of the indefinite, endless leisure of the winter holiday – but first, the military striking clock.

Once a year we were taken to see the clock strike noon – an event in our lives as colourful, and traditional, and as fixed and immovable in the calendar of pageantry as Trooping the Colour. Everybody who was anybody assembled, a few minutes before twelve, on the patch of worn tiles incorporating an advertisement for tomato sausages done in tasteful mosaic, beneath that military striking clock.

There was me, and Jack Corrigan, and the crippled lad from No. 43, and there was even Albert Skinner – whose father never took him anywhere, not even to the Education Office to explain why he'd been playing truant.

Albert Skinner, with his shaved head and his shirt-lap hanging out of his trousers, somehow attached himself, insinuated himself, like a stray dog. You'd be waiting at the tram stop with your mother, all dolled up in your Sunday clothes for going into town and witnessing the ceremony of the military striking clock, and Albert, suddenly, out of nowhere, would be among those present.

'Nah, then, kid.'

And your mother, out of curiosity, would say – as she was meant to say – 'You're never going into town looking like that, are you, Albert?'

And Albert would say: 'No. I was, only I've lost my tram fare.'

And your mother, out of pity, would say – as she was meant to say – 'Well, you can come with us. But you'll have to tidy yourself up. Tuck your shirt in, Albert.'

So at Christmastime Albert tagged on to see the military striking clock strike noon. And after the mechanical soldiers of the King had trundled back into their plaster-of-Paris garrison, he, with the rest of us, was allowed to press his nose to the fabulous toyshop window.

Following a suitable period of meditation, we were then treated to a bag of mint imperials – *'and think on, they're to share between you'* – and conveyed home on the rattling tram. And there, thawing out our mottled legs by the fireside, we were supposed to compose our petitions to Father Christmas.

Dear Father Christmas, for Christmas I would like . . .

'Don't know what to put,' we'd say at length to one another, seeking some kind of corporate inspiration.

'Why don't you ask him for a sledge? I am.'

'Barmpot, what do you want a sledge for? What if it doesn't snow?'

'Well – a cricket bat and stumps, and that.'

'Don't play cricket at Christmas, barmpot.'

Albert Skinner said nothing. Nobody, in fact, said anything worth saying during those tortured hours of voluntary composition.

With our blank jumbo jotters on our knees, we would suck our copying-ink pencils until our tongues turned purple – but it wasn't that we were short of ideas. Far from it: sledges, cricket bats with stumps and that, fountain pens, dynamos, cinematographs complete with Mickey Mouse films – the fact of the matter was, there was too much choice.

For the fabulous toyshop, which sparked off our exotic and finally blank imaginations, was the nearest thing on this earth to Santa's Workshop. It was like a bankruptcy sale in heaven. The big clockwork train ran clockwise and the small electric train ran anti-clockwise, and there was Noah's Ark, and a tram conductor's set, and a junior typewriter revolving on a brightly lit glass shelf, and a fairy cycle hanging from the ceiling on invisible wires, and a tin steam roller, and the *Tip-Top Annual* and the *Film Fun Annual* and the *Radio Fun Annual* and the *Jingles Annual* and the *Joker Annual* and the *Jester Annual*, and board games, and chemistry sets, and conjuring sets, and carpentry sets – everything, in short, that the modern boy would give his eye-teeth for.

Everything that Albert Skinner would have given his eye-teeth for, in fact, and much that Albert Skinner would never get. And not only him. There were items that no reasonable modern boy expected to find in his Christmas pillow-case – not even though he bartered every tooth in his head and promised to be a good lad till kingdom come.

The centrepiece of the fabulous toyshop's window display was always something out of the reach of ordinary mortals, such as the Blackpool Tower in Meccano, or a mechanical carousel with horses that went up and down on their brass poles like the real thing, or Windsor Castle made of a million building bricks, or Buckingham Palace with nobs on – floodlit. None of us had to be told that such luxuries were beyond Father Christmas's price range.

This year the window featured a splendid model of the *Queen Mary*, which had recently been launched on Clydebank. It was about four feet long, with real lights in the portholes, real steam curling out of the funnels, and a crew, and passengers, and lifeboats, and cabin trunks, all to scale – and clearly it was not for the likes of us.

Having seen it and marvelled at it, we dismissed this expensive dream from our minds, sucked our copying-ink pencils and settled down to list our prosaic requests – for Plasticine, for farmyard animals that poisoned you when you licked the paint off, and for one pair of roller skates between two of us.

All of us, that is to say, except Albert Skinner. Having considered several possibilities, and taken advice on the rival merits of a racing track with eight electric sports cars and a glove puppet of Felix the Cat he'd rather fancied, Albert calmly announced that he'd given thought to all our suggestions and he was asking Father Christmas for the *Queen Mary*.

This, as you might imagine, was greeted with some scepticism.

'What – that one in the Arcade window? With all the lights and the steam coming out and that? You've never asked for that, have you?'

'Yeh – course I have. Why shouldn't I?'

'He's blinking crackers. Hey, Skinno, why don't you ask for them soldiers that march in and out and bang that clock? Because you've more chance of getting them than that *Queen Mary*.'

'If I'd wanted them soldiers, I'd have asked for them. Only I don't. So I've asked him for the *Queen Mary*.'

'Who – Father Christmas?'

'No – him on the Quaker Oats Box, who do you think?'

'Bet you haven't, man. Bet you're having us on.'

'I'm not – God's honour. I've asked him for the *Queen Mary*.'

'Let's see the letter, then.'

'Can't – I've chucked it up the chimney.'

'Yeh – bet you have. Anyway, your dad won't get it for you – he can't afford it.'

'What's it got to do with him? I'm asking Father Stinking Rotten Christmas for it, not me dad. Dozy.'

'What else have you asked for, Skinno?'

'Nowt. I don't want owt else. I just want the *Queen Mary*. And I'm getting it, as well.'

Little else was said at the time, but privately we thought Albert was a bit of an optimist. For one thing, the *Queen Mary* was so big and so grand and so lit-up that it was probably not even for sale. For another, we were all well aware that Father

Christmas's representative in the Skinner household was a sullen, foul-tempered collier who also happened to be unemployed.

Albert's birthday present, it was generally known, had been a pair of boots – instead of the scooter on which, at that time, he had set his heart.

Even so, Albert continued to insist that he was getting the *Queen Mary* for Christmas. 'Ask my dad,' he would say. 'If you don't believe me, ask my dad.'

None of us cared to broach the subject with the excitable Mr Skinner. But sometimes, when we went to his house to swop comics, Albert would raise the matter himself.

'Dad, I am aren't I? Aren't I, Dad? Getting that *Queen Mary* for Christmas?'

Mr Skinner, dourly whittling a piece of wood by the fireside after the habit of all the local miners, would growl without looking up: 'You'll get a clout over the bloody earhole if you don't stop chelping.'

Albert would turn complacently to us. 'I am, see. I'm getting the *Queen Mary*. Aren't I, Dad? Dad? Aren't I?'

Sometimes, when his father had come home from the pub in a bad mood (which was quite often), Albert's pleas for reassurance would be met with a more vicious response. 'Will you shut up about the bloody *Queen* swining *Mary*!' Mr Skinner would shout. 'You gormless little git, do you think I'm made of money?'

Outside, his ear tingling from the blow his father had landed on it, Albert would bite back the tears and declare stubbornly: 'I'm still getting it. You wait till Christmas.'

Christmas Eve was but a fortnight off by then. Most of us had a shrewd idea, from hints dropped by our mothers, what Father Christmas would be bringing us – or, in most cases, not bringing. 'I don't think Father Christmas can manage an electric train set this year, our Terry. He says they're too expensive. He says he might be able to find you a tip-up lorry.'

Being realists, we accepted our lowly position on Father Christmas's scale of priorities – and we tried our best to persuade Albert to accept his.

'You're not *forced* to get that *Queen Mary*, you know, Skinno.'

'Who says I'm not?'

'My mam. She says it's too big to go in Father Christmas's sack.'

'Yeh, well, that's all *she* knows. Because he's fetching Jacky Corrigan a fairy cycle – so if he can't get the *Queen Mary* in his sack, how can he get a stinking rotten fairy cycle?'

'Yeh, well he isn't fetching me a fairy cycle at all, clever-clogs, he's fetching me a John Bull printing outfit. 'Cos he told my mam.'

'I don't care what he told her, or what he didn't tell her. He's still fetching me that *Queen Mary*.'

The discussion was broken up by the sudden appearance of Mr Skinner at their scullery window. 'If I hear one more bloody word from you about that bloody *Queen Mary*, you'll get nothing for Christmas! Do you hear me?' And there the matter rested.

A few days later the crippled lad at No. 43 was taken by the Church Ladies Guild to see the military striking clock in the City Arcade, and when he came home he reported that the model of the *Queen Mary* was no longer in the window of the fabulous toyshop.

'I know,' said Albert, having confirmed that his father was out of earshot. 'I'm getting it for Christmas.'

And indeed, it seemed the only explanation possible. The fabulous toyshop never changed its glittering display until after Boxing Day – it was unheard of. Some minor item might vanish out of the window – the Noah's Ark, perhaps, or a farmyard, or a game of Monopoly or two. There was a rational explanation for this: Father Christmas hadn't enough toys to go round and he'd been obliged, so to speak, to call on his sub-contractors. But the set-piece, the Blackpool Tower made out of Meccano or the carousel with the horses that went round and round and up and down – that was never removed; never. And yet the *Queen Mary* had gone. What had happened? Had Father Christmas gone mad? Had Mr Skinner bribed him – and if so, with what? Had Mr Skinner won the football pools? Or was it that Albert's unswerving faith could move mountains – not to mention ocean-going liners with real steam and real lights in the portholes? Or was it, as one cynic among us insisted, that the *Queen Mary* had been privately purchased for some pampered grammar school lad on the posher side of town?

'You just wait and see,' said Albert.

And then it was Christmas morning; and after the chocolate pennies had been eaten and all the kitchens in the street were awash with nut-shells and orange peel, we all flocked out to show off our presents – sucking our brand-new torches to make our cheeks glow red, or brandishing a lead soldier or two in the pretence that we had a whole regiment of them indoors. Those who had wanted wooden forts were delighted with their painting books; those who had prayed for electric racing cars were content with their Dinky toys; those who had asked for roller skates were happy with their pencil boxes; and there was no sign of Albert.

No one, in fact, expected to see him at all. But just as we were asking each other what Father Christmas could have brought him – a new jersey, perhaps, or a balaclava helmet – he came bounding, leaping, jumping, almost somersaulting into the street. 'I've got it! I've got it! I've got it!'

Painting books and marbles and games of Happy Families were abandoned in the gutter as we clustered around Albert, who was cradling in his arms what seemed on first inspection to be a length of wood. Then we saw that it had been roughly carved at both ends, to make a bow and stern, and that three cotton-reels had been nailed to it for funnels. A row of tintacks marked the Plimsoll line, and there were stuck-on bits of cardboard for the portholes. The whole thing was painted over in sticky lamp-black, except for the lettering on the portside.

'*The Queen Mary*,' it said. In white, wobbling letters. Capital T, small h, capital E. Capital Q, small u, capital E, capital E, small n. Capital M, small a, capital R, small y. Penmanship had never been Mr Skinner's strong point.

'See!' crowed Albert complacently. 'I told you he'd fetch me it, and he's fetched me it.'

Our grunts of appreciation, though somewhat strained, were genuine enough. Albert's *Queen Mary* was a crude piece of work, but clearly many hours of labour, and much love, had gone into it. Its clumsy contours alone must have taken night after night of whittling by the fireside.

Mr Skinner, pyjama-jacket tucked into his trousers, had come out of the house and was standing by his garden gate. Albert, in a rush of happiness, ran to his father and flung his arms around him and hugged him. Then he waved the *Queen Mary* on high.

'Look, Dad! Look what I've got for Christmas! Look what Father Christmas has fetched me! You knew he would, didn't you, all this time!'

'Get out of it, you soft little bugger,' said Mr Skinner. He drew contentedly on his empty pipe, cuffed Albert over the head as a matter of habit, and went indoors.

KING JOHN'S CHRISTMAS

A. A. MILNE

King John was not a good man –
   He had his little ways.
And sometimes no one spoke to him
   For days and days and days.
And men who came across him,
   When walking in the town,
Gave him a supercilious stare,
Or passed with noses in the air –
And bad King John stood dumbly there,
   Blushing beneath his crown.

King John was not a good man,
   And no good friends had he.
He stayed in every afternoon ...
   But no one came to tea.
And, round about December,
   The cards upon his shelf
Which wished him lots of Christmas cheer,
And fortune in the coming year,
Were never from his near and dear,
   But only from himself.

King John was not a good man,
   Yet had his hopes and fears.
They'd given him no present now
   For years and years and years.
But every year at Christmas,
   While minstrels stood about,
Collecting tribute from the young
For all the songs they might have sung,
He stole away upstairs and hung
   A hopeful stocking out.

King John was not a good man,
   He lived his life aloof;
Alone he thought a message out
   While climbing up the roof.
He wrote it down and propped it
   Against the chimney stack:
'TO ALL AND SUNDRY – NEAR AND FAR –
F. CHRISTMAS IN PARTICULAR.'
And signed it not 'Johannes R.'
But very humbly, 'JACK.'

'I want some crackers,
   And I want some candy;
I think a box of chocolates
   Would come in handy;
I don't mind oranges,
   I do like nuts!
And I SHOULD like a pocket-knife
   That really cuts.
And, oh! Father Christmas, if you love me at all,
Bring me a big, red india-rubber ball!'

King John was not a good man –
   He wrote this message out,
And gat him to his room again,
   Descending by the spout.
And all that night he lay there,
   A prey to hopes and fears.
'I think that's him a-counting now,'
   (Anxiety bedewed his brow.)
'He'll bring one present, anyhow –
   The first I've had for years.'

'Forget about the crackers,
   And forget about the candy;
I'm sure a box of chocolates
   Would never come in handy;
I don't like oranges,
   I don't want nuts,
And I HAVE got a pocket-knife
   That almost cuts.

But, oh! Father Christmas, if you love me at all,
Bring me a big, red india-rubber ball!'

King John was not a good man –
   Next morning when the sun
Rose up to tell a waiting world
   That Christmas had begun,
And people seized their stockings,
   And opened then with glee,
And crackers, toys and games appeared,
And lips with sticky sweets were smeared,
King John said grimly: 'As I feared,
   Nothing again for me!'

'I did want crackers,
   And I did want candy;
I know a box of chocolates
   Would come in handy;
I do love oranges,
   I did want nuts.
I haven't got a pocket-knife –
   Not one that cuts.
And, oh! if Father Christmas had loved me at all,
He would have brought a big, red india-rubber ball!'

King John stood by the window,
   And frowned to see below
The happy bands of boys and girls
   All playing in the snow.
A while he stood there watching,
   And envying them all ...
When through the window big and red
There hurtled by his royal head,
And bounced and fell upon the bed,
   An india-rubber ball!

AND OH, FATHER CHRISTMAS,
  MY BLESSINGS ON YOU FALL
    FOR BRINGING HIM
      A BIG, RED,
      INDIA-RUBBER
      BALL!

Very Well Sung, Boys!

Here is a set of three children's stories— though, to tell the truth, all three have delighted quite as many adults as children. The Wind in the Willows, inspired title for an inspired book, was written by Kenneth Grahame when Secretary of the Bank of England, for his son Alistair. The animals in it, naïve Mole, kindly Rat, worldly Badger and capricious Toad, all seem distinctly human, and indeed nothing could be more human than Mole's delight at the arrival of the field-mice in their red comforters to sing their carols outside his house. Next, a short, odd, vivid story from the pen of that rum genius Hans Andersen. He was livid when a grateful country wanted to honour him with a statue showing him surrounded by children; his stories, he argued vehemently, were universal. Any visitor to Copenhagen can see for himself that the children were duly removed; and on reflection, this bitter and brilliant Christmas yarn is hardly suitable for children at all, though it concerns one. Then that celebrated moment in Little Women when the girls give up their Christmas breakfast to feed a starving German immigrant family. The evening festivities seem to have atoned for that early deprivation.

THE WIND IN THE WILLOWS

KENNETH GRAHAME

At last the Rat succeeded in decoying him to the table, and had just got seriously to work with the sardine-opener when sounds were heard from the fore-court without – sounds like the scuffling of small feet in the gravel and a confused murmur of tiny voices, while broken sentences reached them – 'Now, all in a line – hold the lantern up a bit, Tommy – clear your throats first – no coughing after I say one, two, three. – Where's young Bill? – Here, come on, do, we're all a-waiting –'

'What's up?' inquired the Rat, pausing in his labours.

'I think it must be the field-mice,' replied the Mole, with a touch of pride in his manner. 'They go round carol-singing regularly at this time of the year. They're quite an institution in these parts. And they never pass me over – they come to Mole End last of all; and I used to give them hot drinks, and supper too sometimes, when I could afford it. It will be like old times to hear them again.'

'Let's have a look at them!' cried the Rat, jumping up and running to the door.

It was a pretty sight, and a seasonable one, that met their eyes when they flung the door open. In the fore-court, lit by the dim rays of a horn lantern, some eight or ten little field-mice stood in a semicircle, red worsted comforters round their throats, their fore-paws thrust deep into their pockets, their feet jigging for warmth. With bright beady eyes they glanced shyly at each other, sniggering a little, sniffing and applying coat-sleeves a good deal. As the door opened, one of the elder ones that carried the lantern was just saying, 'Now then, one, two, three!' and forthwith their shrill little voices uprose on the air, singing one of the old-time carols that their forefathers composed in fields that were fallow and held by frost, or when snow-bound in chimney corners, and handed down to be sung in the miry street to lamp-lit windows at Yule-time.

CAROL

Villagers, all, this frosty tide,
Let your doors swing open wide,
Though wind may follow, and snow beside,
Yet draw us in by your fire to bide;
    Joy shall be yours in the morning!

Here we stand in the cold and the sleet,
Blowing fingers and stamping feet,
Come from far away you to greet –
You by the fire and we in the street –
Bidding you joy in the morning!

For ere one half of the night was gone,
Sudden a star has led us on,
Raining bliss and benison –
Bliss to-morrow and more anon,
Joy for every morning!

Goodman Joseph toiled through the snow –
Saw the star o'er a stable low;
Mary she might not further go –
Welcome thatch, and litter below!
Joy was hers in the morning!

And then they heard the angels tell
'Who were the first to cry Nowell?
Animals all, as it befell,
In the stable where they did dwell!
Joy shall be theirs in the morning!'

The voices ceased, the singers, bashful but smiling, exchanged sidelong glances, and silence succeeded – but for a moment only. Then, from up above and far away, down the tunnel they had so lately travelled was borne to their ears in a faint musical hum the sound of distant bells ringing a joyful and clangorous peal.

'Very well sung, boys!' cried the Rat heartily. 'And now come along in, all of you, and warm yourselves by the fire, and have something hot!'

'Yes, come along, field-mice,' cried the Mole eagerly. 'This is quite like old times! Shut the door after you. Pull up that settle to the fire. Now, you just wait a minute, while we – O, Ratty!' he cried in despair, plumping down on a seat, with tears impending. 'Whatever are we doing? We've nothing to give them!'

'You leave all that to me,' said the masterful Rat. 'Here you, with the lantern! Come over this way. I want to talk to you. Now, tell me, are there any shops open at this hour of the night?'

'Why, certainly, sir,' replied the field-mouse respectfully. 'At this time of the year our shops keep open to all sorts of hours.'

'Then look here!' said the Rat. 'You go off at once, you and your lantern, and you get me –'

Here much muttered conversation ensued, and the Mole only heard bits of it, such as — 'Fresh, mind! — no, a pound of that will do — see you get Buggins's, for I won't have any other — no, only the best — if you can't get it there, try somewhere else — yes, of course, home-made, no tinned stuff — well then, do the best you can!' Finally, there was a chink of coin passing from paw to paw, the field-mouse was provided with an ample basket for his purchases, and off he hurried, he and his lantern.

The rest of the field-mice, perched in a row on the settle, their small legs swinging, gave themselves up to enjoyment of the fire, and toasted their chilblains till they tingled; while the Mole, failing to draw them into easy conversation, plunged into family history and made each of them recite the names of his numerous brothers, who were too young, it appeared, to be allowed to go out a-carolling this year, but looked forward very shortly to winning the parental consent.

The Rat, meanwhile, was busy examining the label on one of the beer-bottles. 'I perceive this to be Old Burton,' he remarked approvingly. '*Sensible* Mole! The very thing! Now we shall be able to mull some ale! Get the things ready, Mole, while I draw the corks.'

It did not take long to prepare the brew and thrust the tin heater well into the red heart of the fire; and soon every field-mouse was sipping and coughing and choking (for a little mulled ale goes a long way) and wiping his eyes and laughing and forgetting he had ever been cold in all his life.

'They act plays too, these fellows,' the Mole explained to the Rat. 'Make them up all by themselves, and act them afterwards. And very well they do it, too! They gave us a capital one last year, about a field-mouse who was captured at sea by a Barbary corsair, and made to row in a galley; and when he escaped and got home again, his lady-love had gone into a convent. Here, *you*! You were in it, I remember. Get up and recite a bit.'

The field-mouse addressed got up on his legs, giggled shyly, looked round the room, and remained absolutely tongue-tied. His comrades cheered him on, Mole coaxed and encouraged him, and the Rat went so far as to take him by the shoulders and shake him; but nothing could overcome his stage-fright. They were all busily engaged on him like watermen applying the Royal Humane Society's regulations to a case of long submersion, when the latch clicked, the door opened, and the field-mouse with the lantern reappeared, staggering under the weight of his basket.

There was no more talk of play-acting once the very real and solid contents of the basket had been tumbled out on the table. Under the generalship of Rat, everybody was set to do something or to fetch something. In a very few minutes supper was ready, and Mole, as he took the head of the table in a sort of dream, saw a lately barren board set thick with savoury comforts; saw his little friends' faces brighten and beam as they fell to without delay; and then let himself loose — for he was famished indeed — on the provender so magically provided, thinking what a happy home-coming this had turned out, after all. As they ate, they talked of old times, and the field-mice gave him the local gossip up to date, and answered as well as they could the hundred questions he had to ask them. The Rat said little or nothing, only taking care that each guest had what he wanted, and plenty of it, and that Mole had no trouble or anxiety about anything.

They clattered off at last, very grateful and showering wishes of the season, with their jacket pockets stuffed with remembrances for the small brothers and sisters at home. When the door had closed on the last of them and the chink of the lanterns had died away, Mole and Rat kicked the fire up, drew their chairs in, brewed themselves a last nightcap of mulled ale, and discussed the events of the long day. At last the Rat, with a tremendous yawn, said, 'Mole, old chap, I'm ready to drop. Sleepy is simply not the word. That your own bunk over on that side? Very well, then, I'll take this. What a ripping little house this is! Everything so handy!'

He clambered into his bunk and rolled himself well up in the blankets, and slumber gathered him forthwith, as a swath of barley is folded into the arms of the reaping-machine.

The weary Mole also was glad to turn in without delay, and soon had his head on his pillow, in great joy and contentment.

THE LITTLE MATCH-GIRL

HANS CHRISTIAN ANDERSEN

It was so dreadfully cold! It was snowing, and the evening was beginning to darken. It was the last evening of the year, too – New Year's Eve. Through the cold and the dark, a poor little girl with bare head and naked feet was wandering along the road. She had, indeed, had a pair of slippers on when she left home; but what was the good of that! They were very big slippers – her mother had worn them last, they were so big – and the little child had lost them hurrying across the road as two carts rattled dangerously past. One slipper could not be found, and a boy ran off with the other – he said he could use it as a cradle when he had children of his own.

So the little girl wandered along with her naked little feet red and blue with cold. She was carrying a great pile of matches in an old apron and she held one bundle in her hand as she walked. No one had bought a thing from her the whole day; no one had given her a halfpenny; hungry and frozen, she went her way, looking so woe-begone, poor little thing! The snow-flakes fell upon her long fair hair that curled so prettily about the nape of her neck, but she certainly wasn't thinking of how nice she looked. Lights were shining from all the windows, and there was a lovely smell of roast goose all down the street, for it was indeed New Year's Eve – yes, and that's what she was thinking about.

Over in a corner between two houses, where one jutted a little farther out into the street than the other, she sat down and huddled together; she had drawn her little legs up under her, but she felt more frozen than ever, and she dared not go home, for she had sold no matches and hadn't got a single penny, and her father would beat her. Besides, it was cold at home, too: there was only the roof over them, and the wind whistled in, although the biggest cracks had been stopped up with straw and rags. Her little hands were almost dead with cold. Ah, a little match might do some good! If she only dared pull one out of the bundle, strike it on the wall, and warm her fingers! She drew one out – Whoosh! – How it spluttered! How it burnt! It gave a warm bright flame, just like a little candle, when she held her hand round it. It was a wonderful light: the little girl thought she was sitting in front of a great iron stove with polished brass knobs and fittings; the fire was burning so cheerfully and its warmth was so comforting – oh, what was that! The little girl had just stretched her feet out to warm them, too, when – the fire went out! The stove disappeared – and she was sitting there with the little stump of a burnt-out match in her hand.

Another match was struck; it burnt and flared, and where the light fell upon it, the wall became transparent like gauze; she could see right into the room where the table stood covered with a shining white cloth and set with fine china, and there was a roast goose, stuffed with prunes and apples, steaming deliciously — but what was more gorgeous still, the goose jumped off the dish, waddled across the floor with knife and

fork in its back, and went straight over to the poor girl. Then the match went out, and there was nothing to see but the thick cold wall.

She struck yet another. And then she was sitting beneath the loveliest Christmas tree; it was even bigger and more beautifully decorated than the one she had seen this last Christmas through the glass doors of the wealthy grocer's shop. Thousands of candles were burning on its green branches, and gaily coloured pictures, like those that had decorated the shop-windows, were looking down at her. The little girl stretched out both her hands — and then the match went out; the multitude of Christmas-candles rose higher and higher, and now she saw they were the bright stars — one of them fell and made a long streak of fire across the sky.

'Someone's now dying!' said the little girl, for her old granny, who was the only one that had been kind to her, but who was now dead, had said that when a star falls a soul goes up to God.

Once more she struck a match on the wall. It lit up the darkness round about her, and in its radiance stood old granny, so bright and shining, so wonderfully kind.

'Granny!' cried the little girl. 'Oh, take me with you! I know you'll go away when the match goes out – you'll go away just like the warm stove and the lovely roast goose and the wonderful big Christmas-tree!' – And she hastily struck all the rest of the matches in the bundle, for she wanted to keep her granny there, and the matches shone with such brilliance that it was brighter than daylight. Granny had never before been so tall and beautiful; she lifted the little girl up on her arm, and they flew away in splendour and joy, high high up towards heaven. And there was no more cold and no more hunger and no more fear – they were with God.

But in the corner by the house, in the cold of the early morning, the little girl sat, with red cheeks and a smile upon her lips – dead, frozen to death on the last evening of the old year. The morning of the New Year rose over the little dead body sitting there with her matches, one bundle nearly all burnt out. She wanted to keep herself warm, they said; but no one knew what beautiful things she had seen, nor in what radiance she had gone with her old granny into the joy of the New Year.

LITTLE WOMEN

LOUISA MAY ALCOTT

Jo was the first to wake in the grey dawn of Christmas morning. No stockings hung at the fireplace, and for a moment she felt as much disappointed as she did long ago, when her little sock fell down because it was so crammed with goodies. Then she remembered her mother's promise, and, slipping her hand under her pillow, drew out a little crimson-covered book. She knew it very well, for it was that beautiful old story of the best life ever lived, and Jo felt that it was a true guide-book for any pilgrim going the long journey. She woke Meg with a 'Merry Christmas', and bade her see what was under her pillow. A green-covered book appeared, with the same picture inside, and a few words written by their mother, which made their one present very precious in their eyes. Presently Beth and Amy woke, to rummage and find their little books also – one, dove-coloured, the other blue; and all sat looking at and talking about them, while the east grew rosy with the coming day.

In spite of her small vanities, Margaret had a sweet and pious nature, which unconsciously influenced her sisters, especially Jo, who loved her very tenderly, and obeyed her because her advice was so gently given.

'Girls,' said Meg seriously, looking from the tumbled head beside her to the two little night-capped ones in the room beyond, 'Mother wants us to read and love and mind these books, and we must begin at once. We used to be faithful about it; but since Father went away, and all this war trouble unsettled us, we have neglected many things. You can do as you please; but *I* shall keep my book on the table here, and read a little every morning as soon as I wake, for I know it will do me good, and help me through the day.'

Then she opened her new book and began to read. Jo put her arm round her, and, leaning cheek to cheek, read also, with the quiet expression so seldom seen on her restless face.

'How good Meg is! Come, Amy, let's do as they do. I'll help you with the hard words, and they'll explain things if we don't understand,' whispered Beth, very much impressed by the pretty books and her sisters' example.

'I'm glad mine is blue,' said Amy; and then the rooms were very still while the pages were softly turned, and the winter sunshine crept in to touch the bright heads and serious faces with a Christmas greeting.

'Where is Mother?' asked Meg, as she and Jo ran down to thank her for their gifts, half an hour later.

'Goodness only knows. Some poor creeter come a-beggin', and your ma went straight off to see what was needed. There never *was* such a woman for givin' away vittles and drink, clothes, and firin',' replied Hannah, who had lived with the family since Meg was born, and was considered by them all more as a friend than a servant.

'She will be back soon, I think; so fry your cake, and have everything ready,' said Meg, looking over the presents which were collected in a basket and kept under the sofa, ready to be produced at the proper time. 'Why, where is Amy's bottle of cologne?' she added, as the little flask did not appear.

'She took it out a minute ago, and went off with it to put a ribbon on it, or some such notion,' replied Jo, dancing about the room to take the first stiffness off the new army-slippers.

'How nice my handkerchiefs look, don't they! Hannah washed and ironed them for me, and I marked them all myself,' said Beth, looking proudly at the somewhat uneven letters which had cost her such labour.

'Bless the child! she's gone and put "Mother" on them instead of "M. March". How funny!' cried Jo, taking up one.

'Isn't it right? I thought it was better to do it so, because Meg's initials are "M. M.", and I don't want anyone to use these but Marmee,' said Beth, looking troubled.

'It's all right, dear, and a very pretty idea – quite sensible, too, for no one can ever mistake now. It will please her very much, I know,' said Meg, with a frown for Jo and a smile for Beth.

'There's Mother. Hide the basket, quick!' cried Jo, as a door slammed, and steps sounded in the hall.

Amy came in hastily, and looked rather abashed when she saw her sisters all waiting for her.

'Where have you been, and what are you hiding behind you?' asked Meg, surprised to see, by her hood and cloak, that Lazy Amy had been out so early.

'Don't laugh at me, Jo! I didn't mean anyone should know till the time came. I only meant to change the little bottle for a big one, and I gave *all* my money to get it, and I'm truly trying not to be selfish any more.'

As she spoke, Amy showed the handsome flask which replaced the cheap one; and looked so earnest and humble in her little effort to forget herself that Meg hugged her on the spot, and Jo pronounced her 'a trump', while Beth ran to the window and picked her finest rose to ornament the stately bottle.

'You see, I felt ashamed of my present, after reading and talking about being good this morning, so I ran round the corner and changed it the minute I was up; and I'm *so* glad, for mine is the handsomest now.'

Another bang of the street door sent the basket under the sofa, and the girls to the table, eager for breakfast.

'Merry Christmas, Marmee! Many of them! Thank you for our books; we read some, and mean to, every day,' they cried, in chorus.

'Merry Christmas, little daughters! I'm glad you began at once, and hope you will keep on. But I want to say one word before we sit down. Not far away from here lies a poor woman with a little new-born baby. Six children are huddled into one bed to keep from freezing, for they have no fire. There is nothing to eat over there; and the oldest boy came to tell me they were suffering hunger and cold. My girls, will you give them your breakfast as a Christmas present?'

They were all unusually hungry, having waited nearly an hour, and for a minute no one spoke; only a minute, for Jo exclaimed impetuously:

'I'm so glad you came before we began!'

'May I go and help carry the things to the poor little children?' said Beth, eagerly.

'*I* shall take the cream and the muffins,' added Amy, heroically, giving up the articles she most liked.

Meg was already covering the buckwheats, and piling the bread into one big plate.

'I thought you'd do it,' said Mrs March, smiling as if satisfied. 'You shall all go and help me, and when we come back we will have bread and milk for breakfast, and make it up at dinner-time.'

They were soon ready, and the procession set out. Fortunately it was early, and they went through back streets, so few people saw them, and no one laughed at the queer party.

A poor, bare, miserable room it was, with broken windows, no fire, ragged bed-clothes, a sick mother, wailing baby, and a group of pale, hungry children cuddled under one old quilt, trying to keep warm.

How the big eyes stared and blue lips smiled as the girls went in!

'*Ach, mein Gott!* it is good angels come to us!' said the poor woman, crying for joy.

'Funny angels in hoods and mittens,' said Jo, and set them laughing.

In a few minutes it really did seem as if kind spirits had been at work there. Hannah, who had carried wood, made a fire, and stopped up the broken panes with old hats and her own cloak. Mrs March gave the mother tea and gruel, and comforted her with promises of help, while she dressed the little baby as tenderly as if it had been her own. The girls, meantime, spread the table, set the children round the fire, and fed them like so many hungry birds – laughing, talking, and trying to understand the funny broken English.

'*Das ist gut!*' '*Die Engelkinder!*' cried the poor things, as they ate, and warmed their purple hands at the comfortable blaze.

The girls had never been called angel children before, and thought it very agreeable, especially Jo, who had been considered a 'Sancho' ever since she was born. That was a very happy breakfast, though they didn't get any of it; and when they went away, leaving comfort behind, I think there were not in all the city four merrier people than the hungry little girls who gave away their breakfasts and contented themselves with bread and milk on Christmas morning.

'That's loving our neighbour better than ourselves, and I like it,' said Meg, as they set out their presents, while their mother was upstairs collecting clothes for the poor Hummels.

Not a very splendid show, but there was a great deal of love done up in the few little bundles; and the tall vase of red roses, white chrysanthemums, and trailing vines, which stood in the middle, gave quite an elegant air to the table.

'She's coming! Strike up, Beth! Open the door, Amy! Three cheers for Marmee!' cried Jo, prancing about, while Meg went to conduct Mother to the seat of honour.

Beth played her gayest march, Amy threw open the door, and Meg enacted escort with great dignity. Mrs March was both surprised and touched; and smiled with her eyes full as she examined her presents, and read the little notes which accompanied them. The slippers went on at once, a new handkerchief was slipped into her pocket, well scented with Amy's cologne, the rose was fastened in her bosom, and the nice gloves were pronounced a 'perfect fit'.

There was a good deal of laughing and kissing and explaining, in the simple, loving fashion which makes these home festivals so pleasant at the time, so sweet to remember long afterwards, and then all fell to work.

The morning charities and ceremonies took so much time that the rest of the day was devoted to preparations for the evening festivities.

Not rich enough to afford any great outlay for private performances, the girls put their wits to work, and — necessity being the mother of invention — made whatever they needed. Very clever were some of their productions — pasteboard guitars, antique lamps made of old-fashioned butter-boats covered with silver paper, gorgeous robes

of old cotton glittering with tin spangle from a pickle factory, and armour covered with the same useful diamond-shaped bits, left in the sheets when the lids of tin preserve-pots were cut out. The furniture was used to being turned topsy-turvy, and the big chamber was the scene of many innocent revels.

No gentlemen were admitted; so Jo played male parts to her heart's content, and took immense satisfaction in a pair of russet-leather boots given her by a friend. These boots, an old foil, and a slashed doublet once used by an artist for some picture, were Jo's chief treasures, and appeared on all occasions. The smallness of the company made it necessary for the two principal actors to take several parts apiece; and they certainly deserved some credit for the hard work they did in learning three or four different parts, whisking in and out of various costumes, and managing the stage besides. It was excellent drill for their memories, a harmless amusement, and employed many hours which otherwise would have been idle, lonely, or spent in less profitable society.

On Christmas night, a dozen girls piled on to the bed, which was the dress-circle, and sat before the blue and yellow chintz curtains in a most flattering state of expectancy. There was a good deal of rustling and whispering behind the curtain, a trifle of lamp-smoke, and an occasional giggle from Amy, who was apt to get hysterical in the excitement of the moment. Presently a bell sounded, the curtains flew apart, and the Operatic Tragedy began.

'A gloomy wood', according to the one play-bill, was represented by a few shrubs in pots, green baize on the floor, and a cave in the distance. This cave was made with a clothes-horse for a roof, bureaus for walls; and in it was a small furnace in full blast, with a black pot on it, and an old witch bending over it. The stage was dark, and the glow of the furnace had a fine effect, especially as real steam issued from the kettle when the witch took off the cover. A moment was allowed for the first thrill to subside; then Hugo, the villain, stalked in with a clanking sword at his side, a slouched hat, black beard, mysterious cloak, and the boots. After pacing to and fro in much agitation, he struck his forehead, and burst out in a wild strain, singing of his hatred for Roderigo, his love for Zara, and his pleasing resolution to kill the one and win the other. The gruff tones of Hugo's voice, with an occasional shout when his feelings overcame him, were very impressive, and the audience applauded the moment he paused for breath. Bowing with the air of one accustomed to public praise, he stole to the cavern, and ordered Hagar to come forth with a commanding 'What ho, minion! I need thee!'

Out came Meg, with grey horse-hair hanging about her face, a red and black robe, a staff, and cabbalistic signs upon her cloak. Hugo demanded a potion to make Zara adore him, and one to destroy Roderigo. Hagar, in a fine dramatic melody, promised both, and proceeded to call up the spirit who would bring the love philtre:

> Hither, hither, from thy home,
> Airy sprite, I bid thee come!
> Born of roses, fed on dew,
> Charms and potions canst thou brew?
>
> Bring me here, with elfin speed,
> The fragrant philtre which I need;
> Make it sweet and swift and strong,
> Spirit, answer now my song!

A soft strain of music sounded, and then at the back of the cave appeared a little figure in cloudy white, with glittering wings, golden hair, and a garland of roses on its head. Waving a wand, it sang:

> Hither I come,
>   From my airy home,
> Afar in the silver moon.
>   Take this magic spell,

And use it well,
Or its power will vanish soon!

And, dropping a small, gilded bottle at the witch's feet, the spirit vanished. Another chant from Hagar produced another apparition – not a lovely one; for, with a bang, an ugly black imp appeared, and, having croaked a reply, tossed a dark bottle at Hugo, and disappeared with a mocking laugh. Having warbled his thanks and put the potions in his boots, Hugo departed; and Hagar informed the audience that, as he had killed a few of her friends in times past, she has cursed him, and intends to thwart his plans, and be revenged on him. Then the curtain fell, and the audience reposed and ate candy while discussing the merits of the play.

A good deal of hammering went on before the curtain rose again; but when it became evident what a masterpiece of stage-carpentering had been got up, no one murmured at the delay. It was truly superb! A tower rose to the ceiling; half-way up appeared a window, with a lamp burning at it, and behind the white curtain appeared Zara in a lovely blue and silver dress, waiting for Roderigo. He came in gorgeous array, with plumed cap, red cloak, chestnut love-locks, a guitar, and the boots, of course. Kneeling at the foot of the tower, he sang a serenade in melting tones. Zara replied, and, after a musical dialogue, consented to fly. Then came the grand effect of the play. Roderigo produced a rope ladder, with five steps to it, threw up one end, and invited Zara to descend. Timidly she crept from her lattice, put her hand on Roderigo's shoulder, and was about to leap gracefully down, when, 'Alas! alas for Zara!' she forgot her train – it caught in the window, the tower tottered, leant forward, fell with a crash, and buried the unhappy lovers in the ruins!

A universal shriek arose as the russet boots waved wildly from the wreck, and a golden head emerged, exclaiming, 'I told you so! I told you so!' With wonderful presence of mind, Don Pedro, the cruel sire, rushed in, dragged out his daughter, with a hasty aside:

'Don't laugh! Act as if it was all right!' – and, ordering Roderigo up, banished him from the kingdom with wrath and scorn. Though decidedly shaken by the fall of the tower upon him, Roderigo defied the old gentleman, and refused to stir. This dauntless example fired Zara: she also defied her sire, and he ordered them both to the deepest dungeons of the castle. A stout little retainer came in with chains, and led them away, looking very much frightened, and evidently forgetting the speech he ought to have made.

Act third was the castle hall; and here Hagar appeared, having come to free the lovers and finish Hugo. She hears him coming, and hides; sees him put the potions into two cups of wine, and bid the timid little servant 'Bear them to the captives in their cells, and tell them I shall come anon.' The servant takes Hugo aside to tell him something, and Hagar changes the cups for two others which are harmless. Ferdinando, the 'minion', carries them away, and Hagar puts back the cup which holds the poison meant for Roderigo. Hugo, getting thirsty after a long warble, drinks it, loses his wits, and, after a good deal of clutching and stamping, falls flat and dies; while Hagar informs him what she has done in a song of exquisite power and melody.

This was a truly thrilling scene, though some persons might have thought that the sudden tumbling down of a quantity of long hair rather marred the effect of the villain's death. He was called before the curtain, and with great propriety appeared, leading Hagar, whose singing was considered more wonderful than all the rest of the performance put together.

Act fourth displayed the despairing Roderigo on the point of stabbing himself, because he has been told that Zara has deserted him. Just as the dagger is at his heart, a lovely song is sung under his window, informing him that Zara is true, but in danger, and he can save her, if he will. A key is thrown in, which unlocks the door, and in a spasm of rapture he tears off his chains, and rushes away to find and rescue his lady-love.

Act fifth opened with a stormy scene between Zara and Don Pedro. He wishes her to go into a convent, but she won't hear of it; and, after a touching appeal, is about to faint, when Roderigo dashes in and demands her hand. Don Pedro refuses because he is not rich. They shout and gesticulate tremendously, but cannot agree, and Roderigo is about to bear away the exhausted Zara, when the timid servant enters with a letter and a bag from Hagar, who has mysteriously disappeared. The latter informs the party that she bequeaths untold wealth to the young pair, and an awful doom to Don Pedro, if he doesn't make them happy. The bag is opened, and several quarts of tin money shower down upon its stage, till it is quite glorified with the glitter. This entirely softens the 'stern sire': he consents without a murmur, all join in a joyful chorus, and the curtain falls upon the lovers kneeling to receive Don Pedro's blessing in attitudes of the most romantic grace.

Tumultuous applause followed, but received an unexpected check; for the cot-bed, on which the 'dress-circle' was built, suddenly shut up, and extinguished the enthusiastic audience. Roderigo and Don Pedro flew to the rescue, and all were taken out unhurt, though many were speechless with laughter. The excitement had hardly subsided, when Hannah appeared, with 'Mrs March's compliments, and would the ladies walk down to supper'.

This was a surprise, even to the actors; and, when they saw the table, they looked at one another in rapturous amazement. It was like Marmee to get up a little treat for them; but anything so fine as this was unheard of since the departed days of plenty. There was ice-cream – actually two dishes of it, pink and white – and cake and fruit and distracting French bonbons, and, in the middle of the table, four great bouquets of hothouse flowers.

It quite took their breath away; and they stared first at the table and then at their mother, who looked as if she enjoyed it immensely.

'Is it fairies?' asked Amy.

'It's Santa Claus,' said Beth.

'Mother did it'; and Meg smiled her sweetest, in spite of her grey beard and white eyebrows.

'Aunt March had a good fit, and sent the supper,' cried Jo, with a sudden inspiration.

'All wrong. Old Mr Laurence sent it,' replied Mrs March.

'The Laurence boy's grandfather! What in the world put such a thing into his head? We don't know him!' exclaimed Meg.

'Hannah told one of his servants about your breakfast party. He is an odd old gentleman, but that pleased him. He knew my father, years ago; and he sent me a polite note this afternoon, saying he hoped I would allow him to express his friendly feeling towards my children by sending them a few trifles in honour of the day. I could not refuse; and so you have a little feast at night to make up for the bread-and-milk breakfast.'

'That boy put it into his head, I know he did! He's a capital fellow, and I wish we could get acquainted. He looks as if he'd like to know us; but he's bashful, and Meg is so prim she won't let me speak to him when we pass,' said Jo, as the plates went round, and the ice began to melt out of sight, with 'Ohs!' and 'Ahs!' of satisfaction.

'You mean the people who live in the big house next door, don't you?' asked one of the girls. 'My mother knows old Mr Laurence; but says he's very proud, and doesn't like to mix with his neighbours. He keeps his grandson shut up, when he isn't riding or walking with his tutor, and makes him study very hard. We invited him to our party, but he didn't come. Mother says he's very nice, though he never speaks to us girls.'

'Our cat ran away once, and he brought her back, and we talked over the fence, and were getting on capitally – all about cricket, and so on – when he saw Meg coming, and walked off. I mean to know him some day; for he needs fun, I'm sure he does,' said Jo decidedly.

'I like his manners, and he looks like a little gentleman; so I've no objection to your knowing him, if a proper opportunity comes. He brought the flowers himself; and I should have asked him in, if I had been sure what was going on upstairs. He looked so wistful as he went away, hearing the frolic, and evidently having none of his own.'

'It's a mercy you didn't, Mother!' laughed Jo, looking at her boots. 'But we'll have another play, some time, that he *can* see. Perhaps he'll help act; wouldn't that be jolly?'

'I never had such a fine bouquet before! How pretty it is!' And Meg examined her flowers with great interest.

'They *are* lovely. But Beth's roses are sweeter to me,' said Mrs March, smelling the half-dead posy in her belt.

Beth nestled up to her, and whispered softly, 'I wish I could send my bunch to Father. I'm afraid he isn't having such a merry Christmas as we are.'

A Most Singular
and Whimsical Problem

'The Adventure of the Blue Carbuncle' is the only Sherlock Holmes story with a Christmas flavour. Holmes is in fine form as he deduces just about all he needs to know of the life and character of Henry Baker merely by studying his old felt hat. Sophisticated nit-pickers may pick their nits (Covent Garden is a fruit, flower, and vegetable market which does not and did not sell fowl) but the period atmosphere is marvellously realized. How spacious to be able to place your ads in no fewer than seven London evening papers at mid-morning, and see them appear the same evening! Here is clear evidence that the turkey has not yet triumphed over the goose as the Englishman's Christmas fare. The story is also noteworthy as one of the fourteen occasions — no less — on which the great detective took the law into his own hands and freed a criminal. 'Send him to gaol now,' he tells Watson 'and you make him a gaolbird for life. Besides, it is the season of forgiveness.'

THE ADVENTURE
OF THE BLUE CARBUNCLE

ARTHUR CONAN DOYLE

I had called upon my friend Sherlock Holmes upon the second morning after Christmas, with the intention of wishing him the compliments of the season. He was lounging upon the sofa in a purple dressing-gown, a pipe-rack within his reach upon the right, and a pile of crumpled morning papers, evidently newly studied, near at hand. Beside the couch was a wooden chair, and on the angle of the back hung a very seedy and disreputable hard felt hat, much the worse for wear, and cracked in several places. A lens and a forceps lying upon the seat of the chair suggested that the hat had been suspended in this manner for the purpose of examination.

'You are engaged,' said I; 'perhaps I interrupt you.'

'Not at all. I am glad to have a friend with whom I can discuss my results. The matter is a perfectly trivial one' (he jerked his thumb in the direction of the old hat), 'but there are points in connection with it which are not entirely devoid of interest, and even of instruction.'

I seated myself in his arm-chair, and warmed my hands before his crackling fire, for a sharp frost had set in, and the windows were thick with the ice crystals. 'I suppose,' I remarked, 'that, homely as it looks, this thing has some deadly story linked on to it — that it is the clue which will guide you in the solution of some mystery, and the punishment of some crime.'

'No, no. No crime,' said Sherlock Holmes, laughing. 'Only one of those whimsical little incidents which will happen when you have four million human beings all jostling each other within the space of a few square miles. Amid the action and reaction of so dense a swarm of humanity, every possible combination of events may be expected to take place, and many a little problem will be presented which may be striking and bizarre without being criminal. We have already had experience of such.'

'So much so,' I remarked, 'that, of the last six cases which I have added to my notes, three have been entirely free of any legal crime.'

'Precisely. You allude to my attempt to recover the Irene Adler papers, to the singular case of Miss Mary Sutherland, and to the adventure of the man with the twisted lip. Well, I have no doubt that this small matter will fall into the same innocent category. You know Peterson, the commissionaire?'

'Yes.'

'It is to him that this trophy belongs.'

'It is his hat.'

'No, no; he found it. Its owner is unknown. I beg that you will look upon it, not as a battered billycock, but as an intellectual problem. And, first as to how it came here. It arrived upon Christmas morning, in company with a good fat goose, which is, I have no doubt, roasting at this moment in front of Peterson's fire. The facts are these. About four o'clock on Christmas morning, Peterson, who, as you know, is a very honest fellow, was returning from some small jollification, and was making his way homewards down Tottenham Court Road. In front of him he saw, in the gaslight, a tallish man, walking with a slight stagger, and carrying a white goose slung over his shoulder. As he reached the corner of Goodge Street a row broke out between this stranger and a little knot of roughs. One of the latter knocked off the man's hat, on which he raised his stick to defend himself, and, swinging it over his head, smashed the shop window behind him. Peterson had rushed forward to protect the stranger from his assailants, but the man, shocked at having broken the window and seeing an official-looking person in uniform rushing towards him, dropped his goose, took to his heels, and vanished amid the labyrinth of small streets which lie at the back of Tottenham Court Road. The roughs had also fled at the appearance of Peterson, so that he was left in possession of the field of battle, and also of the spoils of victory in the shape of this battered hat and a most unimpeachable Christmas goose.'

'Which surely he restored to their owner?'

'My dear fellow, there lies the problem. It is true that "For Mrs Henry Baker" was printed upon a small card which was tied to the bird's left leg, and it is also true that the initials "H.B." are legible upon the lining of this hat; but, as there are some thousands of Bakers, and some hundreds of Henry Bakers in this city of ours, it is not easy to restore lost property to any one of them.'

'What, then, did Peterson do?'

'He brought round both hat and goose to me on Christmas morning, knowing that even the smallest problems are of interest to me. The goose we retained until this morning, when there were signs that, in spite of the slight frost, it would be well that it should be eaten without unnecessary delay. Its finder has carried it off therefore to fulfil the ultimate destiny of a goose, while I continue to retain the hat of the unknown gentleman who lost his Christmas dinner.'

'Did he not advertise?'

'No.'

'Then, what clue could you have as to his identity?'

'Only as much as we can deduce.'

'From his hat?'

'Precisely.'

'But you are joking. What can you gather from this old battered felt?'

'Here is my lens. You know my methods. What can you gather yourself as to the individuality of the man who has worn this article?'

I took the tattered object in my hands, and turned it over rather ruefully. It was a very ordinary black hat of the usual round shape, hard and much the worse for wear. The lining had been of red silk, but was a good deal discoloured. There was no maker's name; but, as Holmes had remarked, the initials 'H.B.' were scrawled upon one side. It was pierced in the brim for a hat-securer, but the elastic was missing. For the rest, it was cracked, exceedingly dusty, and spotted in several places, although there seemed to have been some attempt to hide the discoloured patches by smearing them with ink.

'I can see nothing,' said I, handing it back to my friend.

'On the contrary, Watson, you can see everything. You fail, however, to reason from what you see. You are too timid in drawing your inferences.'

'Then, pray tell me what it is that you can infer from this hat?'

He picked it up, and gazed at it in the peculiar introspective fashion which was characteristic of him. 'It is perhaps less suggestive than it might have been,' he remarked, 'and yet there are a few inferences which are very distinct, and a few others which represent at least a strong balance of probability. That the man was highly intelletual is of course obvious upon the face of it, and also that he was fairly well-to-do within the last three years, although he has now fallen upon evil days. He had foresight, but has less now than formerly, pointing to a moral retrogression, which, when taken with the decline of his fortunes, seems to indicate some evil influence, probably drink, at work upon him. This may account also for the obvious fact that his wife has ceased to love him.'

'My dear Holmes!'

'He has, however, retained some degree of self-respect,' he continued, disregarding my remonstrance. 'He is a man who leads a sedentary life, goes out little, is out of training entirely, is middle-aged, has grizzled hair which he has had cut within the last few days, and which he anoints with lime-cream. These are the more patent facts which are to be deduced from his hat. Also, by the way, that it is extremely improbable that he has gas laid on in his house.'

'You are certainly joking, Holmes.'

'Not in the least. Is it possible that even now when I give you these results you are unable to see how they are attained?'

'I have no doubt that I am very stupid; but I must confess that I am unable to follow you. For example, how did you deduce that this man was intellectual?'

For answer Holmes clapped the hat upon his head. It came right over the forehead and settled upon the bridge of his nose. 'It is a question of cubic capacity,' said he: 'a man with so large a brain must have something in it.'

'The decline of his fortunes, then?'

'This hat is three years old. These flat brims curled at the edge came in then. It is a hat of the very best quality. Look at the band of ribbed silk, and the excellent lining. If this man could afford to buy so expensive a hat three years ago, and has had no hat since, then he has assuredly gone down in the world.'

'Well, that is clear enough, certainly. But how about the foresight, and the moral retrogression?'

Sherlock Holmes laughed. 'Here is the foresight,' said he, putting his finger upon the little disc and loop of the hat-securer. 'They are never sold upon hats. If this man ordered one, it is a sign of a certain amount of foresight, since he went out of his way to take this precaution against the wind. But since we see that he has broken the elastic, and has not troubled to replace it, it is obvious that he has less foresight now than formerly, which is a distinct proof of a weakening nature. On the other hand, he has endeavoured to conceal some of these stains upon the felt by daubing them with ink, which is a sign that he has not entirely lost his self-respect.'

'Your reasoning is certainly plausible.'

'The further points, that he is middle-aged, that his hair is grizzled, that it has been recently cut, and that he uses lime-cream, are all to be gathered from a close examination of the lower part of the lining. The lens discloses a large number of hair-ends, clean cut by the scissors of the barber. They all appear to be adhesive, and there is a distinct odour of lime-cream. This dust, you will observe, is not the gritty, grey dust of the street, but the fluffy brown dust of the house, showing that it has been hung up indoors most of the time; while the marks of moisture upon the inside are proof positive that the wearer perspired very freely, and could, therefore, hardly be in the best of training.'

'But his wife – you said that she had ceased to love him.'

'This hat has not been brushed for weeks. When I see you, my dear Watson, with a week's accumulation of dust upon your hat, and when your wife allows you to go out in such a state, I shall fear that you also have been unfortunate enough to lose your wife's affection.'

'But he might be a bachelor.'

'Nay, he was bringing home the goose as a peace-offering to his wife. Remember the card upon the bird's leg.'

'You have an answer to everything. But how on earth do you deduce that the gas is not laid on in the house?'

'One tallow stain, or even two, might come by chance; but, when I see no less than five, I think that there can be little doubt that the individual must be brought into frequent contact with burning tallow – walks upstairs at night probably with his hat in one hand and a guttering candle in the other. Anyhow, he never got tallow stains from a gas jet. Are you satisfied?'

'Well, it is very ingenious,' said I, laughing; 'but since, as you said just now, there has been no crime committed, and no harm done save the loss of a goose, all this seems to be rather a waste of energy.'

Sherlock Holmes had opened his mouth to reply, when the door flew open, and Peterson the commissionaire rushed into the compartment with flushed cheeks and the face of a man who is dazed with astonishment.

'The goose, Mr Holmes! The goose, sir!' he gasped.

'Eh! What of it, then? Has it returned to life, and flapped off through the kitchen window?' Holmes twisted himself round upon the sofa to get a fairer view of the man's excited face.

'See here, sir! See what my wife found in its crop!' He held out his hand, and displayed upon the centre of the palm a brilliantly scintillating blue stone, rather smaller than a bean in size, but of such purity and radiance that it twinkled like an electric point in the dark hollow of his hand.

Sherlock Holmes sat up with a whistle. 'By Jove, Peterson,' said he, 'this is treasure-trove indeed! I suppose you know what you have got?'

'A diamond, sir! A precious stone! It cuts into glass as though it were putty.'

'It's more than a precious stone. It's *the* precious stone.'

'Not the Countess of Morcar's blue carbuncle?' I ejaculated.

'Precisely so. I ought to know its size and shape, seeing that I have read the advertisement about it in *The Times* every day lately. It is absolutely unique, and its value can only be conjectured, but the reward offered of a thousand pounds is certainly not within a twentieth part of the market price.'

'A thousand pounds! Great Lord of mercy!' The commissionaire plumped down into a chair, and stared from one to the other of us.

'That is the reward, and I have reason to know that there are sentimental considerations in the background which would induce the Countess to part with half of her fortune if she could but recover the gem.'

'It was lost, if I remember aright, at the Hotel Cosmopolitan,' I remarked.

'Precisely so, on the twenty-second of December, just five days ago. John Horner, a plumber, was accused of having abstracted it from the lady's jewel-case. The evidence against him was so strong that the case has been referred to the Assizes. I have some account of the matter here, I believe.' He rummaged amid his newspapers, glancing over the dates, until at last he smoothed one out, doubled it over, and read the following paragraph:

'Hotel Cosmopolitan Jewel Robbery. John Horner, 26, plumber, was brought up upon the charge of having upon the 22nd inst., abstracted from the jewel-case of the Countess of Morcar the valuable gem known as the blue carbuncle. James Ryder, upper-attendant at the hotel, gave his evidence to the effect that he had shown Horner up to the dressing-room of the Countess of Morcar upon the day of the robbery, in order that he might solder the second bar of the grate, which was loose. He had remained with Horner some little time but had finally been called away. On returning he found that Horner had disappeared, that the bureau had been forced open, and that the small morocco casket in which, as it afterwards transpired, the Countess was accustomed to keep her jewel, was lying empty upon the dressing-table. Ryder instantly gave the alarm, and Horner was arrested the same evening; but the stone could not be found either upon his person or in his rooms. Catherine Cusak, maid to the Countess, deposed to having heard Ryder's cry of dismay on discovering the robbery, and to having rushed into the room, where she found matters were as described by the last witness. Inspector Bradstreet, B Division, gave evidence as to the arrest of Horner, who struggled frantically, and protested his innocence in the strongest terms. Evidence of a previous conviction for robbery having been given against the prisoner, the magistrate refused to deal summarily with the offence, but referred it to the Assizes. Horner, who had shown signs of intense emotion during the proceedings, fainted away at the conclusion, and was carried out of court.'

'Hum! So much for the police-court,' said Holmes thoughtfully, tossing aside his paper. 'The question for us now to solve is the sequence of events leading from a rifled jewel-case at one end to the crop of a goose in Tottenham Court Road at the other. You see, Watson, our little deductions have suddenly assumed a much more important and less innocent aspect. Here is the stone; the stone came from the goose, and the goose came from Mr Henry Baker, the gentleman with the bad hat and all the other characteristics with which I have bored you. So now we must set ourselves very seriously to finding this gentleman, and ascertaining what part he has played in this little mystery. To do this, we must try the simplest means first, and these lie undoubtedly in an advertisement in all the evening papers. If this fail, I shall have recourse to other methods.'

'What will you say?'

'Give me a pencil, and that slip of paper. Now, then: "Found at the corner of Goodge Street, a goose and a black felt hat. Mr Henry Baker can have the same by applying at 6.30 this evening at 221B Baker Street." That is clear and concise.'

'Very. But will he see it?'

'Well, he is sure to keep an eye on the papers, since, to a poor man, the loss was a heavy one. He was clearly so scared by his mischance in breaking the window, and by the approach of Peterson, that he thought of nothing but flight; but since then he must have bitterly regretted the impulse which caused him to drop his bird. Then, again, the introduction of his name will cause him to see it, for every one who knows him will direct his attention to it. Here you are, Peterson, run down to the advertising agency, and have this put in the evening papers.'

'In which, sir?'

'Oh, in the *Globe, Star, Pall Mall, St James's Gazette, Evening News, Standard, Echo,* and any others that occur to you.'

'Very well, sir. And this stone?'

'Ah, yes, I shall keep the stone. Thank you. And, I say, Peterson, just buy a goose on your way back, and leave it here with me, for we must have one to give to this gentleman in place of the one which your family is now devouring.'

When the commissionaire had gone, Holmes took up the stone and held it against the light. 'It's a bonny thing,' said he. 'Just see how it glints and sparkles. Of course it is a nucleus and focus of crime. Every good stone is. They are the devil's pet baits. In the larger and older jewels every facet may stand for a bloody deed. This stone is not yet twenty years old. It was found in the banks of the Amoy River in Southern China, and is remarkable in having every characteristic of the carbuncle, save that it is blue in shade, instead of ruby red. In spite of its youth, it has already a sinister history. There have been two murders, a vitriol-throwing, a suicide, and several robberies brought about for the sake of this forty-grain weight of crystallized charcoal. Who would think that so pretty a toy would be a purveyor to the gallows and the prison? I'll lock it up in my strong-box now, and drop a line to the Countess to say that we have it.'

'Do you think this man Horner is innocent?'

'I cannot tell.'

'Well, then, do you imagine that this other one, Henry Baker, had anything to do with the matter?'

'It is, I think, much more likely that Henry Baker is an absolutely innocent man, who had no idea that the bird which he was carrying was of considerably more value than if it were made of solid gold. That, however, I shall determine by a very simple test, if we have an answer to our advertisement.'

'And you can do nothing until then?'

'Nothing.'

'In that case I shall continue my professional round. But I shall come back in the evening at the hour you have mentioned, for I should like to see the solution of so tangled a business.'

'Very glad to see you. I dine at seven. There is a woodcock, I believe. By the way, in view of recent occurrences, perhaps I ought to ask Mrs Hudson to examine its crop.'

I had been delayed at a case, and it was a little after half-past when I found myself in Baker Street once more. As I approached the house I saw a tall man in a Scotch bonnet, with a coat which was buttoned up to his chin, waiting outside in the bright semicircle which was thrown from the fanlight. Just as I arrived, the door was opened, and we were shown up together to Holmes's room.

'Mr Henry Baker, I believe,' said he, rising from his arm-chair, and greeting his visitor with the easy air of geniality which he could so readily assume. 'Pray take this chair by the fire, Mr Baker. It is a cold night, and I observe that your circulation is more adapted for summer than for winter. Ah, Watson, you have just come at the right time. Is that your hat, Mr Baker?'

'Yes, sir, that is undoubtedly my hat.'

He was a large man, with rounded shoulders, a massive head, and a broad, intelligent face, sloping down to a pointed beard of grizzled brown. A touch of red in nose and cheeks, with a slight tremor of his extended hand, recalled Holmes's surmise as to his habits. His rusty black frock-coat was buttoned right up in front, with the collar turned up, and his lank wrists protruded from his sleeves without a sign of cuff or shirt. He spoke in a low staccato fashion, choosing his words with care, and gave the impression generally of a man of learning and letters who had had ill-usage at the hands of fortune.

'We have retained these things for some days,' said Holmes, 'because we expected to see an advertisement from you giving your address. I am at a loss to know now why you did not advertise.'

Our visitor gave a rather shamefaced laugh. 'Shillings have not been so plentiful with me as they once were,' he remarked. 'I had no doubt that the gang of roughs who assaulted me had carried off both my hat and the bird. I did not care to spend more money in a hopeless attempt at recovering them.'

'Very naturally. By the way, about the bird – we were compelled to eat it.'

'To eat it!' Our visitor half rose from his chair in his excitement.

'Yes; it would have been no use to anyone had we not done so. But I presume that this other goose upon the sideboard, which is about the same weight and perfectly fresh, will answer your purpose equally well?'

'Oh, certainly, certainly!' answered Mr Baker, with a sigh of relief.

'Of course, we still have the feathers, legs, crop, and so on of your own bird, if you so wish . . .'

The man burst into a hearty laugh. 'They might be useful to me as relics of my adventure,' said he, 'but beyond that I can hardly see what use the *disjecta membra* of my late acquaintance are going to be to me. No, sir, I think that, with your permission, I will confine my attentions to the excellent bird which I perceive upon the sideboard.'

Sherlock Holmes glanced across at me with a slight shrug of his shoulders.

'There is your hat, then, and there your bird,' said he. 'By the way, would it bore you to tell me where you got the other one from? I am somewhat of a fowl fancier, and I have seldom seen a better-grown goose.'

'Certainly, sir,' said Baker, who had risen and tucked his newly gained property under his arm. 'There are a few of us who frequent the Alpha Inn near the Museum – we are to be found in the Museum itself during the day, you understand. This year our good host, Windigate by name, instituted a goose-club, by which, on consideration of some few pence every week, we were to receive a bird at Christmas. My pence were duly paid, and the rest is familiar to you. I am much indebted to you, sir, for a Scotch bonnet is fitted neither to my years nor my gravity.' With a comical pomposity of manner he bowed solemnly to both of us, and strode off upon his way.

'So much for Mr Henry Baker,' said Holmes, when he had closed the door behind him. 'It is quite certain that he knows nothing whatever about the matter. Are you hungry, Watson?'

'Not particularly.'

'Then I suggest that we turn our dinner into a supper, and follow up this clue while it is still hot.'

'By all means.'

It was a bitter night, so we drew on our ulsters and wrapped cravats about our throats. Outside, the stars were shining coldly in a cloudless sky, and the breath of the passers-by blew out into smoke like so many pistol shots. Our footfalls rang out crisply and loudly as we swung through the doctors' quarter, Wimpole Street, Harley Street, and so through Wigmore Street into Oxford Street. In a quarter of an hour we were in Bloomsbury at the Alpha Inn, which is a small public-house at the corner of one of the streets which run down into Holborn. Holmes pushed open the door of the private bar, and ordered two glasses of beer from the ruddy-faced, white-aproned landlord.

'Your beer should be excellent if it is as good as your geese,' he said.

'My geese!' The man seemed surprised.

'Yes. I was speaking only half an hour ago to Mr Henry Baker, who was a member of your goose-club.'

'Ah! yes, I see. But you see, sir, them's not *our* geese.'

'Indeed! Whose, then?'

'Well, I get the two dozen from a salesman in Covent Garden.'

'Indeed! I know some of them. Which was it?'

'Breckinridge is his name.'

'Ah! I don't know him. Well, here's your good health, landlord, and prosperity to your house. Good night.'

'Now for Mr Breckinridge', he continued, buttoning up his coat, as we came out into the frosty air. 'Remember, Watson, that though we have so homely a thing as a goose at one end of this chain, we have at the other a man who will certainly get seven years' penal servitude, unless we can establish his innocence. It is possible that our inquiry may but confirm his guilt; but, in any case, we have a line of investigation which has been missed by the police, and which a singular chance has placed in our hands. Let us follow it out to the bitter end. Faces to the south, then, and quick march!'

We passed across Holborn, down Endell Street, and so through a zigzag of slums to Covent Garden Market. One of the largest stalls bore the name of Breckinridge upon it, and the proprietor, a horsy-looking man, with a sharp face and trim side-whiskers, was helping a boy to put up the shutters.

'Good evening. It's a cold night,' said Holmes.

The salesman nodded, and shot a questioning glance at my companion.

'Sold out of geese, I see,' continued Holmes, pointing at the bare slabs of marble.

'Let you have five hundred tomorrow morning.'

'That's no good.'

'Well, there are some on the stall with the gas fire.'

'Ah, but I was recommended to you.'

'Who by?'

'The landlord of the "Alpha".'

'Ah, yes; I sent him a couple of dozen.'

'Fine birds they were, too. Now where did you get them from?'

To my surprise the question provoked a burst of anger from the salesman.

'Now then, mister,' said he, with his head cocked and his arms akimbo, 'what are you driving at? Let's have it straight, now.'

'It is straight enough. I should like to know who sold you the geese which you supplied to the "Alpha".'

'Well, then, I shan't tell you. So now!'

'Oh, it is a matter of no importance; but I don't know why you should be so warm over such a trifle.'

'Warm! You'd be as warm, maybe, if you were as pestered as I am. When I pay good money for a good article there should be an end to the business; but it's "Where are the geese?" and "Who did you sell the geese to?" and "What will you take for the geese?" One would think they were the only geese in the world, to hear the fuss that is made over them.'

'Well, I have no connection with any other people who have been making inquiries,' said Holmes carelessly. 'If you won't tell us the bet is off, that is all. But I'm always ready to back my opinion on a matter of fowls, and I have a fiver on it that the bird I ate is country bred.'

'Well, then, you've lost your fiver, for it's town bred,' snapped the salesman.

'It's nothing of the kind.'

'I say it is.'

'I don't believe you.'

'D'you think you know more about fowls than I, who have handled them ever since I was a nipper? I tell you, all those birds that went to the "Alpha" were town bred.'

'You'll never persuade me to believe that.'

'Will you bet, then?'

'It's merely taking your money, for I know that I am right. But I'll have a sovereign on with you, just to teach you not to be obstinate.'

The salesman chuckled grimly. 'Bring me the books, Bill,' said he.

The small boy brought round a small thin volume and a great greasy-backed one, laying them out together beneath the hanging lamp.

'Now then, Mr Cocksure,' said the salesman, 'I thought that I was out of geese, but before I finish you'll find that there is still one left in my shop. You see this little book?'

'Well?'

'That's the list of the folk from whom I buy. D'you see? Well, then, here on this page are the country folk, and the numbers after their names are where their accounts are in the big ledger. Now, then! You see this other page in red ink? Well, that is a list of my town suppliers. Now, look at that third name. Just read it out to me.'

'Mrs Oakshott, 117 Brixton Road — 249,' read Holmes.

'Quite so. Now turn that up in the ledger.'

Holmes turned to the page indicated. 'Here you are, "Mrs Oakshott, 117 Brixton Road, egg and poultry supplier." '

'Now, then, what's the last entry?'

' "December 22. Twenty-four geese at 7s. 6d." '

'Quite so. There you are. And underneath?'

' "Sold to Mr Windigate of the 'Alpha' at 12s." '

'What have you to say now?'

Sherlock Holmes looked deeply chagrined. He drew a sovereign from his pocket and threw it down upon the slab, turning away with the air of a man whose disgust is too deep for words. A few yards off he stopped under a lamp-post, and laughed in the hearty, noiseless fashion which was peculiar to him.

'When you see a man with whiskers of that cut and the "Pink 'Un" protruding out of his pocket, you can always draw him by a bet,' said he. 'I dare say that if I had put a hundred pounds down in front of him that man would not have given me such complete information as was drawn from him by the idea that he was doing me on a wager. Well, Watson, we are, I fancy, nearing the end of our quest, and the only point which remains to be determined is whether we should go on to this Mrs Oakshott tonight, or whether we should reserve it for tomorrow. It is clear from what that surly fellow said that there are others besides ourselves who are anxious about the matter, and I should...'

His remarks were suddenly cut short by a loud hubbub which broke out from the stall which we had just left. Turning round we saw a little rat-faced fellow standing in the centre of the circle of yellow light which was thrown by the swinging lamp, while Breckinridge the salesman, framed in the door of his stall, was shaking his fists fiercely at the cringing figure.

'I've had enough of you and your geese,' he shouted. 'I wish you were all at the devil together. If you come pestering me any more with your silly talk I'll set the dog at you. You bring Mrs Oakshott here and I'll answer her, but what have you to do with it? Did I buy the geese off you?'

'No; but one of them was mine all the same,' whined the little man.

'Well, then, ask Mrs Oakshott for it.'

'She told me to ask you.'

'Well, you can ask the King of Proosia, for all I care. I've had enough of it. Get out of this!' He rushed fiercely forward, and the inquirer flitted away into the darkness.

'Ha, this may save us a visit to Brixton Road,' whispered Holmes. 'Come with me, and we will see what is to be made of this fellow.' Striding through the scattered knots of people who lounged round the flaring stalls, my companion speedily overtook the little man and touched him upon the shoulder. He sprang round, and I could see in the gaslight that every vestige of colour had been driven from his face.

'Who are you, then? What do you want?' he asked in a quavering voice.

'You will excuse me,' said Holmes blandly, 'but I could not help overhearing the questions which you put to the salesman just now. I think that I could be of assistance to you.'

'You? Who are you? How could you know anything of the matter?'

'My name is Sherlock Holmes. It is my business to know what other people don't know.'

'But you can know nothing of this?'

'Excuse me, I know everything of it. You are endeavouring to trace some geese which were sold by Mrs Oakshott, of Brixton Road, to a salesman named Breckinridge, by him in turn to Mr Windigate, of the "Alpha," and by him to his club, of which Mr Henry Baker is a member.'

'Oh, sir, you are the very man whom I have longed to meet,' cried the little fellow, with outstretched hands and quivering fingers. 'I can hardly explain to you how interested I am in this matter.'

Sherlock Holmes hailed a four-wheeler which was passing. 'In that case we had better discuss it in a cosy room rather than in this wind-swept market-place,' said he. 'But pray tell me, before we go further, who it is that I have the pleasure of assisting.'

The man hesitated for an instant. 'My name is John Robinson,' he answered, with a sidelong glance.

'No, no; the real name,' said Holmes sweetly. 'It is always awkward doing business with an *alias*.'

A flush sprang to the white cheeks of the stranger. 'Well, then,' said he, 'my real name is James Ryder.'

'Precisely so. Head attendant at the Hotel Cosmopolitan. Pray step into the cab, and I shall soon be able to tell you everything which you would wish to know.'

The little man stood glancing from one to the other of us with half-frightened, half-hopeful eyes, as one who is not sure whether he is on the verge of a windfall or of a catastrophe. Then he stepped into the cab, and in half an hour we were back in the sitting-room at Baker Street. Nothing had been said during our drive, but the high, thin breathings of our new companion, and the claspings and unclaspings of his hands, spoke of the nervous tension within him.

'Here we are!' said Holmes cheerily, as we filed into the room. 'The fire looks very seasonable in this weather. You look cold, Mr Ryder. Pray take the basket chair. I will just put on my slippers before we settle this little matter of yours. Now, then! You want to know what became of those geese?'

'Yes, sir.'

'Or rather, I fancy, of that goose. It was one bird, I imagine, in which you were interested – white, with a black bar across the tail.'

Ryder quivered with emotion. 'Oh, sir,' he cried, 'can you tell me where it went to?'

'It came here.'

'Here?'

'Yes, and a most remarkable bird it proved. I don't wonder that you should take an interest in it. It laid an egg after it was dead – the bonniest, brightest little blue egg that ever was seen. I have it here in my museum.'

Our visitor staggered to his feet, and clutched the mantelpiece with his right hand. Holmes unlocked his strong-box, and held up the blue carbuncle, which shone out like a star, with a cold, brilliant, many-pointed radiance. Ryder stood glaring with a drawn face, uncertain whether to claim or to disown it.

'The game's up, Ryder,' said Holmes quietly. 'Hold up, man, or you'll be into the fire. Give him an arm back into his chair, Watson. He's not got blood enough to go in for felony with impunity. Give him a dash of brandy. So! Now he looks a little more human. What a shrimp it is, to be sure!'

For a moment he had staggered and nearly fallen, but the brandy brought a tinge of colour into his cheeks, and he sat staring with frightened eyes at his accuser.

'I have almost every link in my hands, and all the proofs which I could possibly need, so there is little which you need tell me. Still, that little may as well be cleared up to make the case complete. You had heard, Ryder, of this blue stone of the Countess of Morcar's?'

'It was Catherine Cusack who told me of it,' said he, in a crackling voice.

'I see. Her ladyship's waiting-maid. Well, the temptation of sudden wealth so easily acquired was too much for you, as it has been for better men before you; but you were not very scrupulous in the means you used. It seems to me, Ryder, that there is the making of a very pretty villain in you. You knew that this man Horner, the plumber, had been concerned in some such matter before, and that suspicion would rest the more readily upon him. What did you do, then? You made some small job in my lady's room – you and your confederate Cusack – and you managed that he should be the man sent for. Then, when he had left, you rifled the jewel-case, raised the alarm, and had this unfortunate man arrested. You then . . .'

Ryder threw himself down suddenly upon the rug, and clutched at my companion's knees. 'For God's sake, have mercy!' he shrieked. 'Think of my father! Of my mother! It would break their hearts. I never went wrong before! I never will again. I swear it. I'll swear it on a Bible. Oh, don't bring it into court! For Christ's sake, don't!'

'Get back into your chair!' said Holmes sternly. 'It is very well to cringe and crawl now, but you thought little enough of this poor Horner in the dock for a crime of which he knew nothing.'

'I will fly, Mr Holmes. I will leave the country, sir. Then the charge against him will break down.'

'Hum! We will talk about that. And now let us hear a true account of the next act. How came the stone into the goose, and how came the goose into the open market? Tell us the truth, for there lies your only hope of safety.'

Ryder passed his tongue over his parched lips. 'I will tell you it just as it happened, sir,' said he. 'When Horner had been arrested, it seemed to me that it would be best for me to get away with the stone at once, for I did not know at what moment the police might not take it into their heads to search me and my room. There was no place about the hotel where it would be safe. I went out, as if on some commission, and I made for my sister's house. She had married a man named Oakshott, and lived in Brixton Road, where she fattened fowls for the market. All the way there every man I met seemed to me to be a policeman or a detective, and for all that it was a cold night, the sweat was pouring down my face before I came to the Brixton Road. My sister asked me what was the matter, and why I was so pale; but I told her that I had been upset by the jewel robbery at the hotel. Then I went into the back-yard, and smoked a pipe, and wondered what it would be best to do.

'I had a friend once called Maudsley, who went to the bad, and has just been serving his time in Pentonville. One day he had met me, and fell into talk about the ways of thieves and how they could get rid of what they stole. I knew that he would be true to me, for I knew one or two things about him, so I made up my mind to go right on to Kilburn, where he lived, and take him into my confidence. He would show me how to turn the stone into money. But how to get to him in safety? I thought of the agonies I had gone through in coming from the hotel. I might at any moment be seized and searched, and there would be the stone in my waistcoat pocket. I was leaning against the wall at the time, and looking at the geese which were waddling about round my feet, and suddenly an idea came into my head which showed me how I could beat the best detective that ever lived.

'My sister had told me some weeks before that I might have the pick of her geese for a Christmas present, and I knew that she was always as good as her word. I would take my goose now, and in it I would carry my stone to Kilburn. There was a little shed in the yard, and behind this I drove one of the birds, a fine big one, white, with a barred tail. I caught it and, prising its bill open, I thrust the stone down its throat as far as my finger could reach. The bird gave a gulp, and I felt the stone pass along its gullet and down into its crop. But the creature flapped and struggled, and out came my sister to know what was the matter. As I turned to speak to her the brute broke loose, and fluttered off among the others.

'"Whatever were you doing with that bird, Jem?" says she.

'"Well," said I, "you said you'd give me one for Christmas, and I was feeling which was the fattest."

'"Oh," says she, "we've set yours aside for you. Jem's bird, we call it. It's the big, white one over yonder. There's twenty-six of them, which makes one for you, and one for us, and two dozen for the market."

'"Thank you, Maggie," says I; "but if it is all the same to you I'd rather have that one I was handling just now."

'"The other is a good three pound heavier," she said, "and we fattened it expressly for you."

'"Never mind. I'll have the other, and I'll take it now," said I.

'"Oh, just as you like," said she, a little huffed. "Which is it you want, then?"

'"That white one, with the barred tail, right in the middle of the flock."

'"Oh, very well. Kill it and take it with you."

'Well, I did what she said, Mr Holmes, and I carried the bird all the way to Kilburn. I told my pal what I had done, for he was a man that it was easy to tell a thing like that to. He laughed until he choked, and we got a knife and opened the goose. My heart turned to water, for there was no sign of the stone, and I knew that some terrible mistake had occurred. I left the bird, rushed back to my sister's, and hurried into the back-yard. There was not a bird to be seen there.

'"Where are they all, Maggie?" I cried.

'"Gone to the dealer's."

'"Which dealer's?"

'"Breckinridge, of Covent Garden."

'"But was there another with a barred tail?" I asked, "the same as the one I chose?"

'"Yes, Jem, there were two barred-tailed ones, and I could never tell them apart."

'Well, then, of course, I saw it all, and I ran off as hard as my feet would carry me to this man Breckinridge; but he had sold the lot at once, and not one word would he tell me as to where they had gone. You heard him yourselves tonight. Well, he has always answered me like that. My sister thinks that I am going mad. Sometimes I think that I am myself. And now – and now I am myself a branded thief, without ever having touched the wealth for which I sold my character. God help me! God help me!' He burst into convulsive sobbing, with his face buried in his hands.

There was a long silence, broken only by his heavy breathing, and by the measured tapping of Sherlock Holmes's finger-tips upon the edge of the table. Then my friend rose, and threw open the door.

'Get out!' said he.

'What, sir! Oh, Heaven bless you!'

'No more words. Get out!'

And no more words were needed. There was a rush, a clatter upon the stairs, the bang of a door, and the crisp rattle of running footfalls from the street.

'After all, Watson,' said Holmes, reaching up his hand for his clay pipe, 'I am not retained by the police to supply their deficiencies. If Horner were in danger it would be another thing, but this fellow will not appear against him, and the case must collapse. I suppose that I am commuting a felony, but it is just possible that I am saving a soul. This fellow will not go wrong again. He is too terribly frightened. Send him to gaol now, and you make him a gaolbird for life. Besides, it is the season of forgiveness. Chance has put in our way a most singular and whimsical problem, and its solution is its own reward. If you will have the goodness to touch the bell, Doctor, we will begin another investigation, in which also a bird will be the chief feature.'

IT'S ALL
THY MERCY AND LOVE,
LORD

Two Celtic Christmases: a gorgeously realized scene from James Joyce's 'The Dead', later published in his collection of short stories Dubliners. *The starving and unknown young Irish writer was glad then to sell them for a pound each; but the readers of the* Irish Homestead *were getting a bargain. Then, Christmas in a remote corner of Wales: a blind old woman, her misshapen son, a simple hare for the Christmas dinner; unpromising material on the face of it, but in* Winter in the Hills, *John Wain puts them together with an enviable delicacy and assurance. Even in this modest setting, the blue flame flickers round the pudding and the light changes from a cheese-cloth white to a warm pink and finally to a glowing crimson; a visual feast made the more poignant and transfixing by Mam's blindness.*

THE DEAD

JAMES JOYCE

A fat brown goose lay at one end of the table and at the other end, on a bed of creased paper strewn with sprigs of parsley, lay a great ham, stripped of its outer skin and peppered over with crust crumbs, a neat paper frill round its shin and beside this was a round of spiced beef. Between these rival ends ran parallel lines of side-dishes: two little minsters of jelly, red and yellow; a shallow dish full of blocks of blancmange and red jam, a large green leaf-shaped dish with a stalk-shaped handle, on which lay bunches of purple raisins and peeled almonds, a companion dish on which lay a solid rectangle of Smyrna figs, a dish of custard topped with grated nutmeg, a small bowl full of chocolates and sweets wrapped in gold and silver papers and a glass vase in which stood some tall celery stalks. In the centre of the table there stood, as sentries to a fruit-stand which upheld a pyramid of oranges and American apples, two squat old-fashioned decanters of cut glass, one containing port and the other dark sherry. On the closed square piano a pudding in a huge yellow dish lay in waiting and behind it were three squads of bottles of stout and ale and minerals, drawn up according to the colours of their uniforms, the first two black, with brown and red labels, the third and smallest squad white, with transverse green sashes.

Gabriel took his seat boldly at the head of the table and, having looked to the edge of the carver, plunged his fork firmly into the goose. He felt quite at ease now for he was an expert carver and liked nothing better than to find himself at the head of a well-laden table.

'Miss Furlong, what shall I send you?' he asked. 'A wing or a slice of the breast?'

'Just a small slice of the breast.'

'Miss Higgins, what for you?'

'O, anything at all, Mr Conroy.'

While Gabriel and Miss Daly exchanged plates of goose and plates of ham and spiced beef Lily went from guest to guest with a dish of hot floury potatoes wrapped in a white napkin. This was Mary Jane's idea and she had also suggested apple sauce for the goose but Aunt Kate had said that plain roast goose without apple sauce had always been good enough for her and she hoped she might never eat worse. Mary Jane waited on her pupils and saw that they got the best slices and Aunt Kate and Aunt Julia opened and carried across from the piano bottles of stout and ale for the gentlemen and bottles of minerals for the ladies. There was a great deal of confusion and laughter and noise, the noise of orders and counter-orders, of knives and forks, of corks and glass-stoppers. Gabriel began to carve second helpings as soon as he had finished the first round without serving himself. Every one protested loudly so that he compromised by taking a long draught of stout for he had found the carving hot work. Mary Jane settled down quietly to her supper but Aunt Kate and Aunt Julia were still toddling round the table, walking on each other's heels, getting in each other's way and giving each other unheeded orders. Mr Browne begged of them to sit down and eat their suppers and so did Gabriel but they said there was time enough so that, at last Freddy Malins stood up and, capturing Aunt Kate, plumped her down on her chair amid general laughter.

When everyone had been well served Gabriel said, smiling:

'Now, if anyone wants a little more of what vulgar people call stuffing let him or her speak.'

A chorus of voices invited him to begin his own supper and Lily came forward with three potatoes which she had reserved for him.

'Very well,' said Gabriel amiably, as he took another preparatory draught, 'kindly forget my existence, ladies and gentlemen, for a few minutes.'

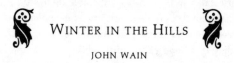

WINTER IN THE HILLS

JOHN WAIN

Christmas Day dawned amid white, freezing mist. As Roger walked along the lane towards Gareth's, the bottles dragged at his pockets. The sun was a low red disc and the mist went all the way up to the sky. Even the tops of the mountains were not wholly clear.

He opened the gate, went across the field, and knocked on the cottage door. It was eleven o'clock; he had timed his arrival with some care, so as to be early enough to help with the preparations but not so early as to intrude on a scene of comfortable late rising. Evidently it was right: Gareth, in his shirt sleeves but shaved and combed, opened the door at once.

'Merry Christmas,' he said gravely.

'That's come true already,' said Roger.

He entered. The old woman was sitting in her accustomed place. She wore the usual brown cardigan, but over it, across her broad fleshless shoulders, she had arranged a fine fringed shawl, decorated with intricate needlework. Perhaps the needle that made those thousands of patient stitches had been her own, half a century earlier; perhaps her eyes, in their days of keenness, had put in all those hours of close and loving observation.

'Nadolig Llawan,' she said.

Roger felt exhilarated. His sense of occasion was roused by her Welsh greeting and her embroidered shawl. Yes, this was to be a special day.

From now on, the three of them spoke in Welsh.

'Sit down,' Gareth commanded, drawing up a chair for Roger. The fire was hot and clear; it must have been lit at least two hours earlier.

'But I want to help,' Roger protested.

'You can do that by keeping Mam company. Nobody's allowed in the kitchen. I'm cooking the feast and what I've got is a secret till I bring it in.'

Roger, willingly allowing Gareth to be captain of his own ship, hung up his overcoat ready to sit down. But first (why not?) he took out the bottle of wine, an excellent hock that he had chosen very deliberately from the stock of the best wine merchant in the district.

'Here's something to wash it down with. It needs to be cold so I'll stand it outside.'

Gareth took the bottle for a moment in his great hand.

'Wine, eh?' he said.

'I thought I'd like to bring something,' said Roger simply.

'I'm a beer man myself. But it does no harm to break out of your habits now and then. I've got a bottle or two of beer in, and to tell you the truth I've opened a couple already, in the kitchen, while I've been doing the vegetables. If I mix my drinks too much, you'll have to put me to bed.'

Laughter forced its way up from the echo-chamber of his chest.

'All cooks drink,' said Roger. 'The heat of the kitchen lets them sweat it out.'

He opened the door and put the bottle outside in the misty morning. A solitary crow alighted, eyed the bottle, and flew disappointedly away.

Closing the door, Roger went and sat beside Mam. Gareth had already disappeared into the kitchen and shut the door firmly.

'Mr Furnivall,' said the old woman.

'I'm here.'

'There's something I want you to do.'

For an instant, Roger felt an anticipatory twinge just above the knee, where her powerful old fingers had gripped him the time before, when she so urgently needed to ask him for news of Gareth's troubles. But there was no urgency this time: on the contrary, her serenity was palpable, authoritative.

'There's a little drawer in the table.'

He looked round and located it. 'Yes,' he said.

'Please open it and tell me what you find.'

He slid the drawer open and took out two thick, round, crinkly shapes. Crepe bandages? No, paper streamers, egad.

'Gareth didn't get anything to decorate the place with,' said the old woman, smiling into the fire. 'I suppose he thinks it doesn't matter because I can't see them and he doesn't mind about such things. But the last time I went down to the shop with Maldwyn, the day before Christmas Eve it was, they said they had two of these big paper streamers left over and nobody would be buying them now and would I take them as a present. I said yes straight away. I thought it was very kind of them, because after all they could have put them back into stock for next year.'

Roger turned the unwieldy packets over in his hands.

'Shall I put them up?' he asked.

'Yes,' she said eagerly. 'Do it while Gareth's in the kitchen. There's a little hammer and some tacks on the sideboard behind me.'

Roger took the hammer and tacks, broke open the first packet, and, seizing a chair to stand on, began working fast and efficiently. In a moment he had the first streamer running right round the four walls. Then he took out the second one and looped it across from the centre to the corners.

'How does it look?' Mam asked.

'Pretty good, to me,' he answered, putting the chair back against the wall. 'I dare say a woman would do it better.'

'What colour are they?'

'One's red and silver, the other's yellow and green.'

She sighed with pleasure and folded her hands.

'I heard you,' Gareth shouted from the kitchen. 'I heard you hammering. What's the game?'

'Just cracking nuts,' Roger called. 'Go back to your work.'

Gareth's chuckle flowed round them as they sat conspiratorially by the fire.

For a few minutes, neither of them spoke, and it crossed Roger's mind to wonder whether Mam would renew her questioning about the state of Gareth's affairs. But, as he glanced across at her calm face, he realized that this was a mistake. Nothing would make her pollute this day with the anxieties of the world.

To draw her on to a topic that she would enjoy, he asked her a question about her late husband and their life together in this house. Her answers were freely informative. Gareth had already told Roger, as they walked towards the cottage on that first visit, that his father had been dead fifteen years. Now Mam added the all-important fact that it was only since his death that her sight had failed her. Their life together had been happy, he could tell that: small frugalities, the saving of candle-ends, a meal of butcher's meat only on Sundays and festivals; but tragedy and disappointment they had been spared – unless, Roger thought, you counted the grief it must have been to them that their only child had proved misshapen. Or was that deeply felt as a grief? Wouldn't he have been, to his mother at any rate, simply her child, simply Gareth? And the father, however it may have hurt him to see the lopsided whelp in its cradle, would have been reassured as the years went by and Gareth grew into a prodigy of strength, a knotted and twisted oak that nothing could push down.

'Have you a photograph of your husband?' he asked Mam.

'Up in my room,' she answered.

It pleased him to think that she kept her Geraint's picture near her bed, where she could reach out and touch it on waking. For that, surely, was the motive. And he forbore to question further. Whether Geraint had been a man big enough to match her size, or the strong gnome he had originally imagined to be the only father for Gareth, would remain mysterious. It was right that some things should be left in the shadows.

A warning whoop from Gareth told Roger to get the table laid. Under Mam's direction he found the thick white cloth, the cutlery, the carving-fork and knife. There were no wine-glasses, but on the dresser he found what seemed to be a medicine glass, which he put beside Mam's place, and ordinary half-pint tumblers for himself and Gareth.

'Appetites ready?' Gareth called from the kitchen. 'We'll be eating in two minutes.'

Roger hurried to the front door. The wine was chilled to exactly the right temperature by the nipping air. A hasty question to Mam, and he was directed to a corkscrew. Working fast, he had just got the cork out and poured the first glass when Gareth flung open the door from the kitchen.

'Clear the way!' he shouted. 'Clear the way for the head cook of the royal household!'

He marched in, holding a large meat-dish proudly high. On it lay a brown richly smoking shape. A delicious smell of delicate roast meat and herbs came with him on his progress to the table.

'A hare!' cried the old woman. 'I can smell it, Gareth! I know I'm right!'

Gareth set down the dish with tender pride.

'Not just an ordinary hare,' he said. 'A hare of the mountain. I snared it myself. I've been very busy these last few days. I snared three, as a matter of fact, but the first two weren't good enough for a feast like this. The first was just a leveret, and the second was an old female, very bony. But this one, ah!'

Roger gazed with reverence at the dish.

'I'll just get the vegetables,' said Gareth, 'while you help Mam to the table and get her settled with everything she needs.'

He disappeared, and came back with a huge pan of roast potatoes, a dish of brussels sprouts, and three plates heated to such a temperature that even his work-inured hands could not hold them without a cloth.

Roger, having installed Mam in her chair on the side nearest the fire, was just about to take his own seat when he noticed that the old woman was sitting very still and upright, with one hand raised for silence.

'Gareth?'

'Yes, Mam?'

'Are you ready for me to say grace?'

Gareth laid down the carving-knife and stood, immobile, beside his chair.

'Say it, Mam.'

'O Lord,' the old woman said, 'here we are just about to eat another good Christmas dinner through Thy mercy and love. I've seen seventy-two Christmases and I've never failed to have something good to eat on them, since I grew my first set of teeth, and it's all Thy mercy and love, Lord.'

Roger salivated as the smell of the roast hare came to his nostrils, but the stillness was profound, and hungry as he was he did not want it to be broken yet.

'This is a special Christmas, Lord, as Thou knowest,' said Mam. 'Our lives have got much more difficult this year and they may get more difficult still, but Thou hast sent into our lives a new friend, who has come from we don't know where, and decided to give us his help we don't know why, but it gives us joy, O Lord, that he is here with us to share our feast this day.'

'Amen,' said Gareth.

'And to remember with us the birth in Bethlehem,' she finished.

They stood for a moment without breaking the spell, and then Mam said briskly, 'Now, Gareth, carve!' And Gareth carved.

'I never knew before,' said Roger with his mouth full, 'that you could roast a hare.'

'I've come round to it,' said Gareth. 'I've stewed 'em and I've cooked 'em with belly of pork. But I think they taste finest of all when they're roasted.'

He drank off his wine.

'Goes well, that.'

'Have some more,' said Roger, pouring.

'I killed this hare cleanly,' said Gareth. 'Snapped his neck like a matchstick. So he didn't lose a drop of blood.'

'How much did he weigh?' Mam asked.

'Before I cut his head and neck off, and skinned him,' said Gareth in a calculating voice, his head slightly on one side, 'I should say about, well, six pounds.'

They ate on in silence for a few minutes.

'It's lucky that Gareth was able to turn his hand to cooking so well,' said Mam, evidently to Roger. 'He never cooked a meal till I started losing my sight.'

'Ah, well, it wasn't sudden,' said Gareth. 'You had plenty of chance to coach me while it was coming on.'

Drinking the last of the wine, Roger looked quickly from one of them to the other. How strong they were, how matter-of-fact and without self-pity. Mam's blindness was a fact they had both accepted, and whatever agony it had caused them was now assimilated and conquered. That she was blind was simply one of the given conditions of life, such as that the mountains were steep, the rocks hard, and the wind from the sea always in their faces.

When they had cleaned out every dish and pushed away their empty plates, Gareth stood up.

'I hope you've kept some room,' he said. 'There's a Christmas pudding.'

'Good God,' said Roger. 'What genius!'

'Oh, it's from the shop,' said Gareth quickly. 'I know when I'm beaten. But I thought Christmas wouldn't be right without it. It's just a little one.'

This was the time, Roger decided, to go to his coat pocket and produce the whisky. They arrived back at the table at the same moment.

'Something to pour over it,' he said, unscrewing the bottle.

'You're the genius,' said Gareth simply.

Roger poured some of the whisky on to the tiny pudding, and Gareth took out a box of matches and lit it. They watched gravely as the small blue halo flickered for a moment.

'It should be brandy really,' Roger apologized.

'I'm sure this is just as good, man.'

The pudding despatched, they stacked the dishes and sat down by the fire to enjoy the sensation of being full-fed, warm, peaceful, and permeated by alcohol.

'Are you in a draught, Mam?'

'Not the least bit.'

Outside, the short day was already sinking downward. Sheep would be penned together for fleecy warmth, and, soon, the mist would condense into freezing drops on the heather. The year was turning, turning on a bleak axle of darkness and cold.

Roger and Gareth were slowly sipping whisky from their tumblers.

'Have a drop more.'

'It keeps the cold out,' Gareth acquiesced.

'Don't be silly, Gareth,' said his mother. 'By this fire there's no cold to keep out.'

'It's lubrication,' said Gareth calmly, pouring a couple of inches into his glass. 'Same as the bus. Keeps condensation out of the cylinders.'

He drank, appreciatively.

They sat in silence for a few minutes. Roger noticed that the light coming in through the window, on the seaward side, had changed from a cheese-cloth white to a rich, warm pink. He was about to remark on it when a sudden qualm about Mam's blindness caused him to keep silent. Was it right to mention a fine sunset when sitting with someone from whose eyes the colour of sunsets had faded for ever?

The light grew richer: from pink it deepened to a wonderful crimson, that glowed in a square on the whitewashed wall behind Gareth's somnolent head. Roger, lifting his glass, saw that his hand was bathed in this same crimson.

'Gareth! Mam!' Roger cried. 'Drink a toast with me: to our victory!'

In his excitement, he stood up.

'Mam hasn't got a drink,' said Gareth. 'Here.'

He took down a glass and poured an inch of whisky for her. The bottle was getting very low now.

'I don't touch strong drink,' she protested.

'No,' said Gareth. 'But you will this time, Mam. Roger's right. He wants us to drink a toast to the best thing we have in the world: our fighting spirit.'

'Christmas,' she sighed, 'and you talk of fighting.'

'We talk of surviving, Mrs Jones,' said Roger.

They raised their glasses. Mam coughed a few times as the whisky went down, but she seemed gladdened by it, or by something: a gentle, reminiscent smile came over her face.

'Ah, Gareth,' she said softly. 'You're Geraint's own son.'

'I hope so, Mam.'

'He'd have said just the same as you. He'd have said that our fighting spirit is the best thing we have.'

Gareth smiled with her, so that it seemed to Roger, watching, that their two faces were very much alike.

'Remember when Prince kicked me?' Gareth asked.

'Yes. I was frightened for you.'

'I never told you what happened afterwards,' said Gareth. 'All these years I never told you, but I'll tell you now.'

'Afterwards?'

'When I got out again,' said Gareth. He turned to Roger. 'We had a horse called Prince, that used to do the work about the place before we had a tractor. He was a good old helper – he knew every stone and blade of grass on the place better than my dad did. But once, when I was a little nipper, six or seven years old, a strange thing happened – he kicked me. I must have been fooling about near his hind legs. The kick was a pretty bad one – it didn't break any bones but it dislocated my arm. I was badly bruised as well, and they put me to bed and I was there for a couple of days at least. When I got up and started running about the place again, I kept very clear of Prince, and my dad must have noticed this, because one morning he called me over to where he and Prince were standing, just outside the stable door. Gareth, he says. Yes, dad. Would you like a shilling, he says. A shilling was a lot of money to me, and he got it out of his pocket and held it up so I could see how it glittered in the sun. It's yours, he says, all you have to do is pick it up – and with that he tosses it down right among Prince's hooves. I looked down and saw it shining there, and Prince's feet looked very big and very hard, and I was still aching from the kick he'd given me, but I wanted the shilling and there was something I wanted more than the shilling, you understand me?'

Roger nodded.

'So I went down among the horse's feet and picked up the shilling,' said Gareth. He had turned his head and was speaking now to Mam. 'The ground was a bit muddy and the first time I went for it it slithered away. But I grabbed again, and Prince kept still as a mouse, and I came up with it and shouted, I did it, I did it, dad! I did it!'

He laughed delightedly.

'And I never knew,' said Mam. 'Did he tell you not to say anything to me?'

'Not he. But I noticed he said nothing about it when we came in for our dinner, and little as I was I understood somehow that if he said nothing it was best for me to say nothing, too.'

There was a silence. Roger thought of the small, misshapen body, bruised and frightened, going down in the mud for the shilling that was to be his bright badge of manhood, shining in the shadows of his mind for ever. The sharp, still-frightened but exultant cry rang in his ears: *I did it, dad! I did it!*

'You did it all right,' he said to Gareth.

'Prince was as good as gold,' said Gareth. 'I was sick with grieving when he died, though I was nearly a man by that time.'

The crimson light had paled, and the sky outside the windows was now almost drained of its magic.

'Let's have some light,' said Gareth, springing up, 'and a cup of good hot tea.'

The afternoon trance was broken: the bustle of cheerful normality was back. The electric light splashed literalness over everything, banished metaphor, showed Gareth as less of a badger or a hawk than a hunchbacked man, Roger as a shabby smiler with an intellectual face, Mam as a placid ebbing life in an armchair.

They drank tea, and Gareth produced another surprise from the mysterious kitchen into which no one but he was allowed: a dark, rich, marzipan-topped Christmas cake.

'Gareth, this is home-made,' said Mam, eating judicially.

'Mrs Arkwright,' said Gareth, nodding. 'She makes cakes for something to do. Half the village gets one.'

Roger had a sudden vision of Mrs Arkwright, alone in her spick-and-span bungalow, mixing dark sugary ingredients in a big china bowl and thinking of people who needed cakes. Under some circumstances, this vision would have seemed to him intensely melancholy, the time-killing of a lonely woman whose only other occupation was quarrelling with the dustmen, but now he saw it in a different light. It made him think of the courage and resourcefulness of human beings, their endless inventiveness, their readiness to fight back against the bitter siege of the years.

'Mrs Arkwright!' he cried. 'Lancashire's gift to Llancrwys!'

'God bless her for a kind heart,' Mam said.

'I hope she gave the dustmen a cake,' said Gareth.

Roger felt light-headed. He was probably drunk; but, if so, what had inebriated him was less the whisky than the strangeness of the day and the delicate flesh of the roasted hare and the sombre splendour of the sunset, and the utterly individual faces of Gareth and Mam, and the thought of Mrs Arkwright and the dustmen and all the rich, inextricable human pattern that could never be unpicked.

'The last time I ate this kind of cake was at a wedding,' he said. The statement was not true, but he listened to it with interest and wondered what other statements he was about to make. And besides, what was true? The brain's truth or the heart's truth?

'I went to a wedding just before I came up here,' he went on. 'It was a tremendously happy occasion. My brother Geoffrey got married to this wonderful girl, Margot. I think they're going to be ideally happy.'

They listened, and he talked on.

'Margot's the most beautiful girl. She has red-gold hair and these amazing green eyes. All sorts of men have been trying to marry her but she stood out for the best. That's Geoffrey — if I do say so myself, being his brother and everything. Of course, he's always overshadowed me. He's some years older, and besides that he's far more intelligent and attractive. But he's always been gentle with me. I never felt jealous of him — all the things he did just seemed to be out of my sphere, so that it never entered my head to compete with him.

'Geoffrey and I lived together,' he went on. 'Of course, I knew I'd lose him sooner or later. The best thing, really. I mean, it's a shame for Geoffrey not to be married and have offspring. He'll be a marvellous father.'

'And you,' said Mam into the kindly silence. 'You'll be looking round for a wife now.'

'And not before it's time,' said Roger heartily. 'I had my eye on one or two up here. But they seem to be all booked.'

'Rhiannon's booked, that's certain,' said Gareth drily. 'That fellow with the aeroplanes'll never leave go of her.'

'Dilwyn? D'you think he'll get her in the end?'

'When she's ready,' said Gareth, nodding, 'she'll come to Dilwyn.'

'Well, I must get married,' said Roger. 'Or I'll feel very out of it, with Geoffrey and Margot setting up house. They've found a wonderful place, in the country. Right off on its own, among the fields. Sixteenth-century, with a paddock and an orchard. They've both lived in London so much that they'll be glad to have quiet and elbow-room in the country. And there's plenty of room for a family.'

Restless, he crossed the room and stood looking out at the long, still line of silver light that rested on the edge of the dark Irish Sea.

'Yes,' he said, so quietly that the others scarcely heard him. 'I've got to get used to doing without Geoffrey now. But he'll be all right with Margot. And it's nice to see two people as happy as that.'

Smiling, he turned and faced Gareth and Mam. 'That's enough about me,' he said.

They drank up the whisky, ate some cold ham, and sat by the fire in a comfortable stupor. Gareth produced an old pack of cards and he and Roger played, unskilfully but with much companionable joking, two or three games of rummy. Finally, at midnight, Roger noticed that Mam was asleep in her chair and judged that it was time to go. Gareth saw him down to the gate.

'No work tomorrow,' he said. 'Have a good lie in.'

'I will,' said Roger. 'Goodnight, and thanks again.'

As he turned away, a slight feeling of strangeness, of displacement, tugged at his consciousness. He had walked a hundred yards through the crisp, clear night before he realized what it was. Both he and Gareth, as the day of celebration ended and their thoughts turned to work, had spoken in English.

Take Fesaunt,
Boare and Chykenne ...

We have had little to interest the dedicated Christmas cook till now; here then is a set of historic dishes. First, Mrs Beeton's Christmas pudding; next the Christmas menu of George and Martha Washington (note how such archetypally American delights as squash, hominy, and cranberry are already listed), then a fourteenth-century recipe for what was then called Christmas pastry but which we would now call pâté. Then, from Spike Milligan's Puckoon, a recipe for Christmas dinner on the 99th day of the Great Siege of Paris. Though Milligan jests, his menu is not far from the truth. Note, however, the magnificent wines still available to wash it down! Finally, Elizabeth David at her most convivial, anecdotal, and magisterial, offers convincing evidence that the Christmas pudding is, of all things, a Mediterranean food.

CHRISTMAS PLUM-PUDDING
Very Good

MRS BEETON

INGREDIENTS   *1 ½* lb of raisins, ½ lb of currants, ¾ lb of breadcrumbs, ½ lb of mixed peel, ¾ lb of suet, 8 eggs, 1 wineglassful of brandy

MODE Stone and cut the raisins in halves, but do not chop them; wash, pick and dry the currants, and mince the suet finely; cut the candied peel into thin slices, and grate down the bread into fine crumbs.

When all these dry ingredients are prepared, mix them well together; then moisten the mixture with the eggs, which should be well beaten, and the brandy; stir well, that everything may be very thoroughly blended, and *press* the pudding into a buttered mould; tie it down tightly with a floured cloth, and boil for five or six hours. It may be boiled in a cloth without a mould, and will require the same time allowed for cooking.

As Christmas puddings are usually made a few days before they are required for table, when the pudding is taken out of the pot, hang it up immediately, and put a plate or saucer underneath to catch the water that may drain from it. The day it is to be eaten, plunge it into boiling water, and keep it boiling for at least two hours; then turn it out of the mould, and serve with brandy sauce. On Christmas Day a sprig of holly is usually placed in the middle of the pudding and about a wineglassful of brandy poured round it, which at the moment of serving, is lighted and the pudding thus brought to the table encircled in flame.

Average cost 4s. *Sufficient* for a quart mould for seven or eight persons. Seasonable on the 25th December, and on various festive occasions till March.

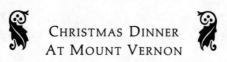

Christmas Dinner At Mount Vernon

GEORGE AND MARTHA WASHINGTON

An Onion Soup call'd the King's Soup
Oysters on the Half Shell   Grilled Salt Roe Herring
Boiled Rockfish
Roast Beef and Yorkshire Pudding   Mutton Chops
Roast Suckling Pig   Roast Turkey with Chestnut Stuffing
Round of Cold Boiled Beef with Horse-radish Sauce
Cold Baked Virginia Ham
Lima Beans   Baked Acorn Squash
Baked Celery with Slivered Almonds
Hominy Pudding   Candied Sweet Potatoes
Cantaloupe Pickle   Spiced Peaches in Brandy
Spiced Cranberries
Mincemeat Pie   Apple Pie   Cherry Pie   Chess Tarts
Blancmange   Plums in Wine Jelly   Snowballs
Indian Pudding
Great Cake   Ice Cream   Plum-Pudding
Fruits   Nuts   Raisins
Port   Madeira

A RECIPE
FOR CHRISTMAS PASTRY

(Presumed AD 1394)

Take Fesaunt, Boare and Chykenne, or Caponne, of eche oone, with two partruchis and two Pygeonnes; and smite hem on peeces and pyke clene away therfrom all ye boonys that ye can, and therewith do into a paste made craftely ynne ye lykenes of a byrdes bodye with ye lyuours and hertys and twy kydneis of shepe and farcys [force-meat] and eyren [eggs] made ynto balles. Cast therto poudre of pepyr, salte, spyce, eysell [vinegar] and funges [mushrooms] pickled and thanne [then] take ye boonys and let hem seethe ynne a pot to make a gode broth for it; with ye hede of oone of ye byrdes stucke at ye oone end of ye paste and a grete tayle at ye other and dyvers of hys longe fedyrs sette ynne cunnynglye alle aboute hym.

PUCKOON

SPIKE MILLIGAN

'Poppa, what was the greatest meal ever served?'

Poppa puzzled at young Sean's question.

'The greatest I don't know but . . .' here he closed his eyes and put his finger on his nose. Suddenly he spoke. 'The meal served at the Tuileries in 1820, I have a copy in my wallet, listen to this; no, better still, I will read you the most extraordinary menu, which proves that the French under no matter what harrowing conditions still attain the heights of civilization.' Poppa donned his glasses and read.

'Dinner served at the Café Voisin, 261 rue Saint-Honoré, on December 25th 1870, 99th day of the siege.'

Here he looked around to observe their surprise, then continued.

Hors-d'œuvres
Butter-Radishes, Stuffed Donkey's Head, Sardines

Soups
Purée of Red Beans with Croûtons
Elephant Consommé

Entrées
Fried Gudgeons, Roast Camel English Style
Jugged Kangaroo
Roast Bear Chops au Poivre

Roasts
Haunch of Wolf, Venison Sauce
Cat Flanked by Rats
Watercress Salad
Antelope Terrine with Truffles
Mushroom Bordelaise
Buttered Green Peas

Dessert
Rice Cake with Jam
Gruyère Cheese

Wines

(Here Poppa's face beamed)

First service
Sherry
Latour Blanche 1861!
Château Palmer 1864!

'Now *second* service,' he emphasized:

Mouton Rothschild 1846!
Romanee Conti 1858!
Grand Porto 1827!

He folded the paper, and patted his brow where an excitement of perspiration had grown. They gathered by the menu that the Paris Zoo had been held in reserve for a Christmas Dinner. At the time young Sean was only seven, and the names of the great wine Châteaux that his father rolled off meant very little to him, but his father's persistence had borne fruit and the whole family were now confirmed lovers of wine.

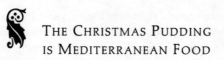

THE CHRISTMAS PUDDING IS MEDITERRANEAN FOOD

ELIZABETH DAVID

A white cube of a house, two box-like rooms and a nice large kitchen. No bath. No plumbing. A well and a fig tree outside the front door and five yards away the Aegean. On the horizon a half circle of the islands of Andros, Tinos, Seriphos. In the village, about three dozen houses, two churches (one Orthodox, one Roman Catholic), one provision shop. Down on the shore one shack of a tavern, and in the village street a more important one, stacked with barrels and furnished with stout wooden tables.

Christo, the owner of this second tavern, was one of the grandees of the village. He operated, in addition to the tavern, a small market garden, and sold his produce in the island's capital seven miles away. He also had a brother-in-law, called Yannaki. Yannaki was that stock Greek village character, the traveller come home after experiencing glamorous doings and glorious events in far-off places. True to type, he spoke a little Anglo-American and, more uncommonly, a little French; he was always on hand to help out if foreigners came to the village. He seemed a kind and cheerful man, rich too; at any rate, he owned a spare donkey and was prepared to lend me this animal, along with a boy to talk to it, so that I could ride into the town when I needed to stock up with fresh supplies of beans and oil, bottled wine, cheese, dried fruit, and boxes of the delicious Turkish Delight which was – still is – a speciality of the island.

Before long it transpired that the greatest favour I could bestow upon Yannaki in return for the loan of his transport would be some tomato soup in tins and perhaps also a jar or two of English 'picklies'.

Handing over to one of the brothers who owned the hotel and the Turkish Delight factory in the capital a bundle of drachmae which would have kept me in wine and cheese for a month, I got in return four tins, vintage, of the required soup. Of English piccalilli, which I took it was what Yannaki meant by picklies, there was no sign nor sniff, and very relieved I was. Many more such exotic luxuries, and it would be cheaper for me to leave my seashore village for Athens and a suite at the Grande-Bretagne.

The tomato soup gave Yannaki and Christo and their families a great deal of pleasure. It was the real thing, no mistaking it. In return I was offered baskets of eggs, lemons, oranges, freshly dug vegetables and salads, glass after glass of wine in the tavern. And, then, next time the picklies? I *was* English wasn't I? Then I should certainly be able to produce these delicacies.

For days I scanned the horizon for sight of an English yacht. I could, in my turn, have bartered fresh vegetables and fruit for the jars of mustard pickles which I knew must grace the table of any English *lordos* grand enough to be roaming the Aegean seas. It was late in the season. That way no yacht came.

Anyone who has experience of the stubborn determination, courteous but quite unrelenting, of an Aegean islander when he has made up his mind about something will understand why, in the end, I was obliged to set to and make those confounded pickles myself.

Into the town then for mustard, vinegar, spices. Long mornings I spent cutting up cauliflower and onions, carrots and cucumbers. Afternoons, I squatted in my kitchen fanning the charcoal fires into a blaze brisk enough to boil the brew. The jars, the only ones I could find, which I had bought to pack the stuff in were of one oke capacity, three pounds, near enough. Also they were of rough earthenware, unglazed, and exceptionally porous. Before I could even give the filled jars away they were half empty again, the liquid all soaked up by that sponge-like clay. Every one had to be replenished with a fresh batch of pickle. To me the mixture seemed fairly odd, but with my village friends it was successful enough. In fact, on the barter system, I could have lived for nothing so long as I was prepared to dedicate my life to pickle-making. Before long, though, it was getting on for December, and references to 'Xmas pudding' began to crop up in the tavern talk. By now I had learned a little more about these kindly village tyrants. If Christmas pudding they wanted, Christmas pudding I should have to give them. But not, so help me, made on the improvized happy-go-lucky system I'd used for the mustard pickles. Once more then into the town (I never could stay five seconds on a horse or a mule or even a bicycle, but by that time I had at least found out how to sit on a donkey and get the animal moving over stony paths and up and down steep hills) to telegraph home for a recipe. When it arrived, it turned out to be one of those which calls for a pound of almost everything you can think of, which was lucky. Simply by multiplying each by three it was all turned into okes. A large-scale Christmas party was now simmering, so there wouldn't, I thought, be an oke too much.

Now, all those with their fine talk of the glories of Old English fare, have they ever actually made Christmas pudding, in large quantities, by Old English methods? Have they for instance ever tried cleaning and skinning, flouring, shredding, chopping beef kidney suet straight off the hoof? Have they ever stoned bunch after bunch of raisins hardly yet dry on the stalk and each one as sticky as a piece of warm toffee? And how long do they think it takes to bash up three pounds of breadcrumbs without an oven in which they could first dry the loaves? Come to that, what would they make of an attempt to boil, and to keep on the boil for nine to ten hours on two charcoal fires let into holes in the wall, some dozen large puddings? Well, I had nothing much else to do in those days and quite enjoyed all the work, but I'd certainly never let myself in for such an undertaking again. Nor, indeed, would I again attempt to explain the principles of a hay-box and the reasons for making one to peasants of whose language I had such a scanty knowledge and who are in any case notoriously unreceptive to the idea of having hot food, or for that matter hot water or hot coffee, hotter than tepid.

All things considered, my puddings turned out quite nicely. The ones which emerged from the hay-box were at just about the right temperature – luke-warm. They were sweet and dark and rich. My village friends were not as enthusiastic as they had been about the mustard pickles. What with so many of the company having participated in the construction of the hay-box, my assurances that the raisins and the currants grown and dried there on the spot in the Greek sun were richer and more juicy than the artificially dried, hygienically treated and much-travelled variety we got at home, my observations on the incomparable island-made candied citron and orange peel (that was fun to cut up too) given me by the neighbours, and the memorable scent of violets and brilliantine given to the puddings by Athenian brandy, a certain amount of the English mystery had disappeared from our great national festive dish.

That *le plum-pudding n'est pas Anglais* was a startling discovery made by a French chef, Philéas Gilbert, round about the turn of the century. No, not English indeed. In this case le plum-pudding had been almost Greek. What I wish I'd known at the time was the rest of Gilbert's story. It seems that with a passing nod to a Breton concoction called *le far* 'obviously the ancestor of the English pudding', an earlier French historian, Bourdeau by name, unable or perhaps unwilling to claim plum pudding for France, says that it is precisely described by Athenaeus in a report of the wedding feast of Caranus, an Argive prince, The pudding was called *strepte*, and in origin was entirely Greek.

I Sent for

a Mince-pie Abroad ...

Now for a whole clutch of diarists. There is a large question mark over The Diary of a Farmer's Wife. It was serialized in four parts in the Farmer's Weekly in 1937 as the diary of Anne Hughes. She, the paper claimed, was the wife of a Hereford farmer, and her diary covered the eighteen months between February 1796 and 1797. Introducing the Penguin edition, Michael Croucher maintains that it is unlikely to be a forgery because Jeanne Preston, who produced the diary when the paper suddenly needed a serial, would not have had the literary ability to fabricate it. I wonder. We could judge better if the diary survived; but Jeanne is thought to have given it away to an American soldier during the war. What we do know is that Jeanne in her youth was befriended by a vigorous old lady called Mary Anne Thomas, née Hughes. Could Mary Anne, asks Croucher, have been Anne's daughter? The dates can be made to fit — just. Yet our credulity is stretched perilously thin. Much more likely, surely, is that Jeanne lapped up wide-eyed the stories Mary Anne spun to her of life at a country farm around the turn of the eighteenth century; and that Jeanne regurgitated them herself when suddenly called on by the Weekly (for whom she wrote already) for a serial. It hardly matters; the diary is excellent value whether it has written provenance or relies on oral tradition.

The Rev. Francis Kilvert's diary, on the other hand, impresses us by its sheer Victorian manliness and muscular Christianity. Indeed, we can still get a sympathetic shiver from his account of taking a morning bath amid the floating ice.

One of the most remarkable entries made by John Evelyn in his diary is that for Christmas Day, 1657. Cromwell was the Protector of England and Christ's Mass was banned. The passage has an eerie modern ring to it; we can feel Evelyn's relief when he is at last pityingly released by his interrogators. It has even been argued that one of our submerged impulses as a race towards nostalgia for Christmas past lies in the loss of many ancient Christmas observances during the years of the protectorate.

Evelyn's contemporary, Samuel Pepys, offers us a fine account of a Christmas Day four years before the Great Fire of London; Charles Lamb takes us to Christ's Hospital (did they have no holidays in those days?); and the young Victoria gives us a typically conscientious account of a royal Christmas. Lehzen was her former governess, Lady Conroy, wife of the Comptroller of her mother's household, Dash her pet spaniel. Her three childhood playmates were Victoire Conroy and Emily Gardiner, both daughters of court officials, and her cousin George Cambridge. Louis, confusingly, was her female attendant. She was seventeen; and in six months would be Queen.

Last, a heart-warming account from Addison, writing in the Spectator under the signature 'L', one of the four code letters (CLIO — the muse of history) with which he signed off all his 274 letters to the paper.

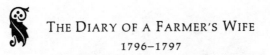

The Diary of a Farmer's Wife
1796–1797

ANNE HUGHES

Dec. ye 23. We have bin verrie bussie with sum goodlie things to eat. Boiled hams and great big mince pies and roast geese and hens and boiled and roasted beef, all reddie for eating. Johns mother be going to make a pudden for carter and shepherd, and I shall give them a big mince pie and apples, so that they can have Christmas fare. Carters wiffe be cumming early to get ready for our visitors who be cumming tomorrow. We shall be verrie bussie, so I shall not have time to write in my book till all over.

Johns mother have made a verrie pretty dish wich she do call meat cake. She did mix flower and butter to a thick paste and put sum on the bottom of a bake tin, this she did cover with the chopt beef and onion and herbs, then more paste, then more meat and flavouring, and paste agen, till the tin be full. Then she do cover all with more paste and cook till done. She do say this do cut like a cake when it be cold with the meat inside. There also be 2 roast hares and pudden with spices and plenty of apple pies and divers things and junkets, cider cake and cinnamon cakes and a rich Christmas cake, Johns mother did bake.

I hope we shall have enough, but I be keeping sum rabbit pies and a big ham ready, in case it be wanted. John will tap the new beer and the honey wine, and we shall have primy rose wine, as well as Eldernberrie, and dandie lyon, so there should be good store.

I do hear John below so must not write more; I do love my little book so do write much and have wrote nearly all the pages, and I dout if I shall start another one, though I do love it.

Dec. ye 27. Christmas be all over now, and our visitors gone, but a right good time we did have, the roads did dry up a bit so not too bad for the travellers, who did cum pack horse. Cusson Tom and Emma, her ladd and his sweetheart Jan, did get here after a journie of hard going Christmas Eve, the rest did cum Christmas morning and all of us to church leaving carters wiffe and Sarahs sister Jane to help Sarah with the dinner to be all ready genst our cumming back, and mother and me did set the tables together in a row and cover them with my linnen table cloths; then we did put the silver and glass and all did look verrie fine. Passon did give a verrie good sermon, telling us to do to others as we would have them do to us, and the world the better place, to which I do agree. The singing did go right heartilie with a great roar, the church bein full, for all do like the young passon and his mother.

Then we out and home to our dinner. John did set at one end with beef and geese, and Farmer Ellis at the other to cut up the hams and so on, which Sarah and Jane did carry round till all served, and all did eat their fill and had plentie. Then John did pass the wine and all did drink each other's healths; then the men did smoke while we ladies did drink our wine and talk of divers things that had happened through the year, not thinking so much had; then the men did say let us dance, so Bill and Jen did play a merrie jig on their fiddles and we did step it out finely; till all breathless, we do sit down laffing much.

Farmer Bliss did say lets have a story, so Passon did tell us a good one that did cause much merriment; then John did say he would tell them the story what happened when his father died, and did tell of the man what stopped him on the road. His mother did say it must have bin Joe Graves who did go to them for shelter when in trouble, and they did hide him for 3 days and he getting off safe at last. Then said Mistress Prue it showed how one good turn did make another.

Then cusson Tom saying we be getting too serious, so Mistress Prue to the spinette to play a merrie tune, and we to dancing once more stepping it right merrilie till Sarah do say its time for tea; whereon we do sit down and do justice to all the good things provided, which did make a brave show and looked verrie good on the dishes; the lights from the tapers in Johns mothers silver candle sticks did light the holly Sarah had put on the table in glasses. All the ladies did like mothers meat cake, and want to know how to make it.

Then we did gather together and play the game of Popp; we did put the chairs in a ringe, the men on one side, the ladies on the other with our hands behind, one holding a apple which be passed from one to another. The man must not speak but do beckon to the lady they think have got the apple; if she have not she do say 'popp' and the man do have to sit on the floor and pay forfitt, till all there; but if he be right he do take the ladie on his knees till the game be played out. After we did play bobbie apple, and snap draggon, the Passon burning his fingers mitilie to get Sarahs plum; all did enjoy it much, and then we did stop a while for sum cakes and wine, and sum songs sung by one and other; then more dancing till supper, then more games and later all home after a really good Christmas which we did all enjoy much with everybody happie. And now this be the last page in my little book. I know not if I shall ever write another one. I do feel I have much to be thankful for, for my life with John and his mother be a verrie happy one.

I do wonder where my little book will go, who may read it. I shall always keep it, and perhaps if God do give me a son he will read it some day and so know what a fine man his father is. So I say good-by to my little book.

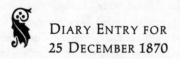

DIARY ENTRY FOR
25 DECEMBER 1870

REV. FRANCIS KILVERT

Sunday, Christmas Day

As I lay awake praying in the early morning I thought I heard a sound of distant bells. It was an intense frost. I sat down in my bath upon a sheet of thick ice which broke in the middle into large pieces whilst sharp points and jagged edges stuck all round the sides of the tub like *chevaux de frise*, not particularly comforting to the naked thighs and loins, for the keen ice cut like broken glass. The ice water stung and scorched like fire. I had to collect the floating pieces of ice and pile them on a chair before I could use the sponge and then I had to thaw the sponge in my hands for it was a mass of ice. The morning was most brilliant. Walked to the Sunday School with Gibbins and the road sparkled with millions of rainbows, the seven colours gleaming in every glittering point of hoar frost. The Church was very cold in spite of two roaring stove fires. Mr V. preached and went to Bettws.

CHRISTMAS DAY, 1657

JOHN EVELYN

I went with my Wife &c: to *Lond*: to celebrate *Christmas day*. Mr. *Gunning* preaching in *Excester* Chapell on 7: *Micha* 2. Sermon Ended, as he was giving us the holy Sacrament, The Chapell was surrounded with Souldiers: All the Communicants and Assembly surpriz'd & kept Prisoners by them, some in the house, others carried away: It fell to my share to be confined to a roome in the house, where yet were permitted to Dine with the master of it, the Countesse of *Dorset*, *Lady Hatton* & some others of quality who invited me: In the afternoone came *Collonel Whaly*, *Goffe* & others from *Whitehall* to examine us one by one, & some they committed to the *Martial*, some to Prison, some Committed. When I came before them they tooke my name & aboad, examind me, why contrarie to an Ordinance made that none should any longer observe the superstitious time of the *Nativity* (so esteem'd by them) I durst offend, & particularly be at *Common prayers*, which they told me was but the *Masse* in *English*, & particularly pray for *Charles stuard*, for which we had no Scripture: I told them we did not pray for *Cha: Steward* but for all *Christian Kings, Princes* & *Governers*: The[y] replied, in so doing we praied for the K. of *Spaine* too, who was their Enemie, & a *Papist*, with other frivolous & insnaring questions, with much threatning, & finding no colour to detaine me longer, with much pitty of my Ignorance, they dismiss'd me: These were men of high flight, and above Ordinances: & spake spitefull things of our B: Lords nativity: so I got home late the next day blessed be God: These wretched miscreants, held their muskets against us as we came up to receive the Sacred Elements, as if they would have shot us at the Altar, but yet suffering us to finish the Office of Communion, as perhaps not in their Instructions what they should do in case they found us in that Action

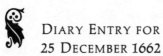

DIARY ENTRY FOR
25 DECEMBER 1662

SAMUEL PEPYS

Had a pleasant walk to White Hall, where I intended to have received the Communion with the family, but I come a little too late. So I walked up into the house, and spent my time in looking over pictures, particularly the ships in King Henry the VIIIth's voyage to Bullaen; marking the great difference between those built then and now. By and by down the chapel again, where Bishop Morley preached upon the song of the Angels, 'Glory to God on high, on earth peace, and good will towards men.' Methought he made but a poor sermon, but long, and, reprehending the common jollity of the Court for the true joy that shall and ought to be on these days, he particularized concerning their excess in playes and gaming, saying that he whose office it is to keep the gamesters in order and within bounds, serves but for a second rather in a duell,

meaning the groome-porter. Upon which it was worth observing how far they are come from taking the reprehensions of a bishop seriously, that they all laugh in the chapel when he reflected on their ill actions and courses. He did much press us to joy in these public days of joy, and to hospitality; but one that stood by whispered in my eare that the Bishop do not spend one groate to the poore himself. The sermon done, a good anthem followed with vialls, and the King come down to receive the Sacrament. But I staid not, but calling my boy from my Lord's lodgings, and giving Sarah some good advice by my Lord's order to be sober, and look after the house, I walked home again with great pleasure, and there dined by my wife's bed-side with great content, having a mess of brave plum-porridge and a roasted pullet for dinner, and I sent for a mince-pie abroad, my wife not being well, to make any herself yet.

CHRISTMAS AT
CHRIST'S HOSPITAL, LONDON

CHARLES LAMB

Let me have leave to remember the festivities at Christmas, when the richest of us would club our stock to have a gaudy day, sitting round the fire, replenished to the height with logs; and the pennyless and he that could contribute nothing, partook in all the mirth and in some of the substantialities of the feasting; the carol sung by night at that time of the year, which, when a young boy, I have so often laid awake from seven (the hour of going to bed) till ten, when it was sung by the older boys and monitors, and have listened to it in their rude chanting, till I have been transported to the fields of Bethlehem, and the song of which was sung at that season by the angels' voices to the shepherds.

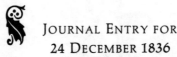

JOURNAL ENTRY FOR
24 DECEMBER 1836

PRINCESS VICTORIA

Saturday, 24 December 1836

I awoke after 7 and got up at 8. After 9 breakfasted, at a little after 10 we left Kensington with dearest Lehzen, Lady Conroy and — Dashy! and reached Claremont at a quarter to 12. Played and sang. At 2 dearest Lehzen, Victoire and I went out, and came home at 20 minutes past 3. No one was stirring about the gipsy encampment except George, which I was sorry for as I was anxious to know how our poor friends were, after this bitterly cold night. Played and sang. Received from dearest, best Lehzen as a Christmas box two lovely little Dresden China figures, two pair of lovely little chased gold buttons, a small lovely button with an angel's head which she used to wear herself, and a pretty music book; from good Louis a beautiful piece of Persian stuff for an album; and from Victoire and Emily Gardiner a small box worked by themselves. Wrote my journal, went down to arrange mamma's table for her. At 6 we dined. Mr Edmund Byng and Mr Conroy stayed here. Mr Byng is going to stay here a night or two. Very soon after dinner mamma sent for us into the gallery, where all the things were arranged on different tables. From my dear mamma I received a beautiful massive gold buckle in the shape of two serpents; a lovely little delicate gold chain with a turquoise clasp; a lovely coloured sketch of dearest Aunt Louise by Partridge copied from the picture he brought and so like her; 3 beautiful drawings by Munn, one lovely seaview by Purser and one cattle piece by Cooper (all coloured), 3 prints, a book called Finden's Tableau, Heath's Picturesque Annual, Ireland; both these are very pretty; Friendship's Offering and the English Annual for 1837, The Holy Land illustrated beautifully, two handkerchiefs, a very pretty black satin apron trimmed with red velvet, and two almanacks. I am very thankful to my dear mamma for all these very pretty things. From dear Uncle Leopold a beautiful turquoise ring; from the Queen a fine piece of Indian gold tissue; and from Sir J. Conroy a print. I gave my dear Lehzen a green morocco jewel case, and the Picturesque Annual; mamma gave her a shawl, a pair of turquoise earrings, an annual, and handkerchiefs. I then took mamma to the Library where my humble table was arranged; I gave her a bracelet made of my hair, and the Keepsake, and Oriental Annual. Stayed up till eleven.

SIR ROGER DE COVERLEY'S CHRISTMAS

JOSEPH ADDISON

Sir Roger, after the laudable custom of his ancestors, always keeps open house at *Christmas*. I learned from him that he had killed eight fat hogs for this season, that he had dealt about his chines very liberally amongst his neighbours, and that in particular he had sent a string of hogs-puddings with a pack of cards to every poor family in the parish. I have often thought, says Sir Roger, it happens very well that *Christmas* should fall out in the middle of winter. It is the most dead uncomfortable time of the year, when the poor people would suffer very much from their poverty and cold, if they had not good cheer, warm fires, and *Christmas* gambols to support them. I love to rejoice their poor hearts at this season, and to see the whole village merry in my great hall. I allow a double quantity of malt to my small beer, and set it a running for twelve days to every one that calls for it. I have always a piece of cold beef and a mince-pye upon the table, and am wonderfully pleased to see my tenants pass away a whole evening in playing their innocent tricks, and smutting one another.

I was very much delighted with the reflexion of my old friend, which carried so much goodness in it. He then launched out into the praise of the late act of parliament for securing the Church of *England*, and told me with great satisfaction, that he believed it already began to take effect, for that a rigid dissenter who chanced to dine at his house on *Christmas* day, had been observed to eat very plentifully of his plumb-porridge.

'THIS,' SAID MR PICKWICK, 'IS INDEED COMFORT'

Now for three English immortals. Christmas brought both hazard and delight to Billy Bunter, the Fat Owl of the Remove in the much-loved Greyfriars School stories. There would be loads of free scoff – but where precisely? In this classic 1930 story from the Magnet, the paper which delighted generations of schoolboys, Bunter has been trying to wangle an invitation for the hols from his schoolfellows. But there is no room for Bunter at Cherry Place, where Bob Cherry's people live; nor at Mauleverer Towers where Lord Mauleverer slums it with his pater and mater; nor anywhere else. Things look pretty bleak for Bunter – till he saves the life of Lord Cavandale, in a series of whopping flukes, twice in one day. The grateful peer invites Bunter to be his guest at Cavandale Abbey. It looks as if Bunter's luck has turned at last. Meanwhile, down at Skeldings, Bertie Wooster is saved by the bell yet again in the vintage story 'Jeeves and the Yule-tide Spirit'. Not only is there a glorious inside account of life in the Drones Club, but an inspired description, even by the Master's Olympian standard, of the fate Bertie had so narrowly missed in the fearsome form of Honoria Glossop; a girl whose laughter sounded 'like waves breaking on a stern and rock-bound coast'. Then on to Christmas at Dingley Dell with that other towering comic figure of English fiction, Mr Pickwick, and the best account it can offer of the hazards and delights of kissing under the Christmas mistletoe. Next, since the lore of the mistletoe is not so well documented in English writing as one would wish, a charming short poem by Walter de la Mare about it; and finally in this section, a seasonal episode from The Diary of a Nobody in which Mr Pooter finds all this kissing under the mistletoe a subversive innovation.

BILLY BUNTER'S CHRISTMAS

FRANK RICHARDS

'Pilkingham!'

'My lord!'

Billy Bunter blinked at the plump, florid, clean-shaven, almost majestic personage who answered to the name of Pilkingham. This personage, evidently the butler of Cavandale Abbey, seemed rather to swim than to walk. Bunter had seen all sorts of conditions of butlers; but he admitted to himself that Pilkingham took the cake. A sense of his own majesty below stairs, mingled with a due sense of the majesty of his master above stairs. In the butler line, Pilkingham was what Fisher T. Fish of the Remove, would have called 'the goods'.

The butler, while he gave his respectful attention to his lordship, eyed Bunter from the corner of one eye. If he was surprised to see a fat schoolboy with a bandaged chin in Lord Cavandale's company, he did not, of course, betray it. No emotion, except that of a self-respecting respect, was ever allowed to appear on Pilkingham's well-trained visage.

'This young gentleman, Master Bunter, will be staying for ... h'm ... some time,' said the peer. 'You will make every arrangement for his comfort.'

'Quite so, my lord.'

'I may tell you, Pilkingham, that this young gentleman has twice saved my life today.'

'Indeed, my lord!'

Bunter's idea was that that ought to have made the butler jump. But Pilkingham did not jump. Only a sudden electric shock could have made Pilkingham jump.

'No doubt you will see it in the evening papers,' said Lord Cavandale. 'An attack was made on me in the train from Lantham. This boy saved my life. I have just been fired on in my own park, possibly – indeed probably – by the same man. Owing to Master Bunter the bullet missed its mark. I am telling you this, Pilkingham, so that you will fully understand that Master Bunter is a very honoured guest in this house.'

Possibly the peer was aware that Pilkingham, on first appearances, did not think much of Master Bunter. He was making the matter quite clear. 'I understand, my lord,' said Pilkingham.

'Very good!'

Lord Cavandale smiled, a kind smile, and Bunter followed Pilkingham. The peer looked after him thoughtfully. Grateful as he was to Bunter for his timely aid in the Lantham train, Lord Cavandale possibly had not been delighted by the fat junior butting into his palatial establishment. Yet if Bunter had not come home with him in the car his lordship knew that he would now be lying with a bullet in his body – dead or dying. Bunter, certainly, had not shown a lot of courage on this second occasion – far from it; but equally certainly, he had saved the peer's life a second time. One obligation piled on another like this could not help but make the peer feel very kindly towards the Owl of Greyfriars. If Bunter's conversation in the car had given the impression that he was a fatuous ass, the peer was unwilling to receive that impression, and tried to dismiss it.

Billy Bunter, owing to his peculiar propensity for butting in where he had no concern, had had a rather unusual experience of various establishments – some of them on a large scale. But Cavandale Abbey was the most tremendous establishment into which Bunter had ever butted. The oak-panelled hall, adorned with armoured figures and priceless statuary, was immense in extent. A double staircase gave access to the oaken gallery that surrounded it on three sides, and from this wide, lofty gallery opened more corridors and staircases than Bunter could have counted. He wondered that the inhabitants never lost their way in the building.

A grave gentleman – whom Bunter later learned was the groom of the chambers – met Pilkingham, and they spoke together in low tones for a few moments, unheard by Bunter. Then Pilkingham swam on again with Bunter at his heels.

A door was opened by the groom of the chambers. Pilkingham stood aside, and Bunter rolled into the room.

It was a large, lofty, pleasant room, overlooking the great park. It was furnished with great elegance and comfort. Already – as if by magic – a manservant was igniting a log fire on a wide hearth. Lofty windows – the middle one a french window – gave on a balcony.

Pilkingham swam in and opened a farther door.

'Your bed-room, sir.'

Bunter realized that he was being accommodated with a sitting-room and a bed-room as well. There was no lack of accommodation at Cavandale Abbey, and no lack of service. No lack of anything as far as Bunter could see.

Pilkingham opened another door.

'Your bath-room, sir.'

There was a private bath-room as well! Bunter, however, did not enthuse. He had no great use for a bath-room.

In the doorway on the corridor a young man appeared, a footman with a professionally wooden face.

'Albert!' said Mr Pilkingham, barely noticing the existence of this young man. 'This is Mr Bunter, upon whom you'll be in personal attendance during his stay.'

Bunter almost chuckled! He was going to have a footman to himself! If only all Greyfriars could have been there to see it!

'This bell, sir,' said Pilkingham, 'will summon Albert should you require him. The telephone, sir, is here.'

There was a telephone, too!

'Dinner, sir, is at seven!' said Pilkingham.

Something – dinner or not – was going to be a jolly long time before seven, Bunter told himself.

'I will take a little refreshment in my room,' said Bunter. 'Nothing much, you know – say, a cold chicken. And a pie! Some asparagus! And pâté de foie gras. A cake or two. Some biscuits. A little fruit! Just a snack to keep me going till dinner.'

If Mr Pilkingham felt any surprise he did not show it.

'Very good, sir.'

Mr Pilkingham swam away.

The fire was now burning nicely, and the servant who had lighted it glided away. Albert remained.

Outside the house the December dusk was deepening.

'Put on the light, James!' said Bunter. He had not forgotten that his personal attendant's name was Albert. But Bunter had a belief that it was aristocratic to forget servants' names.

'When the dickens is the grub coming?' added Bunter peevishly.

'The – the what?'

'I mean the cold collation. I'm hungry,' said Bunter. 'Look here, you cut off and buck them up, George!'

'Certainly, sir.'

Albert cut off, closing the door softly behind him. Billy Bunter stretched out his fat toes to the fire, and grinned. Some fellows might have been put out by a stately butler like Pilkingham and an army of menservants in livery. Not Bunter! Bunter flattered himself that he knew how to handle servants. The thing was to let the menials see that a fellow was accustomed to this sort of thing, and thought nothing of it. That, Bunter had no doubt, he was doing. He was feeling happy and satisfied. He might not, perhaps, have felt so satisfied could he have heard what Albert respectfully murmured to Mr Pilkingham and what Mr Pilkingham condescendingly said in reply to Albert. Fortunately, he could not hear.

There was a discreet tap on the door.

It opened.

Albert re-entered, followed by two other servants bearing trays. Billy Bunter's eyes glistened behind his big spectacles.

With soft and silent footsteps the servants placed a table beside Bunter, and set the table. Bunter sat up and took notice. At a glance he saw that the grub was going to be good at Cavandale Abbey. It was only a 'cold collation,' but it was excellent; and, still more to the point, it was ample.

Billy Bunter proceeded to enjoy himself.

There was no doubt that he was in clover. He kept Albert in the room to wait upon him while he ate; and Albert was kept fairly busy. Albert was a well-trained young

man, trained under the skilled and experienced Pilkingham; but surprise, and then astonishment dawned on his wooden face as Bunter travelled through the foodstuffs. He wondered whether Mr Bunter was ever going to finish and whether he would burst before he had finished, or after he had finished.

Bunter finished at last. He finished with regret, for there were still foodstuffs on the table. But even Bunter had a limit.

'Herbert!'

'Sir!'

'You may bring me a box of cigarettes.'

The table was cleared – Bunter had not left much to clear except crockery – and Bunter leaned back in an armchair and lighted a cigarette. He was not at Greyfriars now; and the gimlet eye of Quelch could not fall upon him. So Bunter could let himself go.

He was careful, however, not to smoke the cigarette through. He had a misgiving that it might disturb the foodstuffs he had packed away.

Guests at Cavandale Abbey had little to complain of. Bunter was going to enjoy his Christmas holidays.

There was no doubt about that! There had been doubt – very serious doubt – but there was none now. Bunter was deeply thankful that he had not been able to hook on to the Bounder for Christmas – that he had failed to glue himself to Harry Wharton & Co. Better than any of these was Christmas with Lord Cavandale – much better! William George Bunter was a pig in clover!

 JEEVES AND THE YULE-TIDE SPIRIT

P. G. WODEHOUSE

The letter arrived on the morning of the sixteenth. I was pushing a bit of breakfast into the Wooster face at the moment and, feeling fairly well-fortified with coffee and kippers, I decided to break the news to Jeeves without delay. As Shakespeare says, if you're going to do a thing you might just as well pop right at it and get it over. The man would be disappointed, of course, and possibly even chagrined: but, dash it all, a splash of disappointment here and there does a fellow good. Makes him realize that life is stern and life is earnest.

'Oh, Jeeves,' I said.

'Sir?'

'We have here a communication from Lady Wickham. She has written inviting me to Skeldings for the festives. So you will see about bunging the necessaries together. We repair thither on the twenty-third. Plenty of white ties, Jeeves, also a few hearty country suits for use in the daytime. We shall be there some little time, I expect.'

There was a pause. I could feel he was directing a frosty gaze at me, but I dug into the marmalade and refused to meet it.

'I thought I understood you to say, sir, that you proposed to visit Monte Carlo immediately after Christmas.'

'I know. But that's all off. Plans changed.'

'Very good, sir.'

At this point the telephone rang, tiding over very nicely what had threatened to be an awkward moment. Jeeves unhooked the receiver.

'Yes? ... Yes, madam ... Very good, madam. Here is Mr Wooster.' He handed me the instrument. 'Mrs Spenser Gregson, sir.'

You know, every now and then I can't help feeling that Jeeves is losing his grip. In his prime it would have been with him the work of a moment to have told Aunt Agatha that I was not at home. I gave him one of those reproachful glances, and took the machine.

'Hullo,' I said. 'Yes? Hullo? Hullo? Bertie speaking. Hullo? Hullo? Hullo?'

'Don't keep on saying Hullo,' yipped the old relative in her customary curt manner. 'You're not a parrot. Sometimes I wish you were, because then you might have a little sense.'

Quite the wrong sort of tone to adopt towards a fellow in the early morning, of course, but what can one do?

'Bertie, Lady Wickham tells me she has invited you to Skeldings for Christmas. Are you going?'

'Rather!'

'Well, mind you behave yourself. Lady Wickham is an old friend of mine.'

I was in no mood for this sort of thing over the telephone. Face to face, I'm not saying, but at the end of a wire, no.

'I shall naturally endeavour, Aunt Agatha,' I replied stiffly, 'to conduct myself in a manner befitting an English gentleman paying a visit –'

'What did you say? Speak up. I can't hear.'

'I said Right-ho.'

'Oh? Well, mind you do. And there's another reason why I particularly wish you to be as little of an imbecile as you can manage while at Skeldings. Sir Roderick Glossop will be there.'

'What!'

'Don't bellow like that. You nearly deafened me.'

'Did you say Sir Roderick Glossop?'

'I did.'

'You don't mean Tuppy Glossop?'

'I mean Sir Roderick Glossop. Which was my reason for saying Sir Roderick Glossop. Now, Bertie, I want you to listen to me attentively. Are you there?'

'Yes. Still here.'

'Well, then, listen. I have at last succeeded, after incredible difficulty, and in face of all the evidence, in almost persuading Sir Roderick that you are not actually insane. He is prepared to suspend judgement until he has seen you once more. On your behaviour at Skeldings, therefore –'

But I had hung up the receiver. Shaken. That's what I was. S. to the core.

Stop me if I've told you this before: but, in case you don't know, let me just mention the facts in the matter of this Glossop. He was a formidable old bird with a bald head and outsize eyebrows, by profession a loony-doctor. How it happened, I couldn't tell you to this day, but I once got engaged to his daughter, Honoria, a ghastly dynamic exhibit who read Nietzsche and had a laugh like waves breaking on a stern and rock-bound coast. The fixture was scratched owing to events occurring which convinced the old boy that I was off my napper; and since then he has always had my name at the top of his list of 'Loonies I have Lunched With'.

It seemed to me that even at Christmas-time, with all the peace on earth and goodwill towards men that there is knocking about at that season, a reunion with this bloke was likely to be tough going. If I hadn't had more than one particularly good reason for wanting to go to Skeldings, I'd have called the thing off.

'Jeeves,' I said, all of a twitter, 'Do you know what? Sir Roderick Glossop is going to be at Lady Wickham's.'

'Very good, sir. If you have finished breakfast, I will clear away.'

Cold and haughty. No symp. None of the rallying-round spirit which one likes to see. As I had anticipated, the information that we were not going to Monte Carlo had got in amongst him. There is a keen sporting streak in Jeeves, and I knew he had been looking forward to a little flutter at the tables.

We Woosters can wear the mask. I ignored his lack of decent feeling.

'Do so, Jeeves,' I said proudly, 'and with all convenient speed.'

Relations continued pretty fairly strained all through the rest of the week. There was a frigid detachment in the way the man brought me my dollop of tea in the mornings. Going down to Skeldings in the car on the afternoon of the twenty-third, he was aloof and reserved. And before dinner on the first night of my visit he put the studs in my dress-shirt in what I can only call a marked manner. The whole thing was extremely painful, and it seemed to me, as I lay in bed, on the morning of the twenty-fourth, that the only step to take was to put the whole facts of the case before him and trust to his native good sense to effect an understanding.

I was feeling considerably in the pink that morning. Everything had gone like a breeze. My hostess, Lady Wickham, was a beaky female built far too closely on the lines of my Aunt Agatha for comfort, but she had seemed matey enough on my arrival. Her daughter, Roberta, had welcomed me with a warmth which, I'm bound to say, had set the old heart-strings fluttering a bit. And Sir Roderick, in the brief moment we had had together, appeared to have let the Yule-tide Spirit soak into him to the most amazing extent. When he saw me, his mouth sort of flickered at one corner, which I took to be his idea of smiling, and he said 'Ha, young man!' Not particularly chummily, but he said it: and my view was that it practically amounted to the lion lying down with the lamb.

So, all in all, life at this juncture seemed pretty well all to the mustard, and I decided to tell Jeeves exactly how matters stood.

'Jeeves,' I said, as he appeared with the steaming.

'Sir?'

'Touching on this business of our being here, I would like to say a few words of explanation. I consider that you have a right to the facts.'

'Sir?'

'I'm afraid scratching that Monte Carlo trip has been a bit of a jar for you, Jeeves.'

'Not at all, sir.'

'Oh, yes, it has. The heart was set on wintering in the world's good old Plague Spot, I know. I saw your eye light up when I said we were due for a visit there. You snorted a bit and your fingers twitched. I know, I know. And now that there has been a change of programme the iron has entered into your soul.'

'Not at all, sir.'

'Oh, yes, it has. I've seen it. Very well, then, what I wish to impress upon you, Jeeves, is that I have not been actuated in this matter by any mere idle whim. It was through no light and airy caprice that I accepted this invitation to Lady Wickham's. I have been angling for it for weeks, prompted by many considerations. In the first place, does one get the Yule-tide spirit at a spot like Monte Carlo?'

'Does one desire the Yule-tide spirit, sir?'

'Certainly one does. I am all for it. Well, that's one thing. Now here's another. It was imperative that I should come to Skeldings for Christmas, Jeeves, because I knew that young Tuppy Glossop was going to be here.'

'Sir Roderick Glossop, sir?'

'His nephew. You may have observed hanging about the place a fellow with light hair and a Cheshire-cat grin. That is Tuppy, and I have been anxious for some time to get to grips with him. I have it in for that man of wrath. Listen to the facts, Jeeves, and tell me if I am not justified in planning a hideous vengeance.' I took a sip of tea, for the mere memory of my wrongs had shaken me. 'In spite of the fact that young Tuppy is the nephew of Sir Roderick Glossop, at whose hands, Jeeves, as you are aware, I have suffered much, I fraternized with him freely, both at the Drones Club and elsewhere. I said to myself that a man is not to be blamed for his relations, and that I would hate to have my pals hold my Aunt Agatha, for instance, against me. Broad-minded, Jeeves, I think?'

'Extremely, sir.'

'Well, then, as I say, I sought this Tuppy out, Jeeves, and hobnobbed, and what do you think he did?'

'I could not say, sir.'

'I will tell you. One night after dinner at the Drones he betted me I wouldn't swing myself across the swimming-bath by the ropes and rings. I took him on and was buzzing along in great style until I came to the last ring. And then I found that this fiend in human shape had looped it back against the rail, thus leaving me hanging in the void with no means of getting ashore to my home and loved ones. There was nothing for it but to drop into the water. He told me that he had often caught fellows that way: and what I maintain, Jeeves, is that, if I can't get back at him somehow at Skeldings – with all the vast resources which a country-house affords at my disposal – I am not the man I was.'

'I see, sir.'

There was still something in his manner which told me that even now he lacked complete sympathy and understanding, so, delicate though the subject was, I decided to put all my cards on the table.

'And now, Jeeves, we come to the most important reason why I had to spend Christmas at Skeldings. Jeeves,' I said, diving into the old cup once more for a moment and bringing myself out wreathed in blushes, 'the fact of the matter is, I'm in love.'

'Indeed, sir?'

'You've seen Miss Roberta Wickham?'

'Yes, sir.'

'Very well, then.'

There was a pause, while I let it sink in.

'During your stay here, Jeeves,' I said, 'you will, no doubt, be thrown a good deal together with Miss Wickham's maid. On such occasions, pitch it strong.'

'Sir?'

'You know what I mean. Tell her I'm rather a good chap. Mention my hidden depths. These things get round. Dwell on the fact that I have a kind heart and was runner-up in the Squash Handicap at the Drones this year. A boost is never wasted, Jeeves.'

'Very good, sir. But –'

'But what?'

'Well, sir —'

'I wish you wouldn't say "Well, sir" in that soupy tone of voice. I have had to speak of this before. The habit is one that is growing upon you. Check it. What's on your mind?'

'I hardly like to take the liberty ...'

'Carry on, Jeeves. We are always glad to hear from you, always.'

'What I was about to remark, if you will excuse me, sir, was that I would scarcely have thought Miss Wickham a suitable —'

'Jeeves,' I said coldly, 'if you have anything to say against the lady, it had better not be said in my presence.'

'Very good, sir.'

'Or anywhere else, for that matter. What is your kick against Miss Wickham?'

'Oh, really, sir!'

'Jeeves, I insist. This is a time for plain speaking. You have beefed about Miss Wickham. I wish to know why.'

'It merely crossed my mind, sir, that for a gentleman of your description Miss Wickham is not a suitable mate.'

'What do you mean by a gentleman of my description?'

'Well, sir —'

'Jeeves!'

'I beg your pardon, sir. The expression escaped me inadvertently. I was about to observe that I can only asseverate —'

'Only what?'

'I can only say that, as you have invited my opinion —'

'But I didn't.'

'I was under the impression that you desired to canvass my views on the matter, sir.'

'Oh? Well, let's have them, anyway.'

'Very good, sir. Then briefly, if I may say so, sir, though Miss Wickham is a charming young lady —'

'There, Jeeves, you spoke an imperial quart. What eyes!'

'Yes, sir.'

'What hair!'

'Very true, sir.'

'And what *espièglerie*, if that's the word I want.'

'The exact word, sir.'

'All right, then. Carry on.'

'I grant Miss Wickham the possession of all these desirable qualities, sir. Nevertheless, considered as a matrimonial prospect for a gentleman of your description, I cannot look upon her as suitable. In my opinion Miss Wickham lacks seriousness, sir. She is too volatile and frivolous. To qualify as Miss Wickham's husband, a gentleman would need to possess a commanding personality and considerable strength of character.'

'Exactly!'

'I would always hesitate to recommend as a life's companion a young lady with quite such a vivid shade of red hair. Red hair, sir, in my opinion, is dangerous.'

I eyed the blighter squarely.

'Jeeves,' I said, 'you're talking rot.'

'Very good, sir.'

'Absolute drivel.'

'Very good, sir.'

'Pure mashed potatoes.'

'Very good, sir.'

'Very good, sir – I mean very good, Jeeves, that will be all,' I said.

And I drank a modicum of tea, with a good deal of hauteur.

It isn't often that I find myself able to prove Jeeves in the wrong, but by dinner-time that night I was in a position to do so, and I did it without delay.

'Touching on that matter we were touching on, Jeeves,' I said, coming in from the bath and tackling him as he studded the shirt, 'I should be glad if you would give your careful attention for a moment. I warn you that what I am about to say is going to make you look pretty silly.'

'Indeed, sir?'

'Yes, Jeeves. Pretty dashed silly it's going to make you look. It may lead you to be rather more careful in future about broadcasting these estimates of yours of people's characters. This morning, if I remember rightly, you stated that Miss Wickham was volatile, frivolous and lacking in seriousness. Am I correct?'

'Quite correct, sir.'

'Then what I have to tell you may cause you to alter that opinion. I went for a walk with Miss Wickham this afternoon: and as we walked, I told her about what young Tuppy Glossop did to me in the swimming-bath at the Drones. She hung upon my words, Jeeves, and was full of sympathy.'

'Indeed, sir?'

'Dripping with it. And that's not all. Almost before I had finished, she was suggesting the ripest, fruitiest, brainiest scheme for bringing young Tuppy's grey hairs in sorrow to the grave that anyone could possibly imagine.'

'That is very gratifying, sir.'

'Gratifying is the word. It appears that at the girls' school where Miss Wickham was educated, Jeeves, it used to become necessary from time to time for the right-thinking element of the community to slip it across certain of the baser sort. Do you know what they did, Jeeves?'

'No, sir.'

'They took a long stick, Jeeves, and – follow me closely here – they tied a darning-needle to the end of it. Then at dead of night, it appears, they sneaked privily into the party of the second part's cubicle and shoved the needle through the bedclothes and punctured her hot-water bottle. Girls are much subtler in these matters than boys, Jeeves. At my old school one would occasionally heave a jug of water over another bloke during the night-watches, but we never thought of effecting the same result in this particularly neat and scientific manner. Well, Jeeves, that was the scheme which Miss Wickham suggested I should work on young Tuppy, and that is the girl you call frivolous and lacking in seriousness. Any girl who can think up a wheeze like that is my idea of a helpmeet. I shall be glad, Jeeves, if by the time I come to bed tonight you have waiting for me in this room a stout stick with a good sharp darning-needle attached.'

'Well, sir –'

I raised my hand.

'Jeeves,' I said. 'Not another word. Stick, one, and needle, darning, good, sharp, one, without fail in this room at eleven-thirty tonight.'

'Very good, sir.'

'Have you any idea where young Tuppy sleeps?'

'I could ascertain, sir.'

'Do so, Jeeves.'

In a few minutes he was back with the necessary informash.

'Mr Glossop is established in the Moat Room, sir.'

'Where's that?'

'The second door on the floor below this, sir.'

'Right-ho, Jeeves. Are the studs in my shirt?'

'Yes, sir.'

'And the links also?'

'Yes, sir.'

'Then push me into it.'

The more I thought about this enterprise which a sense of duty and good citizenship had thrust upon me, the better it seemed to me. I am not a vindictive man, but I felt, as anybody would have felt in my place, that if fellows like young Tuppy are allowed to get away with it the whole fabric of Society and Civilization must inevitably crumble. The task to which I had set myself was one that involved hardship and discomfort, for it meant sitting up till well into the small hours and then padding down a cold corridor, but I did not shrink from it. After all, there is a lot to be said for family tradition. We Woosters did our bit in the Crusades.

It being Christmas Eve, there was, as I had foreseen, a good deal of revelry and what not. First, the village choir surged round and sang carols outside the front door, and then somebody suggested a dance, and after that we hung around chatting of this and that, so that it wasn't till past one that I got to my room. Allowing for everything, it didn't seem that it was going to be safe to start my little expedition till half past two at the earliest: and I'm bound to say that it was only the utmost resolution that kept me from snuggling into the sheets and calling it a day. I'm not much of a lad now for late hours.

However, by half past two everything appeared to be quiet. I shook off the mists of sleep, grabbed the good old stick-and-needle and off along the corridor. And presently, pausing outside the Moat Room, I turned the handle, found the door wasn't locked, and went in.

I suppose a burglar – I mean a real professional who works at the job six nights a week all the year round – gets so that finding himself standing in the dark in somebody else's bedroom means absolutely nothing to him. But for a bird like me, who has had no previous experience, there's a lot to be said in favour of washing the whole thing out and closing the door gently and popping back to bed again. It was only by summoning up all the old bull-dog courage of the Woosters, and reminding myself that if I let this opportunity slip another might never occur, that I managed to stick out what you might call the initial minute of the binge. Then the weakness passed, and Bertram was himself again.

At first when I beetled in, the room had seemed as black as a coal-cellar: but after a bit things began to lighten. The curtains weren't quite drawn over the window and I could see a trifle of the scenery here and there. The bed was opposite the window, with the head against the wall and the end where the feet were jutting out towards where I stood, thus rendering it possible after one had sown the seed, so to speak, to make a quick getaway. There only remained now the rather tricky problem of locating the old hot-water bottle. I mean to say, the one thing you can't do if you want to carry a job like this through with secrecy and dispatch is to stand at the end of the fellow's bed, jabbing the blankets at random with a darning-needle. Before proceeding to anything in the nature of definite steps, it is imperative that you locate the bot.

I was a good deal cheered at this juncture to hear a fruity snore from the direction of the pillows. Reason told me that a bloke who could snore like that wasn't going to be awakened by a trifle. I edged forward and ran a hand in a gingerly sort of way over the coverlet. A moment later I had found the bulge. I steered the good old darning-needle on to it, gripped the stick, and shoved. Then, pulling out the weapon, I sidled towards the door, and in another moment would have been outside, buzzing for home and the good night's rest, when suddenly there was a crash that sent my spine shooting up through the top of my head and the contents of the bed sat up like a jack-in-the-box and said:

'Who's that?'

It just shows how your most careful strategic moves can be the very ones that dish your campaign. In order to facilitate the orderly retreat according to plan I had left the door open, and the beastly thing had slammed like a bomb.

But I wasn't giving much thought to the causes of the explosion, having other things to occupy my mind. What was disturbing me was the discovery that, whoever else the bloke in the bed might be, he was not young Tuppy. Tuppy has one of those high, squeaky voices that sound like the tenor of the village choir failing to hit a high note. This one was something in between the last Trump and a tiger calling for breakfast after being on a diet for a day or two. It was the sort of nasty, rasping voice you hear shouting 'Fore!' when you're one of a slow foursome on the links and are holding up a couple of retired colonels. Among the qualities it lacked were kindliness, suavity, and that sort of dove-like cooing note which makes a fellow feel he has found a friend.

I did not linger. Getting swiftly off the mark, I dived for the door-handle and was off and away, banging the door behind me. I may be a chump in many ways, as my Aunt Agatha will freely attest, but I know when and when not to be among those present.

And I was just about to do the stretch of corridor leading to the stairs in a split second under the record time for the course, when something brought me up with a sudden jerk. One moment, I was all dash and fire and speed; the next, an irresistible force had checked me in my stride and was holding me straining at the leash, as it were.

You know, sometimes it seems to me as if Fate were going out of its way to such an extent to snooter you that you wonder if it's worth while continuing to struggle. The night being a trifle chillier than the dickens, I had donned for this expedition a dressing-gown. It was the tail of this infernal garment that had caught in the door and pipped me at the eleventh hour.

The next moment the door had opened, light was streaming through it, and the bloke with the voice had grabbed me by the arm.

It was Sir Roderick Glossop.

The next thing that happened was a bit of a lull in the proceedings. For about three and a quarter seconds or possibly more we just stood there, drinking each other in, so to speak, the old boy still attached with a limpet-like grip to my elbow. If I hadn't been in a dressing-gown and he in pink pyjamas with a blue stripe, and if he hadn't been glaring quite so much as if he were shortly going to commit a murder, the tableau would have looked rather like one of those advertisements you see in the magazines, where the experienced elder is patting the young man's arm, and saying to him, 'My boy, if you subscribe to the Mutt-Jeff Correspondence School of Oswego, Kan., as I did, you may some day, like me, become Third Assistant Vice-President of the Schenectady Consolidated Nail-File and Eyebrow Tweezer Corporation.'

'You!' said Sir Roderick finally. And in this connection I want to state that it's all rot to say you can't hiss a word that hasn't an 's' in it. The way he pushed out that 'You!' sounded like an angry cobra, and I am betraying no secrets when I mention that it did me no good whatsoever.

By rights, I suppose, at this point I ought to have said something. The best I could manage, however, was a faint, soft bleating sound. Even on ordinary social occasions, when meeting this bloke as man to man and with a clear conscience, I could never be completely at my ease: and now those eyebrows seemed to pierce me like a knife.

'Come in here,' he said, lugging me into the room. 'We don't want to wake the whole house. Now,' he said, depositing me on the carpet and closing the door and doing a bit of eyebrow work, 'kindly inform me what is this latest manifestation of insanity?'

It seemed to me that a light and cheery laugh might help the thing along. So I had a pop at one.

'Don't gibber!' said my genial host. And I'm bound to admit that the light and cheery hadn't come out quite as I'd intended.

I pulled myself together with a strong effort.

'Awfully sorry about all this,' I said in a hearty sort of voice. 'The fact is, I thought you were Tuppy.'

'Kindly refrain from inflicting your idiotic slang on me. What do you mean by the adjective "tuppy"?'

'It isn't so much an adjective, don't you know. More of a noun, I should think, if you examine it squarely. What I mean to say is, I thought you were your nephew.'

'You thought I was my nephew? Why should I be my nephew?'

'What I'm driving at is, I thought this was his room.'

'My nephew and I changed rooms. I have a great dislike for sleeping on an upper floor. I am nervous about fire.'

For the first time since this interview had started, I braced up a trifle. The injustice of the whole thing stirred me to such an extent that for a moment I lost that sense of being a toad under the harrow which had been cramping my style up till now. I even went so far as to eye this pink-pyjamed poltroon with a good deal of contempt and loathing. Just because he had this craven fear of fire and this selfish preference for letting Tuppy be cooked instead of himself should the emergency occur, my nicely-reasoned plans had gone up the spout. I gave him a look, and think I may even have snorted a bit.

'I should have thought that your man-servant would have informed you,' said Sir Roderick, 'that we contemplated making this change. I met him shortly before luncheon and told him to tell you.'

I reeled. Yes, it is not too much to say that I reeled. This extraordinary statement had taken me amidships without any preparation, and it staggered me. That Jeeves had been aware all along that this old crumb would be the occupant of the bed which I was proposing to prod with darning-needles and had let me rush upon my doom without a word of warning was almost beyond belief. You might say I was aghast. Yes, practically aghast.

'You told Jeeves that you were going to sleep in this room?' I gasped.

'I did. I was aware that you and my nephew were on terms of intimacy, and I wished to spare myself the possibility of a visit from you. I confess that it never occurred to me that such a visit was to be anticipated at three o'clock in the morning. What the devil do you mean,' he barked, suddenly hotting up, 'by prowling about the house at this hour? And what is that thing in your hand?'

I looked down, and found that I was still grasping the stick. I give you my honest word that, what with the maelstrom of emotions into which his relevation about Jeeves had cast me, the discovery came as an absolute surprise.

'This?' I said. 'Oh, yes.'

'What do you mean. Oh yes? What is it?'

'Well, it's a long story –'

'We have the night before us.'

'It's this way. I will ask you to picture me some weeks ago, perfectly peaceful and inoffensive, after dinner at the Drones, smoking a thoughtful cigarette and ...'

I broke off. The man wasn't listening. He was goggling in a rapt sort of way at the end of the bed, from which there had now begun to drip on to the carpet a series of drops.

'Good heavens!'

'– thoughtful cigarette and chatting pleasantly of this and that ...'

I broke off again. He had lifted the sheets and was gazing at the corpse of the hot-water bottle.

'Did you do this?' he said in a low, strangled sort of voice.

'Er – yes. As a matter of fact, yes. I was just going to tell you –'

'And your aunt tried to persuade me that you were not insane!'

'I'm not. Absolutely not. If you'll just let me explain.'

'I will do nothing of the kind.'

'It all began –'

'Silence!'

'Right-ho.'

He did some deep-breathing exercises through the nose.

'My bed is drenched!'

'The way it all began –'

'Be quiet!' He heaved somewhat for awhile. 'You wretched, miserable idiot,' he said, 'kindly inform me which bedroom you are supposed to be occupying?'

'It's on the floor above. The Clock Room.'

'Thank you. I will find it.'

'Eh?'

He gave me the eyebrow.

'I propose,' he said, 'to pass the remainder of the night in your room, where, I presume, there is a bed in a condition to be slept in. You may bestow yourself as comfortably as you can here. I will wish you good-night.'

He buzzed off, leaving me flat.

Well, we Woosters are old campaigners. We can take the rough with the smooth. But to say that I liked the prospect now before me would be paltering with the truth. One glance at the bed told me that any idea of sleeping there was out. A goldfish could have done it, but not Bertram. After a bit of a look round, I decided that the best chance of getting a sort of night's rest was to doss as well as I could in the armchair. I pinched a couple of pillows off the bed, shoved the hearth-rug over my knees, and sat down and started counting sheep.

But it wasn't any good. The old lemon was sizzling much too much to admit of anything in the nature of slumber. This hideous revelation of the blackness of Jeeves's treachery kept coming back to me every time I nearly succeeded in dropping off: and, what's more, it seemed to get colder and colder as the long night wore on. I was just wondering if I would ever get to sleep again in this world when a voice at my elbow said 'Good-morning, sir,' and I sat up with a jerk.

I could have sworn I hadn't so much as dozed off for even a minute, but apparently I had. For the curtains were drawn back and daylight was coming in through the window and there was Jeeves standing beside me with a cup of tea on a tray.

'Merry Christmas, sir!'

I reached out a feeble hand for the restoring brew. I swallowed a mouthful or two, and felt a little better. I was aching in every limb and the dome felt like lead, but I was now able to think with a certain amount of clearness, and I fixed the man with a stony eye and prepared to let him have it.

'You think so, do you?' I said. 'Much, let me tell you, depends on what you mean by the adjective "merry". If, moreover, you suppose that it is going to be merry for you, correct that impression. Jeeves,' I said, taking another half-oz. of tea and speaking in a cold, measured voice, 'I wish to ask you one question. Did you or did you not know that Sir Roderick Glossop was sleeping in this room last night?'

'Yes, sir.'

'You admit it!'

'Yes, sir.'

'And you didn't tell me!'

'No, sir. I thought it would be more judicious not to do so.'

'Jeeves –'

'If you will allow me to explain, sir.'

'Explain!'

'I was aware that my silence might lead to something in the nature of an embarrassing contretemps, sir —'

'You thought that, did you?'

'Yes, sir.'

'You were a good guesser,' I said, sucking down further Bohea.

'But it seemed to me, sir, that whatever might occur was all for the best.'

I would have put in a crisp word or two here, but he carried on without giving me the opp.

'I thought that possibly, on reflection, sir, your views being what they are, you would prefer your relations with Sir Roderick Glossop and his family to be distant rather than cordial.'

'My views? What do you mean, my views?'

'As regards a matrimonial alliance with Miss Honoria Glossop, sir.'

Something like an electric shock seemed to zip through me. The man had opened up a new line of thought. I suddenly saw what he was driving at, and realized all in a flash that I had been wronging this faithful fellow. All the while I supposed he had been landing me in the soup, he had really been steering me away from it. It was like those stories one used to read as a kid about the traveller going along on a dark night and his dog grabs him by the leg of his trousers and he says 'Down, sir! What are you doing, Rover?' and the dog hangs on and he gets rather hot under the collar and curses a bit but the dog won't let him go and then suddenly the moon shines through the clouds and he finds he's been standing on the edge of a precipice and one more step would have – well, anyway, you get the idea: and what I'm driving at is that much the same sort of thing seemed to have been happening now.

It's perfectly amazing how a fellow will let himself get off his guard and ignore the perils which surround him. I give you my honest word, it had never struck me till this moment that my Aunt Agatha had been scheming to get me in right with Sir Roderick so that I should eventually be received back into the fold, if you see what I mean, and subsequently pushed off on Honoria.

'My God, Jeeves!' I said, paling.

'Precisely, sir.'

'You think there was a risk?'

'I do, sir. A very grave risk.'

A disturbing thought struck me.

'But, Jeeves, on calm reflection won't Sir Roderick have gathered by now that my objective was young Tuppy and that puncturing his hot-water bottle was just one of those things that occur when the Yule-tide Spirit is abroad – one of those things that have to be overlooked and taken with the indulgent smile and the fatherly shake of the head? What I mean is he'll realize that I wasn't trying to snooter him, and then all the good work will have been wasted.'

'No, sir. I fancy not. That might possibly have been Sir Roderick's mental reaction, had it not been for the second incident.'

'The second incident?'

'During the night, sir, while Sir Roderick was occupying your bed, somebody entered the room, pierced his hot-water bottle with some sharp instrument, and vanished in the darkness.'

I could make nothing of this.

'What! Do you think I walked in my sleep?'

'No, sir. It was young Mr Glossop who did it. I encountered him this morning, sir, shortly before I came here. He was in cheerful spirits and enquired of me how you were feeling about the incident. Not being aware that his victim had been Sir Roderick.'

'But, Jeeves, what an amazing coincidence!'

'Sir?'

'Why, young Tuppy getting exactly the same idea as I did. Or, rather, as Miss Wickham did. You can't say that's not rummy. A miracle, I call it.'

'Not altogether, sir. It appears that he received the suggestion from the young lady.'

'From Miss Wickham?'

'Yes, sir.'

'You mean to say that, after she had put me up to the scheme of puncturing Tuppy's hot-water bottle, she went away and tipped Tuppy off to puncturing mine?'

'Precisely, sir. She is a young lady with a keen sense of humour, sir.'

I sat there, you might say stunned. When I thought how near I had come to offering the heart and hand to a girl capable of double-crossing a strong man's honest love like that, I shivered.

'Are you cold, sir?'

'No, Jeeves. Just shuddering.'

'The occurrence, if I may take the liberty of saying so, sir, will perhaps lend colour to the view which I put forward yesterday that Miss Wickham, though in many respects a charming young lady –'

I raised the hand.

'Say no more, Jeeves,' I replied. 'Love is dead.'

'Very good, sir.'

I brooded for a while.

'You've seen Sir Roderick this morning, then?'

'Yes, sir.'

'How did he seem?'

'A trifle feverish, sir.'

'Feverish?'

'A little emotional, sir. He expressed a strong desire to meet you, sir.'

'What would you advise?'

'If you were to slip out by the back entrance as soon as you are dressed, sir, it would be possible for you to make your way across the field without being observed and reach the village, where you could hire an automobile to take you to London. I could bring on your effects later in your own car.'

'But London, Jeeves? Is any man safe? My Aunt Agatha is in London.'

'Yes, sir.'

'Well, then?'

He regarded me for a moment with a fathomless eye,

'I think the best plan, sir, would be for you to leave England, which is not pleasant at this time of the year, for some little while. I would not take the liberty of dictating your movements, sir, but as you already have accommodation engaged on the Blue Train for Monte Carlo for the day after tomorrow –'

'But you cancelled the booking?'

'No, sir.'

'I thought you had.'

'No, sir.'

'I told you to.'

'Yes, sir. It was remiss of me, but the matter slipped my mind.'

'Oh?'

'Yes, sir.'

'All right, Jeeves. Monte Carlo ho, then.'

'Very good, sir.'

'It's lucky, as things have turned out, that you forgot to cancel that booking.'

'Very fortunate indeed, sir. If you will wait here, sir, I will return to your room and procure a suit of clothes.'

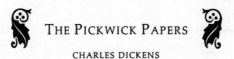

THE PICKWICK PAPERS

CHARLES DICKENS

From the centre of the ceiling of this kitchen, old Wardle had just suspended, with his own hands, a huge branch of mistletoe, and this same branch of mistletoe instantaneously gave rise to a scene of general and most delightful struggling and confusion; in the midst of which, Mr Pickwick, with a gallantry that would have done honour to a descendant of Lady Tollimglower herself, took the old lady by the hand, led her beneath the mystic branch, and saluted her in all courtesy and decorum. The old lady submitted to this piece of practical politeness with all the dignity which befitted so important and serious a solemnity, but the younger ladies, not being so thoroughly imbued with a superstitious veneration for the custom: or imagining that the value of a salute is very much enhanced if it cost a little trouble to obtain it: screamed and struggled, and ran into corners, and threatened and remonstrated, and did everything but leave the room, until some of the less adventurous gentlemen were on the point of desisting, when they all at once found it useless to resist any longer, and submitted to be kissed with a good grace. Mr Winkle kissed the young lady with the black eyes, and Mr Snodgrass kissed Emily, and Mr Weller, not being particular about the form of being under the mistletoe, kissed Emma and the other female servants, just as he caught them. As to the poor relations, they kissed everybody, not even excepting the plainer portions of the young-lady visitors, who, in their excessive confusion, ran right under the mistletoe, as soon as it was hung up, without knowing it! Wardle stood with his back to the fire, surveying the whole scene, with the utmost satisfaction; and the fat boy took the opportunity of appropriating to his own use, and summarily devouring, a particularly fine mince-pie, that had been carefully put by, for somebody else.

Now, the screaming had subsided, and faces were in a glow, and curls in a tangle, and Mr Pickwick, after kissing the old lady as before mentioned, was standing under the mistletoe, looking with a very pleased countenance on all that was passing around him, when the young lady with the black eyes, after a little whispering with the other young ladies, made a sudden dart forward, and, putting her arm round Mr Pickwick's neck, saluted him affectionately on the left cheek; and before Mr Pickwick distinctly knew what was the matter, he was surrounded by the whole body, and kissed by every one of them.

It was a pleasant thing to see Mr Pickwick in the centre of the group, now pulled this way, and then that, and first kissed on the chin, and then on the nose, and then on the spectacles: and to hear the peals of laughter which were raised on every side; but it was a still more pleasant thing to see Mr Pickwick, blinded shortly afterwards with a silk handkerchief, falling up against the wall, and scrambling into corners, and going through all the mysteries of blind-man's buff, with the utmost relish for the game, until at last he caught one of the poor relations, and then had to evade the blind-man himself, which he did with a nimbleness and agility that elicited the admiration and applause of all beholders. The poor relations caught the people who they thought would like it, and, when the game flagged, got caught themselves. When they were all tired of blind-man's buff, there was a great game at snap-dragon, and when fingers enough were burned with that, and all the raisins were gone, they sat down by the huge fire of blazing logs to a substantial supper, and a mighty bowl of wassail, something smaller than an ordinary wash-house copper, in which the hot apples were hissing and bubbling with a rich look, and a jolly sound, that were perfectly irresistible.

'This,' said Mr Pickwick, looking round him, 'this is, indeed, comfort.'

 ## MISTLETOE

WALTER DE LA MARE

Sitting under the mistletoe
(Pale green, fairy mistletoe)
One last candle burning low,
All the sleepy dancers gone,
Just one candle burning on,
Shadows lurking everywhere:
Someone came, and kissed me there.

Tired I was; my head would go
Nodding under the mistletoe
(Pale green, fairy mistletoe)
No footstep came, no voice, but only,
Just as I sat there, sleepy, lonely,
Stooped in the still and shadowy air,
Lips unseen – and kissed me there.

THE DIARY OF A NOBODY

GEORGE AND WEEDON GROSSMITH

DECEMBER 24.   I am a poor man, but I would gladly give ten shillings to find out who sent me the insulting Christmas card I received this morning. I never insult people; why should they insult me? The worst part of the transaction is, that I find myself suspecting all my friends. The handwriting on the envelope is evidently disguised, being written sloping the wrong way. I cannot think either Gowing or Cummings would do such a mean thing. Lupin [his son] denied all knowledge of it, and I believe him; although I disapprove of his laughing and sympathizing with the offender. Mr Franching would be above such an act; and I don't think any of the Mutlars would descend to such a course. I wonder if Pitt, that impudent clerk at the office, did it? Or Mrs Birrell, the charwoman, or Burwin-Fosselton? The writing is too good for the former.

CHRISTMAS DAY.   We caught the 10.20 train at Paddington, and spent a pleasant day at Carrie's [his wife's] mother's. The country was quite nice and pleasant, although the roads were sloppy. We dined in the middle of the day, just ten of us, and talked over old times. If everybody had a nice, *un*interfering mother-in-law, such as I have, what a deal of happiness there would be in the world. Being all in good spirits, I proposed her health; and I made, I think, a very good speech.

I concluded, rather neatly, by saying: 'On an occasion like this – whether relatives, friends, or acquaintances – we are all inspired with good feelings towards each other. We are of one mind, and think only of love and friendship. Those who have quarrelled with absent friends should kiss and make up. Those who happily have *not* fallen out, can kiss all the same.'

I saw the tears in the eyes of both Carrie and her mother, and must say I felt very flattered by the compliment. That dear old Reverend John Panzy Smith, who married us, made a most cheerful and amusing speech, and said he should act on my suggestion respecting the kissing. He then walked round the table and kissed all the ladies, including Carrie. Of course one did not object to this: but I was more than staggered when a young fellow named Moss, who was a stranger to me, and who had scarcely spoken a word through dinner, jumped up suddenly with a sprig of mistletoe, and exclaimed: 'Hulloh! I don't see why I shouldn't be in on this scene.' Before one could realize what he was about to do, he kissed Carrie and the rest of the ladies.

Fortunately the matter was treated as a joke, and we all laughed; but it was a dangerous experiment, and I felt very uneasy for a moment as to the result. I subsequently referred to the matter to Carrie, but she said: 'Oh, he's not much more than a boy.' I said that he had a very large moustache for a boy. Carrie replied: 'I didn't say he was not a nice boy.'

DECEMBER 26.   I did not sleep very well last night; I never do in a strange bed. I feel a little indigestion, which one must expect at this time of the year. Carrie and I returned to Town in the evening. Lupin came in late. He said he enjoyed his Christmas, and added: 'I feel as fit as a Lowther Arcade fiddle, and only require a little more "oof" to feel as fit as a £500 Stradivarius.' I have long since given up trying to understand Lupin's slang, or asking him to explain it.

DEAR OLD FRIEND

AND ABSENTEE ...

Next, some Christmas letters. Thomas Manning was an old school friend of Charles Lamb's from his days at Christ's Hospital. He was a celebrated traveller and one of the first Englishmen to master the Chinese language. He was away in the Far East when Lamb wrote to him in 1815, offering him mock condolences for being so far away from an English Christmas.

John Keats, on the other hand, had love on his mind on Christmas Day 1818 and gives us a vivid – some would say disenchanted – picture of his lady-love, Fanny Brawne.

Macaulay's Christmas is remarkable because it was his last. On the 28th December he wrote his final letter, enclosing £25 to a poor clergyman, and died that evening.

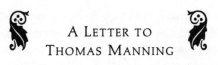
December 25th 1815

Dear Old Friend and Absentee,

This is Christmas Day, 1815, with us; what it may be with you I don't know; the 12th June next year perhaps; and if it should be the consecrative season with you, I don't see how you can keep it. You have no turkeys; you would not desecrate the season by offering up a withered Chinese Lantern instead of the Savoury grand Nrofolcian Holocaust that smokes all around my nostrils at this moment from a thousand firesides. Then what puddings have you? Where will you get holly to stick in your

Churches, or Churches to stick your dried tea leaves (that must be the substitute) in? What memorials you can have of the Holy time I see not. A chopped missionary or two may keep up the thin idea of Lent and the Wilderness; but what standing evidence have you of the Nativity?

'Tis our rosy-cheeked homestalled divines, whose faces shine to the tune of 'Unto us a Child was born,' faces fragrant with the mince-pies of half a century, that alone can authenticate the cheerful mystery. I feel my bowels refreshed with the holy-tide; my zeal is great against the unedified heathen. Down with the Pagodas, down with the Idols – Ching-Chong-fo – and his foolish Priesthood. Come out of Babylon, O my friend, for her time is come, and the child that is native and the proselyte of her gates, shall kindle and smoke together. And in sober sense what makes you so long from among us, Manning?

You must not expect to see the same England again which you left.

A LETTER TO HIS SISTER

JOHN KEATS

Friday, December 25th 1818

... I think of going into Hampshire this Christmas to Mr Snook's – they say I shall be very much amused – but I don't know – I think I am too huge a mind for study – I must do it – I must wait at home and let those who wish to come to see me, I cannot always be (how do you spell it?) trapsing ...

Shall I give you Miss Brawne? She is about my height – with a fine style of countenance of the lengthened sort – she wants sentiment in every feature – She manages to make her hair look well – her nostrils are fine – though a little painful – her mouth is bad and good – her profile is better than her full-face which indeed is not full but pale and thin, without showing any bone. Her shape is very graceful and so are her movements – her arms are good, her hands baddish – her feet tolerable. She is not seventeen – but she is ignorant – monstrous in her behaviour, flying out in all directions – calling people such names that I was forced lately to make use of the term Minx – this I think, not from any innate vice but from a penchant she has for acting stylishly – I am, however, tired of such style, and shall decline any more of it ...

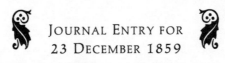

JOURNAL ENTRY FOR
23 DECEMBER 1859

LORD MACAULAY

This morning I had scarcely left my closet when down came the ceiling in large masses. I should certainly have been stunned, probably killed, if I had stayed a few minutes longer. I stayed by my fire, not exerting myself to write, but making Christmas calculations, and reading. An odd declaration by Dickens that he did not mean Leigh Hunt by Harold Skimpole. Yet he owns that he took the light externals of the character from Leigh Hunt, and surely it is by those light externals that the bulk of mankind will always recognize character. Besides, it is to be observed that the vices of Harold Skimpole are vices to which Leigh Hunt had, to say the least, some little leaning, and which the world generally imputed to him most unsparingly. That he had loose notions of *meum* and *tuum*, that he had no high feeling of independence, that he had no sense of obligation, that he took money whenever he could get it, that he felt no gratitude for it, that he was just as ready to defame a person who had relieved his distress as a person who had refused him relief – these were things which, as Dickens must have known, were said, truly or falsely, about Leigh Hunt, and had made a deep impression on the public mind. Indeed, Leigh Hunt had said himself, 'I have some peculiar notions about money. They will be found to involve considerable differences of opinion with the community, particularly in a commercial country. I have not that honour of being under obligation which is thought an essential refinement in money matters.' This is Harold Skimpole all over. How then can Dickens doubt that Harold Skimpole should be supposed to be a portrait of Leigh Hunt?

And It Came to Pass in Those Days . . .

Now for the Nativity itself. We begin with the passage in Isaiah which presages it, and the Gospel which tells it best. It seems to overawe many writers and the anthologies are full of trite poetry and prose on the theme. Yet T. S. Eliot's 'Journey of the Magi' has its own curious haunting quality while G. K. Chesterton's 'A Christmas Carol' has a simple lyric beauty reminiscent of Swinburne; meanwhile Ian Serraillier brings a welcome informality to the hallowed scene and in 'The Four Wise Men' Michel Tournier has the brilliantly odd notion of telling the story through the eyes of the ass.

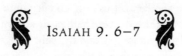

Isaiah 9. 6–7

For unto us a child is born, unto us a son is given: and the government shall be upon his shoulder: and his name shall be called Wonderful, Counsellor, The mighty God, The everlasting Father, The Prince of Peace. Of the increase of his government and peace there shall be no end, upon the throne of David, and upon his kingdom, to order it, and to establish it with judgment and with justice from henceforth even for ever. The zeal of the Lord of hosts will perform this.

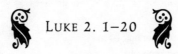

Luke 2. 1–20

And it came to pass in those days, that there went out a decree from Caesar Augustus, that all the world should be taxed. (And this taxing was first made when Cyrenius was governor of Syria.) And all went to be taxed, every one into his own city. And Joseph also went up from Galilee, out of the city of Nazareth, into Judaea, unto the city of David, which is called Bethlehem; (because he was of the house and lineage of David:) to be taxed with Mary his espoused wife, being great with child. And so it was, that, while they were there, the days were accomplished that she should be delivered. And she brought forth her firstborn son, and wrapped him in swaddling clothes, and laid him in a manger; because there was no room for them in the inn. And there were in the same country shepherds abiding in the field, keeping watch over their flock by night. And, lo, the angel of the Lord came upon them, and the glory of the Lord shone round about them: and they were sore afraid. And the angel said unto them, Fear not: for, behold, I bring you good tidings of great joy, which shall be to all people. For unto you is born this day in the city of David a Saviour, which is Christ the Lord. And this shall be a sign unto you; Ye shall find the babe wrapped in swaddling clothes, lying in a manger. And suddenly there was with the angel a multitude of the heavenly host praising God, and saying, Glory to God in the highest, and on earth peace, good will toward men. And it came to pass, as the angels were gone away from them into heaven, the shepherds said one to another, Let us now go even unto Bethlehem, and see this thing which is come to pass, which the Lord hath made known unto us. And they came with haste, and found Mary, and Joseph, and the babe lying in a manger. And when they had seen it, they made known abroad the saying which was told them concerning this child. And all they that heard it wondered at those things which were told them by the shepherds. But Mary kept all these things, and pondered them in her heart. And the shepherds returned, glorifying and praising God for all the things that they had heard and seen, as it was told unto them.

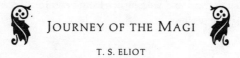

Journey of the Magi

T. S. ELIOT

'A cold coming we had of it,
Just the worst time of the year
For a journey, and such a long journey:
The ways deep and the weather sharp,
The very dead of winter.'
And the camels galled, sore-footed, refractory,
Lying down in the melting snow.
There were times we regretted
The summer palaces on slopes, the terraces,
And the silken girls bringing sherbet.
Then the camel men cursing and grumbling
And running away, and wanting their liquor and women,
And the night-fires going out, and the lack of shelters,
And the cities hostile and the towns unfriendly
And the villages dirty and charging high prices:
A hard time we had of it.
At the end we preferred to travel all night,
Sleeping in snatches,
With the voices singing in our ears, saying
That this was all folly.

*

Then at dawn we came down to a temperate valley,
Wet, below the snow line, smelling of vegetation,
With a running stream and a water-mill beating the darkness,
And three trees on the low sky.
And an old white horse galloped away in the meadow.
Then we came to a tavern with vine-leaves over the lintel,
Six hands at an open door dicing for pieces of silver,
And feet kicking the empty wine-skins.
But there was no information, and so we continued
And arrived at evening, not a moment too soon
Finding the place; it was (you may say) satisfactory.

All this was a long time ago, I remember,
And I would do it again, but set down
This set down
This: were we led all that way for
Birth or Death? There was a Birth, certainly,
We had evidence and no doubt. I had seen birth and death,
But had thought they were different; this Birth was
Hard and bitter agony for us, like Death, our death.
We returned to our places, these Kingdoms,
But no longer at ease here, in the old dispensation,
With an alien people clutching their gods.
I should be glad of another death.

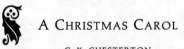

A CHRISTMAS CAROL

G. K. CHESTERTON

The Christ-child lay on Mary's lap,
    His hair was like a light,
(O weary, weary were the world,
    But here is all aright.)

The Christ-child lay on Mary's breast,
    His hair was like a star.
(O stern and cunning are the kings,
    But here the true hearts are.)

The Christ-child lay on Mary's heart,
    His hair was like a fire.
(O weary, weary is the world,
    But here the world's desire.)

The Christ-child stood at Mary's knee,
    His hair was like a crown,
And all the flowers looked up at him,
    And all the stars looked down.

THE MAYOR
AND THE SIMPLETON

IAN SERRAILLIER

They followed the star to Bethlehem –
Boolo the Baker, Barleycorn the farmer,
old Darby and Joan, a small boy Peter, and
a simpleton whose name was Innocent.
Over the snowfields and the frozen rutted lanes
they followed the Star to Bethlehem.

Innocent stood at the stable door
and watched them enter. A flower
stuck out of his yellow hair; his mouth gaped open
like a drawer that wouldn't shut.
He beamed upon the child where he lay
among the oxen, in swaddling clothes in the hay,
his blue eyes shining steady as the Star overhead;
beside him old Joseph and
Mary his mother, smiling.
                                    Innocent was delighted.

They brought gifts with them – Boolo, some fresh crusty loaves
(warm from the baking) which he laid
at the feet of the infant Jesus, kneeling
in all humility.
                                    Innocent was delighted.

Barleycorn brought two baskets – one with a dozen eggs,
the other with two chickens – which he laid
at the feet of the infant Jesus, kneeling
in all humility.
                                    Innocent was delighted.

Darby and Joan brought apples and pears from their garden,
wrapped in her apron and stuffed
in the pockets of his trousers; the little boy
a pot of geraniums – he had grown them himself.
And they laid them

at the feet of the infant Jesus, kneeling
in all humility.
                                    Innocent was delighted.

The mayor rolled up in his coach with a jingle of bells
and a great to-do. He stepped out with a flourish
and fell flat on his face in the snow. His footmen
picked him up and opened his splendid
crimson umbrella. Then he strutted to the door,
while the white flakes floated down
and covered it with spots. He was proud of his umbrella
and didn't mean to give it away.

Shaking the snow off on to the stable floor,
the mayor peered down at the child where he lay
among the oxen, in swaddling clothes in the hay,
his blue eyes shining steady as the Star overhead,
beside him old Joseph and
Mary his mother, smiling.
                                    Innocent was puzzled.

And the mayor said: 'On this important occasion
each must take a share in the general thanksgiving.
Hence the humble gifts – the very humble gifts –
which I see before me. My own contribution
is something special – a speech. I made it up myself and I'm sure
you'll all like it. Ahem. Pray silence for the mayor.'

'Moo, moo,' said the oxen.
                          'My fellow citizens,
the happy event I refer to – in which we all rejoice –
has caused a considerable stir
in the parish . . .'
                     'in the whole world,' said a voice.
Who spoke? Could it be Innocent, always so shy,
timid as a butterfly, frightened
as a sparrow with a broken wing? Yes, it was he.
Now God had made him bold.

'I fear I must start again,' said the mayor.
'My fellow citizens, in the name of the people of this parish
I am proud to welcome one
who promises so well . . .'

'He is the Son of Heaven,'
said Innocent.
            The mayor took no notice.
'I prophesy a fine future for him,
almost – you might say – spectacular.
He'll do us all credit. At the same time I salute in particular
the child's mother, the poor woman who ...'
    'She is not poor but the richest, most radiant
of mothers.'
    'Simpleton, how dare you interrupt!'
snapped the mayor.

But God, who loves the humble, heard him not.
He made him listen, giving Innocent the words:
'Mr Mayor, you don't understand. This birth
is no local event. The child is Jesus,
King of kings and Lord of lords.
A stable is his place and poverty his dwelling-place –
yet he has come to save the world. No speech
is worthy of him ...'
                        'Rubbish!' said the mayor.
'I took a lot of trouble. It's a rare
and precious gift, my speech – and now
I can't get a word in edgeways.'

'Rare and precious, did you say? Hear what the child
has brought to *us* – peace on earth, goodwill toward men.
O truly rare and precious gift!'
    'Peace on earth,' said the neighbours,
'goodwill toward men. O truly rare
and precious gift!' They knelt in humility,
in gratitude to the child who lay
among the oxen, in swaddling clothes in the hay,
his blue eyes shining steady as the Star overhead,
beside him old Joseph and
Mary his mother, smiling.

The mayor was silent. God gave the simpleton
no more to say. Now
like a frightened bird
over the snowfields and the frozen rutted lanes

he fluttered away. Always, as before, a flower
stuck out of his yellow hair; his mouth gaped open
like a drawer that wouldn't shut.
He never spoke out like that again.

As for the mayor, he didn't finish his speech.
He called for his coach, and drove off, frowning,
much troubled. For a little while
he thought of what the simpleton had said.
But he soon forgot all about it, having
important business to attend to in town.

 THE FOUR WISE MEN

MICHEL TOURNIER

I had to tell you all this, because otherwise you wouldn't understand my state of mind
that winter's day, when I arrived in Bethlehem — that's a small town in Judaea — with
my master. The whole province was in a turmoil, because the Emperor had ordered a
census of the population, and everybody and his family had to go back to the place
they came from to register. Bethlehem is hardly more than a big village perched on the
top of a hill, the sides of which are terraced and covered with little gardens with dry-
stone retaining walls. In the spring and at normal times it's probably a nice enough
place to live in, but at the onset of winter and with all this census bustle, I certainly
missed my stable at Djela, our home village. My master and mistress had been lucky

enough to find a place for themselves and their two children in a big inn that was humming like a beehive. Alongside of the main building there was a kind of barn where they probably stored provisions. In between there was a narrow passage, leading nowhere, with a sort of thatched roof made by throwing armfuls of reeds on top of some crossbeams. Under this precarious shelter some feeding troughs had been set up and the ground had been strewn with litter for the beasts belonging to the guests at the inn. That was where they tethered me, next to an ox who had just been unharnessed from a cart. I don't mind telling you that I've always had a horror of oxen. I admit they haven't an ounce of malice in them, but unfortunately my master's brother-in-law owns one. At ploughing time the two brothers-in-law help each other out, and that means harnessing us to the plough together, though it's expressly forbidden by law. That is a very wise law, because, take it from me, nothing could be ghastlier than working in that sort of team. The ox has his pace — which is slow — and his rhythm — which is steady. He pulls with his neck. The ass — like the horse — pulls with his crupper. He works spasmodically, in fits and starts. To team him up with an ox is to put a ball and chain on his legs, to curtail his energy — which he hasn't got so much of to begin with.

But that night there was no question of ploughing. Travellers turned away from the inn had invaded the barn. I strongly suspected that they wouldn't leave us in peace for long. And pretty soon, true enough, a man and a woman slipped into our improvised stable. The man was an old fellow, some kind of artisan. He had kicked up a big fuss, telling everyone who would listen that if he had to register in Bethlehem for the census, it was because his family tree — twenty-seven generations no less — went back to King David, who himself had been born in Bethlehem. Everybody laughed in his face. He'd have had more chance of finding lodging if he had mentioned the condition of his very young wife, who seemed dead tired and very pregnant besides. Taking straw from the floor and hay from the feeding troughs, he put together a kind of pallet between the ox and me, and laid the young woman down on it.

Little by little, everybody found his place and the noise died down. Now and then the young woman moaned softly and that's how we found out that her husband's name was Joseph. He comforted her as best he could, and that's how we found out that her name was Mary. I don't know how many hours passed, because I must have slept. When I woke up, I had a feeling that a big change had taken place, not only in our passageway, but everywhere, even, so it seemed, in the sky, glittering tatters of which shone through our miserable roof. The great silence of the longest night of the year had fallen on the earth, and it seemed as though, for fear of breaking the silence, the earth had stopped the flow of its waters and the heavens were holding their breath. Not a bird in the trees. Not a fox in the fields. Not a mole in the grass. The eagles and the wolves, whatever had beak or claw, watched and waited, with hunger in their bellies and their eyes fixed on the darkness. Even the glowworms and fireflies masked their light. Time had given way to a sacred eternity.

Then suddenly, in less than an instant, something enormous happened. An irrepressible thrill of joy traversed heaven and earth. A rustling of innumerable wings made it plain that swarms of angelic messengers were rushing in all directions. The thatch over our heads was lit up by the dazzling train of a comet. We heard the crystalline laughter of the brooks and the majestic laughter of the rivers. In the desert of Judaea swirls of sand tickled the flanks of the dunes. An ovation rose from the terebinth forests and mingled with the muffled applause of the hoot owls. All nature exulted.

What had happened? Hardly anything. A faint cry had been heard, coming from the dark, warm pallet, a cry that could not have come from a man or a woman. It was the soft wailing of a newborn babe. Just then, a column of light came to rest in the middle of the stable: the Archangel Gabriel, Jesus's guardian angel, had arrived. The moment he got there, he took charge, so to speak. At the same time, the door opened, and one of the maids from the inn came in, supporting a basin of warm water on her hip. Without hesitation she knelt down and bathed the child. Then she rubbed it with salt to toughen the skin, swaddled it, and handed it to Joseph, who set it down on his knees, in token of paternal recognition.

You have to hand it to Gabriel, his efficiency was remarkable. Meaning no disrespect to an archangel, I have to tell you that for the past year he hadn't let any grass grow under his feet. He was the one who announced to Mary that she would be the mother of the Messiah. He was the one who set the kindly old Joseph's suspicions to rest. And it was he, later on, who would dissuade the Three Kings from making their report to Herod, and organize the little family's flight into Egypt. But that's getting ahead of my story. Just then he was playing the majordomo, the master of joyous ceremonies in that lowly place, which he transfigured, pretty much the way the sun turns the rain into a rainbow. In his very own person he went about waking the shepherds in the country nearby. At first, as you might expect, he gave them quite a turn. But then, laughing to reassure them, he announced the big news, and summoned them to the stable. Stable? That seemed strange, but it also put those simple folk at their ease.

When they started pouring in, Gabriel arranged them in a semicircle and helped them to come forward, one by one, kneel on one knee, pay their respects, and proffer their good wishes. And saying those few words was no joke for those silent men, who as a rule speak only to their dogs or the moon. Stepping up to the crib, they set down the products of their toil, clotted milk, small goat's cheeses, butter made from ewe's milk, olives from Galgala, sycamore figs, and dates from Jericho, but neither meat nor fish. They spoke of their humble sufferings, epidemics, vermin, and animal pests. Gabriel blessed them in the name of the Child, and promised them help and protection.

Neither meat nor fish, I said. But one of the last shepherds stepped forward with a little ram, barely four months old, wrapped around his neck. He knelt down, deposited his burden on the straw, then raised himself to his full height. The country people recognized Silas the Samaritan, a shepherd, to be sure, but also a kind of hermit, reputed among the simple folk for his wisdom. He lived all alone with his dogs and his beasts, in a mountain cave near Hebron. Everyone knew that he wouldn't come down from his wilderness for nothing, and when the archangel signalled him to speak, they all listened.

'My lord,' he began, 'some people say I withdrew to the mountains because I hated men. That's not true. It wasn't hatred of mankind but love of animals that made me a hermit. But when someone loves animals, he has to protect them from the wickedness and greed of men. It's true, I'm not the usual kind of husbandman. I neither sell nor kill my beasts. They give me their milk. I make it into cream, butter, and cheese. I sell nothing. I use these gifts according to my needs and give the rest – the greater part – to the poor. If tonight I've obeyed the angel, who woke me and showed me the star, it's because of the rebellion in my heart, not only against the ways of my society, but worse, against the rites of my religion. Unfortunately, this thing goes back a long way, almost to the beginning of time, and it would take a great revolution to bring about a change. Has the revolution happened tonight? That's what I've come to ask you.'

'It has happened tonight,' Gabriel assured him.

'I'll start with Abraham's sacrifice. To test Abraham, God commanded him to offer Isaac, his only son, as a burnt offering. Abraham obeyed. He took the child and climbed a mountain in the land of Moriah. The child was puzzled: They had brought wood, they had brought the fire and the knife, but where was the lamb for the burnt offering? Wood, fire, knife ... There, my lord, are the accursed stigmata of man's destiny!'

'There will be more,' said Gabriel gloomily, thinking of the nails, the hammer, and the crown of thorns.

'Then Abraham built an altar, laid the wood in order, and bound Isaac and laid him on the altar upon the wood. And he set his knife on the child's white throat.'

'But then,' Gabriel interrupted, 'an angel came and stayed his arm. That was me.'

'Yes, of course, good angel,' said Silas. 'But Isaac never recovered from the fright of seeing his own father holding a knife at his throat. The blue flash of the knife blasted his eyes; his eyesight was poor as long as he lived, and at the end he went stone blind. That's why his son Jacob was able to deceive him and pass for his brother Esau. But that's not what bothers me. Why couldn't you content yourself with stopping the child-killing? Did blood have to flow? You, Gabriel, supplied Abraham with a young ram, which was killed and offered up as a burnt offering. Couldn't God do without a death that morning?'

'I admit that Abraham's sacrifice was a failed revolution,' said Gabriel. 'We'll do better next time.'

'Actually,' said Silas, 'we can go further back in sacred history and trace Yahweh's secret passion to its source. Remember Cain and Abel. The two brothers were at their devotions. Each offered up products of his labour. Cain was a tiller of the soil, he offered up fruits and grain, while Abel, who was a shepherd, offered up lambs and their fat. What happened? Yahweh turned away from Cain's offering and welcomed Abel's.

Why? For what reason? I can see only one: It was because Yahweh hates vegetables and loves meat! Yes, the God we worship is hopelessly carnivorous!

'And we honour Him as such. Consider the temple at Jerusalem in its splendour and majesty, that sanctuary of the radiant divinity. Did you know that on some days it's drenched in steaming fresh blood like a slaughterhouse? The sacrificial altar is a huge block of rough-hewn stone, with hornlike protuberances at the corners and traversed with runnels to evacuate the blood of the victims. On the occasion of certain festivals the priests transform themselves into butchers and massacre whole herds of beasts. Oxen, rams, he-goats, even whole flocks of doves are shaken by the spasms of their death agony. They are dismembered on marble tables, and the entrails are thrown into a brazier. The whole city is infested with smoke. Some days, when the wind is from the north, the stench spreads as far as my mountain and my beasts are seized with panic.'

'Silas the Samaritan,' said Gabriel, 'you have done well to come here tonight to watch over the Child and worship him. The complaints of your animal-loving heart will be heard. I've said that Abraham's sacrifice was a failed revolution. Soon the Father will sacrifice the Son again. And I swear to you that this time no angel will stay His hand. All over the world from now on, even on the smallest of islands, and at every hour of the day till the end of time, the blood of the Son will flow on altars for the salvation of mankind. This little child you see sleeping in the straw – the ox and the ass do well to warm Him with their breath, for He is in truth a lamb. From now on there will be no other sacrificial lamb, because He is the Lamb of God, who alone will be sacrificed in *saecula saeculorum*.

'Go in peace, Silas. As a symbol of life you may take with you the young ram you have brought. More fortunate than Abraham's, he will testify in your herd that from now on the blood of animals will no longer be shed on God's altars.'

After this angelic speech there was a thoughtful pause that seemed to make a space around the terrible and magnificent event the angel had announced. Each in his own way and according to his powers tried to imagine what the new times would be like. But then a terrible jangling of chains and rusty pulleys was heard, accompanied by a burst of grotesque, ungainly, sobbing laughter. That was me, that was the thunderous bray of the ass in the manger. Yes, what would you expect, my patience was at an end. This couldn't go on. We'd been forgotten again; I'd listened attentively to everything that had been said, and I hadn't heard one word about asses.

Everybody laughed – Joseph, Mary, Gabriel, the shepherds, Silas the hermit, the ox, who hadn't understood one thing – and even the Child, who flailed merrily about with His four little limbs in His straw crib.

'Don't let it worry you,' said Gabriel. 'The asses will not be forgotten. Obviously you don't have to worry about sacrifices. Within memory of priest no one has ever seen an ass offered up on an altar. That would be too much honour for you poor humble donkeys. And yet great is your merit, beaten, starved, crushed under the weight of your burdens. But don't imagine that your miseries escape the eye of an archangel. For instance, Kadi Shuya, I distinctly see a deep, festering little wound behind your left ear. Day after day your master prods it with his goad. He thinks the pain will revive your flagging vigour. Ah, poor martyr, every time he does it, I suffer with you.'

The archangel pointed a luminous finger at my right ear and instantly the deep, festering little wound that had not escaped him closed. What's more, the skin that covered it was now so hard and thick that no goad would ever make a dent in it. Then and there I tossed my mane with enthusiasm and let out a triumphant bray.

'Yes, you humble and friendly companions of man's labour,' Gabriel went on, 'you will have your reward and your triumph in the great story that's starting tonight.

'One day, a Sunday – which will be known as Palm Sunday – the Apostles will find a she-ass and her colt in the village of Bethany near the Mount of Olives. They will loose them and throw a cloak on the back of the foal – which no one will yet have mounted – and Jesus will ride it. And Jesus will make His solemn entry into Jerusalem, through the Golden Gate, the finest of the city's gates. The people will rejoice and acclaim the Nazarene prophet with cries of Hosannah to the Son of David! And the foal will tread a carpet of palm branches and flowers that the people will have laid over the paving stones. And the mother ass will trot in the rear of the procession, braying to all and sundry: "That's my foal! That's my foal!" for never will a mother ass have been so proud.'

So for the first time in history someone had given a thought to us asses, someone had stopped to think about our sufferings of today and joys of tomorrow. But before that could happen an archangel had to come all the way down from heaven. Suddenly I didn't feel alone any more, I'd been adopted by the great Christmas family. I was no longer the outcast whom no one understood. What a beautiful night we could all have spent together in the warmth of our sacred poverty! How late we would have slept next morning! And what a fine breakfast we'd have had!

Too bad! The rich always have to butt in. The rich are insatiable, they want to own everything, even poverty. Who could ever have imagined that this wretched family, camping between an ox and an ass, would attract a king? Did I say a king? No, three kings, authentic sovereigns, from the Orient, what's more! And really, what an outrageous display of servants, animals, canopies...

The shepherds had gone home. Once again silence enveloped that incomparable night. And suddenly the village streets were full of tumult. A clanking of bridles and stirrups and weapons; purple and gold glittered in the torchlight; shouts and commands rang out in barbarous languages. And most marvellous of all: the astonishing silhouettes of animals from the ends of the earth, falcons from the Nile, greyhounds, green parrots, magnificent horses, camels from the far south. Why not elephants while they were about it?

At first a lot of us went out and looked. Curiosity. There had never been such a show in a Palestinian village. You have to hand it to them – when it came to stealing our Christmas, the rich spared no expense. But in the end too much is enough. We went back inside and barricaded ourselves and some beat it across the hills and fields. Because, you see, unimportant people like us can expect no good of the great. Better steer clear of them. For a farthing dropped here and there, how many whippings fall to the lot of the beggar or ass who crosses a prince's path!

That's the way it looked to my master. Awakened by the ruckus, he gathered up his family and belongings, and I saw him elbowing his way into our improvised stable. My master knows his own mind, but he's a man of few words. Without so much as opening his mouth, he untied me and we left that noisy village before the kings marched in.

Father Christmas has played a surprisingly modest part in this book; but here now he is enchantingly introduced by G. K. Chesterton in his cheering fable 'The Shop of Ghosts'. Charles Dickens too has a small part in the tale, and so brings us naturally to the book that started it all, A Christmas Carol, by general acclaim the finest, clearest, and warmest account of the English festival ever written. There are those who find Tiny Tim somewhat rebarbative, but there is no gainsaying the sheer sensuous joie de vivre *of the descriptive passages: the ultra-white almonds, the candied fruits spotted with molten sugar, the moist and pulpy figs, the French plums, blushing in their modest tartness. Dickens is often accused of inventing Christmas as we know it; if he did, this is where it happened.*

The Shop of Ghosts
A Good Dream

G. K. CHESTERTON

Nearly all the best and most precious things in the universe you can get for a halfpenny. I make an exception of course, of the sun, the moon, the earth, people, stars, thunderstorms, and such trifles. You can get them for nothing. But the general principle will be at once apparent. In the street behind me, for instance, you can now get a ride on an electric tram for a halfpenny. To be on an electric tram is to be on a flying castle in a fairy tale. You can get quite a large number of brightly coloured sweets for a halfpenny.

But if you want to see what a vast and bewildering array of valuable things you can get at a halfpenny each, you should do as I was doing last night. I was glueing my nose against the glass of a very small and dimly lit toy-shop in one of the greyest and leanest of the streets of Battersea. But dim as was that square of light, it was filled (as a child once said to me) with all the colours God ever made. Those toys of the poor were like the children who buy them; they were all dirty; but they were all bright. For my part, I think brightness more important than cleanliness; since the first is of the soul, and the second of the body. You must excuse me; I am a democrat; I know I am out of fashion in the modern world.

As I looked at that palace of pigmy wonders, at small green omnibuses, at small blue elephants, at small black dolls, and small red Noah's arks, I must have fallen into some sort of unnatural trance. That lit shop-window became like the brilliantly lit stage when one is watching some highly coloured comedy. I forgot the grey houses and the grimy people behind me as one forgets the dark galleries and the dim crowds at a theatre. It seemed as if the little objects behind the glass were small, not because they were toys, but because they were objects far away. The green omnibus was really a green omnibus, a green Bayswater omnibus, passing across some huge desert on its ordinary way to Bayswater. The blue elephant was no longer blue with paint; he was blue with distance. The black doll was really a negro relieved against passionate tropic foliage in the land where every weed is flaming and only man is black. The red Noah's ark was really the enormous ship of earthly salvation riding on the rain-swollen sea, red in the first morning of hope.

Every one, I suppose, knows such stunning instants of abstraction, such brilliant blanks in the mind. In such moments one can see the face of one's own best friend as an unmeaning pattern of spectacles or moustaches. They are commonly marked by the two signs of the slowness of their termination. The return to real thinking is often as abrupt as bumping into a man. Very often indeed (in my case) it is bumping into a man. But in any case the awakening is always emphatic and, generally speaking, it is always complete. Now, in this case, I did come back with a shock of sanity to the consciousness that I was, after all, only staring into a dingy little toy-shop; but in some strange way the mental cure did not seem to be final. There was still in my mind an unmanageable something that told me that I had strayed into some odd atmosphere, or that I had already done some odd thing. I felt as if I had worked a miracle or committed a sin. It was as if I had (at any rate) stepped across some border in the soul.

To shake off this dangerous and dreamy sense I went into the shop and tried to buy wooden soldiers. The man in the shop was very old and broken, with confused white hair covering his head and half his face, hair so startlingly white that it looked almost artificial. Yet though he was senile and even sick, there was nothing of suffering in his eyes; he looked rather as if he were gradually falling asleep in a not unkindly decay. He gave me the wooden soldiers but when I put down the money he did not at first seem to see it; then he blinked at it feebly, and then he pushed it feebly away.

'No, no,' he said vaguely. 'I never have. I never have. We are rather old-fashioned here.'

'Not taking money,' I replied, 'seems to me more like an uncommonly new fashion than an old one.'

'I never have,' said the old man, blinking and blowing his nose; 'I've always given presents. I'm too old to stop.'

'Good heavens!' I said. 'What can you mean? Why, you might be Father Christmas.'

'I am Father Christmas,' he said apologetically, and blew his nose again.

The lamps could not have been lighted yet in the street outside. At any rate, I could see nothing against the darkness but the shining shop-window. There were no sounds of steps or voices in the street; I might have strayed into some new and sunless world. But something had cut the cords of common sense, and I could not feel even surprise except sleepily. Something made me say 'You look ill, Father Christmas.'

'I am dying,' he said.

I did not speak, and it was he who spoke again.

'All the new people have left my shop. I cannot understand it. They seem to object to me on such curious and inconsistent sort of grounds, these scientific men, and these innovators. They say that I give people superstitions and make them too visionary; they say I give people sausages and make them too coarse. They say my heavenly parts are too heavenly; they say my earthly parts are too earthly; I don't know what they want I'm sure. How can heavenly things be too heavenly, or earthly things too earthly? How can one be too good, or too jolly? I don't understand. But I understand one thing well enough. These modern people are living and I am dead.'

'You may be dead,' I replied. 'You ought to know. But as for what they are doing – do not call it living.'

A silence fell suddenly between us which I somehow expected to be unbroken. But it had not fallen for more than a few seconds when, in the utter stillness, I distinctly heard a very rapid step coming nearer and nearer along the street. The next moment a figure flung itself into the shop and stood framed in the doorway. He wore a large white hat tilted back as if in impatience; he had tight bright old-fashioned pantaloons, a gaudy old-fashioned stock and waistcoat, and an old fantastic coat. He had large wide-open luminous eyes like those of an arresting actor; he had a fiery nervous face, and a fringe of beard. He took in the shop and the old man in a look that seemed literally a flash, and uttered the exclamation of a man utterly staggered.

'Good lord!' he cried out; 'it can't be you! It isn't you! I came to ask where your grave was.'

'I'm not dead yet, Mr Dickens,' said the old gentleman, with a feeble smile; 'but I'm dying,' he hastened to add reassuringly.

'But, dash it all, you were dying in my time,' said Mr Charles Dickens, with animation; 'and you don't look a day older.'

'I've felt like this for a long time,' said Father Christmas.

Mr Dickens turned his back and put his head out of the door into the darkness.

'Dick,' he roared at the top of his voice, 'he's still alive.'

Another shadow darkened the doorway, and a much larger and more full-blooded gentleman in an enormous periwig came in, fanning his flushed face with a military hat of the cut of Queen Anne. He carried his head well back like a soldier, and his hot face had even a look of arrogance, which was suddenly contradicted by his eyes, which were as humble as a dog's. His sword made a great clatter, as if the shop were too small for it.

'Indeed,' said Sir Richard Steele, ' 'tis a most prodigious matter, for the man was dying when he wrote about Sir Roger de Coverley and his Christmas Day.'

My senses were growing dimmer and the room darker. It seemed to be filled with new-comers.

'It hath ever been understood,' said a burly man, who carried his head humorously and obstinately a little on one side – I think he was Ben Jonson – 'It hath ever been understood, consule Jacobo, under our King James and her late Majesty, that such good and hearty customs were fallen sick, and like to pass from the world. This greybeard most surely was no lustier when I knew him than now.'

And I also thought I heard a green-clad man, like Robin Hood, say in some mixed Norman French, 'But I saw the man dying.'

'I have felt like this a long time,' said Father Christmas in his feeble way again.

Mr Charles Dickens suddenly leant across to him. 'Since when?' he asked. 'Since you were born?'

'Yes,' said the old man, and sank shaking into a chair. 'I have been always dying.'

Mr Dickens took off his hat with a flourish like a man calling a mob to rise.

'I understand it now,' he cried; 'you will never die.'

A CHRISTMAS CAROL

CHARLES DICKENS

Awaking in the middle of a prodigiously tough snore, and sitting up in bed to get his thoughts together, Scrooge had no occasion to be told that the bell was again upon the stroke of One. He felt that he was restored to consciousness in the right nick of time, for the especial purpose of holding a conference with the second messenger despatched to him through Jacob Marley's intervention. But, finding that he turned uncomfortably cold when he began to wonder which of his curtains this new spectre would draw back, he put them every one aside with his own hands, and lying down again, established a sharp look-out all round the bed. For he wished to challenge the Spirit on the moment of its appearance, and did not wish to be taken by surprise, and made nervous.

Gentlemen of the free-and-easy sort, who plume themselves on being acquainted with a move or two, and being usually equal to the time-of-day, express the wide range of their capacity for adventure by observing that they are good for anything from pitch-and-toss to manslaughter; between which opposite extremes, no doubt, there lies a tolerably wide and comprehensive range of subjects. Without venturing for Scrooge quite as hardily as this, I don't mind calling on you to believe that he was ready for a good broad field of strange appearances, and that nothing between a baby and rhinoceros would have astonished him very much.

Now, being prepared for almost anything, he was not by any means prepared for nothing; and, consequently, when the Bell struck One, and no shape appeared, he was taken with a violent fit of trembling. Five minutes, ten minutes, a quarter of an hour went by, yet nothing came. All this time, he lay upon his bed, the very core and centre of a blaze of ruddy light, which streamed upon it when the clock proclaimed the hour; and which, being only light, was more alarming than a dozen ghosts, as he was powerless to make out what it meant, or would be at; and was sometimes apprehensive that he might be at that very moment an interesting case of spontaneous combustion, without having the consolation of knowing it. At last, however, he began to think – as you or I would have thought at first; for it is always the person not in the predicament who knows what ought to have been done in it, and would unquestionably have done it too – at last, I say, he began to think that the source and secret of this ghostly light might be in the adjoining room, from whence, on further tracing it, it seemed to shine. This idea taking full possession of his mind, he got up softly and shuffled in his slippers to the door.

The moment Scrooge's hand was on the lock, a strange voice called him by his name, and bade him enter. He obeyed.

It was his own room. There was no doubt about that. But it had undergone a surprising transformation. The walls and ceiling were so hung with living green, that it looked a perfect grove; from every part of which, bright gleaming berries glistened. The crisp leaves of holly, mistletoe, and ivy reflected back the light, as if so many little mirrors had been scattered there; and such a mighty blaze went roaring up the chimney, as that dull petrification of a hearth had never known in Scrooge's time, or Marley's, or for many and many a winter season gone. Heaped up on the floor, to form a kind of throne, were turkeys, geese, game, poultry, brawn, great joints of meat, sucking-pigs, long wreaths of sausages, mince-pies, plum-puddings, barrels of oysters, red-hot chestnuts, cherry-cheeked apples, juicy oranges, luscious pears, immense twelfth-cakes, and seething bowls of punch, that made the chamber dim with their delicious steam. In easy state upon this couch, there sat a jolly Giant, glorious to see; who bore a glowing torch, in shape not unlike Plenty's horn, and held it up, high up, to shed its light on Scrooge, as he came peeping round the door.

'Come in!' exclaimed the Ghost. 'Come in! and know me better, man!'

Scrooge entered timidly, and hung his head before this Spirit. He was not the dogged Scrooge he had been; and though the Spirit's eyes were clear and kind, he did not like to meet them.

'I am the Ghost of Christmas Present,' said the Spirit. 'Look upon me!'

Scrooge reverently did so. It was clothed in one simple green robe, or mantle, bordered with white fur. This garment hung so loosely on the figure, that its capacious breast was bare, as if disdaining to be warded or concealed by any artifice. Its feet, observable beneath the ample folds of the garment, were also bare; and on its head it wore no other covering than a holly wreath, set here and there with shining icicles. Its dark brown curls were long and free; free as its genial face, its sparkling eye, its open hand, its cheery voice, its unconstrained demeanour, and its joyful air. Girded round its middle was an antique scabbard; but no sword was in it, and the ancient sheath was eaten up with rust.

'You have never seen the like of me before!' exclaimed the Spirit.

'Never,' Scrooge made answer to it.

'Have never walked forth with the younger members of my family; meaning (for I am very young) my elder brothers born in these later years?' pursued the Phantom.

'I don't think I have,' said Scrooge. 'I am afraid I have not. Have you had many brothers, Spirit?'

'More than eighteen hundred,' said the Ghost.

'A tremendous family to provide for!' muttered Scrooge.

The Ghost of Christmas Present rose.

'Spirit,' said Scrooge submissively, 'conduct me where you will. I went forth last night on compulsion, and I learnt a lesson which is working now. Tonight, if you have aught to teach me, let me profit by it.'

'Touch my robe!'

Scrooge did as he was told, and held it fast.

Holly, mistletoe, red berries, ivy, turkeys, geese, game, poultry, brawn, meat, pigs, sausages, oysters, pies, puddings, fruit, and punch, all vanished instantly. So did the room, the fire, the ruddy glow, the hour of night, and they stood in the city streets on Christmas morning, where (for the weather was severe) the people made a rough, but brisk and not unpleasant kind of music, in scraping the snow from the pavement in front of their dwellings, and from the tops of their houses, whence it was mad delight to the boys to see it come plumping down into the road below, and splitting into artificial little snow-storms.

The house fronts looked black enough, and the windows blacker, contrasting with the smooth white sheet of snow upon the roofs, and with the dirtier snow upon the ground; which last deposit had been ploughed up in deep furrows by the heavy wheels of carts and waggons; furrows that crossed and re-crossed each other hundreds of times where the great streets branched off; and made intricate channels, hard to trace in the thick yellow mud and icy water. The sky was gloomy, and the shortest streets were choked up with a dingy mist, half thawed, half frozen, whose heavier particles descended in a shower of sooty atoms, as if all the chimneys in Great Britain had, by one consent, caught fire, and were blazing away to their dear hearts' content. There was nothing very cheerful in the climate or the town, and yet there was an air of cheerfulness abroad that the clearest summer air and brightest summer sun might have endeavoured to diffuse in vain.

For the people who were shovelling away on the house-tops were jovial and full of glee; calling out to one another from the parapets, and now and then exchanging a facetious snowball — better-natured missile far than many a wordy jest — laughing heartily if it went right and not less heartily if it went wrong. The poulterers' shops were still half open, and the fruiterers' were radiant in their glory. There were great, round, pot-bellied baskets of chestnuts, shaped like the waistcoats of jolly old gentlemen,

lolling at the doors, and tumbling out into the street in their apoplectic opulence. There were ruddy, brown-faced, broad-girthed Spanish Onions, shining in the fatness of their growth like Spanish Friars, and winking from their shelves in wanton slyness at the girls as they went by, and glanced demurely at the hung-up mistletoe. There were pears and apples, clustered high in blooming pyramids; there were bunches of grapes, made in the shopkeepers' benevolence to dangle from conspicuous hooks, that people's mouths might water gratis as they passed; there were piles of filberts, mossy and brown, recalling, in their fragrance, ancient walks among the woods, and pleasant shufflings ankle deep through withered leaves; there were Norfolk Biffins, squab and swarthy, setting off the yellow of the oranges and lemons, and, in the great compactness of their juicy persons, urgently entreating and beseeching to be carried home in paper bags and eaten after dinner. The very gold and silver fish, set forth among these choice fruits in a bowl, though members of a dull and stagnant-blooded race, appeared to know that there was something going on; and, to a fish, went gasping round and round their little world in slow and passionless excitement.

The Grocers'! oh the Grocers'! nearly closed, with perhaps two shutters down, or one; but through those gaps such glimpses! It was not alone that the scales descending on the counter made a merry sound, or that the twine and roller parted company so briskly, or that the canisters were rattled up and down like juggling tricks, or even that the blended scents of tea and coffee were so grateful to the nose, or even that the raisins were so plentiful and rare, the almonds so extremely white, the sticks of cinnamon so long and straight, the other spices so delicious, the candied fruits so caked and spotted with molten sugar as to make the coldest lookers-on feel faint and subsequently bilious. Nor was it that the figs were moist and pulpy, or that the French plums blushed in modest tartness from their highly-decorated boxes, or that everything was good to eat and in its Christmas dress; but the customers were all so hurried and so eager in the hopeful promise of the day, that they tumbled up against each other at the door, crashing their wicker baskets wildly, and left their purchases upon the counter, and came running back to fetch them, and committed hundreds of the like mistakes, in the best humour possible; while the Grocer and his people were so frank and fresh that the polished hearts with which they fastened their aprons behind might have been their own, worn outside for general inspection, and for Christmas daws to peck at if they chose.

But soon the steeples called good people all, to church and chapel, and away they came, flocking through the streets in their best clothes, and with their gayest faces. And at the same time there emerged from scores of bye-streets, lanes, and nameless turnings, innumerable people, carrying their dinners to the bakers' shops. The sight of these poor revellers appeared to interest the Spirit very much, for he stood with Scrooge beside him in a baker's doorway, and taking off the covers as their bearers passed, sprinkled incense on their dinners from his torch. And it was a very uncommon kind of torch, for once or twice when there were angry words between some dinner-carriers who had jostled each other, he shed a few drops of water on them from it, and their good humour was restored directly. For they said it was a shame to quarrel upon Christmas Day. And so it was! God love it, so it was!

In time the bells ceased, and the bakers were shut up; and yet there was a genial shadowing forth of all these dinners and the progress of their cooking, in the thawed blotch of wet above each baker's oven; where the pavement smoked as if its stones were cooking too.

'Is there a peculiar flavour in what you sprinkle from your torch?' asked Scrooge.

'There is. My own.'

On the threshold of the door the Spirit smiled, and stopped to bless Bob Cratchit's dwelling with the sprinkling of his torch. Think of that! Bob had but fifteen 'Bob' a-week himself; he pocketed on Saturdays but fifteen copies of his Christian name; and yet the Ghost of Christmas Present blessed his four-roomed house!

Then up rose Mrs Cratchit, Cratchit's wife, dressed out but poorly in a twice-turned gown, but brave in ribbons, which are cheap and make a goodly show for sixpence; and she laid the cloth, assisted by Belinda Cratchit, second of her daughters, also brave in ribbons; while Master Peter Cratchit plunged a fork into the saucepan of potatoes, and getting the corners of his monstrous shirt collar (Bob's private property, conferred upon his son and heir in honour of the day) into his mouth, rejoiced to find himself so gallantly attired, and yearned to show his linen in the fashionable Parks. And now two smaller Cratchits, boy and girl, came tearing in, screaming that outside the baker's they had smelt the goose, and known it for their own; and basking in luxurious thoughts of sage and onion, these young Cratchits danced about the table and exalted Master Peter Cratchit to the skies, while he (not proud, although his collars nearly choked him) blew the fire, until the slow potatoes bubbling up, knocked loudly at the saucepan-lid to be let out and peeled.

'Whatever has got your precious father then?' said Mrs Cratchit. 'And your brother, Tiny Tim! And Martha warn't as late last Christmas Day by half-an-hour.'

'Here's Martha, mother!' said a girl, appearing as she spoke.

'Here's Martha, mother!' cried the two young Cratchits. 'Hurrah! There's *such* a goose, Martha!'

'Why, bless your heart alive, my dear, how late you are!' said Mrs Cratchit, kissing her a dozen times, and taking off her shawl and bonnet for her with officious zeal.

'We'd a deal of work to finish up last night,' replied the girl, 'and had to clear away this morning, mother!'

'Well! Never mind so long as you are come,' said Mrs Cratchit. 'Sit ye down before the fire, my dear, and have a warm, Lord bless ye!'

'No, no! There's father coming,' cried the two young Cratchits, who were everywhere at once. 'Hide, Martha, hide!'

So Martha hid herself, and in came little Bob, the father, with at least three feet of comforter exclusive of the fringe, hanging down before him; and his threadbare clothes darned up and brushed, to look seasonable; and Tiny Tim upon his shoulder. Alas for Tiny Tim, he bore a little crutch, and had his limbs supported by an iron frame!

'Why, where's our Martha?' cried Bob Cratchit, looking round.

'Not coming,' said Mrs Cratchit.

'Not coming!' said Bob, with a sudden declension in his high spirits; for he had been Tim's blood horse all the way from church, and had come home rampant. 'Not coming upon Christmas Day!'

Martha didn't like to see him disappointed, if it were only in joke; so she came out prematurely from behind the closet door, and ran into his arms, while the two young Cratchits hustled Tiny Tim, and bore him off into the wash-house, that he might hear the pudding singing in the copper.

'And how did little Tim behave?' asked Mrs Cratchit, when she had rallied Bob on his credulity, and Bob had hugged his daughter to his heart's content.

'As good as gold,' said Bob, 'and better. Somehow he gets thoughtful, sitting by himself so much, and thinks the strangest things you ever heard. He told me, coming home, that he hoped the people saw him in the church, because he was a cripple, and it might be pleasant to them to remember upon Christmas Day, who made lame beggars walk, and blind men see.'

Bob's voice was tremulous when he told them this, and trembled more when he said that Tiny Tim was growing strong and hearty.

His active little crutch was heard upon the floor, and back came Tiny Tim before another word was spoken, escorted by his brother and sister to his stool before the fire; and while Bob, turning up his cuffs – as if, poor fellow, they were capable of being made more shabby – compounded some hot mixture in a jug with gin and lemons, and stirred it round and round and put it on the hob to simmer; Master Peter, and the two ubiquitous young Cratchits went to fetch the goose, with which they soon returned in high procession.

Such a bustle ensued that you might have thought a goose the rarest of all birds; a feathered phenomenon, to which a black swan was a matter of course – and in truth it was something very like it in that house. Mrs Cratchit made the gravy (ready beforehand in a little saucepan) hissing hot; Master Peter mashed the potatoes with incredible vigour; Miss Belinda sweetened up the apple-sauce; Martha dusted the hot plates; Bob took Tiny Tim beside him in a tiny corner at the table; the two young Cratchits set chairs for everybody, not forgetting themselves, and mounting guard upon their posts, crammed spoons into their mouths, lest they should shriek for goose before their turn came to be helped. At last the dishes were set on, and grace was said. It was succeeded by a breathless pause, as Mrs Cratchit, looking slowly all along the carving-knife, prepared to plunge it in the breast; but when she did, and when the long expected gush of stuffing issued forth, one murmur of delight arose all round the board, and even Tiny Tim, excited by the two young Cratchits, beat on the table with the handle of his knife, and feebly cried Hurrah!

There never was such a goose. Bob said he didn't believe there ever was such a goose cooked. Its tenderness and flavour, size and cheapness, were the themes of universal admiration. Eked out by apple-sauce and mashed potatoes, it was a sufficient dinner for the whole family; indeed, as Mrs Cratchit said with great delight (surveying one small atom of a bone upon the dish), they hadn't ate it all at last! Yet every one had had enough, and the youngest Cratchits in particular, were steeped in sage and onion to the eyebrows! But now, the plates being changed by Miss Belinda, Mrs Cratchit left the room alone – too nervous to bear witnesses – to take the pudding up and bring it in.

Suppose it should not be done enough! Suppose it should break in turning out! Suppose somebody should have got over the wall of the back-yard, and stolen it, while they were merry with the goose – a supposition at which the two young Cratchits became livid! All sorts of horrors were supposed.

Hallo! A great deal of steam! The pudding was out of the copper. A smell like a washing-day! That was the cloth. A smell like an eating-house and a pastrycook's next door to each other, with a laundress's next door to that! That was the pudding! In half a minute Mrs Cratchit entered – flushed, but smiling proudly – with the pudding, like a speckled cannon-ball, so hard and firm, blazing in half of half-a-quartern of ignited brandy, and bedight with Christmas holly stuck into the top.

Oh, a wonderful pudding! Bob Cratchit said, and calmly too, that he regarded it as the greatest success achieved by Mrs Cratchit since their marriage. Mrs Cratchit said that now the weight was off her mind, she would confess she had had her doubts about the quantity of flour. Everybody had something to say about it, but nobody said or thought it was at all a small pudding for a large family. It would have been flat heresy to do so. Any Cratchit would have blushed to hint at such a thing.

At last the dinner was all done, the cloth was cleared, the hearth swept, and the fire made up. The compound in the jug being tasted, and considered perfect, apples and oranges were put upon the table, and a shovel-full of chestnuts on the fire. Then all the Cratchit family drew round the hearth, in what Bob Cratchit called a circle, meaning half a one; and at Bob Cratchit's elbow stood the family display of glass. Two tumblers, and a custard-cup without a handle.

These held the hot stuff from the jug, however, as well as golden goblets would have done; and Bob served it out with beaming looks, while the chestnuts on the fire sputtered and cracked noisily. Then Bob proposed:

'A Merry Christmas to us all, my dears. God bless us!'

Which all the family re-echoed.

'God bless us every one!' said Tiny Tim, the last of all.

He sat very close to his father's side upon his little stool. Bob held his withered little hand in his, as if he loved the child, and wished to keep him by his side, and dreaded that he might be taken from him.

'Spirit,' said Scrooge, with an interest he had never felt before, 'tell me if Tiny Tim will live.'

'I see a vacant seat,' replied the Ghost, 'in the poor chimney-corner, and a crutch without an owner, carefully preserved. If these shadows remain unaltered by the Future, the child will die.'

'No, no,' said Scrooge. 'Oh, no, kind Spirit! say he will be spared.'

'If these shadows remain unaltered by the Future, none other of my race,' returned the Ghost, 'will find him here. What then? If he be like to die, he had better do it, and decrease the surplus population.'

Scrooge hung his head to hear his own words quoted by the Spirit, and was overcome with penitence and grief.

'Man,' said the Ghost, 'if man you be in heart, not adamant, forbear that wicked cant until you have discovered What the surplus is and Where it is. Will you decide what men shall live, what men shall die? It may be, that in the sight of Heaven, you are more worthless and less fit to live than millions like this poor man's child. Oh God! to hear the Insect on the leaf pronouncing on the too much life among his hungry brothers in the dust!'

Scrooge bent before the Ghost's rebuke, and trembling cast his eyes upon the ground. But he raised them speedily, on hearing his own name.

'Mr Scrooge!' said Bob; 'I'll give you Mr Scrooge, the Founder of the Feast!'

'The Founder of the Feast indeed!' cried Mrs Cratchit, reddening. 'I wish I had him here. I'd give him a piece of my mind to feast upon, and I hope he'd have a good appetite for it.'

'My dear,' said Bob, 'the children! Christmas Day.'

'It should be Christmas Day, I am sure,' said she, 'on which one drinks the health of such an odious, stingy, hard, unfeeling man as Mr Scrooge. You know he is, Robert! Nobody knows it better than you do, poor fellow!'

'My dear,' was Bob's mild answer, 'Christmas Day.'

'I'll drink his health for your sake and the Day's,' said Mrs Cratchit, 'not for his. Long life to him! A merry Christmas and a happy new year! He'll be very merry and very happy, I have no doubt!'

The children drank the toast after her. It was the first of their proceedings which had no heartiness. Tiny Tim drank it last of all, but he didn't care twopence for it. Scrooge was the Ogre of the family. The mention of his name cast a dark shadow on the party, which was not dispelled for full five minutes.

After it had passed away, they were ten times merrier than before, from the mere relief of Scrooge the Baleful being done with. Bob Cratchit told them how he had a situation in his eye for Master Peter, which would bring in, if obtained, full five-and-sixpence weekly. The two young Cratchits laughed tremendously at the idea of Peter's being a man of business; and Peter himself looked thoughtfully at the fire from between his collars, as if he were deliberating what particular investments he should favour when he came into the receipt of that bewildering income. Martha, who was a poor apprentice at a milliner's, then told them what kind of work she had to do, and how many hours she worked at a stretch, and how she meant to lie abed tomorrow morning for a good long rest; tomorrow being a holiday she passed at home. Also how she had seen a countess and a lord some days before, and how the lord 'was much about as tall as Peter;' at which Peter pulled up his collars so high that you couldn't have seen his head if you had been there. All this time the chestnuts and the jug went round and round; and by-and-bye they had a song, about a lost child travelling in the snow, from Tiny Tim, who had a plaintive little voice, and sang it very well indeed.

There was nothing of high mark in this. They were not a handsome family; they were not well dressed; their shoes were far from being water-proof; their clothes were scanty; and Peter might have known, and very likely did, the inside of a pawnbroker's. But they were happy, grateful, pleased with one another, and contented with the time; and when they faded, and looked happier yet in the bright sprinklings of the Spirit's torch at parting, Scrooge had his eye upon them, and especially on Tiny Tim, until the last.

Bread and Butter Letter

My first thanks must, of course, go to John Simmons. It was his letter, as I explained in the introduction, that gave birth to this book; may he find readings in it for his supper club for many years to come. Peter Carson of Penguin said yes to the idea as soon as it was put to him, and has been a doughty guide, counsellor and friend during its making. John Denny of Penguin contributed more valuable ideas and did the day-to-day editing with skill and care.

For their meticulous work on the text I am much indebted to Gillian Bate and Donna Poppy; Anne-Marie Ehrlich researched the pictures that Judy Gordon turned into such elegant pages; Rachel Pyper made sure all this loving work meshed together; Dotti Irving and Clare Harington proved (indeed are still proving) what intelligent promotion can do for a book.

I shall not be the first writer to thank the staff of the London Library for their patience, expertise, and good humour; let me simply record my debt with all the others. Westminster Library too was unfailingly and endlessly helpful. My daughter Amanda Smith researched with her usual brisk dispatch and my wife Mary Schoenfeld Smith was invaluable in helping us get the final balance right.

Next I should like to thank Mary Macintosh and her *puellae doctae* at the Elgin Bookshop off the Portobello Road. They not only rustled up obscure books with crisp authority; they contributed many of their own valuable ideas as well. Happy is the man who has such a bookshop by his own front door.

Finally, I am particularly grateful to John Julius Norwich for so generously lending me all the material he has used for the service of readings and carols he does each year in Liverpool Cathedral. This not only opened up some rich new seams for us; it also enabled us to be the first to publish in hard covers his delicious parody of 'The Twelve Days of Christmas'. Though the maker of that enchanted argosy *Christmas Crackers* may well be surfeited with delights, I like to hope he too may find something for a future carol service in our pages.

THANKS, GENTLE READERS

Although many people put forward ideas for this book, its heart is made up of suggestions from readers of my Sunday Times *column. Warm thanks to each and every one of them.*

Christina Allen
Audrey Anderson
E. Bagnall
The Rev. Hugh Bailey
Rosemary Bartlett
A. G. Bennett
Anita R. Bevan
Mrs Nicola Bevan
Peter Binder
Lorna Brooks
Beryl Bugler
Margaret Carr
Mrs Maureen Crook
Ray Danby
Stephen d'Arcy
Bernard Davies (Sherlock Holmes Society)
Richard Douglas-Grey
Brian Dowling
Mrs A. M. Drury
B. L. Field
Mrs Barbara Golding
Margaret Grant Cormack
Barbara M. Hancock
Barbara Hare
Marion Hatch
Mrs Margaret Hill
Phyl Histon
Alan Hockley
Patricia Horner
John Hubbard
Louise Izzard
Allan C. Jones
Daniel Jones
William Kimball
Martin Kneapp

Peter Lancaster-Brown
David Langshaw
L. W. Ludlam
Mrs Ruth Main
Hilary McGowan
John McKeown
Dr B. N. McQuade
Mr P. J. Meade
Kevin Mellor
Celia Middleton
R. J. Miller
Joan Moncrieff
Edward A. Murphy
John O'Byrne
Brian O'Gorman
Mrs Jennifer Orwin
Mrs Manon Owen
Mrs Celia Pottinger
Elizabeth Poynton
The Rev. P. Pridham
Mary M. Redman
Anthony Rota
Doreen Sherman
Mrs Ann Smith
Brian Stevenson
John R. Talbot
Mrs Teddie Thom
I. Noël Treavett
Janet Watson
William White
Robin Wickham
L. Wilson
H. Worth
Margaret Worthington

THANKS, GENTLE WRITERS

I am indeed grateful to all of the following for permission to reproduce their copyright material in *The Christmas Reader*:

The extract from *Ending Up* by Kingsley Amis reprinted by permission of the author and Jonathan Cape Ltd; 'The Little Match-Girl' from *Hans Christian Andersen's Fairy Tales: A Selection* translated by L. W. Kingsland (World's Classic Paperback, 1984) reprinted by permission of Oxford University Press, © Oxford University Press, 1959; 'A Remaining Christmas' by Hilaire Belloc reprinted by permission of A. D. Peters & Co. Ltd; 'Christmas Day in the Cookhouse' (Billy Bennett) reproduced by permission of Paxton Music Ltd; 'Christmas' by John Betjeman reprinted by permission of John Murray (Publishers) Ltd; extracts from the Authorized King James Version of the Bible, which is Crown Copyright in the United Kingdom, are reprinted by permission of Eyre & Spottiswoode (Publishers) Ltd, Her Majesty's Printers, London; the letter by Captain R. J. Armes from *Christmas Truce* by Malcolm Brown and Shirley Seaton reprinted by permission of the authors, Leo Cooper and Martin Secker & Warburg Ltd; 'A Christmas Memory' by Truman Capote reprinted by permission of Hamish Hamilton Ltd and Random House Inc.; 'My Antonia' by Willa Cather (new paperback edition, The Virago Press Ltd, 1980 reprinted by permission of Curtis Brown Ltd, London, Copyright Willa Cather, 1918; 'A Christmas Carol' and 'The Shop of Ghosts' by G. K. Chesterton reprinted by permission of Miss D. E. Collins; 'Christmas in Vermont' by Alistair Cooke reprinted by permission of the author and The Bodley Head Ltd; the letter from *The Noël Coward Diaries* edited by Graham Payn and Sheridan Morley reprinted by permission of Weidenfeld & Nicolson Ltd; 'The Three Law Masses' (Chapter 17) from *Letters from my Windmill* by Alphonse Daudet translated by Frederick Davies (Penguin Classics, 1978, pp. 158–67 reprinted by permission of Penguin Books Ltd, © Frederick Davies, 1978; 'The Christmas Pudding is Mediterranean Food' from *Spices, Salts and Aromatics in the English Kitchen* by Elizabeth David (Penguin Handbooks, revised edition, 1975, pp. 208–11) reprinted by permission of Penguin Books Ltd; © Elizabeth David, 1970; 'Mistletoe' by Walter de la Mare reprinted by permission of the Literary Trustees of Walter de la Mare and The Society of Authors as their representative; the extract from *Monsieur* by Lawrence Durrell reprinted by permission of Faber & Faber Ltd; 'Old Sam's Christmas Pudding' by Marriott Edgar reproduced by permission of EMI Music Publishing Ltd, London W C2 0LD, Copyright 1949 Francis Day & Hunter Ltd; 'The Journey of the Magi' from *Collected Poems 1909–1962* by T. S. Eliot reprinted by permission of Faber & Faber Ltd; from *A Child in the Forest* by Winifred Foley reprinted by permission of BBC Publications and Century Hutchinson Ltd; the extract from *The Diary of a Farmer's Wife 1796–1797* ('A Dish for Cross Husbands') by Anne Hughes (Penguin Books, 1981, pp. 102–6) reprinted by permission of Penguin Books Ltd, Copyright Mollie Preston 1937, © 1964, 1980; the extract from 'The Dead' from *Dubliners* by James Joyce reprinted by permission of Jonathan

Cape Ltd and The Society of Authors as the literary representatives of the Estate of James Joyce; the extract from *Kilvert's Diary* edited by William Plomer reprinted by permission of Mrs Sheila Hooper and Jonathan Cape Ltd; 'Christmas in India' from *The Definitive Edition of Rudyard Kipling's Verse* reprinted by permission of the National Trust for Places of Historic Interest or Natural Beauty and Macmillan London Ltd; the extract from *Cider with Rosie* by Laurie Lee reprinted by permission of the author and The Hogarth Press; 'The Christmas Tree' from *Collected Poems* by C. Day Lewis reprinted by permission of The Hogarth Press and Jonathan Cape Ltd and the Executors of the Estate of C. Day Lewis; the extract from *How We Lived Then* edited by Norman Longmate reprinted by permission of the editor; 'All the Days of Christmas' by Phyllis McGinley reprinted by permission of Curtis Brown Ltd, New York, © The Hearst Corporation, 1958; the extract from *The Winds of Change* by Harold Macmillan reprinted by permission of Macmillan Accounts & Administration Ltd; 'Christmas Shopping' from *The Collected Poems of Louis MacNeice* reprinted by permission of Faber & Faber Ltd; the Christmas menu from *Puckoon* by Spike Milligan reprinted by permission of Michael Joseph Ltd in association with M. & J. Hobbs as publisher; 'King John's Christmas' from *Now We Are Six*, 1927, reprinted by permission of Methuen Childrens Books Ltd and McLelland & Stewart Ltd; 'The Twelve Days of Christmas' by John Julius Norwich reprinted by permission of the author; 'It is a Debauch', an extract from *The Collected Essays of George Orwell*, reprinted by permission of the Estate of the late Sonia Brownell Orwell and Martin Secker & Warburg Ltd; from *Billy Bunter's Christmas* by Frank Richards reprinted by permission of Howard Baker Press Ltd; 'Dancing Dan's Christmas' from *Runyon on Broadway* by Damon Runyon reprinted by permission of Constable Publishers; 'The Mayor and the Simpleton' by Jan Serrailler from *Belinda and the Swans* reprinted by permission of the author and Jonathan Cape Ltd, Copyright Ian Serrailler and Jonathan Cape Ltd, 1952; 'An Atrocious Institution', an extract from 'Mrs Tanqueray Plays the Piano' in *Shaw's Music* reprinted by permission of The Society of Authors on behalf of the Bernard Shaw Estate; the extract from 'A Child's Christmas in Wales' by Dylan Thomas reprinted by permission of David Higham Associates Ltd; 'The Four Wise Men' by Michel Tournier reprinted by permission of Collins Publishers; the extract from *The Growing Pains of Adrian Mole* by Sue Townsend reprinted by permission of Methuen London Ltd; the extract from *Winter in the Hills* by John Wain reprinted by permission of the author; 'Albert and the Liner' by Keith Waterhouse, in the anthology *Dandelion Clocks* edited by Alfred Bradley and Kay Jamieson, reprinted by permission of Michael Joseph Ltd; 'Jeeves and the Yule-tide Spirit' from *Very Good Jeeves* by P. G. Wodehouse reprinted by permission of the Executors of the Estate of Lady Wodehouse and the Hutchinson Group Ltd.

THANKS, GENTLE ARTISTS

We have tried wherever we could to use period drawings in *The Christmas Reader*, but where that proved impossible we have commissioned modern artists to illustrate the text. My warmest thanks to them and to all those who provided us with the illustrations listed below:

Pages 3, 98, 101, 105, 142, 253, 255 and 284, drawings by Randolph Caldecott in *Old Christmas, From the Sketchbook of Washington Irving*, 1875; pp. 17, 29, 95, 196, 257 and 287, reproduced by courtesy of The Mary Evans Picture Library; pp. 21, 37, 159, 241, 259, 300 and 313, reproduced by courtesy of The Mansell Collection; pp. 23, 27, 85, 111, 133, 145, 153, 156, 167, 239, 285 and 296, reproduced by courtesy of The Christmas Archives; p. 45, *The Virgin and Child with the Infant St John*, a fifteenth-century woodcut, Hamburg S.1137; p. 49, relief by Sally Seymour, © 1985; pp. 50 and 151, from *St Nicholas* Magazine, 1907, 1908; pp. 55, 73, 127 and 129, woodcuts by Vera Smith, © 1985; pp. 58 and 87, details from *Christmas in France* by F. Meaulle, 1875; p. 80, drawing by Nicholas Bentley from *Furthermore* by Damon Runyon, 1938, reproduced by permission of Constable & Co. Ltd; p. 107, woodcut by Pierre Gringore from *Castell of Labour*, c. 1505; pp. 117 and 119, drawings by George du Maurier from *Trilby*, 1894; pp. 137, 177 and 182, drawings by Zafer Baran, © 1985; p. 140, drawing by Clare Winsten from *G. B. S. 90: Aspects of Bernard Shaw's Life and Work*, 1946, reproduced by courtesy of Hutchinson Publishing Co. Ltd; p. 147, woodcut from Petrus de Rivo, *Opus Responsivum*, 1488; p. 162, woodcut from Bartholomaeus Anglicus, *All the Proprytees of Thynges*, 1495; p. 170, reproduced by courtesy of The Robert Opie Collection; pp. 187, 189 and 194, drawings by E. H. Shepard, copyright under the Berne Convention, reproduced by permission of Curtis Brown Ltd, London; pp. 201 and 307, from *Harper's Weekly*, 1880, 1881; pp. 207, 211, illustrations by Sidney Paget in the *Strand* Magazine, Vol. III, 1892; pp. 242, 245 and 249, drawing by Vana Haggerty, © 1985; p. 252, drawing by Brian Walker from *The Diary of a Farmer's Wife 1796–1797*, Countrywise Books, 1964, © Brian Walker 1964; p. 264, drawing from *Billy Bunter's Christmas* by Frank Richards reproduced by permission of Howard Baker Press Ltd; p. 267, illustration from the *Strand* Magazine, Vol. LXXLV, 1927; p. 291, woodcut from *Legenda Sanctorum Trium Regum*, 1490.

THANKS, GENTLE ARTISTS

We have tried wherever we could to use period drawings in *The Christmas Reader*, but where that proved impossible we have commissioned modern artists to illustrate the text. My warmest thanks to them and to all those who provided us with the illustrations listed below:

Pages 3, 98, 101, 105, 142, 253, 255 and 284, drawings by Randolph Caldecott in *Old Christmas, From the Sketchbook of Washington Irving*, 1875; pp. 17, 29, 95, 196, 257 and 287, reproduced by courtesy of The Mary Evans Picture Library; pp. 21, 37, 159, 241, 259, 300 and 313, reproduced by courtesy of The Mansell Collection; pp. 23, 27, 85, 111, 133, 145, 153, 156, 167, 239, 285 and 296, reproduced by courtesy of The Christmas Archives; p. 45, *The Virgin and Child with the Infant St John*, a fifteenth-century woodcut, Hamburg S.1137; p. 49, relief by Sally Seymour, © 1985; pp. 50 and 151, from *St Nicholas* Magazine, 1907, 1908; pp. 55, 73, 127 and 129, woodcuts by Vera Smith, © 1985; pp. 58 and 87, details from *Christmas in France* by F. Meaulle, 1875; p. 80, drawing by Nicholas Bentley from *Furthermore* by Damon Runyon, 1938, reproduced by permission of Constable & Co. Ltd; p. 107, woodcut by Pierre Gringore from *Castell of Labour*, c. 1505; pp. 117 and 119, drawings by George du Maurier from *Trilby*, 1894; pp. 137, 177 and 182, drawings by Zafer Baran, © 1985; p. 140, drawing by Clare Winsten from *G. B. S. 90: Aspects of Bernard Shaw's Life and Work*, 1946, reproduced by courtesy of Hutchinson Publishing Co. Ltd; p. 147, woodcut from Petrus de Rivo, *Opus Responsivum*, 1488; p. 162, woodcut from Bartholomaeus Anglicus, *All the Proprytees of Thynges*, 1495; p. 170, reproduced by courtesy of The Robert Opie Collection; pp. 187, 189 and 194, drawings by E. H. Shepard, copyright under the Berne Convention, reproduced by permission of Curtis Brown Ltd, London; pp. 201 and 307, from *Harper's Weekly*, 1880, 1881; pp. 207, 211, illustrations by Sidney Paget in the *Strand* Magazine, Vol. III, 1892; pp. 242, 245 and 249, drawing by Vana Haggerty, © 1985; p. 252, drawing by Brian Walker from *The Diary of a Farmer's Wife 1796–1797*, Countrywise Books, 1964, © Brian Walker 1964; p. 264, drawing from *Billy Bunter's Christmas* by Frank Richards reproduced by permission of Howard Baker Press Ltd; p. 267, illustration from the *Strand* Magazine, Vol. LXXLV, 1927; p. 291, woodcut from *Legenda Sanctorum Trium Regum*, 1490.

INDEX OF AUTHORS AND TITLES